MIND SET

by Gary Gentile

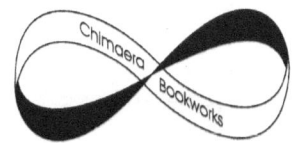

Chimaera Bookworks

Chimaera Bookworks
P.O. Box 57137
Philadelphia, PA 19111

Additional copies of this book may be purchased from the same address by sending a check or money order in the amount of $20 U.S. for each copy (plus $3 postage per order, not per book, in the U.S. Inquire for shipping cost to foreign countries). Alternatively, copies may be purchased from the author's website, and paid by credit card:

http://www.ggentile.com

The cover photographs were taken by the author.

International Standard Book Numbers (ISBN)
1-883056-27-6
978-1-883056-27-8

Original copyright - 1991

Printed in the U.S.A.

Preamble

In 1990, a little known and played-down incident occurred which changed the course of history.

As the Soviet Union stood on the brink of disruption, Russian spies infiltrated U.S. intelligence centers in a last-ditch effort to obtain secret information which, they hoped, would solidify the nation's weakening political structure by providing communism with the edge that was needed to curb the growth of capitalism while permitting the expansion of Russian influence throughout the world.

Only by demonstrating its technological superiority could the Soviet Union retain its solidarity while devoting its considerable excess energy to world domination.

Of all the revolutionary sciences and technologies, the Soviet Union led the race in only one esoteric area - that of the latent powers of the human mind. Russian advances in extra sensory perception far exceeded similar studies in countries that were dominated by religious faith, where the occult was anathema.

In America, the arcane mental sciences received little more than derision from academics who were grounded in the quest for knowledge that was based upon accepted natural laws. Inscrutable pseudoscience drew stern repudiation.

But not all research of the mind lacked the potential for practical application . . .

Chapter 1

" . . . out-of-body experience, which initiated my interest in this line of research, although I wasn't a doctor then. I began by studying hallucinatory drugs that created dissociative feelings in the patient, then experimented with the distortion of consciousness caused by sensory deprivation—"

"Did you ever *test* any of these drugs?" The curly-haired reporter scribbled hastily on his notepad, then waited expectantly for a response. "I mean, on yourself?"

The reception hall was densely packed with doctors milling like cattle in a corral and making just as much noise. The background chatter covered a range of topics, snippets of which wafted through the air like disembodied excerpts from esoteric medical texts. The only people not wearing suits were the women, who were attractively but simply attired in dresses or blouse-and-skirt combos; no high heels.

To offset his professional imagery, Blaine Mitchell sported a Care Bear tie and wore a yellow smile button on his left lapel. "No. My studies in that area were purely academic. There is enough literature on the subject to—"

"But your description was so real, so—so *vivid*." The reporter curled his lips into a half-baked smile that expressed accusation rather than compliment. He was becoming increasingly annoying, not just because he persisted in going on to the next question before Blaine completed his reply to the last, but because he was not satisfied with the answers unless they conformed to the preconceived notions that he wanted verified. "And I don't mean only in your highfalutin medical lingo, but in common language. You talk as if you've *been* there."

Blaine could see that the interview was not going in any direction he cared to follow, but, short of being impolite, he could not see any way of terminating it. He was uncomfortable discussing the results of his laboratory tests with the media; they seldom cared about his work, and often ignored the real issues in order to pick on points salient to their readers or viewers. On the other hand, if he did not clarify his statements, the resultant stories turned out as distorted as the electro-chemically-induced levels of consciousness he was trying to define. He jiggled nervously with the key ring in his right coat pocket.

"The endorphin response is what we would portray as a natural high. If you were listening to my talk you would have heard me make that analogy—"

"Oh, yes." The mousy reporter flipped back several pages, squinted behind thick, rimless lenses, and paraphrased his penciled cuneiform. "Accident victims and soldiers in the field don't feel pain because of body chemicals like adrenaline and morphine, and canoers get hooked on it and build up a tolerance to fear."

Blaine groaned inwardly and rolled his eyes. He could not prevent his fists from clenching. "I said that people suffering injuries *may* temporarily experience a decreased sensitivity to pain due to endorphins—endogenous morphine-like natural analogues—released from the pituitary to combat pain the way adrenaline is released in times of fear to prepare an animal to fight or flee. And canoe*ists*—" He emphasized the "ists." "—need adrenaline to give them the strength to get them through a long and difficult series of rapids. It is runners who build up a tolerance to pain because of the continuous release of endorphins. I did not say they become addicted to—"

"Well, okay, but that's pretty much the same thing, only in different words. That's a wild idea—getting drunk without having to buy booze. But how do you make any money out of it?"

By now Blaine was completely frustrated and losing control of his scientific poise. "Pure research is never conducted for monetary gain. The ultimate goal is the increase in knowledge that may lead to less human suffering—" This time he interrupted himself. Philosophical sentiment was bound to be wasted on a person so out of phase with reality. Putting things into perspective, he realized that whatever this narrow-minded reporter put in his newspaper was not likely to affect the scientific community. Blaine's peers had all been subjected to media mediocrity, and certainly would not react unfavorably to such childish misinterpretations. He decided instead to have some fun. "Have you read my paper, or did the multisyllabic symmetry confuse you?"

"Well, actually—"

"Then perhaps we should discuss brain death, a subject with which you are undoubtedly more familiar." A few titters in the audience informed him that he had hit his mark. "You remember that I began my talk with a discussion of the levels of consciousness, the clinical definition of death, an outline of the neurochemical system, the pharmacological treatment of pain, then the psychobiological explanations of natural and non-addictive painkillers." He tapped on the notepad. "Are you getting all this down?"

The reporter's weak jaw went slack. He looked down, then stared up into Blaine's sparkling green eyes as if he were suddenly confronting a stranger. "Uh, I—"

"Never mind. But I would like to offer a free medical opinion." He leaned close and whispered conspiratorially into the reporter's ear. "You are not schizophrenic."

The reporter's jaw dropped completely. "I'm not what?"

Blaine winked, leaned back, and stood up straight in his blue serge three-piece suit. "The latest research demonstrates that schizophrenia is probably caused by the inability of the brain to filter unnecessary information, that the schizophrenic brain is overwhelmed with stimuli due to the unlimited access of neurotransmitters to nerve cells—a chemical dysfunction you certainly do not manifest. On the contrary, you tolerate so little interference from your environment that your conscious level is practically insubordinate." Titters became light laughter. Once again Blaine tapped the loosely held notepad. "You can quote me on that."

He took three steps to the side and was immediately swallowed up by the resonant crowd. Blaine hated the conventions. Not only did he have to put up with the likes of reporters who wanted only to fill back-page columns or flesh out local broadcasts without the least attempt at accuracy, but he had to defend his ongoing research projects from fellow neurologists who were envious of the large grants that backed Blaine's work. As he dodged his way to an open wall with some breathing space he had the uneasy feeling that he was being watched.

"Alone at last. I've been trying to get your attention all evening."

Out of the volcano and into the lava flow. Marybeth Maples was a brilliant computer analyst and program designer. She was cute in a simplistic way—thin and shapely, with short hair that gave her a boyish appearance. Blaine respected her highly, and even, he had to admit, enjoyed working with her. But she could also drone on forever about absolutely nothing; she was the queen of trivial conversation. Once away from the job, she kept all pretenses to academia firmly hidden behind long and obviously fake eyelashes. The purple paint on her lids was decidedly tacky for any female over the age of thirteen.

"Waving while I'm at the podium is not appropriate behavior." Blaine was still annoyed at the continued smiles and finger wiggles she blandished during his lecture; at a minimum it was distracting. He felt that a woman in her thirties, and with her position of responsibility at the Institute, should show a little more maturity. "Were you trying to embarrass me?"

If she felt the least bit churlish she disguised it perfectly. "I thought the featured speaker could use a little encouragement from the hometown audience. Who did you have for a cheerleader at Berkeley?" Her high-pitched voice stood out against the general hubbub like a harp amidst a band of bassoons. "And where've you been hiding yourself all week? Tilda said you phoned from California and said your departure was delayed. I've called your place half a dozen times and got nothing but that monotonous recording of yours. Really, Blaine, you should try to be more original. And why use it if you don't return your calls?"

An incendiary device went off at the base of Blaine's spine. The heat rose up his backbone and burned his face. Crystal chandeliers twenty feet overhead lit the large room brightly, so he had to hope that his recent suntan was dark enough to disguise his blush.

"Because I haven't been home yet. I—I needed—a little time off. You know—to put life into perspective and . . . to stretch out unused muscles." Blaine avoided eye contact with Marybeth. He glanced over her head into the sea of familiar faces, looking for someone he could signal with raised brows to come and say hello. At the moment he would even consider reopening his conversation with the goggle-eyed reporter whose attention span was shorter than that of a two-year-old, but his questions were far less penetrating, and answers were practically unnecessary.

"Gosh, Blaine, you should have let me know. I've got enough vacation time saved up to take off for months. I would have spared you a few days. We could have met halfway, say, in Denver, and gone skiing or something."

It was the "or something" that Blaine was afraid of. In the five years of their association he had seen her practically every single day, and in all that time she had never let up on him. She had asked him to dinner, to the movies, to plays and shows, and to weekends at the beach, and each time he had explained softly and patiently that he thought it was better to keep their relationship on a professional basis. That added up to nearly two thousand days of negative feedback, and still she had not gotten the message. She had a crush on him that refused to be crushed.

His voice was getting hoarse. In addition to lecturing for an hour to a prestigious gathering of neurologists, neurosurgeons, physiobiologists, psychotherapists, and a scant number of psychiatrists, followed by an hour-long question-and-answer period, he had spent another two hours surrounded by a hostile rabble discussing experimental procedures and defending his conclusions. Marybeth, who conducted interviews and performed the statistical analyses for his work, seemed oblivious to the night's unending attacks on his reputation and professional standing.

"Sorry, Marybeth, I just needed to get away from work and—the work-related environment. They hammered me almost as hard at Berkeley as they did here. And I knew that once the *Journal* came out they'd crucify me tonight because they'd have their objections already formulated." He spread his arms expansively. "You saw the result."

"Yes, and Mighty Joe isn't going to like all the publicity you're getting. But you still should have called. You know I'm always available if you want to talk."

She was certainly available but she always did the talking; Blaine had to listen. "I'm sorry, but—you understand."

He could tell by the expression on her face that she did not. Her feelings were hurt and there was nothing he could do about it. He glanced away uncomfortably. He thought someone was staring at him, but as he gazed into the surrounding faces he saw no hostile or irate doctors or Ph.D.'s ready to pounce on him.

"Speaking of Young, where is he? I've got all the print-outs he wanted in my car."

Changing the subject did not work. With Marybeth, it never did. "At a wedding reception." Her voice was as sweet as a lemon.

"What?" It bothered Blaine that the head of the Institute was not present at his lecture, especially since it was receiving so much notoriety. The recognition was certain to reflect on all the Institute's programs one way or another. Blaine humphed with resignation. "I guess I shouldn't have expected him to back me."

Marybeth's stare was icy. "His daughter got married today."

"Oh." It was just like Young not to mention it. He never spoke about his family, and never asked his coworkers about theirs. He was strictly business, a doctor-turned-administrator who could not stand being upstaged by junior staff members, and who never supported an idea that was not his own. Consequently, he ran the Institute with a fist of rusted iron. "In that case I guess it's okay—"

A passer-by locked shoulders with Blaine, side-stepped for balance, and reached out to steady himself. His pudgy cheeks creased vertically in an expressionless grin. "Pardon me, sir. I guess I wasn't looking where—"

"Don't worry about it." Blaine dismissed the incident with a shake of the head. "You can't get through this crowd without bumping into someone."

The stranger placed well-manicured fingers to his forehead, rumpled short blond hair, and squinted his steely blue eyes. "Just the same—I'm sorry." He glanced at Marybeth. "Ma'am." A moment later he was gone.

Blaine picked up where he left off. "Is he planning to show up at all?" Marybeth shrugged. "I doubt it. You know he's not happy about the situation. With you getting all the credit and publicity—"

"It's not me, it's the program. The Institute will benefit—"

"Excuse me, Dr. Mitchell."

The young man who stood before him was a couple inches taller than Blaine. His short brown hair was somewhat ruffled, his face was covered with thin stubble, and the knot of his tie was loose. The drab sport coat was way out of place.

"Yes. Can I help you?"

"Would you please check your pockets to see if anything is missing?" He phrased the sentence like a question but his voice made it a command.

Blaine stood still for several seconds while the import of his words sank in. Then he quickly reached for his breast pocket. He was relieved to find his wallet in place. He pulled it out, opened it, and did a cursory check of its contents. All his money and credit cards were there.

"Check your other pockets, please."

Blaine raised his eyebrows, but replaced his wallet and did as he was told. "Hmmm. Now where did I put—" He remembered playing with them not too long ago.

"What is it? What did he take?"

"I'm not sure, but—" His hands went in and out of his pockets so fast that he looked like a man with a bad case of hives. "I can't find—" By now he was sure of it. He stared up at the intruder. "My keys are missing. But—"

"I think that man just picked your pocket."

"What man?"

"The one who 'accidentally' bumped into you."

Blaine had already forgotten the incident. Now he conjured in his mind a picture of the stranger. "I don't—know him."

Marybeth was ever astute. "I don't think we know *you*, either. You're not a visiting doctor."

"No, I'm—" He pulled an identification wallet out of his breast pocket and let the bottom fold drop. A silver badge glinted in the light. "—Special Agent Foley. I've been assigned to watch for suspicious-looking characters." He snapped the wallet shut. "Dr. Mitchell, would you please accompany me outside? I think we should go check on your vehicle."

"By all means."

Foley led the way to the glass doors, shoving softly but firmly through the throngs of prattling practitioners. Blaine stayed on his tail so as not to let the press of people close in before he could get through. Friends and acquaintances frowned at his abrupt decampment. The shabbily dressed reporter watched in consternation.

Marybeth stood alone and astonished for only a moment. Then she shouted, "Wait for me." She swung her purse strap over her shoulder and clicked on low heels across the white marble floor.

The air outside was bitterly cold. Stars shone down

through a cloudless sky with clarity typical of New England winters. The blond brick facade of Langdon Hall was tastefully lighted, but the portico was overbearingly bright. Blaine squinted. Beyond the curved driveway, the campus parking lot was illuminated by mercury vapor lamps atop thirty-foot aluminum poles.

"There he goes." Foley pointed to the man running between the rows of parked Mercedes and BMWs.

"That's where I'm parked."

The far end of the lot was empty. With the students on Christmas break most of the battered Fords and souped-up Chevys were in other parts of the state. Except for the doctors attending the conference, only guards and maintenance personnel were likely to be on the grounds or in the deserted buildings.

"There's only one way out," Marybeth announced.

The parking lot was shaped like a large kidney bounded on one side by trees and on the other side by dormitories. The assembly hall was situated at the spout of the kidney. The broad driveway provided easy access without curbs and lane restrictions.

Blaine saw the stranger stop next to his blue Plymouth sedan. The beige coat and blond head were clearly visible in the overhead light from the adjacent pole. The man bent over, and a moment later Blaine heard the sound of a door being wrenched open. Then the man jumped inside and slammed the door shut.

If Blaine was half a step behind Foley it was only because Marybeth had wrapped her arm around his. Blaine had no sooner struggled free than a powerful explosion ripped through his car. He was knocked back more by shock value than by shock wave. In the act of falling he saw every detail in extreme slow motion.

A titanic ball of flame spread outward and upward like a miniature atomic blast. Cars on both sides and the one in front were engulfed in a blossoming yellow cloud. The Plymouth's black-vinyl roof was completely detached, and flew up into the air like a tumbling surfboard. The hood, spinning like a top, scythed through the forest, shredding naked sycamores as if they were blades of grass. The trunk lid clattered across the macadam and ricocheted off the rear end of a dark green Continental, then smashed into the second story of the girl's dorm between two windows; it dropped to the lawn with a dull thump.

The force of the blast felled the lamp pole across two rows of parked cars, crushing several of them under expended kinetic energy. All the lights in the lot went out, but that was hardly noticeable in the glare of the still-expanding fireball.

Foley dived to the ground and covered his head with his hands. Blaine's rump hit the cold cement; he rolled instinctively to soften the blow and to protect his face. Marybeth went down beside him. Blaine slithered on top of her and shielded her face and torso with his body as machine parts and bits of metal rained down upon them. Flaming brands that were pieces of upholstery fluttered in the air like large flakes of ash from a stirred bonfire.

Blaine's ears were still ringing when he sat up and stared dumbfounded at the devastation. His car was little more than a smoking chassis, in the middle of what looked like the aftermath of a demolition derby. The parking lot was littered with burning fiberglass and molten blobs of plastic. Glass shards lay everywhere.

"My car," he choked, when comprehension finally dawned upon him. "He blew up my car."

Chapter 2

"Holy Christ!" Foley climbed up to his hands and knees, and stared with disbelief at the burning field of debris.

Marybeth struggled to get Blaine off of her. She punched him aside when he moved too slowly to suit her. If she was ruffled by the explosive events she did not show it. "What brand of anti-theft devise was that?"

Blaine paid her no mind. He pulled his legs under him and leaned up on one arm, slowly surveying the parking-lot-turned-junkyard. "My car. Why did he—"

"Wake up, Blaine," said Marybeth. "He didn't blow up your car; it was blown out from under him."

Blaine was still dazed. "But—why?"

Marybeth stood up and pulled him to his feet. "You must have really pissed somebody off with that paper of yours."

Blaine stared at her as if she had suddenly turned Martian. "You must be joking?"

"Maybe. But somebody else isn't." She dusted off her tight-fitting skirt as if it were the most important thing in the world. The back of her sheer silk blouse was torn in several places, exposing smooth white skin. Goosebumps on her bare arms were the size of peas.

Blaine's peripheral perceptions were temporarily blinded; the narrow scope of tunnel vision permitted only limited awareness of his surroundings. He flashed back to a war zone half a planet away: a jungle phantasmagoria that existed within the depths of his mind and that surfaced with alarming regularity. Bombs had a place there; in the civilized world they did not. He forced himself to concentrate on the present. Mental processes work at phenomenal speeds; within seconds he was in control and playing the part of a doctor tending a potential patient.

"Foley, are you okay?" He rushed to the man's side and prevented him from getting up the rest of the way.

"Don't move until I examine you. I want to check for broken bones."

For the second time in the same minute Blaine was pushed away. "I'm all right. Just—" The special agent climbed unsteadily to his feet. He was visibly shaken, and had great difficulty forming his words. "Just—I wasn't—expecting that."

"What *did* you expect?" Marybeth wanted to know. "What were you looking for?" She jerked her head in the direction of Langdon Hall. "In there. We've never had security guards for lecture engagements before."

The portico was rapidly filling with babbling spectators emerging from the reception room. The reporter stood in stunned detachment, with mouth agape and arms hanging loosely at his side. The raging fire was so fierce that Blaine could feel the heat against his face.

"No. I know. That is—there was a call—I was assigned—"

Blaine screamed angrily, "If there was a bomb threat goddamn it you should have warned us befo—"

Came the sound of squealing tires. The black Cadillac that turned on two wheels off the street and into the driveway was barreling straight toward the arguing trio. All three leaped behind the dull blue Chrysler at the end of the row. Foley and Marybeth got their legs intertwined and went down headlong. Blaine jumped over them, slipped on a patch of ice, and crashed painfully into the adjacent parked car; a fortunate grab for the door handle saved him from falling.

The Cadillac skidded to a halt in front of the crowded portico. Curious doctors contained further curiosity and stepped back like a well-trained chorus line. The Caddy's headlights limned Blaine, Foley, and Marybeth. Two big, swarthy-looking men got out of the still-rocking car. Each wore heavy brown overcoats buttoned to the neck, sharply creased trousers, and highly polished wingtips. Their black hair was slicked back as if they had just stepped out of a Vitalis commercial. Both held pistols in gloved hands so huge that the guns looked like toys.

The leader waved his automatic carelessly. "Hey, Mitchell. Come wit' us." His voice was a deep guttural bass that could have been an audition for Satchmo. "Don' give us no trouble an' yer frien's'll live to see daylight."

The other man stepped forward with a slight limp. His Colt .45 held a steady bead on Blaine's chest. "Make it quick, an' nobody gets whacked."

Blaine's heart skipped a beat. His hands felt instantly clammy and, despite the cold, his body was bathed in sweat; beads of perspiration formed on his forehead, and his armpits soaked his shirt. He did not like guns pointing at him. Worse yet, he hated the emasculating predicament of not having one to point back. He remained crouched with the skin of his left palm stuck to the metal door handle.

"Who the hell are you?"

Both toughs were taken aback at his effrontery. Foley disentangled himself from Marybeth and slowly rose to his knees. In the icy air the doubly frozen tableau was partially obscured by the condensation of heavy breathing.

Satchmo took a deep breath. "Mister, you wanna reach yer next birthday you better get inna car."

With both Caddy doors open the dome light was on; no one else was in the car. Silhouetted in the twin headlight beams Blaine could not make out the features of either opponent, neither of whom cared about the stampede of people rushing to get back inside the building. Their guns gave them complete command of the situation. Blaine pondered his next move.

"What do you want?" Foley shouted.

Satchmo shifted his aiming point. "I wan' Mitchell to get inna car or I'm gonna blow yer balls off. That plain enough?"

The gimp never let his piece lose sight of Blaine's chest. "An' make it fast. We ain't got all night."

Marybeth made a few gasping sounds that indicated her frame of mind. She sat on the macadam with her legs folded to her side and her arms clenched tightly under her dainty breasts. Whether she shook from fear or the cold was impossible to tell.

Blaine released his grip on the door handle and lost some skin in the process. The physical pain was minor compared to the tremor in his heart. He could feel the blood throbbing through his veins. These men meant business. He took a step forward, then another, and another. He passed between Foley and Marybeth, never taking his eyes off the dark circle above the neck of the man who held him at gunpoint.

Then came more screeching wheels, and every eye turned toward the source. A brand-new, shiny Ford pickup truck executed a perfect blocking maneuver by locking its breaks and skidding sideways into the driveway entrance. A man wearing brown corduroys, a red plaid flannel shirt, a cowhide vest, and a cocked Stetson hat, stepped out of the passenger side with measured precision, and without preamble lowered the barrel of an Uzi and pulled the trigger.

High-speed bullets hit the two gunmen before either could fire back. As lead slammed into flesh, both men were picked up bodily and flung aside like papier-mâché dolls let loose in the wind. They hit the ground broken and bleeding. Satchmo's voice was silenced forever; the other's limp would never bother him again.

Blaine ducked behind the Chrysler's trunk as the Uzi turned in his direction and cut a mean swath just over his head. He heard distinctly the hollow claps made by air coming together in the wake of close calls. Steel-jacketed projectiles tore into fenders and blew out windows with a cacophony that was deafening. Glass particles fell like a shower of meteorites.

The cowboy swung the Uzi toward the front of Langdon Hall. He aimed high, firing above the people clawing their way through the front door. He shattered every pane of glass in the lobby before emptying the magazine, but hit no one. Alongside the portico the lone reporter groveled in the bushes with his face in the dirt; he never once looked up. The cowboy locked and loaded a full magazine.

Foley ripped open his coat, reached inside, and fumbled awkwardly to get his .38 revolver out of its holster. Like a character in a cop show, he leveled it and shouted, "Freeze."

The reply was a burst of bullets whose aim was more determined than the last. Foley ducked behind the fender just in time. The barrage of lead impacting the doors and side panels bounced the Chrysler around as if were a Tonka toy.

Lying under the trunk with an exhaust pipe in his face, Blaine could see the cowboy from the kneecaps down: he strode toward them steadily, firing short controlled bursts. Behind him, the driver of the pickup lighted a stick of dynamite and threw it overhand down the length of the now-empty portico. The poor reporter jumped up and raced around the corner of the building just as the stick detonated. The blast knocked out the support stanchions and collapsed the metal-and-stucco structure in front of the doorway. The machine-gunner kept on coming.

Blaine kicked Foley hard in the back. "Shoot him, damn it! Shoot him! He's gonna get us."

Foley slumped against the rear tire. He stared first at Blaine sprawling on the macadam, then at Marybeth curled into a ball half under the other parked car; she was wide-eyed and working her mouth soundlessly. Fear, not cold. Foley pulled the gun tight against his chest and bounced on the balls of his feet, preparing to spring.

The rat-tat-tat and the fear of imminent death made it nearly impossible to think. But Blaine stopped Foley before he exposed his head to the deadly onslaught. He pointed hard. "Underneath. Get his legs."

Foley appeared dazed, but nodded with fearful understanding. He dropped flat, took careful aim, and fired at timed half-second intervals. His second shot went through the ankle of the cowboy's leather boot. The force of the bullet flung back his leg and tripped him. He hit the blacktop on all fours. Foley's fourth shot went through his forearm and into his upper leg.

The man collapsed just in time for Foley's sixth shot to tear off his stiff-brimmed Stetson. The man lay till.

In the sudden silence Foley fell back next to Marybeth. He stared at the revolver as if it were a writhing rattlesnake. "Oh, my God."

Blaine watched the cowboy's hatless backup grab another Uzi off the pickup's front seat and point it decisively. "Reload, Foley. There's another one out there." Blaine was not impressed by the special agent's conduct under fire. "Hurry!"

"I—I—I'm out of ammo."

"You're out—" Blaine could hardly believe his ears. He twisted his head and looked out from under the car. The other gunman was slinking around the front of the pickup, cautious now that his partner was down and knowing that his target was armed and dangerous. When Blaine twisted back he saw Marybeth holding out a shaking hand and pointing finger. He followed the line of travel to Satchmo's .45 lying on the ground.

Flames reached the gas tank of one of the burning autos behind them. It exploded violently, sending shrapnel into the air along with spumes of blazing gasoline. Blaine used the distraction to his advantage. He rolled onto his knees and knuckles and took off like an Olympic sprinter. In one smooth motion he dashed across the Caddy's headlight beams, scooped up the loose pistol, and did a low shoulder roll that took him out of the gunman's line of sight.

A short burst of fire kept him huddled behind the Caddy's engine and front wheel. As soon as the bullets stopped he shuffled past the open door to the rear of the car and poked his head up over the fender in time to see the machine-gunner swing into the seat of the pickup, intent on escape instead of completing his deadly mission.

As the Ford squealed out of the driveway and into the street, Blaine stretched his upper body across the Caddy's trunk lid and peered over the sights of the automatic. His hands felt like blocks of ice, and his body trembled. Nevertheless, he pulled the trigger and kept pulling it until the hammer fell on an empty chamber. He got off seven shots. He was gratified to see the rear window blasted out as the pickup rounded the corner and disappeared.

Blaine was numb from shock and cold. He backed away from the car, and from the icy metal that felt like the surface of a glacier. He gawked at the amount of destruction that had occurred in the past five minutes. His Plymouth was little more than a smoldering hulk. Three other cars were still burning, and several more had been flattened. Langdon Hall's portico lay in ruins and the glass front of the building was blown in.

And three men lay dead on the blacktop.

Not soon would Blaine Mitchell be invited back to give another lecture.

He stumbled past the Caddy's open door feeling intensely alive after successful combat. His adrenaline was still pumping strong. He saw Foley help Marybeth to her feet; both were ragged but appeared unhurt. Blaine's medical training took hold; without thinking, he stooped by the gimp and placed frozen fingers on his carotid.

At the same instant he heard a whoosh go by his head, followed by a thump in the Caddy's front fender. He spun around in time to see a man wearing a football helmet lower his cane and duck around the far corner of the building. Blaine instinctively raised the pistol and pulled the trigger. The gun was still empty.

"Damn!" He dropped the gun like a hot coal, picked up the gimp's piece, aimed, and fired. A large chunk of blond brick separated from the wall about five feet from the ground. He waited two seconds for the man to reappear. Then he turned and ran for the cowboy.

"Dr. Mitchell, what—" Foley threw up his arms protectively and caught the pistol that Blaine tossed at him.

A moment later Blaine had his hands on the Uzi. He pilled out the magazine to make sure it still held ammunition, then slammed it back in. He shouldered the weapon, pulled it hard into his shoulder, and blasted off another chunk of brick just to let the would-be killer know that he was well armed.

"Blaine!" Marybeth was pointing at the opposite end of Langdon Hall, where the reporter had taken flight.

A huge black man wearing a dark trench coat slowed to a stop under the diffused light at the corner of the building. The pistol clasped in his hand was aimed at Blaine. "Drop it!"

The Uzi responded the same way in Blaine's hands as it had in the cowboy's. Bullets burped out in a continuous stream. The black man twisted and jumped back behind the building. Two rounds whined off brick, the others cleaved silently and invisibly through the air.

"Let's get the hell out of here!" Blaine took Marybeth's wrist and dragged her along the aisle between parked cars. He hunkered low as they crossed the open space beyond. "Foley! Come *on!*"

Foley caught up with them at the next line of cars. He kept looking over his shoulder at both ends of Langdon Hall. "What the hell is going on?"

"You tell me. This is your assignment." With one hand on Marybeth's hand and the other on the Uzi, Blaine ran out onto the grass that bordered the parking lot.

After the initial prompt Marybeth needed no further encouragement. She ran as fast as Blaine despite the impediment of improper footwear. She was breathing hard but was not out of breath. "Into the woods. Quick! Before they cut us off." She took back her hand and led the way through the trees. "There's a bike trail at the bottom of the hill."

Oaks and sycamores spread bare branches skyward. Starlight penetrated the forest with a starkness that was devoid of warmth and comfort. The hard ground was carpeted with twigs and leaves that crunched underfoot, and branches broken off during the last ice storm. The slope was clear of entanglements but frost made footing treacherous. Blaine found it impossible to keep his balance. He skidded halfway down the hill on the seat of his pants, and had the bruises to prove it.

"Hold it," Foley called in a coarse whisper when they reached the macadam path. He held the captured pistol loosely in his hand. "Where are we going?"

Marybeth shook uncontrollably from the cold, and her teeth chattered between words. "Right now I'm just trying to get away."

"Good idea." Blaine put the Uzi on the ground, took off his suit coat, and held it out for Marybeth. "Here, put this on."

She slid her arms into the sleeves and buttoned the coat tight. "Thanks." Blaine retrieved the Uzi, and cradled it in his arm as he hunched over for warmth. "So where to now?"

"The path comes down from the road and winds along the creek until it reaches a walking bridge, then goes either left or right. Left crosses the creek and meanders through the woods, right heads up to the back of the dorms and classrooms."

Blaine clenched and unclenched his stiffened fingers like a cat working out on a scratching post. His joints ached horribly. "I'm for heat."

Foley rubbed his hands together as best he could without letting go of the gun. "Good idea."

"Then follow me." Marybeth took charge of the situation as if she had been running military escape-and-evasion courses all her life. "And keep those guns ready."

They traveled abreast with Marybeth in the middle.

Blaine tried to ignore the cold and concentrate on his surroundings. The trees cast weird shadows that took on nightmarish shapes. The forest could have been a painted backdrop for a college play, or a surrealistic canvas. The creek was frozen solid: a silver thread that glinted like the skin of an eel. Fortunately there was not a breath of wind or the cold would have felt more intense.

"So what's going on here, Foley?" Blaine kept his voice at a discrete whisper. "What's this assignment you're on? And how did we get involved in it?"

Foley had recovered his composure. "I wish the hell I knew. I was sent out to question you about a death threat we received."

"Who am I supposed to have threatened?"

"Nobody. We got an anonymous phone call that said *your* life was in danger and that you needed protection."

"Who are 'we'?"

"The FBI. It happens all the time, Dr. Mitchell. We've even got a hotline for this sort of thing. Ordinarily we send it through channels and pass it along to the local police, which we did, and they check it out. They ask you if you have any enemies, received any threats yourself, that sort of thing. Only this time we found out you'd been missing since your last lecture. That gave the case a higher status rating and, because of the interstate angle, kicked it back into our lap. Local authority just doesn't have the resources to conduct an investigation from one side of the country to the other. So I was sent out here to look for you."

"To see if I'd deliver my own lecture."

"Exactly. We didn't know what else to do short of interviewing everyone who attended your Berkeley talk, where you were last reported seen. That would have been the next step if you hadn't shown up tonight."

Blaine shook his head. "All this from a phone call?"

"And your disappearance. So, where were you all week, Dr. Mitchell?"

"Forget about that and tell me why all these terrorists are out to get me? Granted my work has created some opposition in the field—"

"Opposition?" Marybeth expostulated in a voice that was a chime among toetaps; she lowered it a few decibels. "You've got half the neurologists in the country clamoring for your blood—" She stopped and explained to Foley, "In the figurative sense, that is." To Blaine, "You haven't seen the mail that's come in rebutting your paper. It's been out since Monday, and a lot of people have been burning the candle at both ends in order to burn both of yours."

"Okay, okay, okay." Blaine washed her words away with a wave of his hands, then remembered he was holding an automatic rifle that had recently been fired at him. "But that's intellectual response. This—this is bombs going off and bullets flying. It's not how scientists shoot down competitive theories. I know some of them are pretty radical, but—"

"Shush." The hand that Marybeth clamped over Blaine's mouth could have belonged to a corpse. Her words came in a barely audible murmur. "There's someone up there. Ahead of us."

Foley pulled her down to a crouch. "I don't see anyone."

"It was only a shadow. By the bridge." Her head shook from more than just the cold. "I can't see him, but I can feel him. It's like a—a presence."

Doubled nearly in half, and balanced on the balls of his feet, Blaine scrutinized the silent forest. "There's someone behind us, too. Someone big who can move like a cat."

Foley summed up their predicament with a single word. "Shit."

Chapter 3

Blaine shoved Marybeth and Foley off the narrow macadam trail and into the bushes. By now his fingers were so cold that he felt only a gnawing pain where he knew they should be. He folded his arms over the Uzi and tucked his hands into his armpits. "We've got to get inside before we freeze to death."

"Blaine, I'm scared."

"You're not alone." Blaine put one arm around Marybeth's shoulders and held her tight, then glanced at Foley.

The special agent grimaced. "Hell, that makes three of us. This is more than I bargained for." He closed the two remaining coat buttons without letting go of the pistol, crawled out through the bushes and looked furtively up and down the trail, then backed into the tiny clearing. "Okay, if I've got the layout clear in my mind, we can intersect the trail to the dorm by cutting diagonally through the woods." He touched Marybeth on the arm and looked deep into her eyes. "Do you think you can make it?"

Through gritted teeth, she stammered, "No, but I'll try."

"Good girl." He held the .45 in front of him. "Dr. Mitchell, I know I'm supposed to be protecting you—and I haven't done a very good job of it so far—but I need your help. Stay close and guard the rear."

Blaine never liked walking point. "Okay, but don't pull any of that 'freeze' crap. We're already frozen. If anyone pops up with a gun, get the drop on him before you start holding a conversation."

"Understood."

The bushes thinned after a few feet. Although the ground was rough and uneven and sprinkled with deadfall, travel was easy in the open forest where the trees were spaced far apart. Blaine felt as if he were walking on amputated stubs—his feet were like two blocks of tenderloin hanging in a meat house; thin socks and dress shoes were not designed for winter hiking, nor did the smooth soles provide traction on the puddles of ice. He wished longingly for his goose-down parka, Thinsulate ski bib, and insulated boots.

When they reached the base of the slope Foley started climbing at an angle. This made the going harder because they sideslipped constantly on loose leaves and frost-covered soil. More than once Blaine's feet slid out from under him, and he fell painfully on his arm and thigh. He felt newfound admiration for Marybeth, whose thin skirt and nylons offered no thermal protection, and who slipped as often but made no complaints and never yelped in pain.

At the crest of the rise the dark silhouette of a building came into view. The three-story brick rectangle showed no lights: the latest attempt at utility savings. In a few days, when the students returned, it would be full of light, life, and longing; now it was a bleak gothic castle complete with fluted colonnades, missing only the gargoyles.

Sirens wailed in the background.

Foley stopped at the tree line. "Where's Langdon Hall from here?"

"On the other side of the campus." Blaine pointed with a clenched fist. "The place should be swarming with fire engines and police cars." He glanced at the iridescent dial of his watch. "We've been out here less than ten minutes. If we cut between these buildings—"

"We're not out of the woods yet."

A dark figure darted across the lawn a hundred yards away, between them and the parking lot. Blaine raised the Uzi for a long shot, but the figure melted into the shadows between buildings before he could control his shaking. Flashing red lights and bursting strobes indicated the presence of emergency vehicles a quarter mile away. But help may as well have been on the far side of the moon.

"Let's go," Blaine suggested. "If we can make it to the back door of the dorm we can hide out and call for reinforcements."

"Okay." Foley pulled Marybeth from her crouch, and ran with one arm around her waist. "Are you all right?"

"I've—been—better."

Blaine followed them across the short-cropped grass where in warmer times students sprawled under the sun and laughed and joked and feigned at studying the hefty texts they carried under their arms. His eyes were riveted on the spot where he had last seen the skulker. He was certain this was the man with the pistol at the corner of the lecture hall. He pattered across the sidewalk that encircled the men's dorm, and raced up the five stone steps to the back door.

"It's locked," Foley said simply.

The door was made of thick oak and iron trim, and could not be knocked down by anything less than a Sherman tank. The book-sized rectangular windows were head high—well out of reach of the inside push bars.

"And probably chained on the inside," Marybeth added.

"It figures," Blaine said, with evident resignation. "They're afraid someone might break in and steal all the toilet paper."

"Can we keep moving? That run added half a calorie to my heat reserve."

"Good idea." Foley started down the steps with Marybeth in tow. "What's that building over—" He drew up short on the pebbled concrete pad.

Blaine could tell by the way he was looking that he had seen something across the field. "What is it?"

"Someone—tall. In that opening." He nodded toward a split in the woods, straight down the sidewalk from the back of the dorm.

"That's where the bike trail comes out of the woods." Marybeth gasped, "The man at the bridge!"

Blaine saw nothing. "They're trying to surround us."

"They've already succeeded."

"Okay, let's outflank them. Foley, head for the back of the classroom building. You watch the woods, I'll make sure the other guy doesn't slip around the dorm and cut us off."

It was only a short jog across a crinkled lawn to the latest phase in campus expansion. What had once been an athletic field was now a series of single-story glass-and-metal classrooms, adjoined by a student laboratory complex.

"This one's locked, too."

Blaine ignored Foley, and smashed in the rear door's large glass panel with the butt of the Uzi. In the stark winter silence the shattering pane sounded like a champagne bottle at a ship christening played over a loudspeaker. He reached in, depressed the push bar, and pulled open the door. "I hope this place is burglar alarmed."

The thermostat could not have been set higher than fifty degrees, but to Blaine the hallway felt like the inside of a pizza oven.

"Oh, God, that feels good," Marybeth muttered.

"I never thought I'd hear you say that." Blaine poked his head into several rooms. Each was filled with neatly arranged one-armed desk chairs facing a plain drawerless table and a clean blackboard. "No telephones."

"The place isn't bugged, either." Foley let go of Marybeth and hurried along the darkened corridor. "But we've got something just as good." He stopped by a fire station consisting of an extinguisher, a coil of hose, a water outlet, and a break alarm. "This should bring them running."

"Hit it. Let's create as much havoc as possible."

Foley broke the glass protector with the pistol barrel, and pulled down the red handle.

Nothing happened.

Blaine waited an acceptable amount of time before asking, "Is this a silent alarm that only signals the fire department?"

"It can't be." Foley indicated the gong near the ceiling. "Only burglar alarms work that way. A fire alarm is supposed to alert the people inside so they can evacuate the building."

"Then what's wrong?" He located a wall switch but dared not flip it up lest the light give away their position. "Isn't it on a separate circuit?"

"He cut it." Marybeth looked small in Blaine's coat. She rubbed her hands over her arms and stamped her feet soundlessly on the linoleum. "He cut the wires."

"How could he? How could he know we'd pull the alarm?"

Foley placed his back against the partition and sank down until his rump touched the heels of his arched feet. "We underestimate this guy. He's been ahead of us all the way. He was even waiting for us at the bridge. Then when we bushwhacked through the woods he took the trail to the dorm and nearly cut us off."

"But how did he know we'd come here?" Blaine hunkered down on the floor opposite him.

"I don't know." After a reflective pause, "I think the black man never lost sight of us, but the other one . . . " Foley slowly shook his head. "Dr. Mitchell, I'll be real honest with you, this whole case is way out of my league. Remember, I came to you for answers. I didn't expect to get caught in the middle of a gang war. So tell me, what kind of people are you involved with? And what have you done to them that they rigged your car and hired this outfit as backup?"

"Nobody!" Blaine practically screamed. "I'm a doctor—a scientist. I'm not mixed up in black market pharmaceuticals, prescription drugs, or malpractice scams. I don't even cheat on my income tax. And I don't want to discuss it further until I know I'm going to live long enough to have breakfast."

Marybeth was still shaking. She plopped down on the floor next to Foley and leaned into him. In a hushed tone, she said, "First of all, I don't think we should be shouting. And secondly, if you think about it, there's more than one outfit, as you put it, after us. Or after

Blaine. Those men in the Cadillac wanted to capture him, the cowboys wanted to kill him. And the other two may not even be in cahoots."

"She's right." Blaine toned down his voice so it did not resonate in his throat. To Foley, "For all I know, these guys might be after *you*. The car thief could have been a coincidence."

"One thing you learn in this business is that there's no such thing as coincidence. Everything that's happened tonight is related somehow. There may be different factions involved, but whatever it is they're after, they think you've got it."

"I—haven't—got—anything."

"Oh, I wouldn't say that," Marybeth chided. Then she held out her hand to Foley. "By the way, I don't think we've been properly introduced. I'm Marybeth Maples."

The special agent managed a weak smile as he shook her hand. "Alexander Foley. Call me Alex."

"Nice to meet you, Alex. Call me Marybeth."

"And call me dead if we don't get out of here soon." Blaine pushed himself upright. The feeling had returned to his extremities, but the pit of his stomach was in dire straits; there were men trying hard to kill him and he did not know why. "This guy knows where we are, so let's not be here. We'll try the next building. He can't cut all the circuits."

He marched along the corridor away from the doorway they had entered. His warmed index finger lay inside the trigger guard, ready at a moment's notice to exert pressure. Alex stood up and helped Marybeth to her feet. He kept his arm around her as they trudged through semidarkness toward the opposite end of the building.

Blaine came to a classroom door that was open. He peered cautiously into the room and out the windows on the other side. Saplings planted in mulch looked like silent sentinels, but nothing out there moved. When Alex and Marybeth reached his position he waved them past. A few seconds later they halted at the doorway leading to a cement courtyard.

Three more prefabricated classrooms lay parallel to the one they were in, each separated by ten yards of grass. The courtyard blended in with a basketball court that bounded the back wall of the administration building: four stories of faded red brick covered with creeping vines, and armored by dense shrubbery. If emergency vehicles were still flashing lights in the parking lot they were not visible from here.

Blaine studied his field of vision. "Okay, we run across to the next classroom and go for the fire alarm."

"Wouldn't it be better to—"

"Just do it!" Blaine pushed the handle and stepped out into the cold, fanning the Uzi from side to side. He took particular care to look to the right, in case the evanescent dark figure was lurking at the end of the dorm. He saw no movement, but noticed a small junction box with an open lid; although the stars did not shine brightly enough to see inside, he assumed it was the alarm control box. He pointed it out to Alex as he and Marybeth emerged from the warm cocoon of the classroom building. He put a finger to his lips, then signaled for them to follow. Alex protested, but Blaine shut him up with a pointed finger and a stern look.

Instead of heading for the next classroom, he ran across the cement toward the basketball court. He did not like being exposed but it was the only way to reach the administration building. He broke no records on the hundred-yard dash only because he did not want to outdistance Alex and Marybeth. Less than half a minute later they squeezed through the giant hedgerow that cloaked the lower level to a height of ten feet. They were totally concealed.

"I thought you said—" Alex started.

"That was for him." Blaine's hoarse whisper was barely perceptible. To him it appeared that they had made the crossing unseen. "A red herring. In case they have a listening device." He strained his ears for sounds of pursuit. He heard a car drive by on the other side of the building. "Come on."

The administration building was surrounded by bushes in the same manner in which a medieval castle was encircled by a water-filled moat. Without explanation Blaine skittered along the vine-covered wall behind the shrubbery, feeling his way with freezing hands. The blackness was absolute. He halted when he reached the corner, made sure Marybeth and Alex were behind him, then made the turn and continued along the hidden highway toward the street that passed by the front of the building. Civilization could not be far away.

Blaine hit the dirt and low-crawled between two fat shrubs. In front of him was a short plot of grass, a cement sidewalk, more grass, a curb, and a two-lane macadam road. Stately spruce trees grew in the grass zone separating the sidewalk from the curb. Fifty feet in either direction creosoted power poles bearing telephone lines and electrical cables also sported incandescent streetlights. Far off to the right the flashing lights of emergency vehicles were faintly visible around the bend of Langdon Hall; the sirens had been turned off. Blaine breathed a sigh of relief that made him forget for the moment the bitter cold.

"Don't be too eager, Dr. Mitchell" Alex plopped down next to him and peered out from under the foliage. "If someone wants you bad enough to hire a multinational guerrilla force, they may not hesitate at sacrificing a hit man to take you out from under the nose of a police battalion."

"I need to hear that as much as I need to hear I've got an inoperable brain tumor." Blaine's chattering teeth broke his words into single syllables. "There's some cosmic mix-up here, someone else these guys are looking for. There's got to be." After a pause, "So, what's our next move?"

"A patrol car's got to come—"

Marybeth burrowed in between the two men; she was shaking like a leaf in a summer gale. "The three of us together don't have enough body heat to show up on infrared. Do you mind if I make a suggestion?"

"You may be the self-proclaimed psychic, but I can

read your mind." Blaine nudged the Uzi out into the open. "Let's march down there and turn ourselves in. We can get heat and protection at the same time."

"I'd give anything for a hot bath."

Alex bit his lower lip, then blew out a stream of condensate. "You're right. We can't stand this much longer. But let me go first."

Blaine conceded with a show of palms. "Be my guest."

No sooner had the special agent crept out from under the bush than he jumped back. "Someone's coming. Long gray overcoat with something strange on his head. No gun."

"Marybeth, stop your teeth from chattering or he'll hear you." Blaine hazarded a peek.

The stranger was coming from the direction of Langdon Hall. When he passed under the streetlight the yellow glow shone down on a tall lanky body clad in white fur and wearing a bulky off white hat with long earflaps; he was carrying a bowling ball bag. Because the light was behind him, his face was a blank. Marybeth stuck her finger between chattering teeth. As the man passed in front of them the muted strains of Tchaikovsky's *1812 Overture* were faintly audible in the frigid air. No one moved until his long, steady gait carried him well past the next streetlight.

"Paranoia rears its ugly head." Blaine turned to Alex. "We can't go through life suspecting everyone in a winter coat and a Walkman."

"He reminded me of the man at the bridge," Marybeth said between chatters.

The special agent let out a breath he had been holding for too long. Lying prone, he slumped so his forehead fell against the hand holding the pistol. I'm beginning to dislike field work."

"How long have you been at it?"

"About two days. This is my first assignment."

"Your first—"

Alex cut Blaine off by rising to his hands and knees and crawling out from under the bushes. "Come on.

Let's go talk to the police. I've got to call headquarters and tell them we've stumbled into a hornet's nest."

Blaine hesitated only long enough to drag Marybeth out from under the shrubbery and help her to her feet. She shivered and hugged her chest, but still refused to utter a complaint. Blaine tagged along behind Alex, all the time keeping a sharp eye in all directions.

"I thought you said you were a special agent?" Blaine said accusingly.

"I am. All field workers are referred to as special agents."

Blaine's anger was undoubtedly an overreaction to the evening's terrifying events. "Great. So they send out a lone rookie who runs out of bullets in the first round. What were you supposed to do—negotiate?"

"This started out as a simple assignment, not an underground war," Alex crescendoed. "Hell, I've never even pulled a gun before except on the firing range. I'm an investigator. I work in an office nine to five, with heat and phones and a pot of coffee on the desk. I collect reports, process paperwork, and conduct computer scans. It's as boring as the daytime soaps." Alex scowled, and convulsed with cold. "But it sure beats the hell out of *this*."

They passed the edge of the administration building. A stone pathway separated it from the rear of Langdon Hall: a facing with no windows. The flashing lights became more obvious. When they rounded the corner of the lecture hall it was like entering a triptych painted by Hieronymus Bosch.

The center of the parking lot was a burned out cinder. Wisps of smoke climbed skyward, collecting overhead in the form of a gray vaporous mushroom. Three fire engines and a hook-and-ladder were strategically located like circled Conestogas preparing for an Indian attack. Small gasoline blazes that dotted the landscape were being chased down by fire fighters who skidded awkwardly on what had been turned into a skating rink by pumping trucks and subfreezing temperatures.

About a dozen patrol cars were parked haphazardly on the grass, seemingly the result of college pranksters; they created an unofficial cordon to keep people in rather than out. In addition to uniformed police, security guards, plainclothes agents, and a pacing swat team, about fifty people—lecture attendees— were amassed around the demolished portico. There was a constant transfusion of people through the shattered windows.

The smell of burnt paint and leather upholstery hung in the air, and mingled with unburned hydrocarbons from the exhausts of waiting ambulances, paddy wagons, and rescue vehicles. The din of shouting doctors and bellowing police officers reminded Blaine of initiation day at a basic training camp.

At the perimeter of the main arena stood the nameless reporter who had so infuriated Blaine with his obtuse observations—was it only half an hour ago? With one hand the reporter dabbed a jagged scar on his temple with a bloody handkerchief, while with the other he gesticulated wildly. Words lost in the surrounding cacophony seemed to interest a slump-shouldered man wearing a felt hat; he listened with a cocked head and took notes on a large white pad attached to a Bakelite clipboard.

When the reporter noticed the approaching trio he let out a scream that brought half a dozen guns swinging in his direction. Once he pointed excitedly at Blaine, the pistols, rifles, and autopump shotguns shifted their aiming point and allowed for Kentucky windage—and the number increased to a score. The slump-shouldered man let the clipboard drop to his side. He raised his right arm in a way that demonstrated complete authority. Not a single cop or swat-team sharpshooter relaxed, but neither did they fill the air with lead.

Blaine and Alex stopped in their tracks, acting as a shield for Marybeth. The policemen stared them down. For a long moment both partisans stood riveted in a Mexican standoff.

Blaine tried his hardest not to move, not to trigger an event, but he was so cold that he could not stop shivering. The Uzi was angled downward and to the side in a position he hoped was not threatening. He realized that they were a scruffy-looking bunch, strangely armed and arrayed and with clothes torn and disheveled.

The officer in charge advanced slowly, leadenly, like a wind-up soldier. Tiny particles of ice clung to a thick mustache. Bushy brows billowed into a creased forehead, lids hung low over dark brown eyes; crow's feet and sagging jowls attested to more than middle age. But the pronounced tired look was completely offset by a penetrating stare that never left Blaine's eyes. He stopped an arm's length away.

"Dr. Mitchell, I presume?"

Like Livingstone confronting Stanley, Blaine could think of nothing more creative to say than, "Yes."

Chapter 4

"Dr. Mitchell."

Blaine heard the muffled voice from a distance. He tried to wake up, but he had been on call for more than twenty hours and was dead tired. He had done three neurological examinations, treated an accident victim with severe head trauma and brain lesions, spent two hours in the OR assisting on a case of a subdural hematoma, admitted a patient with Parkinson's disease, and read CAT scans until he was bleary-eyed; and that was in addition to morning rounds and afternoon meetings with physical therapists. He could not face an emergency case now; he might botch the diagnosis.

"Dr. Mitchell."

He knew the voice would not stop nagging until he answered. He reached out for the telephone and instead encountered the fleshy part of Marybeth's inner thigh. That jolted him to instant alertness. He jerked back like a kid caught with his hand in a cookie jar. Marybeth's eyes rolled dreamily as she stretched out on the sofa and turned the other way, dragging most of the blankets with her.

Special Agent Alexander Foley looked down from his six-foot-two height. The smile on his face was not inviting, but the two cups of coffee he held in his hands and the bag of doughnuts clutched under his arm certainly were. The smell alone of black brew was enough to evoke memories of long days of internship.

Blaine reached out automatically. "Thanks. And for services rendered you can call me Blaine."

"Which services are those? Dragging you through a frozen battlefield, or bringing you a coffee?"

"Both. But right now for the coffee." Blaine sat up and sipped over the top of the Styrofoam cup; the liquid burned his lips but he drank it anyway. "I'll take a doughnut, too."

Alex sat down on the only chair, and leaned against

the table on which he placed the white paper bag and the other cup of coffee. There was no other furniture in the room. "Marybeth, I've got one for you, too."

If she heard him she did not acknowledge. She lay curled up like a cat under three layers of wool.

Alex shrugged. "Chocolate or jelly?"

Blaine took back a bit of blanket so it covered his left shoulder. "Surprise me." He took what was proffered and bit into it without looking. He munched and swallowed, and washed it down with a swig of coffee. "So, what's the verdict? Am I in hot water or just a steam bath?"

Alex laughed. "You know, you don't talk like a doctor."

"How does a doctor talk?"

"I don't know. I guess, in language that normal people don't use and can't understand. Infarctions rather than contractions. Like the medical terminology you used at your lecture."

"You were there?"

"Hanging on every word, even the one's I never heard of."

Blaine took another bite and another swig. "The first thing you have to learn about doctors is that they all start out as people. Only the one's on their way to godhood leave their humanity in medical school"

Alex laughed again. "You reamed out that reporter the same way."

"You were there, too?"

"Right by your side. It didn't seem like the appropriate time to interrogate you about anonymous death threats, but I hovered around in case anyone made a move on you. If I'd been a little sharper I'd have caught that pickpocket before he got to you."

"Thereby sealing my fate."

"In retrospect, yes. But—"

"You also saved my ass from that cowboy in the parking lot." Alex jerked a thumb at Marybeth. "Her ass, too."

Alex bit his lip and stared sightlessly at one of the four blank walls. Several seconds passed before he could bring himself to speak. "Dr. Mitchell, er, Blaine, er, I'm sorry I—froze on you out there—"

"Don't worry about it, Alex. It was cold enough to freeze the buns off a bunny." He stuffed the last bit of doughnut in his mouth, stood up, took two steps across the room, and rustled through the bag for another. "Never apologize for being human. It's a trait that we can't live without."

Alex humphed. "Has anyone ever told you that you have great bedside manner?"

Blaine thought about it for a moment. "As a matter of fact . . .

Alex smiled with a faint blush and shook his head. Blaine chomped his way through the second doughnut.

After a prolonged silence Marybeth sat up and opened her eyes. "All right, you two, what's going on behind my back?"

"I knew she was awake." Blaine scooped up the other cup of coffee and held it out for her. "Here, take this." When she hesitated, he added, "Doctor's orders."

She gave him a baleful eye, but took the cup. "Oh, it feels so good in my hands. I think I'll just hold it."

"That's always been your problem, Marybeth." Before she could reply, Blaine went on, "So what's the news from headquarters?"

Alex tilted his head. "It's too early to tell. The day shift won't be coming on till eight o'clock." He glanced at his watch. "Three more hours. It'll be a while before my report is processed. In the meantime, Captain Lawson has the entire police department on the scene, and he's checking out leads. You are a very unpopular person right now."

"I was pretty popular a few hours ago."

"Among certain factions. But there are quite a few people who haven't gotten to bed yet. Lawson won't release a soul till each and every one has been interrogated. It's a madhouse downstairs."

Blaine whistled. "You're talking about several hundred busy and high-strung doctors, some with planes to catch."

"The one's with early flights are getting priority treatment. Lawson's pulled cops off the beat to help with the paperwork, and dragged others out of bed; they're down there now writing field reports instead of speeding tickets. And the parking lot is sealed till further notice. Those who drove to the lecture last night have had their cars impounded till a bomb squad can defuse them all."

"Does that mean you think I wasn't the prime target?"

"No, it means we're covering all bases. I've discussed this pretty thoroughly with Lawson and, while we haven't reached any conclusions yet, it's obvious that you are directly involved in this case."

"Now wait just a—"

Alex held up his hands defensively. "Don't get me wrong. I'm not accusing you of anything. What I'm saying is that, for reasons not yet established, certain factions and/or individuals have been led to believe that your work is important enough to require the kind of attention that it got last night."

"My work?" Blaine practically shouted.

"Okay, that's an assumption on my part. Lawson doesn't agree with me by a long shot. But let's suppose, from the investigator's perspective, that you have a clean slate—that your personal record demonstrates no irregularities of a criminal nature. And I'm going out on a limb here because I haven't even seen your personnel file; this whole thing blew up so fast."

"No pun intended."

There was not even a hint of humor in Alex's tone or expression. For the moment he was all special agent. "As far as I'm concerned, you're an innocent bystander someone is trying to kill. And that's all. Until I get some background data, anything else is open to interpretation. The chief handed me a cover sheet, told me to check you out, you turned up missing, and that seemed to verify foul play along the line. I called your house and got a recording, I called your office and was told that you wouldn't be in till Saturday, but that you were giving a very important lecture Friday night and were expected to be there. You know the rest."

Blaine mulled over Alex's summation. "My work routine is certainly no secret. Anyone could have called and gotten the same information. The only thing no one knew is that after the Berkeley conference I went backpacking in Yosemite. It was a spur-of-the-moment decision."

"You still should have called me," Marybeth piped in. The blankets slipped to her waist; she still wore Blaine's blue coat.

Blaine craned his neck and raised his eyebrows. "I told you. They lambasted me so hard out there that I wanted to stretch my mind and muscles before facing another antagonistic audience. Of course, I never expected such a hostile reception." He took a deep draft of coffee. "Pun intended."

"How can you be so casual when people are trying to kill you?"

"It's easy now that it's over. Last night's experience was shocking, perhaps terrifying, but today I'm feeling the flush of post-traumatic exhilaration. I'm damned happy to be alive, and you should be, too. Doctor's orders."

Marybeth scowled as she took her first sip of coffee.

Alex had no time for nonsense. "Excuse me, Blaine, but I'd like to go over a few things with you while they're still fresh in your mind. We need to establish some kind of motivation for the threats on your life."

Blaine acknowledged with a nod. "We're way beyond the threat stage."

The special agent was all business. He fished a microcassette recorder from his coat pocket and pressed a red button on its side. "I'm taping this for the record, so I won't have to take notes. First of all, did you recognize any of the men who attacked you in the parking lot last night?"

Blaine shook his head. "No, I never saw any of them before."

"Did you notice any of them at your lecture, either

in the audience or during the reception?"

"No."

"Did you see any of them at Berkeley? Could they have been following your lecture circuit?"

"Not that I recall."

"Have you ever seen them, or men dressed like them, at your office or hanging around your house?"

"No."

"Could they have been patients of yours at one time?"

"I haven't practiced medicine for ten years. But still, none of their faces are familiar."

"How about the pickpocket? Had you noticed him at all during the evening?"

"No. I was besieged by colleagues and didn't pay much attention to who was beyond my immediate field of view."

"Do you remember what you were talking about just prior to him bumping in to you?"

Blaine thought for a moment. "Sorry. No." Then, after a pause, "Wait a minute. Wasn't it about—" He looked at Marybeth. "Weren't we talking about Young's daughter getting married?"

"That's right!" Marybeth explained to Alex, "J. Worthington Young is the head of the Institute. He—"

"Pardon me." To Blaine, "Didn't you mention having a print-out for him in your car?" The special agent made it sound like a statement.

"Oh, that's right. It was a copy of the computer file on our latest analyses. I took it with me to California in order to update my lecture format. The original data in my paper—"

"Wait, wait, wait. I'm getting confused by all these dates and updates, papers and lectures. Can you give me a brief description and chronology?" When Blaine pinched his eyes questioningly, Alex went on, "Remember what I said—if these people are not after you for personal transgressions, they must be after something you're working on."

Blaine shrugged. "I follow your reasoning. And I

don't object to your line of inquiry. It's just difficult to condense ten years of work into twenty-five words or less. Furthermore, I find it impossible to believe that my work at the Institute is a matter of life and death."

"Blaine!" Marybeth objected, spilling her coffee in sudden agitation. "Your work is *only* about life and death."

"In a clinical sense, yes." To Alex, "A lot of our research is based upon the climactic response of terminally ill patients."

"Excuse me, doctor," Alex frowned. "Climactic response? Are you talking about sexual activity among the dying?"

Now it was Blaine's turn to be serious. "No, I'm talking about the chemical changes and hormonal releases that occur when a person expires, an event that triggers bizarre neurotransmissions that are observable in EEG tracings, quantifiable in a holistic concept of brain function, and repeatable in laboratory tests."

"Repeatable? You mean, you make people die more than once?" Alex's expression changed to one of dismay. "I'm sorry, I didn't mean—"

"That's okay. I was unclear. I'm so used to discussing these issues with my colleagues that I sometimes forget our terminology has become so specialized. We also work with lab animals: rats, white mice, and chimpanzees."

The relief was evident on Alex's face. "What? No guinea pigs?"

"They're out of vogue." Blaine swallowed the last of his coffee. "What all this is leading up to is human brain research, both autonomic and in interrelationship with the body and mind, the study of neurological disease and cure, the affects of perception on consciousness, the manifestation of distortions—"

"Okay, okay. You're getting beyond me."

"I wasn't being pedantic, Alex, I was just trying to explain the nature of the work being conducted at the Institute."

"I heard your lecture last night, and I think I got

more out of it than that reporter did."

"That's not saying much. Besides, as you've already seen, my particular research on artificially induced changes in the levels of consciousness and the mitigation of sensory pain has reached a stage of controversy that is not related to other projects under investigation at the Institute. Actually, there's not as much debate about my approach to methodology as there is about certain peripheral findings and resultant philosophical implications—"

"Blaine?" Alex held out his hands once again. "Let's move on to chronology."

"Right. First of all, understand that all our work is funded by private grant, and for that money we are expected to produce results. I don't mean we have to make discoveries or prove theories, although that is the ultimate goal of any scientific research project, but we do have to file monthly program reports—so our benefactors can keep tabs on how their money is being spent. In addition, all researchers are expected to publish the results of their work in bona fide journals—it helps others working on similar projects to know what else is going on in the field. That way we can reduce the amount of duplication of effort while permitting others to refute or corroborate results by independent experiment and analysis.

"In the interests of economy I sometimes submit my research papers as my progress report. Everything goes over Young's desk for approval, and he—his secretary, really—does the actual mailing. Last month's report was submitted to the *Neurological Journal*, which promised immediate publication." Blaine humphed. "That doesn't mean that they agreed with my findings, only that they found them 'speculatively intriguing.' Our computer modem transmits the manuscript directly to their automatic typesetter so there's no chance of typographical errors not made by me or by the review board. The *Journal* was published last week, mailed over the weekend, and arrived on most subscribers' desks on Monday.

"In the interim Marybeth worked up some subsequent analyses which, although she disagrees with my interpretations—" She wrinkled her nose at him. "—I incorporated in my Berkeley lecture on Saturday—two days before it came out in print. Then I took off for the mountains for a week, flew in late yesterday afternoon, and drove directly to the college—stopping for dinner along the way, and diddling over my coffee long enough to arrive too late to get into any heated discussions before I had the opportunity to speak my mind. And, as you have already said, you know the rest. So where does that leave us?"

Alex switched off the tape machine. "Off the record?" He waited for Blaine to nod before going on. "I haven't got a clue."

During the silence that persisted in the room for perhaps half a minute, Blaine listened to the sounds beyond the sheetrocked partitions: a continuous din of clattering typewriters, ringing telephones, grating file drawers, and a shouting match of discordant voices. He peered at the soggy coffee grounds that were sloshing at the bottom of the Styrofoam cup, searching for answers to which he did not even know the questions.

Twenty-four hours ago he had been at the height of ecstasy: warm, cozy, successful, secure in his place in the world. Now control of his life seemed to have been taken away from him—as it had once before. Someone—or something—was slashing at his reins and driving him in a direction he did not want to go. For a man who had a solid purpose in life it was a feeling he could not live with. He found it alarming how quickly the stable human condition could be reduced to raw stimulus response.

A doctor is no stranger to adversity, Blaine less than most. For practically his entire adult life he had dealt with death on a daily basis, from Asian jungles to operating rooms. If a lawyer who defends himself has a fool for a client, a doctor who heeds his own medical advice should get a second opinion. It was time to ask for a prescription.

"So where does that leave us?"

Alex pursed his lips. "What would you say to a patient who asked that question halfway through an exam?"

"I'd say let's do a complete work-up, run some tests, and see what turns up."

"And that's what we're doing. We need more information before we can determine what these people are after. There are bodies to identify, vehicle registrations to trace, weapons' serial numbers to check out. Those are the lab tests in the arsenal of law enforcement. It's neither an easy nor a short process. Meanwhile we keep the patient in a guarded condition."

"Meaning?"

"Protective custody is the best medicine. Police escort allows more freedom but is open to infection. Surveillance is usually nothing more than an invitation to incurable disease. The hot line is a placebo."

"So I've got a choice of everything from ICU to out-patient clinic."

The special agent nodded. "Depending upon the severity of the illness." Blaine could not help but smile. "You know something, Alex? You've got a pretty good bedside manner yourself."

The shrug was barely noticeable. "The rush of events has forced my learning curve. I just want you to be aware of all the variables in this case. So far we know practically nothing, but we can't take a devil-may-care attitude. Captain Lawson's got his men and computers working overtime trying to—"

The door burst open and framed the sour-looking police captain. "Did I hear my name?"

Marybeth perked up sharply. "There was mention of the devil."

Lawson glowered at her. "Still with the sharp tongue, young lady?"

During the initial interrogation Marybeth had expressed herself with growing exacerbation that had not endeared her to the captain. "I think victims should be treated with more respect than you hold for your Friday night drunks and commonplace lowlifes."

Despite his perpetual stoop, the heavy, dark brown three-piece fit the captain well; only the pants legs were a bit baggy—a style that had not been seen in decades, and probably an indication of the age of the suit. He jerked a thumb at Alex. "The only reason you're not in the tank is because you had a federal agent with you to verify your statements." He promptly ignored her and turned to Blaine. "Have you ever heard of Dr. Blaine Mitchell?"

Blaine pinched his eyes in consternation.

"Dr. Blaine Appleton Mitchell?"

"N—no. My middle name is Thomas."

"Is he any relation?"

"Not that I'm aware of."

Captain Lawson referred to the torn computer printout he held in his hand, and read in a monotone, "Blaine Appleton Mitchell, age 63, doctor of pathology at Boston Central, was being investigated for possible underground drug connections. He owned a forty-two foot sloop that he sailed out of Boston Harbor, allegedly used to smuggle illegal substances picked up from offshore drop-offs. The Coast Guard caught him under suspicious circumstances and, although he had no incriminating evidence on board, after being told he was under surveillance he turned himself in to the local narcotics division and admitted that he was involved over his head and wanted out. He was plea bargaining for a reduced or suspended sentence."

Lawson's weathered face was impassive, as if he were listing the ingredients on a cereal box. "He was about to spill his guts about a lot of big-time people."

Blaine felt a wave of relief that was as powerful as that felt by a man who, indicted for murder, just received a verdict of not guilty.

The FBI agent was ever alert. "Pardon me, Captain, but did you say 'was'?"

There was still no expression on the Captain's face. "He died in his sleep Wednesday night. The autopsy report says cardiac arrest."

Chapter 5

"I hate feds."

It was the first time that Blaine had heard any emotion in Captain Lawson's voice, and, although the words were tinged with anger, they demonstrated a kind of communication that was at least slightly removed from machine language. The captain's face remained as obdurate as granite.

"Sir, I'm not trying to supersede your authority or undermine your jurisdiction. On the contrary, I invite your cooperation. But you must understand that this case is now a federal matter and must be handled by federal agents who are used to this kind of—"

"You think my people are incompetent? I'll have you know that the police in this department are among the best-trained investigators in the business. Just because we're a backwater county without a major city doesn't mean—"

"Captain Lawson, please listen to reason." Alex Foley leaned on bleached knuckles over the captain's paper-strewn desk. "Until we have more facts we cannot assume that this is a simple case of mistaken identity. Granted it looks that way now, but even if it is there are still antagonistic factions that might not be aware of the error."

"Mr. Foley, please don't insult me by putting assumptions in my mouth. I know what's going on. And I wasn't suggesting that we place an ad in the *Morning Chronicle* to announce the confusion and let Dr. Blaine go back to his rounds—or whatever he does at the Brain Lab. But until the Commissioner tells me otherwise, you're being tolerated as a guest."

Blaine listened to the slowly building crescendo with growing discomfort. "Perhaps it hasn't occurred to you that my life is more than a territorial dispute between—"

Captain Lawson held up an authoritative hand.

"Hold on, Dr. Mitchell." To Alex, "If you would like to call in your agents to *confer* with this department, I have no objection."

"That's acceptable to me. I'm not trying to take over—"

"*But*, I also want complete coordination. That means priority access to FBI computer files and duplicate copies of all investigative reports."

"You've got it. I'll even see to it that you get my pre-assignment memoranda and Dr. Blaine's case file—when it comes in. For your eyes only."

For a long moment Captain Lawson was silent. With all his demands met so easily he seemed not to know what to say next. "Very well." Now he could afford to be magnanimous. "And I'll make sure that you get photocopies of everything this department does in connection with this case. Dr. Mitchell, you had a comment to make?"

Admittedly, Blaine had never given much thought to police bureau politics, but he quickly perceived that it was just as hierarchical as the medical profession. Every occupation had its pecking order. Now that Alex and Lawson seemed to have established a protocol, his previous dissatisfaction evaporated.

"Yes. I'd like to go home." As an afterthought, he added, "And I'd like some protection."

Lawson cast gimlet eyes at the FBI man. "Foley."

"I'm going to stay with you—for a little while, at least, until we know what's going on. Captain, how soon can headquarters expect a pathology report?"

"The medical examiner is still doing autopsies—"

"Forget that, Captain. Fax the fingerprints and mug shots right away and let us do a computer scan. The sooner we know who the jokers are the better we'll know how to deal with the situation. If you want to accept the responsibility I'll assign you as local liaison. All reports will be routed through your office so you'll have first sight of everything. That way I can continue my field work while you hold the fort. I'll check in with you periodically."

If Captain Lawson was satisfied with Alex's cooperation before, now he was ecstatic. He almost showed it. "Okay."

Alex retrieved the tape recorder from his pocket and handed it to the police captain. "Thanks for the loan. There's not much there that you don't already know, but I've added same observations that I think bear looking into. Please see that a transcript gets sent to headquarters."

Lawson popped out the microcassette. "Okay. Anything else?"

Marybeth spoke up for the first time. She looked more refreshed now that she had washed her face and hands, combed her hair, and reapplied her make-up. "How about transportation?"

Things were moving a little too fast for Blaine, or too tangential, "Wait just a nanosecond. Before you call us a cab and kick us out into the cold, I'd like to discuss the issue of protection."

The special agent leaned nonchalantly against the captain's desk. "I'll be within arm's reach at all times, until a relief arrives who can—"

"I don't think you get my point." Blaine stared unwaveringly into Alex's eyes. "I appreciate your dedication and welcome your presence." To Lawson, "I'll even take a police escort if I can get it." Back to Alex, "But I'd feel a hell of a lot better if I had some personal protection. You know, like a gun?"

Alex was hurt, but Blaine could not afford to worry about the agent's feelings of insecurity when his own life was at stake. A person recovers from a bruised psyche quicker than from a case of steel-jacketed lead poisoning.

"Excuse me, Dr. Mitchell," said Captain Lawson implacably. "But after listening to your account of last night's events I'm not convinced you're the kind of man to be trusted with a loaded weapon. You're a bit hot-headed for my tastes."

"You mealy-mouthed son of a—" Blaine leaped to his feet so fast that the captain lurched back in his creaky swivel chair and rolled into the cluttered window sill behind him. "Have you forgotten that I was robbed, bombed, shot at, chased through the woods—"

Lawson recovered himself quickly. "Calm down, Dr. Mitchell. Calm down." The expression on his face and the tone of his voice remained inviolable. "I know you've been through a lot, and I can appreciate how you feel, but you're acting like a battered housewife who wants to set up a machine gun in her living room after getting a court order against her husband. You're not in the jungle any more. You can't shoot at everything that moves. This is a civilized country full of civilized people, and I don't want any of them shot accidentally because you mistook them for boogiemen."

"What the hell do you mean, boogiemen?" Blaine shouted. "I've studied dream states long enough to know the difference between reality and a nightmare—"

"Blaine." Marybeth's voice was serene, and in that serenity lay strength. "Blaine. All the captain's trying to say is—"

"Dr. Mitchell, don't you see how on edge you are?"

"Yes. And I also see a need to stay on edge. Let me recapitulate." Blaine stuck out fingers as he made his points. "One: a man picks my pocket and tries to steal my car. Two: my car is booby-trapped and only by a fluke am I not in it when it goes off. Three: two men try to kidnap me at gunpoint. Four: two cowboys don't even ask questions, they just try to gun me down in cold blood. Five: a sniper with a silencer shoots at me from behind." Blaine held up his other hand and extended his pinky. "And six: another guy pistol-whips a reporter, then comes after me in case everyone else misses. Now maybe five and six are working together because they tried to corner us in the woods, but I still count at least five enemy denominations out to get me, and goddamn it, I want a gun to protect myself."

During the long ensuing silence a pigeon landed on the outside window ledge and cooed disconsolately.

Captain Lawson inhaled deeply. "I see your point, Dr. Mitchell, and I don't blame you for being upset, but

I'm not allowed to issue side arms to overwrought citizens no matter how pressing the need. To do so would be a tacit implication to take the law into their own hands. This is not a vigilante community. That's why we have laws, police, judges, juries, and trials."

"Great! Would you please explain that to the men who are after my hide? I don't think they understand the rules of engagement."

"However, I cannot prevent you from picking up an application for a permit to carry a firearm. You can get one at the front desk."

"Captain, I don't own a gun. I've *never* owned a gun."

"You can always borrow one." There was not a hint of expression on Captain Lawson's face. He rummaged through the papers on his desk and found a red box of bullets. "Mr. Foley, if you will fill out the proper requisition form I can issue you this ammunition for that six-shooter of yours. You don't have to do it now."

Alex took the box. "Thanks, Captain. I appreciate it."

"Next time, carry at least one reload with you."

"Right."

"And—" Lawson yanked open a desk drawer, lifted out the tray, and pulled out a holstered Glock 9-millimeter, two cardboard cartons of cartridges, and a leather case full of cleaning tools and extra seventeen-shot magazines already loaded. "—in case that's not enough you can borrow my own personal piece. I've got others."

"Uh, thanks."

"I've got to keep the Uzi for evidence." Captain Lawson glanced at Blaine, then returned his penetrating gaze to Alex. "The Glock has more kick than that Smith & Wesson of yours. Think you can handle it?"

Alex cocked a brow. "In a pinch."

"I'd also like to have a couple of detectives tag along, to run interference."

"I'd be glad to have them."

"Dr. Mitchell, is that okay with you?"

Blaine maintained a facade of indifference. "If you think it's necessary."

"You never can tell. The world is full of crazies with hostile tendencies. Mr. Foley, those men will take instructions from you."

"Thank you."

Marybeth cut right through the subvocal innuendo. "Now that everyone's happy, can we leave?"

"Any time, Ms. Maples."

"Can you release Mr. Foley's car from impoundment?"

"Uh, I don't think that's a good idea." Alex looked sheepish. "We shouldn't move anything from the scene of the crime until the investigation team has completed its report. And besides—" He faltered for a moment while he worked his jaw. "—that Chrysler we were hiding behind was my car. From the motor pool. It might not be too comfortable with all that extra ventilation."

Blaine turned to Marybeth. "Don't tell me you parked in the lot, too."

"Right next to you."

As Blaine thought back on it he could remember her car going through its death throes. "The insurance companies are going to love us."

Again Captain Lawson inhaled deeply. "I shouldn't do this because all three of you are on a high-risk policy, but I'll see if highway patrol can spare an unmarked vehicle."

Thirty minutes later they sat across the front seat of a four-door sedan. Alex Foley cranked over the pre-warmed engine. Marybeth sat in the middle with her bare toes stuck in the heating vent. Blaine rode shotgun—literally; in his lap was a cardboard box full of papers, preliminary reports, and a small armory.

"Please drive carefully," Captain Lawson cautioned. "It wouldn't look good if you got a moving violation in a department vehicle."

"Tell it to the judge." Blaine was feeling better after a second cup of coffee. He was looking forward to a shower and a change of clothes. Sleep for the moment was out of the question, but he had gotten by on less when he was Chief Neurosurgeon at Hansen Medical.

Alex signaled by blinking his high beams. The detective in front pulled away from the curb and made a U-turn across the deserted street. Alex did the same. The maneuver was repeated by the follow-up detective. The three cars cruised eastward in the predawn cold along a route already cleared by patrolmen on the graveyard shift.

The fainter stars faded from sight as the sky slowly pinked. A lone condensation trail marred the cloudless horizon. During the night the temperature had dropped to the single digits, but still there was not a breath of air. When touched by passing headlights, hoarfrost that veneered the ground sparkled like angel's hair.

"So what's the prognosis, Alex? Is there any chance I'm a fall guy for that other doctor?"

"Even if his death wasn't suspicious I'd have to say no."

"What's suspicious about a cardiac arrest?" Marybeth gasped. "It's the second highest cause of death in the forty-eight states."

"The timing. Remember what I said about coincidences. In this business they can never be ignored. Pathologist Mitchell died only twenty-four hours after our office was tipped off. The caller did not specify a middle name, but did mention the Institute for Higher Research in Perceptual Functions of the Brain. That has to be you."

"Unless the Good Samaritan didn't know himself."

"There you go making chauvinistic assumptions," Marybeth chided.

"What chauvinism?"

"Alex never once said the person who dropped the quarter was male." Blaine leaned past Marybeth and confided in Alex, "Watch her. She's got a childhood scar that's still a festering sore." To Marybeth, "Pardon my English idiom."

She stuck out her tongue.

Alex ignored the repartee. "Of course, since we don't

know who the caller was or what he or she knows, it's possible that he or she thought it was meant for you and not the pathologist. The caller may have made the wrong assumption."

"So did a whole bunch of other people."

"True, but the initial misinformation may have originated from the same source. If this pathologist was about to incriminate a lot of rich businessmen—that is, uh, business people—and political figures, and hit men were hired to protect their reputations, and one of the guilty parties found out about the conspiracy of murder and wanted to prevent it without getting directly involved—moralistically, drug dealing is a long way from homicide—then he or she may have decided to stave off the execution."

"That's an awful lot of ifs."

Alex laughed. "Now you know why it's better to wait for more information before proposing theories. I usually have a gut feeling about cases, but that only gives me direction. There's still a lot of field work to be done."

"Do you think those dead men will tell us anything?"

"You'd be surprised how much we can learn from a corpse. We track bodies like you track antibodies. Stomach contents might tell us when and where he last ate. Or she." He glanced quickly at Marybeth, but she was busy rubbing her ankles. "The same with food caught between the teeth or in the gums. Dirt stuck to his shoes might reveal where he came from. . . . "

"Real Sherlock Holmes stuff."

"Only much more sophisticated. I hardly need to explain forensic medicine to *you.*"

Blaine shrugged it off. Throughout his life he had encountered people who thought that because he was a doctor he knew absolutely everything there was to know about sickness, disease, injury, and the practically limitless malfunctions of the human and animal body. Pet owners were always asking him to look at their dogs, cats, and canaries. Acquaintances wanted advice on pimples, sore feet, thinning hair, rashes, heart palpitations, glandular complaints, indigestion, lower back pain, boils, distemper, lumbago, and organic disorders. Those who knew he worked at the Institute often asked for opinions about neighbors or relatives who were "not right" in the head. He gave simple advice and suggested that they see a specialist. He tried to be friendly.

"The only one who won't do us any good is the pickpocket."

"He already did his part," Blaine interjected.

"Fingerprint tracing and mug shot comparisons require fingers and a face. The largest pieces we found of *him* were a burned piece of skull, a section of torso, and a femur. They're still out there scraping the parking lot for—"

"Alex! Please!" Marybeth flipped the fan switch up a notch and wriggled her toes in the hot air flow. "You don't need to go into the gory details."

"Sorry."

"I hate to sound like an anxious patient," Blaine said. "But how long will it take to get some positive ID on these guys?"

"We could have something today if they're on file. Our central computer classifies fingerprints by whirl patterns that—"

Blaine held up a hand. "Spare me the itemized account."

"You'll have to pardon me for rambling. I do that kind of work all the time—for field operatives—and I sometimes get carried away with the sheer technology we have at our fingertips—" Alex paused, but said nothing about puns. "Nothing personal, Blaine, but there have been times in the past two days that I wished I was back at headquarters. I never knew how good I had it."

"It's the green-grass/fence syndrome. Marybeth, are you sure you want to come in today?"

Greensborough was not a big city, but neither was it a sleepy rural community. It was spread out rather than up, was paved with grass rather than concrete, and had more groves than buildings. Every crime imaginable was perpetrated within its boundaries, but on a scale commensurate with its population. Its biggest claim to fame was Westmoreland University, which brought in students from all over the country—students who were more eager for a pastoral setting than for the credentials of larger and more well-respected colleges. The Institute was responsible for the high percentage of scientific types in an otherwise typical cross section of middle class society.

"You're not the only workaholic." She slipped on her shoes with a grimace. "But don't expect me at eight o'clock sharp, and don't expect me to be in the best of moods."

"Can we send a car to pick you up?" Alex stopped behind the lead detective, in front of a small Cape Cod with a neatly trimmed lawn. "Or swing by on our way in?"

I'll borrow Mother's car. She doesn't like to drive on Saturday because the college doesn't have class. Drag racers, you know."

"But the kids are gone for semester break."

"Tell her that."

Blaine stepped out into the bitter cold with the large box in his hands. Marybeth slid across the seat, stood quickly, and dashed along the flagstone walk to the front door.

"Hey, what about my coat?"

"I'll drop it off at the cleaner's."

"What about the pants and vest?"

She inserted her key. "Unless you want to give them to me now, you'll have to take them in yourself." She pushed open the door, turned, and waved.

Blaine waved back. Marybeth's mother waved from the picture window. Blaine rolled his eyes, got back in the car, and slammed the door. He put the box on the seat between him and Alex. "Home, James. This has been a rough night."

"For all of us."

Blaine's housing development was just outside of

town. The sprawling single-unit dwellings were constructed from four basic design plans, and were tastefully spaced throughout the natural pine forest. Curving driveways connected the houses like a spider web bracing droplets of dew. The faded brick facades gave the structures strength as well as a rustic flavor; each house had an attached, wooden garage. No overhead wires marred the pastoral beauty. Dumpsters were tactfully concealed in earthen revetments covered naturally with dried pine needles the color of burnt sienna.

Detective number one pulled onto the left side of the concrete apron, facing the garage door. Alex parked next to him, and detective number two boxed him in with his wheels partially on the lawn. Blaine suffered no disillusions about the maneuver; it might seem like overkill, but after last night, "over" was better than "under."

"Correct me if I'm wrong, Blaine, but weren't your keys vaporized over about an acre of Westmoreland's parking lot?"

Blaine smirked. "Not to worry. I have such a nasty habit of losing my keys that I keep an extra set hanging in that mulberry bush."

Although first light had given way to sunrise, the bright yellow ball was yet hidden by the trees. Any warming affect was purely psychological. Blaine dashed out of the car and rummaged frantically through the bush with quickly freezing fingers.

"I don't understand. The only way you can get home is to drive, so how can you lose your house key when it's on the same ring as your car keys?"

"It takes genius." Blaine located the key, managed to get it in the lock despite trembling hands, and pushed his way inside. The living room was neat; with nothing in it but a chair, a sofa, and one end table without a lamp, it could not be otherwise. "I also lock them in the car a lot."

Alex signaled to the two detectives waiting in their cars, and closed the door. "Simple decor."

"I don't like clutter."

Blaine slipped the key into his pants pocket and rubbed his hands vigorously. "Are you going to watch me take a shower, or can I have the bathroom to myself for a few minutes?"

"You can have your privacy. In the mean time I'd like to read that paper you wrote that caused so much controversy."

"In the study." Blaine led the way past the kitchen and bathroom to the end of a short hallway. The bedroom was the smaller room on the right, and faced the back of the house; it was furnished sparingly with a double bed, a bureau, and a chest of drawers. The larger room was the study, filled to capacity with a massive oak desk, a computer console, three filing cabinets, and floor-to-ceiling bookshelves. With shades drawn across the window the room was as dark as the rest of the house. He turned on the ceiling light from the switch at the door. "I'm connected to the Institute's mainframe so I can work at home when—"

The man in Blaine's desk chair sat with his head slumped forward on the ink blotter. Both arms were spread out in front of him as if he had fallen asleep while tidying loose papers. There was no blood.

Alex drew his gun so fast that the friction singed the leather holster.

Blaine advanced slowly, expecting at any second that the man would wake up, yawn, brush off his beige suit, comb his short, blond hair, and apologize for the intrusion. But there was no movement, no sound, no telltale sign of breathing. Although he knew intellectually that nothing less than an examination of vital signs could establish a clinical diagnosis, Blaine had enough experience with death to know it when he saw it. He touched the man's wrist, then his neck.

"No pulse."

The peculiar rigidity of the skin was a sign of rigor mortis.

"Dead about eight hours."

He rolled the man's head to the side. One blue eye stared sightlessly from under the half-closed lid. Beige, blond, and blue suddenly joined in a cohesive color pattern that jutted Blaine's memory. For a moment he was lost in a pastel world between reality and nightmare. Had he dreamt about this man, or seen him through the short-circuiting process of déjà vu?

Then he remembered all too clearly. "It's the pick-pocket!"

Chapter 6

The icy fist on Blaine's neck yanked him back so hard that he nearly suffered a cervical fracture. He was forcibly dragged aside, out of the room, and into the hall.

"Don't touch anything!" Alex commanded through gritted teeth. He stuck his revolver into the bedroom for an instant, then spun around sharply and pointed it past the kitchen and bathroom. "*Nothing*, you hear?"

"Alex, he's not going to come back to life. He can't hurt us."

"And maybe his murderer's hiding under the bed or standing in the shower."

That made Blaine think twice. Chills rode his spine like a train on a cog railway. He had a sudden urge to race out of the house and into the open, where he could see the world in all its starkness and confront those who were skulking after him.

Alex did his best to help. He propelled Blaine into the living room, then turned and covered their rear, fanning his gun across the open-counter kitchen. The only sound audible was the soft hum of the heater and the special agent's hard breathing.

"At least let me get my parka—"

"Nothing!" Alex let go of Blaine's neck only long enough to twist the doorknob. Then he grabbed Blaine's shirt collar and shoved him outside. He used his gun hand to shut the door behind him.

Both detectives popped out of their cars at the same time.

Alex hustled Blaine forward, shouting, "Get on the radio and tell Lawson there's a dead body in there. And watch that door. No one goes in, no one comes out." The tension on his face was evident.

Tired of feeling like a kitten in its mother's mouth, Blaine struggled free of Alex's iron grip. He was not used to being manhandled, but under the circumstances he was gratified to see the special agent taking a firm hold of the situation.

"Get in the car!"

Blaine was already halfway there. "You don't have to shout." Nothing could keep him out in that cold dressed the way he was. After sliding into the seat, the first thing he did was to take out the Glock, slam in a full clip, and flip off the safety. Then he closed the door.

"Sorry, Blaine. Maybe I overreacted, but—"

"Don't worry about it." He pulled back the receiver and chambered a round. "Just keep doing your job and we'll all live happily ever after."

"*Christ* I'm scared. I wish I knew what the *hell* was going on."

"No chance this is a coincidence, I guess?"

Alex's stare could have stopped a herd of water buffalo.

"I didn't think so." An odd calm came over Blaine. The gun fit neatly into his right palm—his left one still hurt from the missing patch of skin—and brought back a flood of memories that last night's shoot-out had been too fleeting to evoke. "So what do we do now?"

Alex switched on the police band radio.

"—don't believe this guy. Death seems to follow him around like he's got it on a leash. Did he take the Hippocratic oath or the hypocritic oath? And I thought Frankenstein—"

"Lawson! Captain Lawson!"

Blaine casually picked up the microphone and handed it to Alex. "You have to push the button."

"Captain Lawson. Foley here. Over."

"No need to shout, son. What is it?"

"Captain, I want a guard posted on Dr. Mitchell's house until a site team from headquarters arrives. Over."

"That body's not going to get up and walk away."

"I don't want anyone going in there, Captain. I've got a crazy hunch about this case. Something weird is going on."

"You've noticed."

"Captain, just do it. This is more important than the Westmoreland parking lot. I'm calling for security clearance on this, with a code one safety imperative."

"What's that supposed to me—"

"Just call headquarters and tell them. They'll know what to do. I—let me think a minute and I'll—over and out." He hung up the mike. "Blaine, this is getting way out of control."

"What do you mean 'getting?' It's gotten."

The radio blared, "Taylor, do what he says. Tape the door and put up a barricade. And stay there until the FBI—"

Alex switched off the radio. His head shook in a continuous nervous tic. "There's no doubt about it. These people, whoever they are, are after *you*—not a penny-ante grass importer. You've got something—"

"You don't know that."

"I know it. I feel it. You've got something they want, or something they think they want, or maybe something they don't want anyone else to have. I'm not quite sure what it is yet, but I heard it in your lecture last night. And it's undoubtedly in your paper, too."

"Electrical stimulation of the brain is hardly just cause for murder, despite the rhetorical phlebotomy you heard to the contrary."

"The what?"

"Bloodletting." Blaine could not help but shudder at the vitriolic diatribe fired at him after the lecture. It was as much a blow to his professional pride as bullets to his body, and, if his hypotheses turned out to be wrong or could be disproven by his rivals, could be every bit as disastrous to his continuance in the field of medicine—the only life he had. In that respect, he was more afraid of losing face in the scientific community than losing his head in Greensborough. A man facing him with a gun was an order of battle he could deal with frontally—a fight which, if lost, was without repercussions.

"There's been enough of that." Alex calmed down visibly. Blaine observed that the agent recuperated from stress more quickly this morning than he had last night. It was a response with which he was all too familiar. "Blaine, that stuff you were saying about morphine receptors and brain pacemakers—was that theoretical?"

"No, it's old hat. It's my new hat approach that has caused such an uproar, and not just because the pacemaker we've developed is worn externally and doesn't have to be surgically implanted. As a biofeedback device it makes superfluous the synthesis of naturally occurring opiates such as enkephalins and endorphins, except perhaps as a first aid measure. The combination of special receptor cells and a circulating neural hormone—"

"You're getting beyond me, doctor, but I think you're on the right track."

Blaine tempered his voice with feigned sarcasm. "Is that your medical opinion?"

"Call it a professional opinion. I think your discoveries have far broader applications than you've had time to consider, and that people other than myself have made the same determination. Your colleagues may be concerned about cutbacks in their own lines of research, maybe even the termination of their projects, but we're dealing with elements who have more in mind than academic studies."

"My patrons obviously agree with you. They've forked over enough money to fund a moon landing, and that's got a lot of people pissed—my boss included. And you're right: we haven't begun to explore the potential of the bypass skullcap, as we call it. Frequency modulation alone—"

"Hold on, Blaine, you're getting beyond me again. But you've got me fired up. I'd like to see your—"

"Better than being fired *on*."

"—lab complex and get a real feel for what you're doing and how you do it. I need to experience this invention of yours before I can understand its significance. Then maybe I'll know what we're up against."

"It's our next stop anyway, if you were planning to

keep me company until reinforcements arrive. But what about—" Blaine pointed the pistol at his study window. "—our twice dead companion? How do you account for that? Cat's may have nine lives, but men don't have two deaths."

Alex looked bewildered. "I don't know. I—I'm a deeply religious person, but in this case I'd be inclined to say that we're dealing with the supernatural."

The shivers that racked Blaine's body were not caused completely by the cold. He was not the least bit superstitious, but finding the intact body of a man he had seen blown to smithereens—and realizing that the time of death in both cases was essentially the same—gave him grave doubts about his conception of life and afterlife.

"Get that engine going, Alex. I've got chills like you wouldn't believe."

"You and me both."

Alex ground the ignition too long. The heater fan was already set on high, where Marybeth had left it, but the blast of hot air did little to dispel the icy atmosphere that pervaded the car.

Blaine put the gun on his lap, and rubbed his hands vigorously in front of the side vent. "There's a logical explanation for all this. I know there is. So let's hurry up and find it."

"I'm with you." Alex switched on the radio.

"—talk about brain transplants is crazy, but then, so is he. For all the trouble he's caused, I wouldn't mind altering his state of consciousness to *un*consciousness. At least then this town—"

"Captain Lawson, come in please."

"What is it, Foley?"

"I need you to call headquarters again."

"Just got off the ringer with them. Your boss is madder than a hornet in a hen house."

"Yes, a field request for a code one safety imperative must have his approval. He'd have been called out of bed for authorization."

"Hell, no. He's mad 'cause no one called him sooner. Says the fireworks 'demonstrated an unanticipated depth of involvement,' or some such nonsense. But you're off the hook because you 'reported the situation promptly through the proper chain of command.' Does he always talk that way?"

He soliloquized to Blaine before he keyed the mike. "At least I've done something right. Maybe I won't lose my job after all."

"As long as I'm alive you've got my vote."

To Lawson, "He's a stickler for departmental decorum. I'll bet he never even raised his voice."

"Not to me, but to listen to him you'd swear he thinks a lingering messenger deserves to be shot. The soft-spoken hombres are the toughest kind. Is Dr. Mitchell with you?"

"Right beside me."

"Then you can tell him he got his man. A farmer reported a pickup truck trying to push down a tree in his front yard. The engine was still running, the transmission was in gear, but the man behind the wheel was stone cold. There was a satchel on the seat with enough explosives in it to level a good-sized town. The patrolman counted five bullet holes in the truck: two in the tailgate, two in the cab, one in the rear window and out the front. One of the bullets in the cab went through the metal and into the man's back. He lived long enough to drive ten miles. Dr. Mitchell, for a man who doesn't own a gun—who's *never* owned a gun—you sure as hell are a crack shot."

Blaine experienced a horrifying sense of satisfaction. In all his years of medical practice he had saved many lives; in fact, he had devoted his career to saving lives. He lost a few patients along the way, but that was to be expected. He was a doctor, not a miracle worker. Then, when he switched from surgery to research, he stopped saving lives in the short term with the hope of saving them in the long term. And despite the medical creed that sought to instill a code of ethics which precluded making value judgments concerning a doctor's patients, the part of him that was human could not help but recognize that the lives he wanted to save were innocent lives worth saving. But when someone tried to kill him . . .

"Just lucky, I guess."

Captain Lawson did not hear the remark because Alex's thumb was not pressing the key. "Feds or not, there's got to be an inquest. It's out of my hands. But Foley's testimony should clear you."

At the moment, judicial inquiries were the least of Blaine's worries. He was more concerned with saving his ass than clearing it.

"Just remember not to go off half cocked. This ain't the army, where you got an open license to kill. The police have to abide by strict rules and regulations designed to protect the public. The discharge of a weapon under *any* circumstances requires an immediate investigation and possible suspension. We've got to do things legally because we are the enforcers of law—"

Blaine hefted the Glock as if it were a newfound toy. "I think he wants to take away my deputy's badge."

"—and order. We always try to talk to a suspected criminal first, and convince him to lay down his arms. Then we read him his rights under the Miranda Act. A person under suspicion is treated with—"

"He's definitely having second thoughts about me."

"—respect and is not to be harmed in any way. He must be brought in for questioning. He has the right to an attorney—"

"What is this? A correspondence course in Boy Scouting?" Blaine grabbed the mike, tapped the key, and turned up the squelch.

The explosion nearly deafened him. A blast of heat seared the right side of his face and peeled the paint off the fenders and door panel. A sheet of flame boiled over the car and washed the windshield for the merest moment before it retreated. The wiper blades were twin streaks of melted rubber.

"Jesus—" Alex started.

Blaine stared out the passenger window at what had once been a police car. The chassis was still there, burning furiously only two feet away, but the body was gone. Even as he looked, charred chunks of framework and pieces of engine block fell like hail. A hot piston drove itself through the windshield between Blaine and Alex, and slammed into the floorboards. Other parts of metal pelted the car for at least fifteen seconds.

The two detectives stood impotently in front of Blaine's house, stretching tape across his door. They could have been slack-jawed statues.

Through the crackling flames Blaine saw two cowboys taking aim with what appeared to be an antitank weapon. "Alex, get the hell—"

The special agent jammed the gearshift lever into reverse at the same time he floored the accelerator. The whining engine threatened to tear itself off its mounting bolts, and the transmission screamed in agony. The car lurched backward, squealed out of the parking spot, and barely got out of the line of fire as the next rocket slammed into the other car's quarter panel. The direct hit demolished the second car the same as it had the first.

The rear wheels of the no-longer unmarked car bounced over the opposite curb so hard that it blew out both tires. Alex never let up on the gas. One second later the trunk wrapped itself around a bristlecone pine. Blaine, crunched against the dashboard by the car's backward momentum, was pitched against the seat with a bone-jarring crash; the impact broke the backrest. As soon as he recovered his senses he yanked back on the door handle to make good his escape; it snapped off like peanut brittle.

"Alex, get out!"

The special agent already had his door open. He tumbled out onto a bed of frozen pine needles. Blaine shoved the cardboard box out the door, hit the ground on a roll, and kept on rolling. Several body-lengths away he twisted into a prone position, swung his gun on the two men taking aim, and fired. They were at least two hundred feet away, and exposed only from the chest up. Blaine's bullets kicked dirt into their faces, forcing them to fire prematurely and duck.

The light armor-piercing round contacted the police car right next to where Blaine had been sitting. If it had hit farther forward it would have detonated against the engine block. But the rocket was fuzed for armor. It went straight through the thin metallic panel and the upholstered seat, and out the closed rear door on the other side. A hundred feet into the woods it exploded against the base of a tall pine, felling it with the ease of a sharp scythe through a single stalk of wheat.

Alex hit the ground by Blaine's side. He took careful aim and squeezed off a shot that whined close above enemy heads. "Let's get in the woods before they reload." His voice was tense but under control.

Blaine looked around to see what the detectives were doing. Both of them were flattened against the driveway like limpets on a rock. They had their guns out and aimed, but were holding their fire. Blaine shouted, "Cover us," then leaped up and made a dash for the tree line. He scooped up the cardboard box along the way.

The detectives laid down a suppressing fire that was not all that accurate, but had a distinct psychological effect. The cowboys were reduced to taking pot shots with Uzis, burping off a few rounds, then hiding like rats in their hole. Blaine and Alex skidded across a frost-covered bed of needles until they reached the protection of a bristlecone pine.

Alex fired one last shot around the trunk of the tree, then his hammer fell on an empty chamber. "Damn! They never run out of bullets in the movies." He flipped out the cylinder and reached into the box for ammunition. "Where's a speed loader when you need one?"

"Welcome to the real world." Blaine deftly released the spent clip and inserted another. He fired a couple of shots into the dirt mound to take the heat off the detectives. Then he stuffed his pockets with bullets and spare magazines. "Let's attack from their flank."

"Let's *what*!" Alex was till shoving in cartridges one at a time. He snapped the cylinder shut, grabbed the box of bullets, and chased after the doctor who was racing across open ground and trying to break the record for the hundred-yard dash. "Blaine, are you crazy? Why not run for cover?"

Blaine was physically exhausted after a week of exceptional outdoor activity, mentally fatigued from an emotionally tense evening and a night with little sleep, and cold enough to freeze the nuts off an iron bridge. "Because I'm pissed."

He dashed from tree to tree until he reached a position only fifty feet from the revetment where a sprawling maple tree offered ample cover. "I don't believe these guys. They're holed up in a dumpster."

Alex crouched behind him. "Why don't we keep them pinned down till backup arrives?"

"Because we don't have a radio and they've got a rocket launcher." He aimed at the top of the mound of dirt and waited for a head to appear before squeezing off a round and knocking off the curious cowboy's ten-gallon hat.

The detectives low-crawled away from the flames of their razed vehicles, taking turns shooting and reloading their revolvers. Sporadic fire from both quarters kept the cowboys temporarily on the defensive.

"You must have nosy neighbors. Someone will call 911."

"And probably be put on hold." Blaine emptied his pockets onto the ground, and between shots forced cartridges into the spare magazines. "Now, are you with me or not?"

Alex fired a shot and took a very deep breath, as if it might be his last. He said reluctantly, "I guess we're both crazy."

Blaine could not contain his smile. "I'm beginning to like you, Alex."

"I'm not sure that's a good sign. Too many people hate you—"

One of the cowboys let loose with his Uzi while the other leaped to the top of the revetment and ran the other way. Bullets chopped through peeling bark and drew about a gallon of syrup before the cowboy swung his gun toward the two detectives.

"Hold it!" Blaine shouted. A split second later he emptied his Glock into the fleeing cowboy; the man was spun completely around by the force of the bullets, and hit the driveway with a thud. "I warned him."

The Uzi came around for a final enfilade, then went silent.

"He's changing magazines." Blaine extended a mental line past the dead cowboy's direction of travel. Parked a hundred feet away in front of a red fire hydrant was a Ford pickup similar to the one used the previous night by the other two cowboys. "Cover me, Alex, or this could be a short friendship."

Before the special agent could object Blaine was on his way. He jammed in a fresh clip on the run, and took a couple of shots at the revetment. Alex and the two detectives did their best to keep the lone cowboy's head inside the dumpster. The tactic worked until the besieged gunman stuck the Uzi over the top of the dirt mound and fired blindly.

Blaine ran around the pickup to use it as cover, then whipped open the passenger door. On the front at lay a canvas satchel held shut with leather straps. Blaine put down his gun and, with fingers numb from the cold, worked open the bag. Inside were long sticks of dynamite, loose blasting caps, a coil of primer cord, a variety of fuzes, timers, detonators, and half a dozen fragmentation grenades.

"Jackpot."

Blaine could have rigged the dynamite with primer cord but went instead for simplicity. He stuffed a grenade into each front pocket, made sure his gun was loaded with a full clip, and waved to Alex to maintain the covering fire. He hunkered down low and gained the protection of a sycamore that was growing on the open side of the revetment, where the trash truck was supposed to back in to lift and empty the dumpster. He had to be careful because he was close to the detectives' line of fire.

There was no time for second thoughts; he was committed. He waited only for a pause in the Uzi's rat-tat-tat, signaled to his companions, and ran headlong for the revetment with the Glock leading the way. He was breathing hard when he reached the dumpster: more from excitement than from exercise. He transferred the gun to his left hand, took out one of the grenades with his right, hooked the pin with the middle finger of his left, pulled, released the spring loaded lever, and counted slowly in his head as he cooked off the grenade, "Zero . . . one . . . two . . . *three—*"

He tossed it fast with a low trajectory in a combination basketball hook shot and volleyball dunk. The dumpster *bonged* when the grenade caromed off the inner steel wall and bounced like a billiard ball in a three-bank shot. Blaine leaped around the edge of the dirt revetment. From inside the dumpster came a clatter of aluminum cans and a frantic rustling of newspapers and trash bags.

Like an echo chamber the dumpster reverberated the sound of the detonation. Some of the blast was directed upward, some was reflected off the reinforced bottom: a spout of dust and debris arced into the air. But most of the fragments ricocheted around the inside of the dumpster like pelting rain on a corrugated tin roof.

Then there was silence.

Alex and the detectives held their fire, and waited expectantly.

Blaine listened for movement inside the dumpster, but nothing stirred. He crept up the sloped revetment by digging the toes of his oxfords into ice-filled divots. Despite the freezing cold, he held the Glock as steady as if it were clamped in a vice. He poked his head warily over the lip of the mound, where the cinderblock wall was topped by a cement lintel. He aimed the gun down into the dumpster before peering into its shadowed depths. Dust lay like a pall.

The cowboy's western wear was shredded confetti, his body a mass of hemorrhaging wounds. In such close confinement the grenade had focused its lethal steel fragments with telling effect. What had once been a living human being was now little more than a tattered rag doll.

"You have the right to remain silent . . . "

Chapter 7

"I hate feds."

"Captain, that's not fair. Your own men will tell you that we did not seek out this engagement. We were ambushed."

"That's what you say. I'm beginning to wonder if you really *were* bushwhacked at the Westmoreland parking lot. Maybe those men didn't chase you into the woods; maybe you went after *them*."

"That's ridiculous. We weren't dressed or armed for open combat."

"You sure made a mess of it this time, though."

The burned-out chassis of two police cars and the shot-up remains of another stood in the background as silent testimonials to the captain's accusations. In addition to the environmental damage the neighborhood had suffered, the two dead bodies added a touch of horror and grim realism to an otherwise fine winter weekend. People from all over the development were there to gawk at the morning's mayhem and demolition.

Blaine broke into the private tête-à-tête with a light rejoinder. "Captain Lawson, have you ever heard of misplaced aggression?"

"And *you*." The lugubrious face was the same as ever, but the eyes were shooting stars. "I should have known better than to let you get near a weapon of any kind."

"What was I supposed to do? Kill them with kindness? Besides, I warned them first and read them their rights."

"Go ahead, mister smart-ass. Make with the jokes like you do in the operating room, or when you're vivisecting monkeys. I don't know what kind of trouble you're in with these people, but I can assure you that after you're done paying up with them you're gonna pay up with me. Them cars cost the taxpayers of this county a lot of goddamn money."

"But you got two pickup trucks in return."

Alex sought to mitigate a situation already gone sour. "Blaine—"

The doctor was having none of it. "Captain, let's remember that I'm the victim here, not some renegade hatchet man. These cowboys are playing for keeps, and they don't care who they kill or what they destroy in order to carry out their plan. For the moment they think that killing me is the answer to their problems, but as Foley will tell you if you'd take the time to listen, they can't be after me for what I've done. They're after me because of what I'm doing—my work at the Institute."

"What? Watching dying people die, like some sick vulture waiting to pluck out their brains. *That* I can understand."

Blaine sensed an underlying hostility that had been brewing in Captain Lawson's breast long before last night's incidents. As soon as he did, his physician's instincts kicked in and he was overwhelmed with the same compassion he felt for any patient hurting from injuries or afflicted with disease. He took his hands out of the pockets of the black fur coat and pleaded with the policeman.

"In all fairness, I don't think you do understand. I know that a lot of my work has been misconstrued by the news media—like that idiot over there." Blaine jerked a thumb at the reporter who was busily interviewing the neighbors; he wore a white gauze pad on the side of his forehead where it had been cut the night before. "But the Institute operates under the strictest code of medical ethics. It does valuable research, and uses only valid and commonly accepted procedures that meet all the criteria of just and humane treatment. Human subjects participate on a volunteer basis, and laboratory animals are properly anesthetized before—"

"Okay, Dr. Mitchell, you've made your point. I just don't like the rodeo show you've been putting on lately. You keep riding broncos and you're bound to get bucked. Now I'll give you some info I got over the radio just a moment ago." He shifted eye contact from Blaine to the FBI man. "Headquarters got a make on those two wops in the Caddy. Seems they've got criminal records as long as the Bill of Rights. Both have mob connections that go way back." He scowled at Blaine. "Now maybe you have to plug that into your Brain Lab computer, but I can add this one in my head." He walked off haughtily to confer with his sergeants.

"The mob? What does he mean, the mob?"

"The Mafia, Blaine. The Cosa Nostra. The Italian underground. Cabiche?"

"What does the Mafia want with me?"

"I sure hope we can find out before they decide to replace your oxfords with cement shoes."

Blaine stared down at the scratched, dirt-smeared leather uppers. He felt a chill come up from the ground; he pulled the long black mink tight around his waist. "I thought Hoover didn't believe in organized crime."

"J. Edgar's dead and so are his misinformed notions. But right now the Mafia is the least of your worries." He tilted his head toward the oncoming reporter.

"I like your wardrobe, Dr. Mitchell. Is it real or synthetic?"

Blaine wanted to talk with the newspaperman as much as he wanted to eat cactus. "It was the best I could come up with on short notice, now that my house has been posted off limits."

"Yes, I understand you found the body of a man at your desk. Do you know what he was doing there?"

"Not much of anything, really. Just sitting."

The reporter was not amused. "And is it true that he was the same man who was blown up in your car last night?"

"Yes, but he's made a remarkable recovery."

The reporter glanced nervously at Alex and back to Blaine. "Do you have any idea who he might be?"

"Only his cosmetic surgeon knows for sure."

The reporter's face turned red in anger. "You know,

your work at the Institute has created quite some turmoil in the papers this past week. Do you think that has anything to do with these attempts on your life?"

Blaine sneered at Alex. "Another mathematician."

"Dr. Mitchell, you're not being very cooperative this morn—"

"That's right, Mr. Jerry Greenstein, and I don't intend to be. I was just handed the early edition of the *Morning Chronicle*, and I don't like what you wrote about last night's events. Your article was sloppy, erroneous, shamefully bigoted, and blatantly self-glorifying. You didn't charge into the sea of battle, you were pushed out the door by the tide of physicians. You didn't dodge any bullets; that cowboy intentionally fired high. You didn't attack that man at the side of the building; you were running like a scared rabbit. And you can't call that scratch on your head a 'gun wound received in battle.'"

By this time Blaine was punching Greenstein so hard with his finger that the reporter was being knocked back by the jackhammer blows. The temples bounced off his ears and his glasses slipped down to the end of his oversized nose.

"If you want to know what a gunshot wound really is, I'd be glad to show you." Blaine flung open the mink coat and whipped the Glock from its holster. He jammed the barrel against the top snap of the reporter's brown cordovan.

"Jesus, Blaine—"

Greenstein blanched, and his lower lip trembled. For perhaps five seconds he quaked like an aspen in a windstorm; then he turned and ran, casting frequent terrified looks over his shoulder.

"It's all right. The safety was on." Blaine holstered the pistol. "Do you think it's significant that Lawson didn't take his gun back?"

Before Alex could think of a response another figure approached them. "Very becoming, Blaine, very becoming." Marybeth ran her eyes admiringly up and down Blaine's precious mink. "Although a bit out of style.

Where do you do your shopping?"

"I'm in no mood for jokes. Is your car here?"

"You don't think I walked?"

Blaine held up the index finger he had just been poking into the reporter's chest. "Hold on a moment." He ran across the lawn to the front door of his neighbor's house, rapped on the oaken panel, and shrugged out of the mink coat.

An elderly woman answered the door. She was gray-haired and way past retirement. She smiled with a grandmotherly warmth that could have softened the pain of the worst scraped knee. "Oh, Dr. Mitchell, I said you could keep it. I don't wear it any—"

"I know, Mrs. Rickles, but it's just not me. And I've got a coat at the office. Thanks very much."

Her Bostonian accent cooed again as she took the mink through the narrowly opened door. "Okay, but if you ever need it—"

He flashed a grin. "I'll come right over and borrow it. Thanks, Mrs. Rickles. And thanks for calling the cops." He turned and ran before she started rambling again about her girlhood on the farm. She paid no attention to all the activity.

To Marybeth, "Where's the car? I'm getting cold."

Marybeth was comfortably dressed in black leather boots, thick woolen slacks, a blue casual jacket, and black leather gloves. She led the way through the line of milling police. "They wouldn't let me drive any closer." She glanced at Alex, then got serious. "Blaine, are you all right?"

Blaine ignored the ogling neighbors and playful kids. "As well as can be under the circumstances."

"But what's going on? Why are all these maniacs out to get you?"

"That's what I'd like to know." Blaine slipped into the front seat of the Dodge Dart and unlocked the rear door for Alex. The engine was running, and the heater was going full blast. "Alex is pretty sure it has to do with our work at the Institute. He thinks—" He stopped reflectively. "Marybeth, what are you doing here? How did you know . . . "

"It was on the radio. You've made the national news."

"Great! Just what I need."

"I came over right away." Marybeth backed up, turned around, and eased the Dart past the long line of parked cars. "Blaine, I know you don't like to hear this kind of stuff, but I've got a creepy feeling—like chills on my neck and butterflies in the pit of my stomach. I—I'm worried about you. Real worried."

Blaine shivered involuntarily. He had always taken a rational approach to life. He distrusted people who relied on "feelings" and who let themselves be guided by complicated belief systems. To him, myth, religion, and superstition were lazy interpretations of misunderstood phenomena. As a staunch pragmatist he had no trouble accepting the simple truth that, in man's present state of knowledge and technology, not all causalities could be explained; he did not need to make up excuses for the unknown and the seemingly unknowable. On the other hand, he had come to respect Marybeth's meditative observations, which he rationalized as subconscious sensibilities. She had a knack for making deductions without all the evidence, for picking up notions without logical extrapolation, for conceiving a whole before she possessed all the parts. Yet, although she often appeared to jump to far-out conclusions, she was often frighteningly intuitive.

"Where are you going, Marybeth?" Alex asked.

As if it were abundantly obvious, she said, "To the Institute, of course." The curved road of the development passed several side streets, then intersected with the main thoroughfare.

"Blaine, you know we shouldn't be doing this without a police escort."

"I know, but I just had to get away from the rubberneckers. It was driving me up a wall. And I wasn't about to ask Captain Lawson to loan me another car. Besides, it's not far."

In Greensborough nothing was far.

Alex twitched nervously in the rear seat. He examined the fields on both sides, and watched for traffic in front and behind. After a couple of minutes he said, "Don't look now, but there's someone following us."

Marybeth's foot faltered on the gas pedal.

"Don't slow down!"

Blaine casually threw his arm over the seat and glanced out the rear window. "He's coming up on us, but that doesn't mean he's following us."

"I know." Alex took out his revolver and rolled down the left window.

"He's accelerating too fast. Marybeth, no matter what happens, don't let him run us into the ditch."

"Alex, you're scaring me."

"Okay, here he comes." Blaine had his pistol cocked and ready. "Marybeth, lower your window."

"Blaine . . . "

"Just do it!"

She did. The stream of arctic air played with her short locks, and blew the collar of her jacket up against her neck. The thick powder and rouge hid her soft natural beauty but could not disguise her fear. Her faint blue eyes were wide.

Alex rested the barrel of his gun on the window ledge. Blaine leaned forward in order to shoot past Marybeth. The nondescript car drew up alongside, then slowed and matched speed. The driver waved. The car fell back and pulled in behind them.

"Shit," Alex muttered, as he fell away from the window.

Blaine snickered and put away his gun. "It's Taylor. Lawson's detective."

Marybeth let out a breath that could have filled a blimp. "You *guys*! Don't *do* that to me."

"Okay, you can close the pneumonia holes." Blaine relaxed and enjoyed the rest of the ride.

The Institute for Higher Research in Perceptual Functions of the Brain—alias the Brain Lab—occupied a spacious twenty-seven acre tract of grassy woodland that in the summer was green and shaded and wonderfully secluded. Even in winter, after the oaks and sycamores had dropped their leaves, the interconnected brick buildings offered cozy privacy because they were set so far back from the road. The shrub-lined driveway was a tenth of a mile long; wooden fences on either side did not keep visitors out of the fields as much as it kept the horses in their corral: a country touch that camouflaged the architectural simplicity and the inner defenses.

The entrance to the grounds proper had all the hallmarks of a secret military installation, complete with concrete columns, a guard shack, and fortified wire gates that were swung shut and locked at night. A ten-foot-high chainlink fence fitted with detection devices and topped with razor-sharp strip wire surrounded the building complex.

"We have a lot of expensive equipment here," said Blaine.

Marybeth rolled down the window as she slowed to a stop. "Good morning, Fred. How are you today?"

The guard was a retired policeman who logged every vehicle that passed through the gates, the times of arrival and departure, and the names of the occupants. The great shock of white hair gave him a grandfatherly appearance. "Just fine, ma'am." He ducked low. "Howdy, Dr. Mitchell."

"Hi, Fred. This is Alex Foley. He'll be working with me today. And the man in the other car is, uh, a detective who is going to help us with some, uh, some disturbances we've been having."

Fred was the resident gardener as well. He spent an hour each day walking the perimeter to pick up wind-blown trash, and to trim the hedges that lined the driveway and the encircling fence. He also came in on Sunday, when the Institute was closed to visitors, to tidy up the grounds more thoroughly. He glanced back. "Looks like Lenny Taylor." To Blaine, "I know most of the policemen hereabouts. Right nice fellow—"

"Fred, we're in a rush today. We'll talk later." Marybeth drove through the gate, knowing he could go on for hours, and wheeled into a parking spot. "Disturbances? Isn't that a bit of an understatement?"

"Like knocking them dead at my lectures? What do you expect me to do, give him a detailed account of the last—" He glanced at his watch. "Do you realize it's only eight-thirty? Even on weekdays I don't come in until nine."

"The privileges of rank." Marybeth parked next to a shiny red Corvette. "Speaking of rank, it looks as if Mighty Joe put in an early appearance."

"He's always here at the crack of dawn. I would be, too, if I had to wake up to his wife."

"Tsk, tsk, tsk. Just because you weren't invited to his daughter's wedding is no reason to make remarks about his marital situation."

Blaine turned to the special agent. "Don't mind the bickering, Alex. It goes on all the time."

"Sounds like my office."

Inside the double glass doors was a large, white-tiled entry that was as sterile as an operating room. Broad alcoves spread out on either side, one a waiting lounge filled with chairs and sofas and magazine racks, the other the receptionist's desk and office area. The dropped-ceiling was white, the plaster walls were white, the switch-plates were white, and the toggles were white. Often, when leaving late at night, Blaine was unable to find the light switches because they blended in so perfectly with the architectural design and color scheme. The furniture and filing cabinets were also white.

The receptionist was thin and shapely, in her early twenties, and could have been Miss October on a Snap-On calendar. Her face advertised more make-up than a cosmetic commercial; her fingernails were dagger length, and painted a bright red to match her flawless lipstick. She sat in the right-side alcove which, with its counter space and medical paraphernalia, was reminiscent of a hospital admitting station. "Good morning Dr. Blaine, Ms. Maples."

Blaine strode by with a smile and a wave. "Hi,

Tilda."

Ogling the receptionist, the detective unbuttoned his trench coat and smoothed back his hair. "Dr. Mitchell, the chief didn't say I had to stay in your pocket. I can wait here for you."

"That's fine. Tilda can direct you to the coffee maker."

They were halfway down the hall before Tilda came running after them. "Oh, Dr. Mitchell, I have some messages for you," she said, in her sexy, high-pitched voice.

He did not slow down. "I'll pick them up later."

"There are quite a few."

"No doubt."

"And Dr. Young wants to see you in his office right away."

"Doesn't he always?"

"He was very specific, Dr. Mitchell. I've never—I've never seen him like this before. He was—quite worked up."

Blaine stopped with his hand on the stairwell door.

"I think you'd better see him," Marybeth singsonged.

Blaine sighed. "I thought showdowns took place at high noon."

"And Ms. Maples?" Tilda struck a poise of indecision. Since she had just borne one bit of bad news, she hesitated before delivering another. "I think the computers are down."

Now it was Marybeth's turn to sigh. Under her breath, "Why doesn't she *know* they're down?" Aloud, "It's probably just your terminal, Tilda, but I'll check it out. Thanks." When they entered the stairwell Marybeth headed down. "Alex, your biggest challenge will be saving him from the wrath of Mighty Joe." She winked, and was gone.

Blaine and Alex went up to the second floor.

By corporate standards Dr. Young's office would not be considered plush. The desk was oak veneered, the chairs were vinyl, the walls were paneled with wood-grained imitation, the window sills were pressboard, and the acoustical tiles were plain white with inset fluorescent fixtures that furnished more than adequate light but had as much ambiance as a basement pull-chain. The wall shelving was the hardware store variety with screwed-in metallic strips, adjustable supports, and stained number two white pine. The expensive leather-bound medical texts and the plethora of modern computer monitors and ancillary equipment more than made up for any deficiencies in appearance. Money was better spent on functional items and laboratory equipment than status imagery.

Joseph Worthington Young was a burly man, balding, dark-complexioned, and as serious in demeanor as Captain Lawson but without the severity of facial expression. The horn-rimmed spectacles corrected his vision for minor nearsightedness.

"Good morning, Joe." Blaine swept into the office the same as he did on any typical workday. "Tilda said you wanted to see me?"

Young eyes constricted into twin beads. He did not seem pleased. "Good morning, Blaine." His voice was lackluster.

"Joe, this is Special Agent Alex Foley."

Young did not seem the least bit surprised. "Good morning, Mr. Foley."

"You can call me Alex, Dr. Young."

"Very well." Young put down his pen and pushed himself up from the desk with his arms, as if his bulk were too much to lift by leg power alone. "Blaine, I—" He paused for several seconds to gather his thoughts, then got right to the point. "I am not at all happy with the, shall we say, adverse publicity you have been bringing down upon this Institute."

Blaine never knew what to expect from his longtime colleague and director of the Institute. He was certainly aware of the older man's unconventional approach to mundane matters, but he was not prepared for what appeared to be a frontal assault that was so out of context with recent events.

"Now do not get me wrong." Young walked around

to the side of his desk and stood with his arms hanging limply at his sides. "I think your research is valuable—extremely valuable. Possibly even fundamental. I personally believe that you have stumbled upon an area of neuroscience that has been sorely neglected in this country, and that may prove to be the last bastion guarding the knowledge of the functions of the brain."

Now Blaine was totally befuddled. What was Mighty Joe Young leading up to?

"I think your team is to be commended for its originality in concept, research design, and execution. But your radical departure from conformance with customary scientific procedure has provoked consternation in the medical community. Furthermore, your, shall we say, extraordinary predictions, given the paucity of demonstrable results, are to many people, the media in particular, somewhat misleading."

"Joe, what is it—"

"Hear me out, Blaine." The interruption caused Young to lose his rhetorical stride. His nose and upper lip twitched nervously. "It is my job to see to it that this Institute upholds its high standing in the field of neurological research. I do that by sanctioning those projects deemed of sufficient scientific merit, by closely monitoring the projects once they are undertaken, by overseeing performance, and by strict adherence to procedures for publication and formal announcement of results. While I must admit that the implications of your team's achievements could be profound, I think it would be prudent if you maintained a lower profile until all the evidence is in and a more thorough examination has been made. Let your applications programs run more analyses—then we will know for certain if your theories are confirmed. And Blaine, back off a bit with the newspapers. Try to be more, shall we say, reserved. Keep your personal opinions segregated from your work here at the Institute. We do not need the kind of adverse publicity you are provoking."

Blaine could have been knocked down by a photon. His jaw dropped, and his hands clenched into fists so tight that his fingernails left deep impressions in the skin of his palms. He was so shocked, so angry, that he could not think of anything to say that would even begin to convey his feelings. He was afraid that if he opened him mouth to protest he would either scream or do nothing more than sputter. So, he did the only thing that it was possible for him to do under the circumstances. He spun on his heel and left.

Chapter 8

The hot water beating against his face and chest was the most exquisite relief in the world—like sight to a blind man, or a reprieve from the electric chair. He luxuriated in the shower, and washed away the dirt, the soil, the perspiration, and the fear of the past twelve hours. After dissolving half a bar of soap on his body, he dialed the shower head to deliver a fine spray against his neck and back, then turned around again and again like pork in a rotisserie. After twenty delicious minutes Blaine Mitchell felt like a new man.

"Alex!"

The FBI man jerked his head up off his shoulder, yanked out his gun, and blinked his eyes in the bright lights of the scrub room. The article he had been reading lay on the floor.

"Sorry, Alex. I didn't mean to startle you." Blaine wrapped a large white bath towel around his waist, then rubbed another one vigorously through his hair. "I called you three times before you woke up."

Alex slipped his revolver into its holster, then rubbed his eyes with the backs of dirt-smudged fingers. "Guess I must have dozed off. Not a good habit for a field agent on the job."

"You can't be alert twenty-four hours a day. I know you were up all night writing reports and talking with Lawson, while Marybeth and I sacked out in the waiting room. Sooner or later you're going to have to get some sleep. But for now, a hot shower will have to suffice."

"Blaine, I can't—"

"You can, and you will. Doctor's orders. Especially if you're going to stick as close to me as you say you are." Blaine took two fresh towels out of the well-stocked linen closet and tossed them to Alex. "Now get in there. You'll feel a whole lot better." He hefted the Glock that had been lying atop his discarded suit, and winked. "I'll play guard for a while."

Reluctantly, Alex gave in. He shed his clothes like a molting crab, letting them fall to the floor as if he had no further use for them in this incarnation. Five minutes was all he took.

The scrub room was large enough to accommodate an entire surgical unit. Since its conversion into a total research facility, operations were no longer performed at the Institute; but staff pathologists and veterinarians often conducted autopsies on the premises. Unneeded operating rooms had been remodeled into locker rooms; each employee had his own closet. Doctors, technicians, and secretaries shared space equally with the maintenance crew and members of the commissary and janitorial departments.

The Institute prided itself on being progressive, and operated as a homogenous whole. Although its doors never closed, most people worked a normal forty-hour week with flexible hours for those who needed them. Doctors, technicians, and research assistants might be in around the clock. Students from Westmoreland University were hired part-time to feed and care for the animals and to do a thousand other necessary but less important tasks.

It was usually pretty quiet on the weekends; those with on-going projects might slip in and use the slackened pace to catch up on paper work.

Alex stepped out of the shower. "You were right. I feel completely refreshed."

Blaine was dressed in surgical greens and clean jogging shoes: his usual garb, although he sometimes wore a smock or lab coat because they had pockets. With a hot washcloth he wiped the excess cream off his face; the blade had left one nick on his chin, but it was small enough not to require anything more than a touch with the styptic pencil to stem the flow of blood. He pushed the aerosol can and a new plastic razor across the sink for Alex. "Anyone who's ever been an intern would have told you the same thing."

The special agent donned a towel and shaved quickly. "No offense, Blaine, but after this assignment I'll be glad to get back to the office and spend the rest of my days processing reports and conducting telephone investigations. Field work isn't all it's cracked up to be."

"That's the second time you've said that." Blaine tossed a set of surgical greens on the sink. "Are you trying to convince *me*, or yourself?"

Alex splashed on a handful of Blaine's aftershave. He ignored the question and pointed to the hospital garb. "I—I can't wear these."

"Why not? They're your size. They're everyone's size."

"Because I have to wear a suit. I can't be caught—"

"In case you haven't noticed, you no longer have a suit." Blaine held up the tattered remains of Alex's pants and jacket; they were ripped practically to shreds. "There's not enough material left to make a hanky. Mine are the same way. It'll save on the cleaning bill."

Alex grimaced at the blackened, singed jacket. "Where did the burns come from?"

"Who knows. When you're under fire you don't remember minor details. You remember only that you survived. Now come with me and I'll get you some footwear." Without waiting for an argument Blaine led the way to the locker room, opened a closet that was not his own, and rummaged through the junk on the floor until he found a pair of sneaks. "Harold and I jog around the compound when the weather's not so bad. He won't mind."

"Blaine, I—"

"No excuses. Let's just say you're working undercover. Field agents do that, don't they?"

"Yes, but, I—I wasn't objecting only to that. It's just that—I really think I should call in for a replacement. I—"

"I know you're tired. So am I. But we're equipped to handle any emergency." He wagged a finger for Alex to follow him into a room that was sectioned off by a windowless door. In the dim glow of a table lamp the four beds looked very appealing. "Later on we can snatch a few winks." He slapped his palm on the closest twin. "They're very comfortable. I sleep here all the time when I'm involved in a project." He indicated another bed whose sheets were mussed. "See, someone slept here last night."

"Blaine, I—that's not what I mean. I—I think it would be better for you if a more experienced operative were to take over this assignment."

"What assignment? After what we've been through we're no longer just an agent and his job. We're friends."

Alex was speechless for several moments. "Blaine, I appreciate that. I really do. But if that's the case, then it's all the more reason to get someone else to cover you. I'm too inexperienced. I'm too—I'm afraid I'll freeze on you again, like I did last night. I—" He fumbled for words like a person coming out of a drugged sleep. "Last night, when I shot—when I shot that man. I only intended to wound him. That's what we're trained to do. That's all I *wanted* to do. But when he fell—right into my line of fire, he—" The agent gulped as if he were swallowing an orange whole. "I didn't mean to kill him. I didn't want to kill him. It was an accident. He just fell . . ."

"So that's what's bothering you." Blaine put both hands on the agent's shoulders, and peered compassionately into fathomless brown eyes. "It's okay to feel this way. You *have* to feel this way, otherwise you wouldn't be human. But don't let the guilt eat you up. You acted out of necessity—to save your life. And mine. And Marybeth's. And that's what counts. I've been around death my whole adult life so I know what I'm talking about. They say the first time you kill is always the worst, but don't believe it. It never gets any better. Death is a constant enemy. But remember this: it's better to be alive with guilt than dead with no feeling at all."

Blaine patted him lightly, and drawled, "Now get dressed, pardner, and meet me in the kitchen." He lifted the pullover and slapped the Glock that was strapped to his waist. "Your iron's in the other room." He did not linger, but let his patient mull over the implications by himself; in Blaine's experience, the best way to handle this kind of situation was not as a confrontation but as an invocation. The only cure for guilt was acceptance.

The smell of sizzling bacon and frying eggs was enough to make Blaine's stomach grumble. He followed his nose into the kitchen where Marybeth was slaving over a hot stove. The commissary department was closed on weekends but the refrigerator was always open.

"I hope you put on a fresh pot of coffee."

Marybeth smiled whimsically. "Have I ever let you down?"

He went straight to the percolator and poured himself a cup of brew. "Never."

The six-slot toaster popped. "Blaine, butter them, will you? The margarine's in the fridge."

"Marybeth, I keep telling you that you butter with butter, not with margarine."

"Just do it." She scraped the eggs off the grill and arranged them on three plates. The men had three eggs each, she had two. "And get the cream while you're there."

The doctor did as he was told. "Yes, ma'am."

"So how was Mighty Joe?"

"Worse than King Kong. Marybeth, I have *never* been so pissed off in my entire life. Here I am dodging bombs and bullets and all he's worried about is my bringing too much adverse publicity on the Institute. He said he didn't care for the newspaper reports. Do you believe that guy?"

Marybeth was so shocked that she dropped the pan of bacon. "What?"

"I can't get over how calloused he was. I didn't expect him to back me—he won't back anything other than his precious computers and their mindless statistical analyses—but he could have at least hinted at some concern about my well-being. The man is totally without decency. Then he went on about my 'team,' and how they 'stumbled' on something that 'may' be significant. Marybeth, I didn't even argue with him. I just got the hell out of there before I exploded. You know, I think I've just 'stumbled' on the explanation for spontaneous human combustion."

"God, he's a cold fish. I knew he was heartless, but I never thought of him as cruel. And he's going to be even less happy when he finds out the computer is locked up."

"What's wrong with it?"

"Don't know." She set the plates on the formica-covered table, piled on the food, and slid into a chair. "It's got a glitch of some kind. I can't get it to boot any files." Marybeth was a genius when it came to computer programming and debugging. She designed and wrote most of the special programs that were used at the Institute. "But I haven't spent much time on it yet."

Blaine sat down and dug into his bacon and eggs. His anger had not curbed his appetite. "Isn't it odd that the director of this Institute has no perception and no brain?"

For once Marybeth did not equate a situation in relation to its effect upon herself. Her voice reflected genuine concern. "He's been acting strange all week; not just aloof, but—bothered. Naturally, I attributed it to his daughter's upcoming marriage and her leaving home. Now I'm not so sure that his problems are that simple. I think he's having marital difficulties."

Blaine was not mollified. "That's no excuse for his abusive indifference."

"No, but it may be an explanation." She carved off a slender piece of bacon and forked it between pencil-thin lips. "Don't misunderstand me. I'm not condoning his actions. But he's got more on his mind than he's willing to admit—even to himself. I have a feeling about it."

"Don't you always?"

She stuck out her tongue.

Blaine scowled as he crunched on his toast. "Even

a person with a severed corpus callosum should have enough sense to separate emotional conflict from true physical danger." In split-brain patients the two hemispheres were unable to communicate, so that each hemisphere operated independently; logic and emotion acted as distinct entities. "And Joe isn't exactly stupid."

Alex entered the kitchen looking pert and prim in his surgical greens and wet-combed hair. Referring to the quick tour of Blaine's office, he said, "What does that sign say on your desk?"

"It doesn't say anything. It can't talk." Without waiting for a comment, Blaine quoted, " 'Is there intelligent life on Earth? Yes, but I'm only visiting.' I saw it on a subway wall."

The special agent sat down at his plate. "Maybe you should introduce Dr. Young to your brain-boost scheme. The one you talked about in your article. Neuronal enhancement and intensification, I think you called it."

Between bites, "Don't make the same mistake that reporter Greenstein made by highlighting the appendiced material and ignoring the substance. I drew some promising extrapolations and suggested peripheral experimentation, but that's a long way from a statement of fact and has nothing to do with our projected research. And like Greenstein, you missed the point. The basis of human intellect is fifteen million neurons, all interacting. As a result of age or injury some of the neurons die, or the interaction process meets interference. I submitted only that a damaged or diseased brain might be rebuilt if we had a clearer understanding of the mechanisms of memory and information-gathering, and could restore the patient's brain to its previous degree of health. I did not state that we could make geniuses out of morons. Although, off the record, it is not neurologically impossible. Our work at present is centered on artificially induced changes in the levels of consciousness and the mitigation of sensory pain."

"Isn't that like mind over matter?"

Blaine wolfed down the last of his meal and got up

to pour more coffee. "It might seem that way but it's not. It's a case of the mind using the brain and the brain protecting the mind."

If Alex was confused before, he was now totally lost. He chewed his food thoughtfully. "That sounds like the blind leading the blind."

"No, it's more like the subconscious telling the intellect how to regulate physiological functions that are normally autonomic—that is, involuntary actions like glandular secretions and the pumping of the heart. For thousands of years doctors have controlled certain malfunctions chemically, such as when they dispense pills to moderate an overactive thyroid or pituitary gland, or inject epinephrine into the heart to stimulate it, or prescribe tranquilizers. One of our study projects concerns disciplining the mind through electronic biofeedback training to treat it's own brain. By fitting a neurometric terminal to the patient's head and focusing electronic pulses directly into the brain, we've been able to achieve . . . " Blaine noticed the glazed look on the agent's face. "Am I losing you?"

"Of course you're losing him. You're using scientific vocabulary on a person who barely understands phonemes—uh, sorry, Alex. No offense meant. It's just that—"

Alex tinkered with his toast. "No, you're quite right." To Blaine, "Maybe you'd better give me a crash course in neuroscience before you show me your lab. Pretend I'm one of your students at Westmoreland."

Marybeth swallowed her last piece of bacon. "That's a mistake, Alex. One class a week has not made him the best of instructors. But look at it this way. Picture the brain as the hardware component of a computer: a plastic housing and hardwired circuitry, diodes and resistors, input terminals and full-color monitors; then picture the mind as an operating system: the software component. See?"

The agent pursed his lips. "Sure."

"No you don't," Blaine objected. "All you see is the common misconception that the human brain is an analogue for an organic computer, to which any neurologist will say hogwash."

Again, Marybeth stuck out her tongue.

"The human brain is not just a three pound lump of protoplasm. It is not just two enlarged cerebral lobes necessary for the manifestation of the mind. Its particular construction is responsible for the *type* of mind we possess. The way it receives stimuli as well as the type of stimuli it receives determine our perception of reality. For example: what we call visible light is only a narrow band on the electromagnetic spectrum, but until a century ago it was the only part of that spectrum that we were aware of. That doesn't mean that the rest of the spectrum didn't exist, only that we had no means of perceiving it. Then along comes radio, radar, sonar, and all of a sudden, after millions of years of dull human consciousness, we detect through instrumentation—an artificial input device—a whole range of frequencies to which we were previously 'blind.' Did stars emit electromagnetic radiation before the invention of the radio telescope? Of course."

"And because sound is molecular vibration, a falling tree makes noise even though there's no one in the forest to hear it," Marybeth added. "But isn't this getting far afield?"

"Perhaps. The point I'm trying to make is that the brain-mind combination is not just a more complicated computer, it is *infinitely* more complicated. A computer is nothing but a keyboard and a central processing unit: a gigantic organizer, like a filing cabinet with fast access to files. The human brain-mind has the ability to conceptualize; it's much more than the simple sum of its parts."

Alex's jaw clamped shut in the middle of a chew. "I think I'm beginning to catch on. You're saying that the computer is not better than the brain—or the brain-mind, as you call it—just because it can calculate faster, any more than a Corvette is better than the human body because it can go a hundred and sixty miles per hour."

"Exactly." Blaine jabbed a finger at Marybeth. "If you had attended some of my lectures you'd know how good a rapport I have with my students." To Alex, "You probably didn't understand my paper because it was written for neurologists, not the lay public. But I can use analogies to explain all the concepts of our work."

The special agent swallowed. "First tell me what the difference is between the brain, the mind, and consciousness."

"The mind and consciousness are used interchangeably to describe the organized totality of psychical structures and processes, in which psychical refers to mental or non-sensory processes such as thinking, cognizance, and self-awareness. Call it the essence of you: your being, or personality, or soul—whatever name appeals to you."

"Karma," Marybeth interjected.

"Or psychoanalytically, the ego: your conception of yourself; the sum of your experience, and the dynamic unity that is the individual. But that's more a discussion for philosophers than scientists. The brain, on the other hand, is generally thought of as the carrier of the mind. It's not just an organ, it's a system: an intricate network of nerve fibers strung throughout the body, each of which carries impulses or messages from remote locations, through the spinal cord and brain stem, to the encephalon; that is, to the part of the central nervous system that resides inside the skull. The triune brain is partially a relic from the past—"

J. Worthington Young stood nervously in the doorway, shifting his overweight body from one flat foot to the other. His arms hung stiffly at his sides, and his hands were balled into tight fists around a rolled up newspaper; his knuckles were bone white. "Pardon me for interrupt—" Eyes as dark as the twin muzzles of a shotgun trained for a target. Despite his obvious discomfort, Young finally settled his gaze on Blaine. "I fear I have made a grievous mistake—" He faltered for a moment. When he continued, his voice was a throaty rasp. "I know how it must seem, but I knew nothing about last night's awful—I just—"

Blaine did not try to ease his boss's distress.

"I just found out about —I just read the *Morning Chronicle*—" Young was practically in tears. Abruptly, he stepped up to the kitchen table and laid his hand upon Blaine's shoulder; his grip was strong and unwavering, like a surgeon's grip on his scalpel. "Blaine, I swear to you, I knew nothing about it until just a few minutes ago. Tilda brought in the paper—"

He let the newspaper unroll on the table in front of Blaine. The front page screamed in forty-eight point headlines: "TERRORIST ATTACK ON WESTMORELAND U". The large black-and-white photo was a blurred time exposure of the university parking lot surrounded by fire fighters directing their hoses at a cluster of burning automobiles. The caption read, "Prominent area scientist involved in shoot-out. *Chronicle* reporter Jerry Greenstein was there."

"I've read it," Blaine said icily. He glanced at the tabloid, then at Young's hand only inches away from his chin. Only once had he and Young made actual physical contact: when they had shaken hands at their first meeting ten years earlier. "Some of it's even true."

Young retracted his hand as if he had just touched a hot iron. "Blaine, I had no idea that—" He backed away and slumped against the tiled wall. "What kind of trouble—are you in?"

Blaine was still galled by Young's previous emotionless dismissal. He remained adamantly silent.

Marybeth ran to Young's side. She placed delicate palms against his suit coat, and looked up into his face like empathy personified. "Joe, are you okay?"

He hung his head like a scolded child. With his gaze fixed upon the floor he slowly shook his great domed pate from side to side. "No, I—" He confronted Blaine with firm resolve. "No matter how strained our relationship has been in the past, no matter what you think of me, you must believe me when I tell you that when you came into my office this morning I knew absolutely nothing about what happened last night at the university. I swear it. I must have sounded like an insouciant fool, considering what you had been through. But I did not know. You must believe that, Blaine. You must."

For a moment, Blaine was persuaded by the sincerity of the director's plea. But he still harbored so much anger that he could not bring himself to speak without fear of going into a rage. He stared at Young like a lion about to pounce on its prey.

"Blaine, I am not unsympathetic to your plight. And I apologize for any misunderstanding. But I—I—I spoke out of ignorance. And I would like to make it up to you. How—how can I help?"

This was an unexpected turn for which Blaine was unprepared. His silence was met with a pinched stare from Marybeth and arched eyebrows from Alex. The ball was in his court. But he was not yet ready play. "You told me that you read about me in the papers."

"I did, but I was talking about the write-ups on your Berkeley conference. The wire service picked up the story, and the *Chronicle* elaborated upon it, I felt, rather freely. Apparently, you drew some conclusions that were not part of your monthly report. The overall reaction among the scientific community was adverse to say the least."

"Joe, you know I always lean to the conservative side when making announcements, especially in my written reports. I never say anything I can't corroborate experimentally. But since that report was written, and the time I went to Berkeley, we substantiated a lot of what we only alluded to before. Research is ongoing. In the final analysis we determined exact frequencies for triggering other amino acid breakdowns."

"But did you have to spread it—" The director nearly swallowed his tongue. "I apologize, Blaine. I—I am confusing issues." Marybeth stepped back as he reached up and rubbed his face with his hands. "It has been a difficult week. What with the letters and phone calls from scientists all over the world, with the Franklin Foundation and the Ford Endowment Society demanding updated records of your research, with my daughter's wedding, and my wife—she has been insufferable—" Young gathered himself together after a brief respite. "Anyway, I realize that my problems are miniscule compared to what you have been through. But please believe me, I knew nothing about last night's assaults. I came here straight from the wedding, worked until two a.m., slept in the guest room, and arose at five. I have been at my desk ever since. Now that I know what has occurred, I want you to understand that you have my full support. If there is anything I can do for you, Blaine, you have only to ask. The resources of the Institute are at your command."

Dr. Young's declaration was tantamount to Napoleon apologizing for his defeat at Waterloo. Now Blaine wanted to speak, but could not think of anything to say.

Chapter 9

The police captain was as lugubrious as ever. "I hate feds." This time the statement was made with dispassion, almost as an afterthought.

Blaine tossed an insulated OR smock at Alex, and struggled into the sleeves of his own. The heavy overcoats were worn while performing brain surgery in air-conditioned operating rooms, when it was necessary to lower the patient's core temperature in order to decrease circulation and reduce the metabolic rate. "My house? What are they doing to my house?"

"When I left, they were tearing it apart piece by piece and going over the pieces with a microscope." Captain Lawson humphed. "They wouldn't even let my men near the place. Hey, Taylor." He breezed by the front desk and yanked the detective's upturned collar. "If you can drag yourself away from the pretty lady I'd like you to follow us back to Dr. Mitchell's house."

"Uh, sure, boss. No problem." Taylor flashed an embarrassed smile at the receptionist. "See you later, Tilda."

She waved with uncertainty.

Lawson pushed through the glass doors into the mid-morning cold. The sun hung in the cloudless sky like a bright yellow balloon filled with helium—which it was. "They had more newfangled gadgets than a World's Fair, and a small task force to operate them. And Ronson says that more men are on the way."

Alex fumbled with the buttons of the smock. "I hope you understand why it has to be that way. It's not that your men aren't competent, it's just that the sophisticated instrumentation requires special training to operate. Ronson is our best electronics expert."

"He's more like an electron if you ask me." He climbed into his car; the engine was running, and the heater fan soughed quietly on its lowest speed. Blaine took the front seat, Alex got in the back. "Got the emotions of a machine."

"If there's anything there to find, he'll find it."

"When I left he was collecting and identifying mouse turds. Put each one in a separate plastic bag like it was a gold nugget."

"I've got mice?" Blaine exclaimed.

Lawson backed the car out of the parking spot, waited for Taylor to do the same, then headed toward the Institute's front gate. Fred nodded pleasantly as they passed the guard shack. "He sucked up every spider and cockroach with a slurp gun and tagged them for lab analysis."

"I've got roaches?"

"You've got trouble, is what you've got." Lawson turned onto the highway at the end of the grounds. Saturday morning traffic was light. "They told me they were going to move out the furniture next, then peel up the carpets. They've got a moving van on the way."

"What the—"

"The body is what interested me, though. I don't believe in reincarnation, but if what you say is true—and I'm not saying I think your slate is clean even if you got a fed to back you up—then we've got an Alfred Hitchcock mystery on our hands. Nothing about this case makes sense. Foley," Lawson glanced into the rearview mirror. "Your chief faxed me the case file—both pages."

"I initiated follow-up lines of investigation before I left for the field. Someone in the Bureau should have picked up on it."

"Nobody touched it till you called in this morning. Anyway, I ran some routine checks and found one interesting item." Lawson paused dramatically, to make sure he had the special agent's curiosity piqued. "The tip-off came from a phone booth in Greensborough."

"What?" Blaine and Alex shouted at the same time.

"The FBI never traced the call."

"That's impossible!" Alex's voice was less than calm. "All incoming calls are logged."

"Oh, the number was there," Lawson said smugly.

"But nobody bothered to see where it came from."

Alex groaned. "Someone's head will roll for this. If I had been handling the in-house investigation I would have checked it first thing. You just type in the number and hit a function key. They probably got some rookie—"

Blaine raised his eyebrows at the special agent.

"I also followed up one of your ideas on the tape recorder. The doc said you were right. The cowboys didn't have vaccination marks."

"There isn't a person in this country, native or naturalized, who hasn't been vaccinated for small pox. It's the law." Blaine questioned the FBI man, "So what does it mean?"

"I suspect they're recruits from some third world nation. If they're illegal aliens our computer won't have any record of them."

"Alex, what made you think of such a thing?"

The special agent shrugged. "It wasn't any brainstorm. A lot of FBI work deals with border crossers and illegal aliens."

Blaine was beginning to realize that police work was as structured as medicine, and every bit as much of a science. "Too bad the ME can't dissect an accent."

"Yes. And as long as we don't know who we're dealing with we don't know what kind of precautions to take."

Blaine stared idly ahead. Through the glare on the windshield he saw rolling fields of turned earth: furrows frozen like permanent waves. Corn husks and dried stalks scattered along the shoulder attested to last year's crop. A muddy van and a pure white limousine passed from the other direction, followed by a rusted, stake-bodied truck with a bed full of antique furniture; but he was more concerned about Ford pickups. Taylor hung back not more than five car-lengths.

"I've taken care of that matter by revoking all leaves and bringing in all off-duty personnel," Captain Lawson said. "Even borrowed a few men from the neighboring counties to help interview the people at your lecture last night. Some of them weren't in the medical field at all. I don't know what's going down, but it sure as hell is something big."

"It sounds as if we're gearing up for World War Three." Blaine suddenly felt that the Glock at his waist was woefully inadequate. "We've already gone from pistols and machine guns to grenades and anti-tank weapons. What's next? Napalm and B-52 strikes?"

The question was academic. Lawson turned the car into Blaine's housing development. Some sections were still under construction; unfinished side streets laden with dirt from graders and dump trucks forked off both sides of the entrance drive. Billboards proudly announced an open house for the weekend. Lawson followed the curved, tree-lined roads to Blaine's cul-de-sac.

"Don't know. But we're keeping everyone under wraps who can't come up with an invitation, till we look into their backgrounds."

A police line had been erected to keep the neighbors and curious onlookers away from the horde of investigators swarming around Blaine's house. The burned-out police cars were still there, but the bodies had been removed to the quickly-filling morgue. The first thing Lawson did upon their arrival was to grab one of his sergeants.

"Post a man on the highway and keep out everybody who doesn't live here. And knock down that open-house billboard. Pronto." To the special agent, "I'm declaring the entire section off-limits. If you don't have a badge, you don't get in here."

"Alex, what are they doing with my things?" Blaine felt a cancerous tumor gnawing away at the pit of his stomach. "It looks like a yard sale."

Two men rolled out Blaine's chest-of-drawers on a dolly, and deposited it on the grass next to the bureau and a pile of clothing. Another man wrote on a clipboard while a photographer took pictures of each item. Two men carried tagged articles up a wooden ramp into an unmarked moving van. Blaine's living room furniture, such as it was, had already been loaded. Most of the kitchen equipment lay in a heap beside the front door.

"Don't panic, Blaine. This is SOP for a code one safety imperative. You'll get everything back in a few weeks."

"Wait a minute! You can't just waltz into my house without a warrant and remove all my belongings."

Alex appeared discomforted. "I thought we had an understanding about the severity of the situation."

"Your house is the scene of a crime, Dr. Mitchell, in which case law enforcement agencies have special prerogative." Captain Lawson added with a smirk, "Besides, an innocent man has nothing to hide."

"I'm not trying to conceal anything from anyone, but I do object to this overt invasion of privacy. At least you could have asked—or warned me."

Alex flipped open his badge to the man guarding the perimeter. "I'm sorry, Blaine. It's my fault. I've been concentrating too much on doing the right thing and making timely decisions to convey to you the investigative routine. This operation is bigger than you think. Look at it like you'd look at a patient under the knife. If you discover a complication after you open him up, you don't cancel the surgery, stitch him back together, wake him up, and have a friendly tête-à-tête; you make an on-the-spot decision and do what's necessary."

"I hate it when you make medical analogies." Blaine allowed himself to be ushered to the open front door. He was immediately halted by a stern-faced man who planted his hand solidly against Blaine's chest. "Excuse me, but I live here."

"Not any more you don't." His voice was a monotone. Over his suit the man wore a lab coat covered with bulging pockets closed with Velcro. His beady eyes were bright and penetrating; his down-turned nose overhung thin, bloodless lips like an eagle's beak; his cheeks were sallow and sunken. "These premises are under federal jurisdiction."

"Now wait just a—"

Alex gently pushed Blaine aside and confronted the

sallow man with his badge. "I'm Special Agent Foley. I called in the security code."

The man acknowledged with a barely perceptible nod. "Ronson. Spec tech. You understand that no one is permitted to enter a code one precaution zone other than the technical specialties team—especially not the code one victim."

"Of course." After a pause, "Captain Lawson said you had files that could be given only to me."

Ronson had a large, sealed letter-sized case slung over his shoulder on an adjustable strap. He pulled it around in front, inserted a ring key into the lock, clicked open the latch, and flipped over the flap. Blaine saw that the fine-grained leather was only a facade for a metallic inner lining; it was a security case for top secret documents.

"Don't be there."

Blaine stepped aside so the furniture movers could get past with their dollies. As he looked inside he noticed that the wall-to-wall carpet was overlaid with aluminum grids, and that four men on their hands and knees, covered with what appeared to be sleeves of armor, poked through the synthetic fibers with magnets, needles, and magnifying lenses. The movers, careful not to get off the jury-rigged sidewalk that extended down the hallway, went into his study. Video cameras mounted on tripods recorded everything.

The thermostat must have been left on, because Blaine could hear the heater fan blowing full blast. Standing at the interface, he felt the heat in front fighting to get past him into the cold outdoors. Then he noticed that all the windows were open, as if the house were being aired or fumigated. He had no chance to protest.

Ronson took out a folder and read off the cover page, "Mitchell, Blaine Thomas; M.D., Ph.D., and an LRRP with so many medals he needs two jackets to wear them all: CIB, DSC, Purple Heart, and about a dozen unit citations and personal commendations. His achievement awards go all the way back to Cub Scouts and glee club, and wind up with enough academic accolades to start his own alphabet. He's chaired international conferences on medicine, specializing in neurology, neuroscience, and neurosurgery. Used to be a hot man with the scalpel until a patient died on the table and he went into research. Widowed ten years. Holds honorary positions on several boards—"

Blaine could not stand having his life history read off in front of him, as if he were a statue instead of a living human being. "Excuse me, but do you know who I am?"

The specialty technician stared at him with half-closed lids. "Case number two nine three stroke one seven stroke four nine."

"For your information I am not a case. I'm a—"

Alex placed a hand on Blaine's shoulder. "Don't take it personally, Blaine. We have cases like you have patients. It's a buzz word in the business. So we don't confuse you with another Dr. Mitchell."

Blaine was not mollified, but did not pursue the issue. A close scrutiny of the spec tech's granite features revealed no sign of emotion, no trace of involvement. Ronson was as cold as the great outdoors. "I'd like to pick up some of my things—if you don't mind." He added emphasis on the last four words. "My parka for one, and my work files."

"I am sorry, Dr. Mitchell, but that is completely out of the question." Ronson removed a transmitter from one of his cargo pockets and placed it to his lips. "Harry, scan the filing cabinet and bring it out." To Blaine, "I cannot permit you inside the house, nor can you be permitted to touch any objects coming out. The only thing you can have is your phone message." He held out two sheets of paper covered with block printing. "I transcribed your answering machine. A lot of people have been trying to get in touch with you this past week."

"Most of them already have." Blaine did not disguise his sarcasm. He took the papers and read down the long list.

"I will need that back, but you can have a photo-copy." To Alex, "They were largely hang-ups, but there were seventeen calls from a gal named Marybeth, and three—all this morning—from Frances Crowley, a doctor in California."

"Is that Francis with an 'i' or Frances with an 'e'?"

Ronson did not grin, nor did his voice conceal any hidden overtones. "An 'e'. I spoke with her myself twenty minutes ago. She was quite concerned about Dr. Mitchell's health, perhaps even distraught." To Blaine, "My impression is that you were having private consultations with her."

"You could say that," Blaine said cautiously.

"Would you like to write down the numbers?"

"It isn't necessary." Blaine handed the papers back to Ronson. "I have a good memory."

To Alex, "I faxed the transcript to HQ. They will check her out."

The special agent held up a ball-point pen. "Where do I sign?"

Ronson produced a printed form whose blank spaces were already filled in. Alex scrawled his signature across the appropriate line. When he handed over the signed sheet of paper, Ronson gave him the folder with Blaine's personal file. Blaine noticed a color photograph of himself on the front, taken at the podium during one of his lecture tours; he did not recognize the background.

A chubby man trundled over the aluminum grid with Blaine's filing cabinet on a dolly. He wheeled it past the knot of men at the door with barely an upward glance, then halted. "Did you want to look in it?"

"The bottom drawer." Blaine kept his hands in his pockets.

Ronson arched his eyebrows. "We have already checked it." He bent down anyway and tugged on the handle; the drawer rolled out on well-oiled roller bearings. "It was empty."

"All my work files are missing." Blaine looked up at Alex. "And the print-outs from the lab, too." He watched as Ronson pulled out the other three drawers. "But my personal files are still here."

Alex nodded. "It all ties in with your work, Blaine. Whoever killed the pickpocket look-alike wanted copies of your technical papers." To Ronson, "Has there been a determination of the cause of death?"

"Thanks, Harry. You can put it in the truck with the rest of the stuff."

After the mover was out of earshot the spec tech spoke crisply, "Ricin."

"Jesus," Alex breathed. His eyes grew to the size of quarters.

"Ricin?" Blaine heard correctly, but could hardly accept the implications. "How was it administered?"

Ronson reached into his satchel and brought out a clear plastic tube the size of a prescription pill bottle. Inside was an ordinary thumb tack. "This was embedded in the desk chair by slicing through the vinyl side and forcing it through the foam padding so that only the tip protruded. When the victim sat at the desk the tack punctured the skin of the gluteus maximus. Death ensued in three to five seconds."

Blaine blanched. He stared at Alex with a combination of awe and dread. "What kind of people are we up against?"

The special agent's slight shrug was almost hidden by the insulated coat. "It's a trick developed by the Russians. Better than bullets, and a hell of a lot quieter. In this case it was used as an antipersonnel mine, only the wrong person tripped it."

"Saved again," Blaine muttered distantly. The irony of having the same man twice trigger booby-traps intended for him was not lost on him. "Is this guy a thief or my benefactor?"

"Hold on here. Can we back up a minute?" Captain Lawson yanked his hands out of the pockets of his overcoat and made a pleading gesture. His eyes darted back and forth like the orbs of a cornered cat. "You're getting beyond me here. What's all this about Ricin and thumb tacks and mines? What're you talking about?"

"Ricin is a poisonous protein extracted from the castor bean and used as a biochemical reagent." Ronson answered. "In concentrated solutions it becomes a highly effective means of assassination. The KGB has been using it for years. A microscopic dose painted on the point of a sharpened instrument creates a weapon so deadly that the slightest pinprick results in nearly instantaneous expiration." There was a hint of admiration in his voice. "It is really quite sophisticated."

"And it means that we're dealing with a highly organized enemy." Alex ran a hand through close-cropped hair. To Ronson, "Were there others?"

The single vertical motion of his head was a conspiratorial affirmative. A slight sideways tilt indicated Blaine and Captain Lawson. "Are they cleared?"

"Under my authority."

"In that case I can show you the lab." Ronson warmed about a degree and a half. At Alex's nod, he led the way to a second moving van parked next to the one being filled with Blaine's furniture and personal belongings. Except for the slit windows and the digital lock on the rear door, the van appeared perfectly normal. The spec tech covered the outer latch with his body while he punched in a coded numerical sequence. The spring mechanism released with a warning buzz and a hiss: the van was pressurized.

When Blaine stepped in through the rear door it was like walking into the cockpit of a 747: only the blue sky and the endless sea of cumulus were missing. Each of the four operators had his own computer console, and wore headphones with slender mouthpieces. Two men were engaged in telephone conversations, another one typed away at his keyboard. Only the man watching the bank of video monitors bothered to look up.

Despite his earlier reticence, Ronson exhibited an eagerness to show off the expensive equipment at his command. He pointed to a complicated array of test tubes, stoppered bottles, and self-contained chemical diagnostic kits. "This is our roving minilab, used to monitor discreet field operations and to conduct automated preliminary analyses of foreign substances. It is a direct outgrowth of the Mariner 9 mission to discover life on Mars, in the early '70's. A cursory on-site examination of the body in the study disclosed an inflamed puncture wound that led us to probe the chair for the inflictive device, which in turn directed the course of our investigation for possible toxic substances. We had a fair idea of what we were looking for." He sounded almost blasé.

The color monitors showed in real-time the meticulous examination of the inside of Blaine's house. The men in the living room had pulled up the carpet, and were going over the padding and plywood floor inch by inch. One man in the kitchen was inspecting each and every drawer, cabinet, nook, and cranny, while another emptied the refrigerator of all its contents and dumped out bottles of condiments and cans of soup and vegetables. The house was being systematically dissected and analyzed.

Ronson explained, "A hypodermic syringe can easily inject poisonous liquids into any kind of sealed container without causing a leak or leaving a telltale mark. We haven't found anything in your food, but with the abundance of other evidence we can't overlook the possibility. We have to destroy everything."

Two men were disassembling Blaine's queen-sized mattress. They shredded the fabric and scraped apart the stuffing, then dumped everything piecemeal into large metal containers. Another team worked in the study, going over the desk and filing cabinets with instruments that looked like Geiger counters but which were obviously not checking for radioactivity. A man wearing metallic gloves was inspecting Blaine's clothing—including his favorite down parka—both visually and electronically.

"So far we have found four other inflictive devices. There may be more." Ronson picked up a clear plastic box sectioned by dividers of the same material; it held four thumb tacks. "One was pushed up through the middle of the mattress, another was secreted in the waist band of a pair of dungarees, and two were lodged in the throw rugs in the bathroom: one by the shower, the other in front of the toilet. Whoever planted them intended to get you either coming or going."

Blaine gulped. If he never again set foot in that house it would be too soon. He had the strange feeling that for the rest of his life every time he got pricked by a splinter of wood he would stop and count to five in order to see if he was going to live. "I've changed my mind about the parka. I'll shiver."

Chapter 10

"I had no idea the FBI had that kind of equipment." There was a hint of respect in Captain Lawson's voice. "Or a reaction team that could be put on location with such speed and expertise."

"We don't advertise it." Alex huddled in the back seat where the heat had trouble reaching. "We can't afford to let everyone know how sophisticated our law enforcement technology is or they'd soon find ways to circumvent it."

"But Foley, I'm a law enforcer. I'm supposed to be part of the team."

"The only way three people can keep a secret is if two of them are dead. That's why we encourage state authorities to call in the FBI on special cases, or to at least submit their evidence and let the FBI handle certain aspects of the investigation. If every cop on the beat had access to our data files, or knew what state-of-the-art equipment we had, word would leak out and someone would write a book about it. Criminals can read, you know. They assimilate police exposes like desert flowers soak up rain. It's best-seller material in the underworld."

Blaine said, "*I'm* impressed."

"Don't get me wrong, Captain. This isn't a power play, and we don't treat local police like country bumpkins. I know you want to be part of this investigation. To be honest with you, the FBI relies heavily on good field investigators. We don't usually solve cases on our own: we collect and collate field reports from dozens of sources so we can look at a case from a big picture perspective. It's a collaborative effort."

Winter scenery passed by unnoticed. Blaine traveled the route between his house and the Institute practically every day. Captain Lawson concentrated on driving. Alex talked.

"Your own initiative proves it. When you checked

out the origin of the tip-off phone call you demonstrated that the FBI is not infallible. No organization is, not just because we're so big that sometimes one hand doesn't know what the other hand is doing, but because we're only human. What we have going for us is a network, with many minds and fingers reaching into criminal corners. And by the way, that was an excellent suggestion you made: to have the Boston doctor's body examined for traces of poison, and to have his house placed off limits until we can get a team in there to check it out. It may come to nothing, but we don't know that yet. Anyway, it shows you're thinking."

"Are you trying to butter me up?" Captain Lawson glanced in the rearview mirror with gimlet eyes, but made no attempt to smile.

Alex thought for a moment. "Possibly. But more likely, I just don't want to alienate you. Or perhaps I want to learn from you. Remember that before this assignment all I ever did was read field reports from officers like yourself, and wonder why they were so incomplete; why the police did not follow lines of reasoning that seemed obvious to me. Now I see how difficult it is on the front line, trying to think and dodge bullets at the same time. I've had a rather rude awakening."

"Foley, you've been more than fair with me. Maybe I don't hate feds after all—at least, not all of them. If my men had gone into that house I'd have had four fatalities on my hands, and nothing to show for it—not even a gun battle. I have to thank you for that."

"We're trained to deal with terrorism and large scale offenses rather than crimes of passion. When it comes to domestic homicide, in most cases the local police are better prepared because they know what's going on in their communities, and who to look for when a crime occurs. The difference between you and me is in areas of expertise."

"Maybe. But I don't mind telling you that my past run-ins with the feds have been a lot less satisfactory. They always end up hogging the headlines and putting my department in the footnotes. Left a bad taste in my mouth."

"Admitted that previous administrations were glory seekers. But the modern day attitude in the Bureau is more progressive. What's important in police work is solving crime, not taking credit for the solution. As you said, we're all on the same team."

Another member of the team honked his horn. Lenny Taylor, keeping a safe distance behind, pulled out into the opposing traffic lane behind a white stretch limousine that was overtaking the lead police car.

"Uh-oh." Blaine instinctively drew his pistol and flipped off the safety. The action was becoming routine.

"Put that gun away, you fool, and get down!" Captain Lawson drew his own gun and held it just below the level of the glass. He was prepared to shoot through the thin door panel if necessary.

Blaine remained defiantly upright. He ignored Lawson's baleful stare and pointed the Glock's barrel at the approaching car. The limousine lurched ahead with the thrust of a powerful engine until it matched the police car's pace. An electric window slid open. Alex rolled down the rear window and thrust out his Smith & Wesson.

A swarthy man with mottled olive skin stuck his head out the window of the limousine, ignored the guns aimed at his face, and smiled. His shout was lost in the wind as he waved for them to pull over.

"What the hell—" Captain Lawson took his foot off the accelerator pedal and let the police car coast. Taylor weaved back and forth with his arm and weapon out the window; fortunately, he held his fire, or there was no telling who or what he might have shot.

The swarthy man withdrew his head as the limousine surged forward. After giving the police car plenty of room, the limousine swung back into the proper traffic lane and gradually pulled off onto the dirt-and-stone shoulder.

Lawson said through gritted teeth, "Careful, careful. Let's see what the man wants before we panic and blow him away. He's innocent till proven guilty." The caution was directed at Blaine.

Blaine lowered his gun, but did not put the safety back on. "Every barrel I've looked down in the past fifteen hours has had moving bullets in it. Coming my way."

"Captain, get Taylor to cover for us." Alex took the initiative and waved for the detective to move past.

Lawson nudged the police car right up to the rear bumper of the limousine. With a screech of tires Taylor skidded to a halt so that his car was catty-cornered to the limousine's front bumper and blocked it in.

The swarthy man poked a highly polished brown shoe out of the left passenger door. He was dressed in a form-fitting tweed suit that was expensive and tailor made. A cold breeze ruffled black, swept-back hair, and made him hunch as he walked back to the three armed men.

Taylor leaped out of his car with his gun pointed at the stranger. "Don't move."

The man ignored him. As he approached Captain Lawson, who stood halfway out of the door with gun in hand, he unbuttoned his coat and pulled it back to reveal a brown matching vest, a dark green tie, and a slender waistline. "As you can see I am unarmed."

Both Blaine and Alex stepped into the open with their guns out. Neither said a word.

Taylor took a position at the front of the limousine and held his service revolver at arms length, with the barrel touching the glass on the driver's side. He peered in through dark-tinted windows. "There's only one of 'em I can see. The driver."

"We are quite alone I assure you. Just my chauffeur and me." He dropped his coat tails and held both hands up at half-mast. His words were clipped, his enunciation precise, almost forced, and he had a tendency to let his words run together. "Anthony Carcione at your service."

The captain's gun held a steady bead on Carcione's chest. "What do you want, Mr. Carcione?" Lawson asked gruffly.

"I would like to speak with Dr. Blaine Mitchell." He looked back and forth between Blaine and Alex, who were dressed identically. "I have information that may help save his life."

"Is that a threat?"

"Not at all. It is an offer. Please—" He lowered his hands a couple inches. "Excuse me, but who are you, if I may ask?"

"Captain Lawson, Greensborough Police Department."

"Ah, Captain Lawson, I understand your—"

Alex holstered his gun and moved in behind Carcione. He ran his hands down Carcione's armpits, torso, crotch, and both legs. "He's clean."

Carcione let his hands drop to his sides. "Very professionally done, for a doctor." To Lawson, "I understand your suspicion and your regard for Dr. Blaine's safety. Please understand that I too have concern for his continued survival."

"And why is that?"

"Captain Lawson, could we continue this conversation in the warm comfort of my car?" After a few seconds of silence, he continued, "You may bring your weapons. And take the time to have your fellow policeman call in my registration. I assure you that everything is quite in order. I am a businessman and rather well known, if not necessarily well liked."

Lawson's gun never wavered. "And why aren't you liked, Mr. Carcione?"

"Because I am a *good* businessman. I make money while my competitors go bankrupt. Please?" He indicated the limousine.

The captain looked first at Alex, then at Blaine. Alex nodded. "Okay, Mr. Carcione." Louder, "Lenny, get on the horn and check out his plates."

Carcione showed a mouthful of white teeth. "This way please." He opened the door for his patrons.

Alex leaned inside and checked out the interior, then nodded to Lawson and Blaine. The rear compartment was like a living room with a low ceiling. The four high-backed swivel chairs that faced inward for conferencing were soft and plush. They would have been comfortable if Blaine had allowed himself to lean into the pile. Instead, he ran his hand along the edge of the seat, feeling for sharp objects, then perched there like a bird about to take flight. When he saw Lawson holster his gun he realized he still held his in a threatening attitude, and put it away.

Carcione, the last one in, settled into the remaining seat and pulled down the armrests. "May I offer you a drink?" He pointed to the well-stocked bar and an electric percolator. "I am having a hot buttered rum myself, but I also have coffee and tea and a variety of wines and liqueurs."

Blaine wondered if his two companions declined for the same reason he did—the possibility of poison. Lawson answered for all of them, "We're on duty."

"Very well." Carcione took his mug off the hot plate and sipped the steaming brew. His fingers were full of gold rings whose large diamonds sparkled in the sunlight. "May I ask which of you doctors is Dr. Blaine?"

Blaine nervously raised his hand.

"And you?"

"Foley."

Carcione nodded. "Dr. Foley, you will pardon me if I direct my attention at your esteemed colleague." To Blaine, "I have been waiting to catch you away from the, shall we say, swarm of federal agents taking over your home. I have a distaste for the FBI."

"Why is that? Are you on the wanted list?" Lawson never pulled his punches.

Carcione had a habit of grinning mirthlessly, a way of disalarming his confidantes without giving away his feelings. "Let us say that they have caused me much grief in the past, and let it go at that."

"What kind of grief?"

He smiled. "You would rather not let it go. Very well." He was as direct as the police captain. "Many of my business associates have had some rather shady dealings in the past. Nothing overtly illegal, you understand, but certainly questionable. Their methods tend to be rather strong on occasion. I, on the other hand, operate my various business interests legitimately, but because of my connections I am grouped with those who are, shall we say, less lawful. Guilt by proximity you might say."

"You're a racketeer."

"Captain Lawson, why the hostility? I have come here to help, yet you insist on persecuting me."

"Let's say that we're a bit touchy today. Recent events have put us on guard."

"That much at least I can understand, if the newspaper accounts are only partway accurate. According to Mr. Greenstein there was quite a clash last night with a variety of assailants."

"Greenstein's a jerk." Blaine found himself speaking without volition. "That little nerd has caused more trouble than he's worth."

"Yes, he has been following your work rather closely this past week, and is directly responsible for some, if not all, of the difficulties you have encountered. It is because of him that I got involved."

"What exactly is your interest in Dr. Mitchell, Mr. Carcione?"

"At last Captain Lawson we come to the point." Carcione let his words run together. "In a word my interest is business. I have a proposition to make to Dr. Mitchell that will benefit both of us. It has to do with his recent developments at the Institute for Higher Research in Perceptual Functions of the Brain."

"Finally, we'll get some answers." Blaine forgot himself and leaned back in the seat, then stiffened. He slowly counted to five before taking another breath. It was a deep inhalation. "What is it about my work that's so all-fired important to so many non-scientists? Why are people dying over it?"

"It has to do with drugs, Dr. Mitchell."

"My work has to do with chemical receptors and electronically induced inhibitors, not drugs."

"A rose by any other name." Carcione flashed his expensive teeth, bought and paid for by illicit wheeling-dealings and excessive profit margins—what he called business acumen.

Other than the acknowledgment of his name, Alex spoke for the first time since entering the limousine. "Are you a drug dealer, Mr. Carcione?"

"No, no, no, Dr. Foley. I am a businessman always on the lookout for new opportunities. Unless I miss my guess, Dr. Mitchell has provided one of those rare opportunities. I simply want to get in on the ground floor by arranging to purchase exclusive rights to Dr. Mitchell's invention before my competitors realize its potential. The early bird gets the worm, you know."

"Forget that Shakespearian stuff," Captain Lawson said. "What does this have to do with saving Dr. Mitchell's life?"

"For a policeman you are quite a negotiator, Captain Lawson. You are wise to ask what I have to offer before coming to the bargaining table. And you are quite right that before we can consummate a deal we must ensure that Dr. Mitchell does not pass on from this world as a result of, shall we say, less ethical adversaries. Dr. Mitchell, first accept my apologies for the strong-arm tactics my subordinates inflicted upon your person—assuming Mr. Greenstein's article was truthful in that regard. They misunderstood their orders and exceeded their authority."

Blaine was in a quandary. "What the hell are you talking about?"

"Permit me to explain. When I first read about your method for altering levels of consciousness by the implantation of electrodes, I was thrilled by the possibilities such a device might have on the open market. Imagine a cure-all painkiller in every household, an artificially chosen level of consciousness that induces in the patient a sense of well-being: a life without pain, without suffering, without stress, and most important-ly, without dependency. It is the answer to society's ills." He spread out his hands. "But you know this already.

"Upon further reading I found that the device is not portable, that it requires a rather large life-support system and power supply: a problem for the present but certainly one not insurmountable in terms of future miniaturization. So, although we have a working model, the question remains how to make it available to the general public." Carcione held up two fingers and flashed his store-bought smile. "I have come up with a solution, but it will require capital to implement. And that, Dr. Mitchell, is where I can help you. My legitimate business is backing ventures with the potential for profit.

"I called you both at home and at the office but could not reach you. I dispatched a representative to Greensborough but he was unable to find you. When I learned that you were slated to return last night I sent escorts to assist my representative. For that I apologize. Luigi Giafaglione and Pasquale DiCristofano were from the old school—"

"Hey!" Lawson burst out suddenly. "They're the two Mafia muscle men who were killed last night at Westmoreland."

In the dead silence that followed, the whoosh of passing cars was barely audible through the limousine's soundproof insulation.

"Please show some respect for the dead, Captain Lawson. They were my henchmen in the most admirable definition of the word. The old ways die hard among the Mafioso. Assuredly Luigi and Pasquale did not have the most progressive of attitudes but that is no reason to blame them for last night's activities. If Mr. Greenstein's article is to be believed, they were victims of circumstance. Dr. Mitchell, forgive me for behavior that might have been misinterpreted as aggression. Any show of force is a holdover from the gang-war days of which they were an inglorious part. But as they are part of the Family, I am honor bound to offer them employment."

Blaine did not know what to say.

"May I continue?"

Staring at the Mafia man who had fingered him with his thugs, Blaine felt that he could do anything he wanted. His nod was little more than a nervous jerk.

"Thank you." Carcione made eye contact with each of the others before continuing. "The late-night radio broadcast was lacking in details but when Luigi and Pasquale did not return to the motel my representative assumed that they were the two men gunned down in the parking lot. He called me immediately. I notified the families of the deceased, initiated an inquiry among my numerous contacts, and left New York for a sleepless ride in the dark. I have been on the telephone almost constantly ever since." He paused dramatically. "But enough small talk. I am sure we have all had more restful nights. Of more importance is the fact that I have learned who the murderers are. They are old enemies of mine who are now enemies of yours. Very dangerous enemies."

Carcione spun his chair around to face the communication console. In addition to the built-in television screen and compact disc player there were three cellular telephones each with an answering machine, a computer monitor and keyboard, a laser printer, and a facsimile receiver. He punched a ten-digit number on the touch-tone telephone. "Bernie, is that information ready for transmission? Good. Send it at once." He disconnected.

To Captain Lawson, "I will give this information to you but not to the FBI. I have had enough of their harassment and will not deal with them. I do however urge you to pass it along so they can help you protect our distinguished doctor, but you must promise not to reveal your source. Agreed?"

The police captain looked directly at Carcione and never batted an eye. "I swear I will not tell the FBI where I got the information."

"Good. Then we have a contract."

The fax machine hummed and clattered as it spat rolled paper over the bale. After three sheets of material curled into Carcione's lap the transmission stopped. He ripped off the last sheet along the grated edge and handed the paper to Blaine. "The fax of life."

Blaine ran his eyes over the newsprint. He saw names, dates, locations, dollar amounts, and miscellaneous news items all of which were meaningless to him and much of which was written in Spanish. He gave the three connected sheets to Lawson, who held them so that Alex could read them as well.

"It is a South American syndicate whose only business is the importation of cocaine into this country. The growing and distilling operation is no secret but is beyond U.S. jurisdiction and is backed by the local regimes supported by its revenues. They have a highly organized smuggling ring with monthly shipments into Miami and Boston. I do not have their exact schedule, only the dates of their next two deliveries. Consider it a bonus."

"Where did you get this—?"

Carcione cut off Lawson like a lawn mower chopping through a blade of grass. "That is not for you to know, Captain Lawson." Carcione's perpetual smile might never have existed. "I offer you the information, not its source, and you would be wise to accept it unquestioningly."

For the first time Blaine saw the police captain knuckle under to another's will. His normally gruff exterior wilted visibly as he was knocked down a notch in the pecking order. He gasped into silence.

Carcione rolled his shoulders, and took a long draught from his mug. "My intelligence network is quite costly. Not in terms of cash but in services I must return. I cannot afford to accumulate too large a debt because in this business loans are not available. Money is easier to obtain than favors."

Still Lawson kept quiet.

To Blaine, "Be warned, Dr. Mitchell. These South American importers are ruthless fanatics who will stop at nothing to ensure the sale of their product. They would blow up a building to kill a cockroach, and send an army if a strike force fails. For all practical purposes they have unlimited resources. Even with the FBI and Greensborough's police department at your disposal your chances of survival are slim to nonexistent. Your best investment is in diversification."

Carcione was no stranger to histrionics. He paused to take a sip of his hot buttered rum while his guests waited for him to continue. Lawson was obviously expectant. Alex appeared calm and indifferent, but his roving eyes observed every gesture, noted every innuendo, took in every suggestion.

Blaine was back on the edge of his seat. "This whole ordeal is a case of mistaken identity," he shouted. "I'm not the Blaine Mitchell who's trafficking drugs. There's another doctor in Boston with the same name and he's the one they're looking for. Only they're too stupid to know it." A sudden idea struck him. "Mr. Carcione, if you have ways of collecting information, can you also leak it?"

The toothy grin returned. "At last we speak the same language, Dr. Blaine. But you are misinformed if you believe that you are not the man they are looking for. I know nothing about this doctor in Boston but I do know that if the newspaper reports are true your machine will put chemical substance marketers out of business. Permanently."

"How?" Blaine pleaded. "How can it do that?"

"Why take opiates when a machine can induce pleasant dreams without harmful side effects?" Carcione spread upturned palms that had never been calloused by physical work. "A person can maintain health *and* sanity without swallowing pills without sniffing powder without injecting liquids through possibly infected needles and without concern for addiction." Carcione's smile returned to its previous proportions. "And we can make it all happen."

At last Blaine saw where Carcione was headed, and knew exactly how he had been misled.

"At first I thought we would construct an assembly-line plant to manufacture individual units for large-

scale distribution but when I discovered how complicated the machinery was I realized that we would need
to establish visitor centers like movie theaters where
the patrons could envision their fantasies mentally
rather than simply viewing them optically. The initial
capital outlay would be considerable but I see no reason why we could not offer the dream machine experience at a price the customer could afford to pay while
reaping commensurate rewards for our investment.
With your brains and my money this could be a remu-
nerative alliance for both of us."

Blaine started to object, but was held in check by
Carcione's upheld hand and aggressive style.

"Anonymity is my stock in trade, Dr. Blaine. I care
nothing about fame. You can have all the prestige and
the justly deserved credit."

"You realize that what I've developed is a medical
device, an anesthetic tool. It won't do what you think it
will do and, despite newspaper accounts to the contrary, it won't put the drug companies out of business."

"Not immediately perhaps but it has the potential.
Yours may be the invention of the century."

Blaine waved him off. "You're talking about developments that may be years in the future—if they're even
possible. You don't need a machine, Mr. Carcione.
You're already dreaming."

"This whole meeting is a scam," Captain Lawson
scowled. "You're using us to get rid of your competitors
and get even for the deaths of your low-life cronies."

Carcione viewed him coolly. He swallowed hard, as
if trying to eat words that he might later regret saying.
In his smooth, even voice, he said, "My friends are dead
and nothing can bring them back. Nor is there money
in revenge. This is strictly business, Captain Lawson,
and business is my life."

This time Lawson did not allow himself to be cowed.
He said nothing, but kept a defiant set to his jaw.

When Carcione reached casually into his breast
pocket Blaine tensed like a batter dodging a wild pitch.
The card that was offered was embossed in gold leaf; on

it were Carcione's name and telephone number, nothing else.

"Call me any time day or night, Dr. Blaine, when you decide to do business. I will instruct my attorneys to submit sample contracts but will not bother you otherwise. When you are prepared to negotiate I trust you will consider my bid. That is all I ask."

Carcione held out his nicely manicured right hand. "Salude."

Chapter 11

"I want to know what the hell this dream machine is all about." Captain Lawson reverted to his normal abrasive personality once he got away from the more powerful influence of Anthony Carcione. He shoved through the glass door of the Institute with enough force to bounce it back from its stops.

Blaine caught the door on the rebound, and wondered if he would have a bruise on his shoulder the next day. "Don't listen to Carcione. He's just another shyster looking to make a fast buck for himself. The trouble is with Greenstein. He started this whole mess by exaggerating the performance level of the neurometric feedback terminal. Now every cutthroat druggie thinks the bypass skullcap is the answer to his dreams—literally."

"Carcione is a highly influential man within uncertain circles." Alex caught up with Blaine in the entry. "His name comes up all the time but we've never been able to catch him at anything. He's what we call an outlaw: he operates outside the framework of strict legality but never does anything overtly criminal. He even claims all his profits and pays his taxes on time."

"Forget Carcione. If we believe what he says, the Mafia is out of the picture. What I want to know is why you didn't radio in that info on the South American gauchos and call in the Marines."

"Did you see all the telemetry equipment he had in that limousine? He's got AM, FM, CB, short wave, long wave, and can probably hear surfers on a Hawaiian wave. It wouldn't surprise me if he picks up military satellite signals. So I didn't want to start broadcasting in the clear, and let him know that an FBI agent had been sitting right across from him posing as a doctor."

"Good afternoon, Dr. Mitchell," Tilda said sweetly. "I've got that list of phone messages for you. The computer is still down but—"

"Pardon me, Miss." Alex reached over the counter top and grabbed the telephone. "How do I get an outside line?"

"Just dial the number. Long distance calls are on the house." Blaine ignored Tilda, who sat with a sheaf of papers in her hand, her mouth agape, and turned to the police captain. "Greenstein made a monumental blunder by ascribing future potential uses of the skullcap to the actual working model, and by misunderstanding the terminology I applied to explain its functions. He's got people believing it's a benign substitute for psychedelic drugs, that it can induce a scripted, hallucinatory experience. Admittedly, at certain frequencies it produces the effect of an out-of-body experience, but that's a useless side effect of our prime research on the conscious release of endorphins through biofeedback stimulus response—"

"Hold on, Doctor. You're losing me with all this scientific mumbo jumbo." Captain Lawson jabbed a finger at Blaine like a goose pecking corn. "All I know is what I hear in town: that you like to watch people die and record it on film, and cut up live chimps so you can make their dicks hard by tickling their brains."

This was not the first time that Blaine found himself on the defensive about the nature of his work. "You've been listening to student part-timers whose love for gallows humor is exceeded only by their fascination for the job. They crack jokes because they can't handle the downbeat reality of caring for sick anthropoids. Don't you think I know they call me the necrophilic voyeur? But they don't mean it in a disparaging way. They just don't see how a person can devote his career to treating terminally ill patients and maintain his sanity. It's their way of getting a grip on the cruelties of life. People die; that's the prediction of birth. Some die quickly and painlessly, others die in slow agony. We don't have to like it, but we do have to live with it. And some of us are lucky enough to be in a position to help those whose fate is a lingering death from cancer or neurological disease."

"Is that how you rationalize it? You call yourself lucky because you get to take deathbed confessions from senile old women?"

"What is your problem, Captain? I'm a doctor. Part of my job is studying the stages of death so I can learn how to mitigate pain in the living and enhance the quality of life for the hopeless. There's nothing wrong with that. And anyway, how is it different from you interviewing bereaved friends and relatives about homicide victims? You badger people in hospital waiting rooms while they're watching a loved one die, without ever considering their grief and mental anguish. And you get paid to do it. Does that make it wrong, because you bought a new car with money earned from the suffering of others?"

The policeman's tongue caught in his throat. He was still trying to form words when Taylor came in and smiled at the receptionist.

Alex interrupted the shouting match with a well-placed diversion. "Headquarters is getting right on the South American angle. Turns out the drug enforcement division has been on their trail for months but could never pin anything on them. This tip from Carcione may blow the lid off their whole operation. DE flipped over the inside scoop. Also told me to watch my ass; these South American dudes are real bad hombres."

"Is that something we didn't already know?" Blaine headed for the stairwell with Alex and Lawson in tow. "Let's get down to the lab so I can give you guys the ten cent tour of the facilities. Perhaps if I can prove to you how innocuous our setup is we can figure out a way to let the underworld know."

"Get Greenstein to write a factual article for a change," Alex suggested.

"I just want to spend five minutes with the twerp when there isn't a battalion of police around. He'll have more than a shiner to show for his troubles."

The basement level of the Institute was a warren of rooms and lab complexes all interconnected by broad corridors. Audible in the background was the chattering of chimpanzees; it was their feeding time, and volunteer students who had not gone home for break tended their needs. A single custodian working overtime was changing tubes in the fluorescent fixtures. Otherwise the rooms were unoccupied.

"Maybe you could hook him up to your brain machine and burn out his mind." The tone of Lawson's voice was definitely accusatory.

Blaine was so tired of hearing the policeman's indictments that he ignored the challenge to argue. He went back a couple of thoughts. "You know, I just figured out what Carcione meant about diversifying. If I were to go public with *all* our data—instead of publishing just an overview paper and giving a couple of introductory lectures--the South American gang would have nothing to gain by killing me."

"I don't think that's exactly what he had in mind." Alex had to skip down the steps two at a time in order to keep up. "What he wanted was for you to give the plans to him so he could start mass production. Of course, his rationale was right. Once the technology is established on a large scale your death would prove nothing."

"So my best insurance policy is to begin disseminating information through the scientific journals, and getting other research facilities to carry on my work." Blaine turned into the kitchen, where a fresh pot of coffee was brewing on the electric percolator. He handed out mugs. "God knows there are enough spin-offs to keep a lot of people busy for years to come."

The clatter of porcelain and silverware brought in Marybeth. She looked a little haggard, and not all from a lack of sleep. She handed Blaine a manila folder. "Here's a hard copy of the file you wanted. But I've got bad news about the computer."

Blaine glanced at the folder, then placed it upside down on the table. He removed his coat and sat down. "Don't tell me it's still locked up."

"Worse than that. It's dead."

He squinted at her. "What do you mean by that?"

Marybeth took a deep breath. "Someone has injected a virus into the program. All our data are gone."

A tingling sensation ran along his spine. "Are you sure it's not just a glitch? Sometimes a power surge will cause a partial memory wipe."

"I've checked everything, Blaine. There are no hardware faults, no electrical spikes, no power breaks, and no physical damage to any of the components. The problem is in the software."

"Have you tried debugging it? Have you run a diagnostics program? Have you called an outside service rep? Have you—"

"Blaine, I've done all that. It's all I've been doing all day. Nothing works. I've tried every access code in the book and a few that aren't. The slate's been wiped clean. Someone has sabotaged the computer quite thoroughly. The only good news is that Mighty Joe wasn't as upset as I thought he would be. Disturbed, yes. But not violent."

At the moment Blaine cared nothing for Young's feelings on the matter. He suddenly felt crushed by the weight of recent events. First he had lost his car, then his house and all its furnishings had been taken away from him, now all his work files—hard copy and magnetic—were missing. Everything he owned, everything he had worked for, everything he had ever done, was gone. He had lost continuity with his past, and faced an uncertain future. Dr. Blaine Thomas Mitchell might never have existed except at this exact moment of awareness. "Cogito ergo sum" was his only contact with reality.

The intensity of the past few hours sapped his energy. He was overcome with fatigue and with the weakness of deep despair. With his elbows resting on the table he dropped his head in his hands. No longer did he know who he was or what he was about. He had become a nonentity. Death seemed to be the only option left to him: a pleasant surcease from the aching memory of life.

He hardly felt the warm touch of Marybeth's hands

on his neck. She kneaded muscles tensed by the awful pressure of the struggle to keep his head above the crashing waves of annihilation. For ten years Blaine had endured holding the hands of patients who were raising the curtain on the final act of a play called life. He had watched impotently as they had gone through the stages of denial and isolation, anger, bargaining, and depression. For him it had been an intellectual exercise that he never actually comprehended. But now that he found himself confronting the inevitable conclusion of the cycle of life, a flash of insight brightened the final stage: acceptance.

"Dr. Mitchell. Oh, Dr. Mitchell." Tilda stood meekly outside the kitchen door, accompanied by Lenny Taylor. "I know you don't want to be bothered by phone calls, but there's a doctor on the line who insists on talking with you."

"Can't you take a message, Tilda? I've got enough problems today without defending my reputation from the medical profession."

"She's been calling all morning. And she's quite— concerned—about you."

In the ensuing silence the humming ballast in the overhead fixture was a symphonic monotone. "Dr. Crowley?"

Tilda nodded.

"Okay, I'll take it in my office."

Marybeth's hands fell away as he pushed himself back from the table. He hunched down the corridor to his darkened sanctum, switched on the fifteen-watt desk light, and eased into his comfortable leather chair halfway hoping to feel the prick of a poisoned dart. He pushed in the flashing light on the telecom set.

"Hello."

"Blaine, is that you?"

"Fran?"

"Good god, Blaine, what's going on out there? I've been worried sick about you."

Blaine forced down the lump in his throat. "It's nothing, Fran. Just a case of mistaken identity."

"But the paper said Westmoreland U was fire-bombed by terrorists during your lecture, that they were after you, that some of the men were machine-gunned by another gang, that the reporter was shot at when he chased them away from the lecture hall, that—"

"It's all an exaggeration, Fran. There's a doctor in Boston who's been smuggling drugs from South America. His name's Blaine Appleton Mitchell. Apparently he fell behind in his payments, or double-crossed his suppliers, and now the dealers are out to get him. They confused him with me because of the similarity of our names. That's all it is. Honest. And that bastard reporter wasn't chasing anyone; he was running like a scared rabbit. He made up most of the story so he could look like a hero."

"What about the attack at your house this morning? It was all over the morning news."

"That was only shortly after dawn. When did they have time to write it up?"

"You must still be on jet lag, darling. We're three hours behind the east coast. You were on television on the eight o'clock report. I was getting dressed when your face came on the screen. God, it was scary. I mean, I woke up next to you just yesterday morning, put you on a plane and sent you across the country, and the next morning there you are back in my bedroom. As soon as the news was over I dashed outside to get the morning paper, and there you were again. Blaine, you're making headlines all over the country. And while we were backpacking you were getting nationwide coverage in the dailies because of your paper on the neurometric feedback terminal."

"That's what's started the mix up. My name got confused with this other Dr. Mitchell. And he's dead."

"*What*?" It was a stifled scream.

"Natural causes, honey. He died in his sleep . . . " Blaine felt the hair on the back of his neck rise like a peacock's tail feathers. He remembered the thumbtack in his bed—a thumbtack tipped with Ricin. He also remembered what Alex said about coincidence. If this was all related . . .

"Blaine, are you sure you're okay? You're not holding back on me, are you? Or underplaying the seriousness—"

"Honest, honey, I'm fine. There's nothing to worry about. I've got more police covering me than the President of the United States. The FBI has put a special investigative team on the case, and they've assigned a bodyguard who won't let me out of his sight—" He looked up and saw the special agent standing in the hall, within earshot. What was it he said about coincidence? "—unless I go into a bathroom without windows." What if the Boston police or the pathologist's relatives stumbled on thumbtacks smeared with Ricin. "Hang on a minute, will you?"

"But darling—"

He covered the mouthpiece with his hand. "Alex, get Lawson in here pronto. He's got to stop anyone from going into Appleton's house. If the same person or group of people who sabotaged my place were responsible for his death, then his house could be—"

Alex held up both hands, palms outward. "I'm way ahead of you, Blaine. I gave strict instructions to the Boston police to post his house, office, automobiles, even his garden shed off limits until a site team arrived. We'll know in a few hours whether his death was tied in with the attempts on your life."

New implications rushed through Blaine's mind like wind through the trees in autumn, and thoughts dropped like dried leaves. This case was getting more complicated with each passing minute.

"—for you. I've got two experiments scheduled for this afternoon, and another in the morning. But I can catch a plane after that and—"

"No, Fran. Don't do that. Don't even think it. Just stay put until this thing blows over. There are too many variables that—"

"So there *is* something you're not telling me, isn't there?"

"No. Yes. There's plenty. It's just that the guys who

are after me don't know that the person they really want isn't me, and that he's already dead. We've got to make contact and let them know. It's—it's very involved." Blaine inspected the raw spot on his palm, where he had lost a piece of skin—was it only last night, or a thousand centuries ago? "We're dealing with a bunch of cowboys who think this is the wild, wild west. Just—just don't—do anything. Sit tight, and I'll keep in touch."

"Are you sure this is the right thing to—"

"Yes, I'm sure. I don't want you involved. I don't want—I don't want to lose you."

"Blaine, what are you talking about? We're already involved—"

"I don't mean that. I mean—I don't want you out here in case things get hot. Okay? Just—sit tight. Really, honey, I've got to go. I've got things to do. I'll—I'll call you."

"Are you sure?"

"Yes, I'm sure. Just—don't worry."

"Darling, I can't not worry about you. I love you."

Blaine hesitated, looked up at Alex. "Me too."

"You love me?"

"Yes."

"Can you say it?"

"Of course, but—Fran, I have to go. I—"

"I love you, Blaine."

"Same here, Fran. Bye."

"Blaine, I—"

He took the receiver away from his ear. He could still hear her voice, but not what she was saying. Full of confused emotion, he eased the phone into the cradle. The line signal stayed on several seconds after he hung up. He wiped sweat off his brow.

"Tough call?"

Blaine sighed deeply. "Yes."

"Dr. Frances Crowley? The woman who left the messages on your home recorder?"

"Yes."

The special agent was silent for several seconds.

"Blaine, I don't mean to pry but—it's important for me to know what's going on." He added hastily, "I don't need intimate details, but if she's involved in any way I can have protection arranged for her. They might try to use her to get to you."

"She's in California, and no one knows we have a—a relationship. It only started a week ago. We met at my lecture at Berkeley. She's a neurosurgeon-turned-researcher, so we have a lot in common. She also likes skiing and backpacking and—and other things." Blaine ran his hands through his hair, wondering what to say—and how much to say.

"I don't want particulars—"

"No, it's okay. I don't mind. Right now, she may be all I have left in the world. She may be all that's keeping me together. I don't know what's going on any more. People out to kill me, steal my files, destroy my computer programs. The next thing you know they'll try to blow up the Institute. Alex, what's happened to my peace of mind? What's happened to my sanity? Yesterday morning I woke up in her—"

"Blaine—"

"It started out so simple. We liked each other, we had our work to share, she invited me to go backpacking at Yosemite, we camped together all week, saw the sights, explored the trails, enjoyed each other's company, rediscovered what it's like to be people instead of doctors. It cleared my head about a lot of things. I spent the last night at her house, got up in the morning to catch a plane east, and came home to bombs, bullets, and land mines. Hell, I thought I left all that in some godforsaken jungle a couple of decades ago. Now I've come full cycle, back to where I was when I was a kid out of high school. Owning nothing, being nobody, facing death on a daily basis. Only this time I'm too smart to just shrug it off. This time I'm not some pimple-faced teenager who thinks he's invulnerable, who thinks only other people die. Now I know what death is: a great nothingness, an infinity of nothingness, an eternity of nothingness. And now I'm afraid of that nothingness."

"You're wrong, Blaine. There's more out there than you realize. This world—this life—is just a stopping place. A testing ground. It's a way station on the trail to fulfillment. And you don't need to worry. When judgment day arrives you'll pass with flying colors."

Marybeth appeared behind Alex, and Lawson behind her. Blaine switched off the desk light and in the darkness rubbed the tears off his cheeks with his shirtsleeve. When he saw the expression on Marybeth's face he knew why the telephone's line signal had remained lighted after he had hung up. But that was unimportant now. What she overheard was her problem. He had more pressing needs to take care of: his life to save, his work to preserve, his long-dead patients to atone for, his newfound love to possess.

A week ago Fran Crowley had undoubtedly saved his life. If he had returned according to schedule, instead of sleeping joyously in her arms, he would have ended up sleeping alone in a poisoned bed. And a moment ago she had just as likely saved him again, this time from the depths of despair.

His admission of fear was the means of overcoming it. It had been building in him ever since last night, but he had ignored it. Now he faced it with new resolve. He had a great deal to live for and plenty of spirit left. He had been too long on the run; now it was time to fight back.

"Let's go to the lab and figure out a plan of attack."

Chapter 12

"We're only just beginning to understand the work-ings of the human brain. In our present state of knowl-edge we know about as much about the processes of thought as Newton knew about falling apples. Don't get me wrong. We've all got ideas about consciousness, but no concrete evidence on what it is or how it came to be or what useful function it serves in evolutionary terms. We call it self-awareness, but that's a philosophical tautology: arguing in a circle, or using a definition as a description. It's like saying that gravity is what makes apples hit the ground; but that only explains what gravity *does*, not what it *is*. We can examine the effect but not the cause. Am I making sense so far?"

Captain Lawson kept his hands at his sides. He was relaxed and characteristically somber. "Police aren't stupid, you know. I've got a degree in criminal psychol-ogy."

Blaine realized he had touched a sore spot. He made a mental note not to touch it again, but did not make any apologies. "Fine. Alex, I think you said you studied criminal law?"

The special agent nodded. "A masters working towards my Ph.D." There was no pretense in his voice. It was a plain statement of fact.

"Then you've both studied enough psychology to know that it's not an exact science. It's not a stab in the dark, either. The mind is a combination of biology, heredity, upbringing, and chemical balance—to say nothing of cultural influence. That's getting far afield for our purposes, so suffice it to say that there can be no clear grasp of human mental processes without a fundamental understanding of the functions of the brain—a statement that some psychiatrists still repudi-ate. But I say that you can't repair an engine without looking under the hood. So let's divorce ourselves from psychiatry and philosophy, and concentrate on neurology: the medical science of the nervous system and its diseases."

"What's this got to do with drugs and dream machines?" Captain Lawson wandered around the laboratory indifferent to Blaine's methodical introduction to the vast array of equipment. "And what's it got to do with stabbing electrodes into dying people's skulls and recording their thoughts instead of letting them die in peace and privacy?"

Blaine sighed. He knew he had his work cut out for him. "First of all, we don't stab electrodes into the skull—we tape power leads onto the scalp. And we can't read or record thoughts, only brain waves at specific frequencies." He found the policeman's continued interruptions disturbing. "Would you let me go about this my own way?"

What Blaine called a laboratory looked more like an operating room only about five times the size and ten times as complex. One entire wall was taken up with computer modules, monitors, and keyboards. The two adjacent walls consisted of life support equipment such as electroencephalographs, electrocardiographs, electromyographs, electro-oculographs, and esoteric devices for biofeedback training: audio oscillators, digital frequency discriminators, and omnidirectional tilt detectors. The fourth wall was bisected by the swinging double doors, on each side of which were adjustable metal shelves containing liquid crystal displays and paper printing machines, isolation amplifiers, electrometers, banks of filter circuits that neutralized local field effects and improved signal-to-noise ratios, and copper plate sensing antennas. Robby the robot would have felt right at home.

Lawson humphed. "You give permanents here, too?"

Instead of an operating table, a multi-adaptable foam-padded chair occupied the center of the room. It sported a headrest topped by a cone-shaped cap similar in appearance to hair dryers in beauty salons, except that teems of wires sprouted from the cap like crab grass on a poorly tended lawn. Thick wads of cables disappeared into the raised gridwork flooring like roots gone astray, and fed the monitoring equipment lining the walls.

"This is the prototype of the bypass skullcap: the large scale model used to design, build, and test the apparatus before improvement and miniaturization. I'll get to it in the proper sequence if you'll let me continue."

"Go ahead." Lawson inspected the mechanical contrivances as if he were looking for clues to a murder. "Don't mind me."

"Thanks." Blaine raised his eyebrows at Alex. "I know you want to try it out, but you've got to know what to expect before I send you on an hallucinatory trip through the pathways of your mind. Otherwise it could scare the hell out of you."

Alex held his hands in a defensive position. "You're the doctor. I'm just here to observe."

"Good." Blaine shuffled along behind Captain Lawson to make certain that he did not tamper with sensitive equipment, or accidentally disrupt sequential phase restrictors that were difficult to recalibrate when knocked out of adjustment. Of course, with the computer down, the monitoring devices—driven by preprogrammed codes—were inoperable.

"Everyone has his own concept of death: what it means, where you go afterwards, if you can come back. Much of what an individual believes about the phenomenon is culturally induced." To Alex, "Are you Catholic?"

"Lutheran."

"Agnostic," mumbled Lawson.

"Okay, but I want to reach a definition of death by going through the stages of life. Let's avoid semantics by agreeing that although crystals absorb minerals and grow as a consequence, they are not alive. They just happen to fit a loose definition of living organisms. True life metabolizes food. Accepting such a simplistic description, let's also avoid semantics by agreeing that biological death is the irreversible cessation of all meta-bolic processes, at which time consciousness in human beings ceases to exist because its carrier—the brain—no longer supports it.

"I haven't said yet what consciousness is, only that it disappears at the time of death because that's how we describe death. Now I'll back up a step and try to explain near-death. Do you remember Aristotle's alle-gorical race between the tortoise and the hare?"

Alex looked dumbfounded. "Is that the one where the fast rabbit dawdled while the slow turtle plodded on toward the finish line, and the turtle won the race because even though he was slow he was steady?"

"No, that's Mother Goose. Aristotle predicted that no matter how fast the rabbit could run, he could never catch up to the tortoise once the tortoise got a head start. It works like this: the rabbit is twice as fast as the tortoise, but doesn't start running until the tortoise is halfway down the track. In the time it takes the rabbit to reach the tortoise's position, the tortoise, still crawl-ing, is three-quarters of the way to the end. When the rabbit reaches that position, the tortoise is seven-eights of the way. When the rabbit reaches the new position, the tortoise is fifteen-sixteenths of the way. When the rabbit gets there, the tortoise is thirty-one-thirty-sec-onds of the way. No matter how hard the rabbit tries, the tortoise is always ahead of him. The rabbit gets closer and closer but never passes the tortoise. In the math books it's called an asymptotic curve."

"In my book it's called bullshit." Captain Lawson stopped meandering and confronted Blaine with dead-pan eyes. "Is this what you so-called scientists do all day? Sit around and recite nursery rhymes?"

"Just *bear* with me, Captain."

"It's your ass that's on the line, not mine. You want to play hopscotch and tiddlywinks, it's okay with me."

"Thank you." Blaine could not disguise his sar-casm. "What I'm trying to analogize is near-death. We know what life is, and we know what death is. What we've been studying here are the stages that lead to death, the final moments of consciousness, that last infinitesimal instant that precedes the irreversible cessation of life—but not necessarily of the body, because we can keep that alive—at least in the sense that if we pump in oxygen, squeeze the heart muscle externally, and inject water and food substitutes, then the body will stay alive. But is that life? Most doctors say no—it's just mechanically forced subsistence. In a similar respect all three of us are dying right now."

"At least one of us is."

Blaine ignored the police captain. "And I don't mean from age. Life requires food, water, and oxygen, in a predetermined supply and constancy. If you go on a hunger strike your body will waste away and die in twenty to thirty days. If you stop drinking you'll be dead in less than a week. If you are deprived of oxygen you won't last more than five minutes. Each of these fuels is necessary for survival within quantifiable parameters. What I'm driving at is this: at what moment when you stop eating or drinking or breathing does death become irretrievable?"

Alex pursed his lips. "I remember reading about starving Arctic explorers who were rescued from the ice, but died anyway from malnutrition despite being given food and medical attention."

"A good example. Many diseases are untreatable as well, but we don't think of a patient as being dead until his vital signs are no longer detectable: heartbeat, blood pressure, and brain activity. In that regard, modern medical science and technology have rendered it increasingly more difficult to define the actual moment of death because we keep pushing the limits of recoverability. If a patient is resuscitated and his heart kept going artificially—that is, despite the failure of the patient's autonomic processes—then biologically the patient is still alive.

"That puts us into a whole new realm of the definition of life, and the distinction between life and death—in this case, the distinction between what was once alive and functioning in a certain manner, and what is now alive but functioning in a different manner. This brings in legal issues, philosophical issues, even religious issues. Is a person truly alive when his body is kept going by external means? Is a person truly alive when we switch off the external means but he continues to breath and pump blood, but cannot gather his own food? A person crippled by accident can't support himself, so society does it for him; do we call him dead?"

Alex shook his head. "You're reaching for extremes."

"No, I'm just trying to explain that there's more to life than we perceive because it all depends upon how we choose to describe it. There's biological life, there's quality of life, there's self-awareness of life, now there's even right to life. We're not single-celled animals floating in a soup of nutrients; we're highly complex multicellular organisms that exist on the microscopic scale by dint of the interdependence of those cells, and on the macroscopic scale in coordination with our fellow man. We're—"

That Blaine was getting carried away by his own fustian was obvious by the expressions on the faces of his companions. "Sorry, sometimes I get on a roll and can't get off. Let's cut to the crux of the matter: human consciousness. What is it, where does it come from, where does it go? Moving up the evolutionary ladder from the amoeba and the paramecium, we'll skip right to the human brain, which consists of three parts. The reptilian brain, or the medulla oblongata, is the oldest evolutionarily; it is the seat of instinct: preprogrammed behavior patterns that cannot be changed during the lifetime of the individual, only through a mutation in the next generation. Wrapped around that is the lower mammalian brain, or the limbic system, which controls automatic bodily functions and, because it affects the expression of emotion, influences our value systems. Finally, on top of that is the neocortex, which is responsible for logical thinking. This triune construction is built up like the layers of an onion. And within these layers reside what we call consciousness."

"At last," Lawson grumbled.

"Let me recite the light bulb analogy that I use with my students. If we equate the glass housing to the human body and the filament to the brain, we can call the glow of light the externalization of consciousness. Give the bulb food—electricity—and we get light. Break the circuit and what happens?"

Lawson remained adamantly silent.

"The light goes out?" Alex ventured.

"Good. At least as a general statement. But if you study a light bulb closely as it's being switched on and off you'll notice that the light doesn't appear and disappear instantaneously. It slowly increases to full brightness, then fades out: just like human consciousness that gradually gains self-awareness somewhere along the route between conception, birth, and maturation; and the death of human consciousness, which doesn't die all at once but goes by degrees. Where does it go? If you believe in God then it goes to heaven; if you're a scientist then it goes out like a light. Permanently."

Alex obviously felt uncomfortable with Blaine's iconoclastic view. "It doesn't offer much hope, does it?"

"Hope for the dead? No. But I'm not a mortician, I'm a doctor. I work with the living. I want to heal the sick, not raise the dead. And—" He raised a finger like a wand. "—I want to be able to save the consciousness like other doctors save the body."

"Is this your brain transplant scheme?" Lawson asked laconically.

"Captain, you're the only one I know who can trivialize infinity." Blaine was barely holding his temper. He was much better off speaking directly to Alex and ignoring Lawson's baited hooks. "Is everything an obscenity to you?"

"I just don't see where any of this is leading."

"Humor me, because we're close to the point of death." If he had his druthers he would have placed a strangle hold on the captain. He turned with a huff toward Alex. "Now, where was I?"

"Saving the consciousness."

"Right. But before we can save the consciousness we have to know what it is. And there's the rub." Blaine slowly shook his head. "We don't have the foggiest notion." He waited for that to sink in before going on. "Okay, perhaps that's an exaggeration. We like to think we know, but I'm a pragmatist. Until I detect it, record it, and reproduce it, I won't quantify it."

Alex squinted. "What about EEG's?"

"Brain waves are only one part of consciousness—a part that we happen to be able, in our present state of technology, to detect. But that doesn't mean that other values, frequencies, or rhythms don't exist. Brain waves pulsated before the invention of the EEG—"

"Like light from the stars and sound in the forest."

"You remember."

Grumpy as ever, Captain Lawson asked, "What the hell are you two talking about?"

"Never mind. Just accept the fact that we do not pretend to know what consciousness is."

"Those pot-smoking hippies think they know," Lawson said gruffly. "Them and their drugs and altered states of consciousness."

"We'll get to that in a moment. First let me go over two more points. When I said that we don't know what consciousness is I didn't mean to imply that we don't know things about it. Now, I don't want to give you an anatomical description of the central nervous system, or the gray matter that's inside that skull of yours—" Blaine looked hard at Captain Lawson. "—so I'll be brief. The brain is a network of fifteen billion nerve cells all interconnected by about a million miles of dendrites, which are like extension cords that receive impulses, both chemical and electrical, from things called synapses. Each nerve cell, or neuron, also transmits impulses to other nerve cells through thin wires called axons. So you've got messages coming in through the synapses, traveling along the dendrites to the neuron, which then communicates along axons to other neurons. The brain is like a bunch of electrically charged meatballs stuck in a bowl of spaghetti. Each neuron is a miniature battery that generates sparks and passes them on to other neurons.

"These sparks, this constant electrical flux, is the process of thought. Memory is a stored galvanic potential. Consciousness is a flow of electrons: the interaction of energy fields within the organ of the brain. Turn off the electricity and the mind collapses like a house of cards; even if the house could be rebuilt you could never get all the cards in the same exact position. The result would be a deviant consciousness, a new personality, a completely different person. That's why I said that when a person dies he is gone irretrievably. All the king's horses and all the king's—"

A glance at Captain Lawson reminded Blaine that now was not the time for fairy tales.

"The mind has no physical attributes. It is ephemeral. It exists only as long as the power that generates it is uninterrupted. There's no coming back from the other side, Alex, because there *is* no other side. There is only existence, and nonexistence. We sustain our individual presence in the short span of time between birth and death. There is nothing else."

The special agent gulped. Captain Lawson glowered. Blaine gathered his thoughts in the silence that followed.

"Again, these are matters for philosophers. What we are studying here is not the death of consciousness, but near-death. Why? Because some very peculiar things occur at that time. Things that we don't understand. Things that occur not to the consciousness directly, but to the brain that supports it—like the filament that supports the light in a bulb. By connecting the bulb to a rheostat and changing the current flow we get a light that glows either dimmer or brighter. Too dim and the light goes out, too bright and the filament burns up."

"Now that I can understand," said Captain Lawson. "It happens to glue sniffers and pill poppers all the time. And the LSD freaks trying to get high end up burning out their brains like a short circuit in a high voltage transformer. Turn themselves into vegetables."

Alex ignored the police captain. "Is this the out-of-body experience you were talking about in your lecture? And the altered states of consciousness?"

"Yes. And what the dear captain says is true. Lysergic acid diethylamide induces an hallucinatory experience, as do many other psychoactive drugs. The problem with LSD is that the effect is linked to the user's expectations. He can have a beneficial trip through his psyche, or he can freak out if he is emotionally unstable—as users generally are. The drug is taken as an escape, not an entertainment. A better example is ketamine, or cyclohexane, an anesthetic that causes the patient to become dissociative."

"How about the Indian peyote cult?"

"Mescaline alters the level of consciousness but doesn't induce a true out-of-body experience. You see, the brain is affected according to the specific chemical or electrical disturbances induced by each particular drug. That in turn affects the mind. And for the record, I prefer the phrase 'level of consciousness' as opposed to 'state of consciousness.' It may sound like a semantic predilection, but it's not. In language a word or phrase often describes an attitude. That's why we say Ms. instead of Miss. The speaker may not intend to convey the connotation of an unmarried woman, but the listener may interpret it that way.

"State of consciousness implies that consciousness is calibrated like rungs on a ladder. Freud differentiated between the id, the ego, and the superego. Many people today claim that there are four states of consciousness: sleeping, dreaming, waking, and transcendental meditation. John Lilly thought there were twelve separate states, but he should have kept to his dolphins instead of going blind on psychedelic drugs. Sanskrit has dozens of words for describing different states of consciousness, and the Indian Buddhists have classified one hundred twenty-one specific mind states. There are other taxonomies as well. Now, just because you have a dozen theories doesn't mean that one of them isn't right. But I think that by talking in terms of 'states,' people tend to believe that you can pick one out like a point on a compass.

"I don't pretend to be a noeticist—one who studies consciousness. I'm a neurologist. I look for an understanding of the mind in the functions of the brain that supports it. It irks my diffident colleagues to no end when I call it being practical. But describing consciousness as having levels is like applying rheostat control to our light bulb: the gradient becomes infinite within its parameters and does not ascribe stages with specific attributes. By being less definite in description it gives us more room to develop working hypotheses. Am I monopolizing the conversation?"

"You are a diarrhea of words and a constipation of ideas." It came off like a well-rehearsed and often-used rebuttal.

"Thank you, Captain. I'm sure many of my colleagues would agree with you." Blaine forced himself not to let the policeman rattle him. "Alex?"

The special agent raised a finger. "Is that why you proposed in your paper doing away with brain wave descriptions, like alpha, beta, delta, and theta, and ascribing frequencies?"

"Exactly. Brain waves have been given arbitrary names according to frequency and power output: cycles per second and the fluctuation in potential. By way of analogy, when we name colors like red and yellow we lose sight of all the shades or orange in between."

"Then I'm with you."

"Good. Then we've arrived at the stage of near-death, and I can demonstrate what it is we're doing here at the Institute." He rushed on before Captain Lawson could insert a derogatory comment. "Certain things happen to the brain under conditions of physical stress. Hit a person in the back of the head and he sees stars. Is his mind propelled into the middle of the Milky Way? No, you've simply jarred the visual analyzer cells located in the primary visual area at the back of the brain. By the same token, give a person certain drugs and his brain tricks his mind with perceptual distortions. His expanded consciousness becomes suprarational and suprasensory; he loses contact with reality and is deluded into believing he has left this plane of existence for another—a higher—mental plane. He may 'hear' his own pronouncement of death, talk with long-dead friends or relatives, re-experience his entire life, or see his god in whatever form he believes it to exist. Sorry, Alex, but I must be purely scientific."

"Sure. I understand."

Blaine pulled no punches. "We categorize all these mystical allusions as mental illusions, or, in a word, hallucination."

"For once we agree on something. But can you get to the point before it gets dull?" Captain Lawson resumed his pacing around the lab.

"A doctor lives on patients, but not so police offi-cers." If Lawson picked up on Blaine's pun he made no notice. "Anyway, the brain produces natural opiates, such as enkephalins, which inhibit pain the same way as endorphins produced by the pituitary gland: by blocking the pain receptors in the central nervous sys-tem. Enkephalins and endorphins are morphine ana-logues: amino acid molecules that are normally part of larger compounds which are broken down under cir-cumstances of pain and severe stress. And the most severe stress a human being will ever encounter is the stress of dying.

"When the body suffers a great enough shock that death becomes imminent, all the built-in protective systems come into play in a last ditch attempt to keep the organism alive. This goes far beyond the simple release of adrenaline during a time of fear. It's a mas-sive response to stimulus. The body and the brain are suddenly flooded with chemicals acting synergistically, and every once in a while this incredible response is enough to 'bring back' a person from what otherwise might have been irreversible clinical death.

"Not unexpectedly, this chemical inundation severely alters the perceptual functions of the brain, and, consequently, the conceptualism of the mind. People have 'come back' with bizarre tales of what they 'saw' when they were clinically dead: long, dark tunnels, bright lights, strange beings. Many people claim to have left their bodies, to have risen above them and gazed down upon them as if they were strangers, to have watched doctors performing CPR, to have felt no pain until they were dragged back down into their resuscitated bodes, to have—"

"Balderdash!" Lawson stuck out his jaw as if it were a battering ram. "Do you *believe* all this crap?"

Blaine maintained an even temper, and said as clearly and as distinctly as possible, "I have to. I've been there myself."

Chapter 13

Sweat poured down Blaine's face in virtual torrents. He blinked it away as long as he could, but was finally forced to duck his head and wipe his brow on his sleeve. The oily residue of insect repellent came off at the same time. Seemingly alerted to the newly opened territory, a mosquito buzzing around his ear wasted no time zeroing in on his forehead just above his left eye. He waited until it landed—which he judged by the decrescendo rather than by feel—before ducking his head again, quickly, and squashing the malaria-carrying insect against his arm. In that simple motion he used more energy than the average mosquito uses in its lifetime. What a waste, he thought.

"Steady, man. Keep it steady." Rogers' deep voice was a barely audible whisper, the merest hush, and was nearly swallowed by the blades of tall elephant grass washing against each other in the gentle morning breeze. The binoculars never left his eyes. "Charlie don't show in the next two hours and we're out of here."

Blaine was stiff after lying in the same position throughout the night: watching, listening, smelling, sensing. He was also suffering the side effects of dextroamphetamine, the stimulant that had helped to keep him awake during the long dark hours; he was coming down with a vengeance, and felt the need to either sleep it off or walk it out. His clothes clung to him like a sodden mass, but after hours of shivering under the starlight with a scope stuck to his eye the heat was a welcome relief.

Below the grassy knoll lay a jungle penetrable only by the narrow trail carved into it by machete: a trail that meandered up the hill and passed fifty feet from where Blaine and his five companions lay concealed. The jungle was alive with hoots, howls, caws, whistles, and raucous squeals, but the only motion so far detected, other than brightly plumaged birds flitting among the branches, was a troop of monkeys that had swung through the tree tops shortly after dawn.

Long range reconnaissance patrols were often boring. But, as lurps always said, the best patrol was a boring patrol. Lack of contact was important military intelligence because it indicated where enemy troops were not operating.

Blaine nearly jumped out of his skin at the sharp slap next to him. It sounded like a rifle crack.

"Damn." Thompson said it in a whisper, but it was much louder than protocol permitted. The grass rustled as he rolled over and into Blaine. "Something bit me, man."

"Keep it down, you idiot." The squiggly veins in Rogers' temples stood out like bloodworms. "You wanna send Charlie a mailgram?"

Thompson rolled up his sleeve to reveal an angry red welt. "What is it, Doc? What got me?"

Blaine inspected the wound in the muscular forearm; it was already beginning to swell. He whispered, "Didn't you see it?"

"No, man. It got away. But it was big."

Rogers crawled over top of Blaine, his weight like that of a bulldozer. "Shut up, Thompson. You tryin' to get us all killed?" Sometimes it took only the faintest noise or the slightest movement to compromise a position.

"Shit, man, there ain't been nobody through here for three days. Charlie ain't come yet he ain't comin' now." Thompson's features were nearly indistinguishable under the thick coating of camouflage paint. "Doc, is it bad?"

"It's a puncture wound of some sort, but not from a snake." Instead of two holes side by side there was only a single red dot, like a lava-filled volcano seen from a geological survey plane. "Probably a sting. How's your hand feel?"

Thompson flexed his fingers. "Strange, man. Like pins and needles."

There was no time to lose. Blaine ripped off his rotted headband and tied it tight above Thompson's bicep. As assistant patrol leader he carried the medical bag, but decided there was no time to dig out the scalpel. This was an emergency. "Rogers, call in the team and get us an early evac."

The team leader took a moment to think about it. "You got it, Doc." He squirreled through the grass to where the other three team members lay in ambush. "Petri, pull in them claymores. Benner, radio base and tell 'em to send a Huey to LZ Baker—asap. Zarzinski, fill in the holes and fluff up the grass."

Blaine slipped his bayonet out of its sheath. It was honed to razor sharpness. "Thompson, bite down on your dog tags because this is going to hurt." With one swift stroke he ran the steel blade across the center of the wound. Thompson gasped, but did not flinch. Blood welled out of the cut, rich and red.

Blaine dropped the bayonet, applied his thumbs to opposite sides of the wound, and squeezed. Thompson gritted his teeth but made not a sound. "Good boy."

There was no froth to the blood or signs of white pus, yet some kind of venom had gotten into Thompson's system and was working its way along his arm. Blaine continued the bloodletting until he was sure he had gotten out all the poison he was going to get. He slit open a first aid packet that he kept in his shirt pocket, slapped a gauze pad over the wound, then laid on crisscrossing strips of adhesive tape. He removed the tourniquet.

"Am I gonna live?"

"I'm afraid so." Blaine sat up and struggled into his seventy-pound rucksack. "Here, let me help you."

Thompson kept clenching and unclenching his fist as Blaine hefted the pack and held it up while Thompson slid his arms through the straps. "My elbow's tingling, too."

"You'll be all right, Thompson. I haven't lost a patient yet." He retrieved his bayonet, wiped it off on his trousers, stuck it into its sheath, and scooped dirt into the shallow depression he had scrabbled out of the ground the day before.

Petri crouched by his side, still wrapping wires around the casing of the antipersonnel mine. "What happened?"

"He got stung by something. It's swelling pretty bad, and tingling."

"It hurts, too, man." It did not come out as a whimper. Thompson was too stoic for that. All members of Long Range Reconnaissance Patrols were handpicked volunteers who could suffer hardships that few other men could even imagine.

"You be all right." Petri slapped Thompson on the back and kneaded the nape of his neck. "Just hang in there, man, an' the big bird'll fly us back to Paradise."

Blaine yanked the ready-access Syrette from around his neck and administered the single dose of morphine. Conditions were less than sterile, but they always were in the jungle. "That'll take the edge off."

"Thanks, man."

It took only five minutes for the lurp team to break camp. It would take close scrutiny to reveal that six men had lain there for more than twelve hours, waiting patiently for an enemy that had not appeared.

Blaine pulled a pillbox from the cargo pocket on his thigh; the hard plastic container held individually wrapped antimalaria pills (dapsone, taken daily, and chloroquine primaquine, weekly), codeine, Darvon, salt tablets, polymagna (an antidiarrheal), and tetracycline. He gave two of the latter to Thompson to combat infection. With his work and ministrations complete, Blaine picked up his M-16 and held it firmly by the pistol grip, with the butt tucked into his armpit.

"No can do, chief." Benner switched off the radio. Both he and Rogers carried PRC-25's. "All the gunships are either out supporting an action to the south, or grounded by weather."

Rogers glanced up at the sky. It was bright blue overhead, with a startling yellow sun nearly at zenith, but storm clouds were rolling in from the south, close to the horizon. "Yeah, well, we'll call 'em again in an hour. Thompson, how you makin' out?"

"Okay, I guess. The doc gimme a shot, an' I still got my own." With his good hand he touched the lanyard around his neck, to which was attached an unused Syrette and dog tags taped together so they would not clang.

"Don't OD it." To Zarzinski, "Hey, Zar, pull it in."

Zarzinski had taken a defensive position close to where the trail emerged from the jungle. He signaled okay with circled thumb and forefinger, then started walking backward with his eyes still on the trailhead. He was rear security.

"Petri, take the point." Rogers readjusted the shapeless brim of his flop hat as the men took their places behind the assigned lead. He did not have to issue orders or instructions: every man knew his job.

The team moved silently through the grass toward the landing zone some five klicks away—three hours travel at the slow pace necessitated by the need for constant alertness. Once out of the field of elephant grass, the men melded into the jungle like wraiths. Their camouflaged fatigues carried no nametapes or insignias of any kind. They walked in single file, not along any trail but by bushwhacking through untrodden territory: over rotten logs, under draping vines, and around trees whose tops were lost in the three-tiered canopy. For the next hour no one spoke a word, or made a sound of any kind. No loose equipment rattled.

When Petri reached a clearing he raised his fist to call a halt. Rogers scrambled past Blaine with a map in hand. He conferred with Petri in low tones, then nodded for him to continue. Petri liked walking point.

Another hour passed in silence. Thompson's left arm hung limply at his side; the fingers dangled uselessly. Despite his obvious discomfort, his eyes were beady beacons of light that took in the surrounding jungle with the intensity of electronic surveillance devices. He kept a firm grip on the captured AK-47, a weapon with advantages in enemy-held country because when fired it did not sound like an American made rifle: the momentary confusion among enemy troops could prove to be their undoing.

Rogers waved them down for a break. The men spread out like the spokes of a wheel, always observing outward.

Blaine took a moment to listen to the sounds of the jungle; if he blocked out the seriousness of their mission, the pristine beauty was almost peaceful. A long-tailed lizard scampered up the trunk of the tree in front of him; horned beetles looking like miniature tanks lumbered along the broken branches that littered the ground. Clouds of unnamed and unknown insects hovered in the underbrush, buzzing like power saws and sounding nearly as loud. Blaine did not sit for fear of what might lie underneath the succulent leaves, but crouched on the balls of his feet. He took a long draft of tepid water, then offered the plastic canteen to Thompson while he peeked under the bandage.

"How's it look, Doc?" Thompson swilled the water inside his cheeks, wetting every part of his mouth before swallowing the iodine-laced brew. He preferred halozone.

"About the same. How's it feel?"

" 'Bout the same."

Blaine placed two fingers in Thompson's palm. "Make a fist."

He did, but it was weak.

"Harder."

He tightened ever so slightly.

"Okay. It's not getting any worse." He felt the top of Thompson's forehead with the back of his hand. "You're running a low grade fever, but it's nothing to worry about." He flashed a mouthful of teeth that hadn't been brushed in three days. "We'll pump you full of antibiotics as soon as we get back. A few days bed rest and you'll be as good as new."

Thompson grinned. Somewhere in the jungle behind him came the sound of a large branch snapping. Thompson leaped into Blaine's arms.

"Hey, Thompson. What're you doing?" Blaine

shoved the man off him. "This is no time to get lovey-dovey—"

Thompson's smile was frozen on his face like a Halloween mask, a grisly caricature that portended neither joy nor happiness. His chest heaved as he tried to gulp down air. Blood dribbled out of his mouth and down his chin. His eyes glazed over. His body went slack as he slipped away to the side.

Blaine grabbed him, and was carried down to the ground. The rucksack slipped away from Thompson's back to reveal a sticky stain on his shirt. The bullet had gone through the pack but had not contacted anything dense enough to prevent it from entering his body. If only he had not given the radio to Rogers.

There came the tat-tat-tat of automatic weapons fire, followed by the dull thud of a grenade launcher. Zarzinski carried an "over and under"—an M-16 with a launcher mounted beneath the barrel, and he was firing both.

"I seen him! I seen him!" shouted Benner. The Sten gun was his weapon of choice; he fired short, controlled bursts like the expert he was, taking time to search for his target between shots.

Both Rogers and Petri joined in the fusillade in order to gain fire superiority over the enemy, or to keep his head down if he was a lone sniper. The grenades were shredding leaves with shrapnel a hundred meters out.

A man clad in black pajamas leaped up barely twenty meters away, fired, and turned. Blaine raised his rifle and clicked off the safety in one practiced motion. He jammed the butt into his shoulder and peered down the sights, leading his target and waiting for him to clear the trees before squeezing the trigger. The rifle burped in his hands, and the enemy guerrilla did a cartwheel and slammed into a thick bole. He dropped out of sight. In three months in the regular infantry and six months with the lurps, Blaine had never had a clearer shot. He looked over his barrel to see if perhaps one of the others had been responsible for the kill, but they were all firing at targets thirty degrees to the right. No one had even seen his man.

Blaine flattened himself to the ground and felt Thompson's carotid for a pulse. There was none. Under the circumstances and in light of probable internal damage, there was no sense in trying cardiopulmonary resuscitation. Thompson was dead and there was no bringing him back. Blaine had about two seconds to feel remorse, and cry over the loss of a friend with whom he had spent many quiet hours. The first tear had just come to his eye when a bullet passed close by his head; the hollow clap as the air closed in on itself shook him out of his reverie. All his instincts came into play as he judged accurately the angle and direction of flight. He redirected his aim, spotted his target, and fired. The slant-eyed guerrilla dropped like a stone.

Bullets laced through the jungle like angry hornets. The cacophony of the firefight was bone chilling because each rifle pop carried with it the potential for death. The *whump* of launched grenades added to the fervor.

Rogers slammed down on the ground next to Blaine. "They got us in a crossfire. We're gonna hightail it back up that ridge and call for extraction. How's Thompson?"

For an answer, Blaine fished Thompson's dog tags from inside his shirt, snapped the chain with a hard jerk, and stuck them in his pocket. Rogers only had time to swallow, and exchange with Blaine a brief look of horror and a nod of acceptance, when there came a whining crescendo from the sky.

"Incoming!"

The mortar blasted a crater in the jungle floor about twenty meters forward of their position. Dirt and leaves and splintered wood erupted in a violent cloud of debris and deadly shrapnel. Another mortar came in right behind it, only closer.

Someone shouted, "They're walkin' 'em in!"

Petri, Benner, and Zarzinski stood up and blasted away in the direction of the enemy as they retreated toward the ridge.

"Come on, Doc." As Rogers rose to his knees he pulled Blaine up with him. "We ain't got time to mourn."

They both scrabbled off through the underbrush, hunched over, slipping and sliding on hands, elbows, knees, and feet. The mortars came in one at a time, walking through the jungle like explosive footsteps. Blaine fell hard against a flat-topped stump and had the wind knocked out of him. He shook his head to clear the ringing in his ears and the stars in his eyes. Rogers grabbed his shirtfront and dragged him past the other three team members.

"I'm okay, just—" Blaine saved his breath for running. As soon as he gained some elevation, he turned and provided cover fire for Petri, Benner, and Zarzinski. In this hopscotch fashion they worked their way up the grade and out of range of the mortars. The loud *whumps* ceased along with the rifle fire. Contact was temporarily broken, but Blaine knew that the enemy was creeping up on them.

Rogers ignored Benner's radio and pulled out his own handset. "Bird Dog. Bird Dog. This is Water Fowl. Come in please. Over."

The reply was instantaneous. "This is Bird Dog. Go ahead Water Fowl. Over."

Convention went by the wayside. "Goddamn it, Bird Dog, you gotta come an' get us. We got Victor Charlies crawling up our ass. Mortars an' heavy automatic weapons fire. Must be at least company strength." He unfolded the creased, grimy, and mold-covered map, looked up the hill, and recited coordinates.

HQ repeated the numbers. "I read you, Water Fowl. Hold on, please. Over."

In the stark silence that followed, Blaine strained every nerve and muscle in an attempt to catch some sign of enemy movement. Without a word, Zarzinski climbed higher up the ridge while Petri and Benner spread out to protect their flanks. The whole jungle sensed the tension in the air—even the insects had stopped chirping. The only motion was that of dust motes swirling in the sunbeams that knifed through the thick triple canopy. Blaine could almost have been looking at a Polaroid picture.

Bird Dog came back in about fifteen seconds, but it seemed like an hour. "Water Fowl. Water Fowl. Got a supply ship rerouted your way. How long can you hold out? Over."

"I'm one man down and low on ammo. Maybe five minutes."

"Make it ten, Water Fowl. He's got to pick up a McGuire Rig. Over."

Rogers knew when further conversation was useless. "Out." He switched frequencies in order to pick up the Huey when it came within range. "Let's get to high ground and dig in."

The team stayed spread out as they raced to the top of the ridge from which they had only minutes before descended. LZ Baker was a small clearing only one kilometer away, but there was no way they could outflank a company of NVA in order to reach the landing zone alive. Their only chance to avoid death or capture was to be hooked out of the jungle by winch.

The climb was hot and tiresome, but Blaine hardly noticed the agony of ascent. He had almost reached the outcrop where Zarzinski crouched at attention when he heard the awful whine of an incoming round. Blaine fell flat and covered his head with his hands. The mortar hit far behind, tearing a swath through the nearby trees and peppering the lower canopy with jagged chunks of steel. As soon as the dust settled the AK's came on line.

Rogers, holding up the rear, spun and fired from the hip on full automatic. Blaine saw black-clad shapes dodging among the trees like shadows. He jammed in a full magazine, got off a few bursts, then heard the whine of an incoming mortar. He hit the ground just as the shell exploded. The whoosh of expanding gases went past like a mad tornado, followed immediately by a hail of shrapnel. He poked up his head as soon as he heard Rogers scream.

"Shit, man. They got me in the ass."

Without thinking, he shrugged off his rucksack and charged down the hill to where his fallen comrade lay. Two enemy soldiers were already drawing beads on Rogers as he clawed his way up the slope. Blaine burped three rounds into each of them, knocking them down like shooting gallery manikins.

"My legs, man. My legs. I can't walk." The team leader dug his fingers into the earth as if he were about to fall off.

Blaine slid down next to him. The backs of Rogers' legs had been macerated with shell fragments and were bleeding profusely, but the radio had protected his vital organs. "You're not hurt bad, Rogers. It's just shock." He yanked off the rucksack and tossed it aside as if it were a bag of cotton. He pulled Rogers up by the armpits. "Get on your knees, man."

Rogers groaned in pain, but managed with Blaine's help to remain upright long enough for Blaine to crawl underneath him. Blaine dragged in his knees, got one arm between Rogers' legs and another around his left arm, and, with superhuman strength, stood up with the team leader on his back. Somehow, he managed to bend over and pick up his rifle. Just in time he glimpsed a sapper crawling through the underbrush about thirty meters away. Holding out his M-16 in one hand, he aimed it like a pistol, pulled the trigger, and put a steel-jacketed bullet through the sapper's head. Then he ran up the hill, past Zarzinski, and deposited his friend in a shallow depression.

Both Benner and Petri fell in from their flanking positions and established a three-man perimeter around Blaine and Rogers.

"We're in the shit, now, man," said Benner. "That chopper don't show in the next two minutes and we're dead meat."

Petri unclipped all the hand grenades from his belt and laid them in neat rows. "They gonna pay for it, though."

As bullets cleaved the foliage, Blaine ripped open

his medical bag and took out compresses and tape. He used his bayonet to slit open the back of Rogers' pants so he could work on him. The jagged wounds were worse than he was willing to admit. He applied direct pressure to the worst of them, one that was suspiciously close to the femoral artery. He held the compress in place with one hand, and used his other hand and his teeth to rip off strips of adhesive tape to lay gauze pads on the adjacent wounds. Rogers was in stable condition but could easily die from systemic shock or loss of blood.

"Incoming!"

Blaine covered Rogers with his own body. The blast was the closest one yet. Dirt and steel sliced through the jungle almost as low as a lawn mower blade.

"I'm hit! I'm hit!" A slab of steel had passed between Petri's upper arm and chest, leaving an awful scar in both. Blood gushed out in torrents.

Blaine still had compresses in his hands, so he slapped one on the side of Petri's chest, just in front of the clavicle, and pinned Petri's arm down over it. "Keep the pressure on, Petri."

Benner was worse. He was leaning against a tree with his hands lying limp in his lap. His neck was covered with blood. He stared wide-eyed at Blaine and tried to speak, but all he did was gurgle. A steel shard had gone completely through his throat. His airway had collapsed, and he was drowning in his own blood.

The madcap firefight was still in full swing. The opposition was shooting everything they had as they assaulted the hill. Only Zarzinski was returning their fire. Blaine pulled the pins from the grenades that Petri had laid out, and lobbed them down the hill. Then he tore open the medical bag and dumped everything on the ground where he could find what he needed. He scooped up a scalpel and a length of plastic tubing.

Blaine had been trained as a medic, and had served in that capacity with the regular infantry. Most of the time all he did was dispense salt tablets and antimalaria pills. The wounds he had treated had been superficial because the outfit had made very little enemy contact; they mostly did guard duty. Now he was about to perform field surgery that was normally done only in a hospital by highly skilled surgeons. His only other choice was to let Benner suffocate.

There was no time to fool with anesthesia; besides, Benner was so far out of it that he was hardly aware of what was going on. Blaine slid the scalpel into Benner's throat just below the Adam's apple.

"What're you doin', man?" Petri yelled.

"A tracheotomy." He carved open a slot as if he were coring an apple. He slid the clear plastic tube into the hole and down the throat, placed his lips on the open end, and puffed in the breath of life. He continued to breathe for Benner until he came around. Then he tied off the tube so it would not fall into the trachea. He did not even consider giving him morphine; any reduction of the cardiovascular rate could prove fatal. He pulled Petri's Syrette off his neck lanyard and let Petri have a shot.

"Huey's coming," Zarzinski announced, as if he were reading it off a train schedule. Then he resumed firing.

"Pop some smoke, damn it." As assistant patrol leader Blaine was now in command. Rogers' radio had been destroyed by the mortar blast, so he used Benner's to make contact with the air. "This is Water Fowl. This is Water Fowl. Do you read me? Over."

"Loud and clear. If you're on top of that ridge you got slopes coming up the north side."

"Blast them, for chrissakes, will you? We're pinned."

"I see purple smoke. Over."

Blaine spun around and saw that Petri had popped a purple smoke canister. "That's us, man. Don't fool around. We need extraction pronto." Now he could hear the distinctive whup-whup-whup of Huey blades charging in from the east. It was the most beautiful sound in the world.

The Huey did not slow down or come to their immediate rescue. Instead it passed below them on the north side of the hill while the door gunner opened up with his M-60 machine gun. Blaine still had not seen the helicopter, but he could track its passage with his ears. The Huey made one pass, turned around, then came back and let the other door gunner have some fun. Blaine tossed down a couple more grenades, then picked up his rifle and fired into the brush.

A shadow passed by. Blaine looked up and saw the Huey hovering directly overhead. He fell back and picked up the handset. "You're above us right now. Drop the rig. We've got wounded to evacuate."

Zarzinski casually reloaded all available weapons, including those of the wounded. Blaine cut the straps off Benner's rucksack. The door gunners continued their harassment fire against the enemy by shooting practically straight down, while the crew chief lowered the McGuire Rig. The pilot maintained his position as the triple harnesses dropped through the jungle canopy. Any sideslipping would either break the cable or drag the rig—including any men in the harnesses—through the branches.

"Zar, give Rogers a hand." Blaine took the first harness and fixed it around Benner's unconscious but still breathing body. Petri was helping with his good hand. Blaine shoved him aside. "You get in the other harness."

Rogers would have objected to going out on the first lift if he had been fully conscious. As it was, he was barely able to keep his eyes open. His hands fumbled ineffectually as Zarzinski strapped him in. Because Petri had to keep his arm clamped to his side he was unable to get the hooks properly snapped. Blaine made sure he was strapped in correctly before double-checking Benner.

The Huey was invisible because of the dense foliage; only a slight darkening of the sky and the cable climbing through the jungle like Jack's beanstalk attested to its position. Blaine called the pilot on the radio and gave him the go-ahead. The helicopter rose vertically until the three men were clear of the trees, then took off to search for a clearing where it could land, get the men out of the rigs, and get them inside the cabin.

It was suddenly very quiet.

"Looks like it's you and me, Mitchell," said Zarzinski.

"Looks that way, Zar." Blaine slapped a full magazine into his M-16, removed the tape from his hand grenades and prepared them for throwing, loaded the abandoned grenade launcher, and selected an orange smoke canister. Then he placed the bayonet on the end of his rifle in case it came down to hand-to-hand. He dropped his web gear.

They had nothing else to say to each other. Blaine retreated into his thoughts as he peered through the leafy foliage for movement, and listened for the crack of a branch underfoot. The waiting game was what lurps played the most, so he was used to it. He thought about Thompson lying out there alone, about what sacrileges the enemy might inflict upon his body. After a moment's reflection he shrugged it off. Thompson was dead, gone, no longer alive. Once a person's tenuous and fragile mind had been snuffed out, for all practical purposes he might never have existed. Blaine accepted this as fact, knew it as ultimate truth. Nothing else made sense in the logical, rationalistic concept of the cosmos. If there was order in the universe, then the continuity of life followed by death was merely part of that order. Blaine was not afraid to die.

"Here they come," Zar whispered.

Blaine felt a twinge of fear. In his heightened sense of awareness he calmly anticipated the human wave assault. Then he heard the soughing in the air, and realized that Zarzinski was referring to the Huey coming back for them. A wave of relief washed over him. If he did not fear death, he at least had respect for the pain that preceded it.

Zar popped the smoke canister. The orange smoke drifted up and out. Blaine keyed the radio, exchanged recognition signals with the pilot, and had him identify the color. The helicopter was no sooner overhead than small weapons fire broke out. Enemy troops lying in ambush were trying to shoot down the Huey and its human cargo. Blaine lobbed his grenades down the side of the hill in the direction of the gunshots. Zar plunked down by his side and added the fury of the grenade launcher and an M-16.

Despite the stream of bullets arcing through the trees, the gutsy pilot hovered in place like a sitting duck while the crew chief lowered the McGuire Rig. Both door gunners plastered the jungle without letting up on the trigger. The air was rent with the sound of chopper blades, exploding grenades, and rifle and machine-gun fire. The jungle seemed to be growing North Vietnamese regulars; they sprouted everywhere like a field of black corn stalks on the move. They seemed intent on over-running the ridge.

The wind shifted; instead of blowing the smoke away from their position, the orange shroud covered them. Blaine squinted through the haze to see if the harness had arrived. A vague shape dangled in mid-air where the smoke was the densest. As Zar kept up the downhill enfilade, Blaine scrambled toward what he thought must be the McGuire Rig. Too late he realized that it was not the harness but a soldier. In that moment of indecision, as he pondered why someone from the Huey would come down in the sling, he saw the man was aiming a wooden-stocked AK-47.

Blaine gasped, raised his rifle, fired, saw a muzzle flash, and felt an incredibly cold, icy sting as the bullet hit him in the chest and went completely through his body and out his back. The force of the shot knocked him down flat. A cloak of blackness descended upon him. All sound ceased. He was suddenly alone in the quiet darkness, in silent tranquility. There was nothing around him but bare black walls. Far, far away glimmered a faint pinpoint of light, like a candle in a coal bin. Blaine soared along the smooth sides of a tunnel faster than a subway car in a tube. He popped out of the end into a world of awful brightness, but the light did not hurt his eyes. He was still in the jungle, only now he floated effortlessly above the ground. He could clearly see the Huey hovering overhead as well as the two men on the ground: one stretched out dead, the other tending to the body.

He felt sorry for the brave enemy soldier. He had paid the ultimate price for his service to his country. But Blaine could not understand why Zarzinski was ripping open his shirt, was placing a compress on his chest, was bending down to kiss him. Then he noticed another body, clad in black, that lay a few meters away: that of a North Vietnamese regular. Only upon close inspection did Blaine realize that the body in Zar's arms was his own. How curious.

A moment later he swooped up past the strangely silent Huey, saw Rogers and Petri and Benner lying injured inside, saw the crew chief handling the extraction cable, saw the door gunners expelling soundless fireflies from the barrels of their guns, saw the impassive faces of the pilot and copilot. Then the Huey was far below, a tiny olive-drab speck in a never-ending jungle of green.

Blaine swooped effortlessly through the upper stratosphere and right out of the solar system. He was surrounded by stars: an endless sea of stars, as plentiful as grains of sand on an endless beach. Nor was he static; he soared through space toward the dense galactic core, where billions and billions of pure white stars shone brightly, packed so tight that they formed one all-encompassing, brilliant, formless mass.

Blaine knew intuitively that once he reached that soundless center he could never leave, that the white light was a point of no return, that it represented the cessation of life. There was no sorrow in this knowledge, no fear, not even remorse; only recognition. Instead, the light was the termination of the pain of living, a return to luxurious nonexistence, the end of a journey begun in the agony of birth.

Death was a nonplace.

With this ultimate enlightenment came doubt.

Despite the peace before him, the serenity offered, the comfort endowed, there was one overriding factor. Blaine did not want to die.

By the volition of some unknown motive force, the noncorporeal entity that was Blaine Thomas Mitchell backed away from the light, zoomed through the galaxy of stars, soared through the solar system, plummeted through the Earth's atmosphere, and was sucked back into his physical body.

He opened his eyes to a world of enduring and unendurable pain.

Chapter 14

"Zarzinski saved my life—or brought me back to life. I don't know which. He plugged up the holes and blew air into my mouth until I started breathing on my own. Then he strapped me into the harness and sent me up. He stayed behind to fight off the assault—I was told this afterwards, of course; I was unconscious. He kept fighting until he either ran out of ammo or was overrun. Nobody knows. For his actions he was given the Medal of Honor the way it was given to most recipients— posthumously." Blaine failed to mention that he himself received the Distinguished Service Cross.

The silence in the lab was so intense that for a moment it rekindled in Blaine the sense of dispassionate dissociation he had just recounted. Alex shuffled his feet uncomfortably and stared at the floor. Captain Lawson was expressionless.

"Anyway, the point of the story is the trauma of near-death. When a person suffers the shock of dying, the brain, starved of oxygen, forces the release of chemicals whose purpose is to preserve the mind—our tenuous stack of cards—until the flow of oxygen can be restored. Kind of like an electric alarm clock with a built-in battery that takes over in case of a power failure. But when this near-death effect kicks in, the level of consciousness of the mind is reduced. It responds to naturally produced stimulants the same way it responds to artificially induced drugs. It hallucinates like hell. I don't for a minute believe I actually left my body on the jungle floor and took off into outer space. But my mind was tricked into believing that it did."

"But Blaine, how do you account for the similarity of incidents among people who've had near-death experiences?" Alex had obviously done his homework. "So many of them report the same episodes that they've been categorized. Such as the out-of-body experience that you just described, or the tunnel with a light at the end."

"How do you explain why a person jerks his arm away from a hot stove?"

"What's that got to do with—"

"Everything, Alex. We're all conditioned with the same reflexes. We all think with the same brain. Out-of-body experience is not all that rare. Psychotics experience it; so do people who practice meditation. It's been manifested during isolation studies by subjects at rest in sensory deprivation tanks. It is a natural mental process that can be triggered by a host of chemical imbalances. And it's been duplicated in the laboratory for years. Stimulating the right temporal lobe of the brain by the lack of oxygen can produce a feeling of detachment or depersonalization which, while not as intense as the true out-of-body experience, proved long before my own work in the area that such an event was reproducible.

"Even the tunnel effect can be explained by ordinary means. If you interrupt the flow of blood to the posterior cerebral artery, which supplies blood to the occipital lobes—the area of the brain responsible for sight—the visual fields collapse and tunnel vision results. It's a natural part of the dying process. It's why people in their last hours often aren't aware of who is around them; you have to stand directly in their line of sight before they can see you. Every physician knows this.

"To go a step farther, there's a distinct similarity between temporal lobe seizures and near-death experience. Again, possibly due to cerebral anoxia; that is, loss of oxygen to the brain. The temporal lobe has a role in memory, and those who have had near-death experiences sometimes talk of panoramic memory and life reviews in which they instantaneously 'remember' every detail of their life, or selected highlights—an incredibly vivid visual imagery."

"That sounds like a deathbed vision," Alex commented. "Or delirium."

"It sounds like lunacy to me." Lawson shoved his

hands deep into his pants pockets and thrust out his jaw. "And if this dream machine of yours kills people and brings them back to life, or takes them close to the point of death, I'll have your ass in jail for malpractice faster than you can say Jack Sprat. Then you won't have to worry about the Mafia or South American drug lords."

"Captain, you make me so mad I could spit nickels." At that, Blaine had trouble controlling his enunciation. "This apparatus does not initiate a physical crisis event; it's an electronic simulator that provokes amino acids in the brain into liberating stress-related hormones that are normally bonded in large molecular strings. It works via direct low-voltage electrical stimulation. With this device, the same naturally occurring opiates released during a near-death trauma can be released upon demand—that is, by conscious will—in order to protect the brain from excessively painful impulses. In short, it nullifies pain, totally and completely."

The police captain pursed his lips. "So it's a sort of super aspirin."

Blaine could do nothing more than roll his eyes. He tried not to scream. "Captain, you're infuriating. The bypass skullcap is a super aspirin the same way the hydrogen bomb is a large firecracker. We're talking a quantum leap over any kind of anesthesia or prescription sedative. It's the ultimate analgesic because it's produced naturally, is nonaddictive, and has no undesirable side effects. It will make all other tranquilizers and anesthetic drugs obsolete, including acupuncture."

"Good God," Alex breathed.

"Now don't get me wrong. It doesn't cure anything. It's not a panacea. It's not even an ameliorative. But for people with chronic pain, for people dying from excruciatingly painful terminal illness, for burn patients and the seriously injured, it can be a godsend. It will completely replace anesthesia, both local and general, in the operating room. And because of a breakthrough in low level EEG detection, it's *that* close to perfection."

Blaine held thumb and forefinger a hair apart, and stabbed them at Captain Lawson. "And your mother helped us get it there."

For the first time since they had met, Blaine saw an expression on Captain Lawson's face that represented emotions other than hostility and aggression. Blaine's many years of dealing with patients who had been forced to accept the horrible news of imminent mortality enabled him to read the policeman's face like the picture pages of a first-grade speller. What began as numbed disbelief quickly turned into a combination of cruel sadness and insecurity, tempered by guilt. Hard man though he was, at this moment Lawson was as vulnerable as a lost child—which in a way he was. Sympathy eased Blaine's anger toward him.

"I'm sorry, Captain. I don't mean to bring back bad memories. But I thought you should know that Helena was a very courageous woman. Marybeth and I spent quite a bit of time with her during her final days. She was lucid right to the end, and exhibited a strength that fails most people when they know the end is near."

Lawson's bushy eyebrows sagged like weighted sand bags. His neck muscles strained as he swallowed the lump in his throat. "I—I'm glad to hear that, Dr. Mitchell. I'm sure you did all you—all you could for her."

"Her life was beyond my control. All I did was administer palliatives to reduce the pain. She even objected to that. She said she wanted to leave this world the same way she came into it—naturally. Did you know that she wanted to be an organ donor?"

Lawson shook his head.

"Due to age and infirmity we couldn't accommodate her last wishes; organs for transplant need to be young and healthy. So she donated her body to science and volunteered for our mind watch program. Like other terminally ill patients at the Center, she permitted us to install monitoring devices in her room so we could detect penultimate chemical changes in her brain and body, and so we could observe and record brain wave patterns and sequences the existence of which at that time we were only beginning to suspect. She had a great love for humanity, a love that played a vital role in developing some of the experimental procedures we've since perfected. You should be proud of her."

Whatever thoughts Captain Lawson had on the matter, he kept to himself. He left the lab without another word.

"You were pretty easy on him, Blaine, considering what he's been putting you through."

"Oh, he's an okay guy. He's just been dealing with criminals for so long it's thwarted his outlook on life." Blaine indicated the manila folder he had tossed unceremoniously on the workbench. "I knew something was bugging him right from the start. The way he came down on me after the shoot-out in the parking lot was more than Greenstein's instigation. And it's gotten worse. I picked up on his innuendoes, and wondered where they were coming from. But Marybeth's the one who figured it out. She remembered Helena Lawson, and put the two names together. Of course, with the computer down she couldn't access the data banks, but we do keep an abbreviated personal file."

Alex rubbed his chin. "I never thought I'd see him wilt like that."

"He's as human as the rest of us, with all the same frailties. He just covers them up better than most. The loss of a loved one affects us all the same way."

"Yes, I can feel for him there. I lost my . . . " The way he trailed off made Blaine think that he must have touched another sore spot. "Your folks?"

Alex lowered his eyes and shook his head grimly. "My wife." Before Blaine could comment, he added quickly. "Oh, it's okay. It was five years ago. I'm over it now."

"No, Alex. That's something you never get over."

"Well, you know what I mean. I still think about her—every now and then—but I'm over the pain and heartbreak. I think I'm even ready to look for someone else. But for a long time I couldn't even imagine seeing another—" He paused for a moment to resolve his thoughts. "It was a car crash. We'd both been drinking a bit—"

Blaine put his hands on Alex's shoulders. "You don't have to relive it for me."

"Yes, I do. I want to tell you about it. I *have* to tell you about it."

"If you need penitence, wait until tomorrow and I'll take you to church. I'm tired of being everyone's confessor. I've got my own problems to take care of. Remember, you're here to help me with mine, not me with yours."

"Blaine, I don't have any sins to confess. The accident wasn't my fault and I don't feel guilty. I wasn't even driving at the time. But you have to hear this because I was severely injured in the crash—went through the windshield because I wasn't wearing a seatbelt—and I had a near-death experience. Not the same as yours, but—"

Blaine pushed the special agent into the specially equipped chair. "Now I'm interested. Have a seat, Alex, and start from the beginning."

Alex stared at the wired armrests and sensor-padded cushions. "Are you going to plug me into your computer—"

"The mainframe's been eaten up by a virus, remember? So relax. No notes, no monitors. Just you and me, mano y mano."

The special agent appeared to be unsettled by the proximity of the recording instrumentation. Instead of easing back into the chair as Blaine did, he perched on the edge of the seat like a pigeon about to flee the coop. He began haltingly, but soon recited in smooth dialogue incidents that must at one time have made quite an impression on him.

"It was a rainy night, and we were coming home from a party. One of Kris's friends had just—well, that doesn't matter. Anyway, we were rounding a curve—turning left—when this guy coming the other way just kept coming straight. I don't know if he fell asleep at the wheel, or what, but he didn't even try to turn. He was driving one of the battlewagons—a Cadillac, or Continental, or something. We were in a subcompact—some foreign piece of junk made out of tinfoil and beeswax. Anyway, he hit us on the driver's side right by the front door. Kris was killed instantly. Crushed to death. I went partway through the glass and was jammed up against the doorpost when the car was spun around and went off the road into a tree. I was pinned in the wreckage.

"Anyway, I remember blacking out. It was strange because at first I could hear everything that was going on around me. Men yelling, women screaming, children crying, dogs barking. We ended up in the front lawn of a farmhouse, woke everyone up, and they all came out to see what they could do. I couldn't see a thing, but I remember smelling gasoline, and thinking: if I don't get out of here I'm going to burn up. Then the sounds faded and I was in a dark room —I mean a pitch-black room, like a coal bin at night. But it wasn't really a room, it was a tunnel. That is, at first I thought it was a room, but it dawned on me that it was really a tunnel. Anyway, I started moving along this tunnel. I don't mean running, or walking—just moving. I wasn't aware of having a body. I just seemed to float along like a boat in a fast current.

"Then I saw this tiny light way down at the end, like I was in a telescope tube looking back at the eyepiece. The light got brighter and brighter until it was like a giant searchlight right in front of me and, somehow, all around me. It was pure white, but it didn't hurt my eyes. I don't even remember blinking. I just accepted it.

"Then this—this being—this being of light came out of it. I don't remember him having a shape. It was just a being of light. A being of purity. I had the feeling it was God. I don't know why. He never said he was God. But he asked me if I was okay, and I said yes. I mean, he didn't speak. He didn't use words. It was as if his thoughts just popped into my head. And I answered him the same way. I felt like I was talking with my mind. Then he asked me if I wanted to go on, if I wanted to go through the light to the other side. I said sure. I didn't even think about my life on Earth, or my wife, or my parents, or my job. None of that mattered. I just knew that I felt so good that I wanted to go on, to see what was on the other side of the light. I wasn't scared. I wasn't even curious. I just knew that that was what I wanted to do.

"All of a sudden Kris was there. She said are you sure, because there's no coming back. I said yes, I want to be with you. She said you don't have to come now because I'll be here forever. And I said I was ready now. Then my grandmother showed up. I don't know where she came from; she was just there. It was great seeing her again. She looked just like I'd seen her last, as a little boy; dressed in a faded print dress and a flowered apron, and wearing black, low-heeled shoes. Her silver hair was tied back in a bun, and it shimmered around her head like a halo. I always loved my grandmother.

"Anyway, she said it isn't your time yet. You have things to do. There are people who need you. You should go back and share your love, and come back when you're done. But I didn't want to go. I wanted to stay with them. But Kris said it was okay, that she'd wait for me. So the being led me back from the light and said it was all for the best. And when I woke up they were pulling me out of the car and putting me on a stretcher."

Alex took a deep breath. "Pretty wild, isn't it?"

"Yes, but also typical. I gather you've read enough on the subject to know that."

"The bestseller material, but never anything scientific. Not like what you do. But because I've been through it, I find it hard to believe it's only a hallucination. God, it was so *real.*"

Blaine spread his hands. "In one sense the experience is a genuine interpretation of what the mind perceives. In the near-death mode the brain is cut off from its physical sensory inputs—sight, sound, taste, smell, and touch—so the information it feeds to the mind is generated from within. You might call it immaculate perception.

"It's also a programmed response: an archetypical imagery from mankind's collective subconscious. The feelings of peace and bliss are the brain's mechanism for dealing with intense pain. And, as you've discovered, an encounter with one's maker is a powerful and transformative experience."

"For me. But you didn't meet your God."

"Because I don't have one. I look for causative reasons for life, for existence, for being, not theological ones. I 'saw' what my mind predetermined I should see: stars, galaxies, the center of the universe. You had a religious experience because that's what you expected. Our different backgrounds and beliefs didn't alter the core experience evoked by the trauma of near-death, only the interpretation of that experience.

"Let's go back to our first meeting, in Westmoreland's parking lot. As an investigator I don't have to tell you how witnesses 'see' events differently. You get five people who all 'saw' the same crime and you get five different versions of what actually occurred. The witnesses aren't lying, they're only interpreting events in terms they can relate to. After ducking bombs and dodging bullets we were both understandably rattled. Then this guy comes out from around the corner of the building and we both jump to conclusions commensurate with our backgrounds and expectations. I saw a man wearing a football helmet and carrying a cane, you saw a man in a furred hat aiming a gun with a silencer. I know what I saw, but I have no reason to disbelieve your story either. So who's right?"

"Probably neither of us."

"Exactly. Take the case of a man blind since birth. A true case. All his life he interpreted objects by touch, by running his hands over them. At the age of forty-eight, a corneal transplant bestowed him with sight. With an alternate means of perception the man had to correlate objects he could now see with how they had always felt. He soon discovered that the dual sensory modes were contradictory. Objects didn't look the way they felt. He became confused. Instead of sight helping him, it distracted him. For him blindness was normal and sight an aberration. The addition of sight was not beneficial; he died within a year of the operation.

"This all goes back to what I was saying before. Our particular type of brain and the kinds of senses we possess determine our perception of the world around us. In that context we can never know the true nature of reality, only the nature of the reality that our brains— our human brains—are capable of perceiving. Different types of brains perceive reality differently—in ways that we can't even imagine. But more to the point, as we die—that is, as the brain is cut off from its sensory inputs—we perceive less of reality, not more of it. The mind withdraws to a locus in the anterior end of the cerebral aqueduct and the posterior end of the fourth ventricle, a place in which it is insulated from external reality. The mind's level of awareness is then limited to its perception of self."

Alex remained rigid both in posture and belief. "Then you're saying that there is no afterlife. That thousands of years of religious faith is only a delusion. A self-delusion. That miracles don't happen and people don't go to heaven when they die. That the church is perpetrating a cruel hoax on mankind."

Blaine realized he was treading on tenuous territory. "I'm saying nothing of the kind. I'm not attacking religion; I've never attacked religion. I've merely focused my attention on science; that is, on the empirical approach to understanding natural phenomena. 'I'm from Missouri, show me.' 'What you see is what you get.' I'm not debunking religious doctrine. The problem I have with religion is that it's not ecumenical. It consists of thousands of belief subsystems that are at best denominational, at worst whimsical. There's no continuity within sects, between sects, or throughout a person's life as he changes sects.

"Perhaps my karma ran over my dogma. I just happen to think that what's important in life is not what a person believes, but how he acts. Or to quote a wise man: 'A religious person follows the teachings of his church, a spiritual person follows the guidance of his soul.' My reductionistic view of near-death experience may prove to be wrong. Perhaps that light at the end of the tunnel is not just the last flash of primal energy, but represents a place we go to. Perhaps death is only an altered state of consciousness. No one knows. At least, no one alive. Some day you and I may find out. But for now, I want to put off that time as long as possible. The curiosity is not killing me."

Alex slouched humbly while he mulled things over in his mind. He appeared noncommittal.

"You don't have to take my word for it." Blaine fumbled with the electrodes on the headset, pursed his lips, thought about the bypass skullcap—the actual production model for which this unit was the prototype—and stood up. The transportable unit was kept in another laboratory down the hall. "Come on. Let's go on a trip."

Chapter 15

"With the mainframe down we can't reproduce the input signals in the prototype unit that are necessary for evoking the actual near-death response—what we call a nonrandom change in the level of consciousness. But because the bypass skullcaps were designed to be transportable they have their own power supply and CPU. They don't have or need massive data storage capability. When we take them to the Center for the Terminally Ill we require only enough memory to record the patient's electrical, chemical and brain wave data; then we bring the units back here and dump the data into the Institute's mainframe, which does the work of collating and analyzing. Marybeth's program, I might add.

"Once we refined the stimulus frequencies and adjusted the electrode locations and distances, we had a self-adjusting unit that could play back previously recorded data—that is, brain wave patterns, or memories, if you will, of the dying act. Pardon me for being so clinical."

"No, that's all right," Alex said. "But let me get this straight. You recorded the brain's functions at the exact moment of death, then digitized the data so you could reproduce it and implant the wave patterns in someone else's consciousness?"

"Approximately. Let me add some more prefatory material before I go on. First, we don't know the precise 'moment' of death because different parts of the body die at different times. Of course we're talking about brain death only, but even then, with all our medical technology, we've been unable to detect an actual 'moment.' Perhaps there is none. Perhaps brain waves drop below the perceptible level of our equipment, but reach a point where life becomes irretrievable—again, due to our present state of technology. I guess if we wanted to define an actual moment it would not be until the last neuron dies. But we know that consciousness disappears long before then."

"So if someone invents more sensitive instrumentation you may have to redefine the moment if you subscribed one now."

"Exactly. And its been happening for years. Decades. People coming back from the dead is an old story, although, I guess I don't have to tell that to a Bible banger. But even in old medical texts there are hundreds of cases of people coming to on their own after they were given up for dead. Nowadays, with CPR, electroshockers, defibrillators, adrenaline injections, and so on, death is ever more elusive. Which is also the reason why the number of recorded instances of near-death experience is constantly growing. If you want to know the truth, most doctors today will readily admit that they don't know exactly when a patient dies. When emergency room doctors no longer detect vital signs, when all resuscitation efforts have failed for what in their mind has been a sufficiently long period of time, they make a judgment call and pronounce the patient dead. Sometimes they make mistakes, and a patient comes back on them; occasionally, after the death certificate is signed. It's quite embarrassing. But the doctor is not to blame. He's only as good as his equipment. If the EEG flatlines he must assume that there's no cerebral activity.

"Now, what we've been doing is making neurometric evaluations of the cerebral and brainstem mechanisms at the 'time' of death. In our studies it didn't matter if the patient was resuscitated because we still get our data on the electrical output and chemical changes externalized by the near-death experience." In aside, "Of course, it matters to the patient." Blaine sometimes felt that his description was too unemotional, too scientific. "We were hampered at first because some brain activity is so deep that surface electrodes don't pick it up. We localized most of these areas in the chimpanzee brain, either by implanting electrodes through the skull or, when that didn't give us enough latitude, by trephining—cutting out sections of bone to expose a larger area of gray matter.

"By continuously refining the focus on specific loci within the neocortex, we eventually developed ways of amplifying deep-seated brain wave activity so the remote sensors in the bypass skullcap could detect them. Basically, it was a matter of the power output of the bypass unit; larger batteries solved the problem." Blaine indicated the suitcase-sized contraption of metal and plastic, and the stout cord leading to a skullcap that looked like an aviator's hat from the Great War. "We call the unit portable because we can wheel it into the hospital, but luggable is probably a more accurate description. It weighs about fifty pounds."

Alex hefted the combination battery box and electronic case. "I see what you mean."

"What raised the largest furor in my paper, and in my lectures, was not the refinement of the brain wave patterns that trigger the release of hormones. We've been doing on that for years, and so have a lot of other researchers. But we found release mechanisms within the brain whose effects have more profound and far-reaching implications."

"You mean, like the out-of-body experience?"

Blaine shrugged it off. "No, that's just a figment of the imagination that scares the pajamas off the patient. We've learned to be very careful with the programming, focusing adjustments, and power output because the illusion of leaving one's body usually causes the patient to lose faith in the practical applications of the bypass skullcap. Marybeth installed a block in the program so the dissociative index can't be triggered accidentally."

Alex pointed to the elaborate headpiece. "Is this bypass skullcap what you referred to in your paper as a prosthetic device: the brain pacemaker?"

"Yes. The original impetus for the establishment of the Institute was research on the control of pain through electrical stimulation of the brainstem: a procedure that's been around for years. People with prolonged and intense pain can find alleviation via

implanted electrodes, a method requiring minor surgery. Then there was the transcutaneous nerve stimu-
lator, or TNS: a high-tech acupuncture device without
the needles. Touch-pads placed on specific areas of the
skin eased the pain of neurogenic pain patients: those
with an endorphin imbalance.

"One of our goals was to devise a way of stimulating
the pain receptors without an invasive procedure, and
with a stronger response than peripheral hormone
stimulation. Hence the bypass skullcap with remote
electrodes that are fine-tuned and powerful enough to
stimulate the brainstem through the skin. As an extra
benefit, the user doesn't look like Frankenstein's mon-
ster, with electrodes sticking out of his neck.

"The next step was to enable chronic pain sufferers
to dissociate themselves from their pain without the
prosthetic device: to take away their crutches, so to
speak. We're doing that through biofeedback training,
in which people learn to monitor their own level of pain
by releasing pain-blocking neurotransmitters without
the aid of the skullcap."

Alex was stunned. "You mean, so people can get
themselves high any time they want just by thinking
about it? By using the power of the mind?"

"Now you sound like Captain Lawson." Blaine
shook his head with evident dissatisfaction. "What did
I tell you about not believing everything you read?
Especially if it's in the newspapers."

"Sorry." Alex put on a suitable expression of cha-
grin. "I guess I was jumping to conclusions."

Blaine nodded in acceptance. "When we get you
plugged in you'll see that you don't get high—despite
Greenstein's shameless prose and Carcione's beliefs to
the contrary. And the South American gang. Their's is
a craved and craven misinterpretation. The bypass
skullcap is as innocuous as a—a—oh, I hate to say
this—an aspirin tablet. But don't tell Lawson I said
that."

Alex held up three fingers. "Scouts honor."

"Thank you. And yes, the mind is a powerful thing,

if you will allow me to use so unscientific a noun. When we look at the brain-mind synergistically—in wholeness rather than by looking at the brain and the mind separately—we see an interrelationship in which each affects the other at the same time each is affected by the other. Remember our oversimplified definitions: the brain regulates the body's autonomic processes and supports the mind; the mind has will, and tells the brain when to move the body. The brain can go on working without the mind, such as when a patient flatlines but his body keeps on breathing and pumping blood. Of course, death is not far behind without external support because the mind is not there to tell the body to get up and find food. Similarly, when the brain dies, the mind's supporting structure collapses; death is practically instantaneous. The brain and the mind are both controlled and controller, with an inherent division of labor.

"What we want to do is strengthen the mind so it can take more control of autonomic bodily functions. Again, this is nothing new. Meditation is a mild form of mind control; conscious relaxation slows the heart rate and lowers blood pressure. For centuries yogis have exhibited phenomenal control over their bodies, and without electronic biofeedback. All of us here at the Institute have practiced enough with the brain bypass units to effect permanent physiological changes: lower respiration, steady pulse, and optimal blood pressure. Jogging isn't all we do to stay in shape."

Alex viewed Blaine suspiciously. "Isn't that going a bit far: like Doctor Jekyll taking his own potions?"

"Come on, Alex. This is the twentieth century, not Victorian England. This is controlled experimentation with sophisticated equipment. Conditioning the subconscious through electronic stimulation is not far removed from psychiatric treatment or transcendental meditation. Besides, it's vitally important that we as doctors fully comprehend the mechanisms of biofeedback training instead of foisting it untried upon the public. The ultimate purpose of the bypass skullcap is not to play peeping Tom on terminally ill patients, but to teach the patients how to control their pain.

"And that's just the short-term goal. By chipping away at the barrier between the brain and the mind we eventually hope to be able to restore full function and mental capacity to victims of stroke, to condition the immune system, to cure aphasia, to accelerate the recovery rate of accident victims, to—" Blaine could tell that Alex was not buying it all. "Didn't you know that patients undergoing surgery recover faster if the anesthesiologist tells him so under anesthesia?"

"No."

"Haven't you heard that the same hormones that elicit the emotions of anger and rage also affect the immune system, and can cause sickness and infection and increase the likelihood of cancer?"

"Not recently."

"All true. We also hope that by restructuring the pathways of the mind we can cure aphasia: to restore to a patient the process of thought and the recognition of identity. It's all possible, Alex. These are all potential uses for the bypass skullcap and biofeedback training."

"Subliminal suggestion I can accept, hormone release I can understand—the mechanism if not volition—and I can sort of see how a person's mind, his personality, can become trapped in the broken pathways of the brain, but what about these brain transplants that Greenstein wrote about?"

Blaine could not hide his frustration. "He picked up on a single sentence at the end of my paper. Lawson spotted it, too, in Greenstein's article. But I only threw that in as a fillip, as a way-out possibility of what future mind research has in store for us. And because Greenstein misconstrued it, I'm afraid that lay readers all over the country are going to believe him in his ignorance."

"If it's not possible, why did you mention it?"

"I didn't. You see, Greenstein did not distinguish between the brain and the mind. The brain can't be transplanted because it's not an isolated organ but an inseparable part of the central nervous system. But the mind, the consciousness, a person's memory, that, if you remember from our earlier discussion, is an interaction of energy fields: a specific construction of electrical potential analogous to the genetic code that controls our heredity and predetermines what our bodies will look like. If we could built a computer with a large enough data storage bank, and record all a person's brain waves and bioelectrical information, we could implant that memory pattern on another brain and wake up the person in a new body. Kind of like reminding someone from a former existence; technically speaking, mental reincarnation, or transmigration."

Alex was silent for a long time. Finally, he breathed, "Wow."

"Now, Greenstein made up all that other stuff: lobotomizing criminals and using them as recipients for transplants, and growing mindless clones as hosts for donors with dying bodies. He even screwed up the terminology. But the point is, although at this stage of development the process is highly speculative, it is possible. Of course, given sufficient time and technology, anything's possible. I'm sure the Wright Brothers never in their wildest dreams envisioned supersonic flight, stealth bombers, and Moon landings. Who knows? A hundred years from now, consciousness transplants may be as common as tonsillectomies. If you think it's frustrating today dealing with women who constantly change their minds, wait until the twenty-second century."

"I heard that, Mr. Chauvinism." Marybeth swept into the room like a breath of fresh air. Her pout was put on. "Blaine, you know I always pick up bad vibes. Why do you persist in testing me when you know I'm nearby?"

"Alex, you certainly understand that feelings are subjective, and don't necessarily depend upon anything going on in the world around us. But did you know that emotions can be so real that they begin to direct our behavior?"

"What's that got to do with the price of eggs?" Marybeth asked.

"Just because you have a crush on me doesn't mean that I'm constantly in touch with your feelings."

Marybeth turned beet red. "You wish."

Seeing that he had embarrassed her more than he intended, Blaine ruffled her hair and pulled her close for a hug. "I'm sorry, Marybeth. You know I love you— like a sister. But as long as you're here I'd like you to act as monitor while I take Alex on a little trip."

It was a moment before Marybeth regained her composure. "All right, but I'll get even with you."

"You've got to stand in line." To Alex, "Let me give you a demonstration of our big breakthrough." He picked up one of the bypass skullcaps, held it out to him, and indicated the barber chair. "Sit down and put this on your head. Marybeth will handle the controls. Remember, she can read your mind."

"With or without the equipment?"

"Either way," she said. To Blaine, "And you quit teasing me or I'll give you a piece of my mind."

"If I had half a mind I'd take it."

Alex seemed uncomfortable as Blaine adjusted the height and tilt of the chair; the light-hearted banter did not ease the strain. He let Marybeth push up the sleeves of the surgical shirt and take his blood pressure. "Now that I'm here I'm not sure I want to go through with this."

"Make up your mind," Marybeth smiled.

He ignored her remark. "Is this going to hurt?"

"Alex, the purpose of the bypass skullcap is to eliminate pain." Blaine placed a stethoscope on Alex's chest, listened, moved it around, listened, and put it away. "Still ticking. Now try to relax. You've had ten times the preparation most patients get, and they never complain."

"But they're probably desperate from the pain they're in. All I've got is a twinge in my back from that car crash, and an overall soreness from last night's exercise—I got banged up a bit."

"Just sit back and enjoy the ride." Blaine pushed him against the cushion. He fitted the skullcap on Alex's head, cinched down the straps, and rocked it back and forth a few times as he ran his fingers over Alex's scalp, like a flamboyant phrenologist. "Marybeth, check the synchronization."

She studied the digital display on the LED screen. "You're getting good at this, Blaine. You got it right the first time."

To Alex, "It's almost impossible to get it on wrong. Instead of using only a couple dozen electrodes like they used to do in the old days, the skullcap is wired with several hundred. The computer is self-calibrating; it's programmed to choose the electrodes closest to the activity centers we're looking for. How's it feel?"

"It's got my hair bunched a little, but other than that it's okay."

"Good. Now we switch on the power. You'll feel some tingles on your scalp, like static electricity. That's normal."

"Yes."

"It's locked in," Marybeth said.

Blaine nodded. "Generate the field."

Marybeth tapped a button.

"The tingles are gone."

"How about that twinge in your back?"

Alex screwed up his face. "I'm not always aware of it. You know, it's one of those things that comes and goes. But—I can't feel it."

"The effect on you is negligible, the same as the effect of—forgive me for saying this—aspirin on a person without a headache."

"Wait a minute. The soreness is gone, too. My legs don't ache any more, as if I've just been given a shot of Demerol. But my mind isn't fuzzy. I can still see perfectly. And hear. And think."

"The brain's peripheral perceptions continue to function despite the blockage of the overpowering input of sensations we interpret as pain. The bypass skullcap has helped you think away your aches and twinges. In that sense you might call it a 'mind set.' "

Alex sounded excited. "In fact, I can't feel anything at all. I mean, I don't have any awareness of my physical body. It's almost as if nothing exists outside my head. But I don't feel—high. I don't have that floating sensation like I do when I take antihistamines, or codeine."

"And that's the beauty of the system. It allows you to retain your equilibrium and mental alertness. And because it blocks pain without the undesirable side effects of chemical medication, it's useless to people with addictive personalities—the people who take drugs for the calming effect, or for fun, or as an escape from reality. The bypass skullcap won't even replace Valium because it offers no emotional relief. It's not a psychiatric tool at all. It simply suspends physiological sensation."

Alex seemed disappointed. "But I thought—there would be more than this. I thought it would—I don't know."

"And that's what everyone else thinks—or wants to think. Thanks to Greenstein. But once we get the units into mass production, we can do so much to alleviate pain in the world. We can give a new quality of life to people with shingles, arthritis, lower back pain, migraine, and on and on and on. And feel this." Blaine scratched Alex's arm with pin.

"I can't. I don't feel a thing."

He stabbed the fleshy part of Alex's upper arm, where doctor's ordinarily insert hypodermic needles.

"Nothing. Not a thing."

He pinched him.

Alex shook his head.

"I could cut you open and remove your appendix, and you'd never notice. At least not the pain. You'd still suffer the physical effects of invasive surgery, and the fear when you saw your guts hanging out, but you'd never feel the cut of the blade."

Alex was obviously overwhelmed. "With a unit like this on his back a soldier in battle could fight until his body dropped out from under him. He'd die before he'd ever know he was wounded."

"That's true," said Marybeth. "But as with every new invention that will forever change the course of human events, there are ethical questions to consider. We don't have the right to delude people with the false belief that no pain means no bodily harm. Marathon runners do extensive damage to their bodies without realizing it because pain is blocked by the natural release of endorphins. That's how they push themselves to the limit of endurance. But a person pushed *beyond* the limits of endurance can die.

"Part of the biofeedback training program we're now developing involves educating chronically ill patients that pain has an important role in survival. If you never felt pain you'd never take your hand out of a fire until it was burned to a crisp. By the same token, the absence of pain via the bypass skullcap is no indication of returning health. I don't know if Blaine explained this to you, but just because you master biofeedback pain reduction doesn't mean you can live that way all the time. It takes intense concentration to force the release of pain-blocking neurotransmitters. You can do it for short periods of time with near total blockage—useful if you break a leg and are waiting to get to a hospital—or you can do it for longer periods of time with only a mitigating effect. The body does not have an infinite supply of chemical reserves, nor can the mind concentrate completely on pain reduction. Everything has its limits."

Alex nodded slowly. "What about the out-of-body experience?"

"None of us have been able to produce the event without the skullcap," said Blaine. "Not that I would want to. It's scary the first time it happens if you're not expecting it, but once you get used to it and can 'watch' it in a detached manner you find that it's no more thrilling than watching television. Are you sure you want to go through with it?"

"Show me everything."

Blaine raised his eyebrows. "Okay. You asked for it." He nodded at Marybeth, who touched a function key on the bypass unit. "You'll get a vague feeling of dissociation as you lose all mental contact with your body. That's the frightening part. But it passes quickly, and puts you in the position of a cameraman filming a movie. Much of what you will experience is what you remember about your surroundings, and how you interpret events that you see and hear—including subconscious interpretations of sounds and their possible meanings. The rest is due to the power of suggestion."

Alex tensed suddenly, and his body convulsed. "Oh, God."

"Take it easy, Alex. I'm right here next to you." Marybeth placed her hand on his arm even though he was pumping so many neurotransmitters that all sense of physical contact was gone. "Remember, this is a conscious dream, an hallucination: something conjured up in your mind."

"Give him more power," Blaine urged.

"God, I'm floating right up out of the chair."

"We've got to give you enough power to ensure subjective autonomy. Otherwise, you'll find it disturbing as you fluctuate between reality and the dream state: when you see through your optic nerve at the same time you're looking through your mind's eye."

"Yes, you're right. After that first 'jolt' of separation the fear is gone. I can roam freely about the room and look down from the ceiling. I can see myself sitting in the chair, I can see you on my right side and Marybeth on my left. She's touching my arm. I can see the whole room, like through a wide-angle lens. I can even see the clock on the wall ticking away, counting time."

"These are all things you saw before we turned on the skullcap and bypassed specific brain wave functions, or things you noted subconsciously and are now remembering. As a trained investigator you should now be able to 'see' many things that you didn't notice before, just as you go through your mind in bed and recall details of the day's events."

"I can even peer into corners and study gadgets I failed to notice before. But it doesn't feel real. I don't feel as if I'm actually there. It's more like you said—like looking at a television screen. Oh, I guess if this were 1950 and I just saw my first TV show I'd be more impressed, but this isn't even as exhilarating as the wraparound theater at the Epcot Center. I'm sorry to have to say this, Blaine, but I'm pretty disappointed. I was expecting an experience more like the one after my car crash."

"If you'll relay that insight to Carcione and the South American gang—and Greenstein—my life will be a whole lot simpler."

"You mean, this is it? This is what all the hullabaloo is about?"

"You got it. Unless we give you a few more watts. That allows the mind to dissociate farther from the body. You can pass through the door and along the corridor."

"What happens if there's a power failure?"

"Never mind."

"That's what I'm afraid of." Alex thought it over for a moment. "Okay, give me a touch more power. Just enough to let me peek outside."

"Be careful. The first time I did this I went right through the roof. Literally. Damn near got run down by a flock of geese. That's why I implanted the suggestion that you travel along the corridor. Go ahead, Marybeth."

She bumped the lever up a notch.

"It's working. I'm out in the corridor now, like a dolly shot in the movies. Hey, I don't remember opening the door."

"The magic of the silver screen," Blaine said. "Why don't you go look for Lawson. He should be skulking around down here somewhere."

"I'm doing it now. I'm checking out the rooms, but I don't really feel in control. It's as if I'm being directed, or like—I guess like watching a motion picture. I'm just letting it happen to me. I have to agree with Greenstein.

You'll never make any money out of this. *Jesus!*"

A gun shot echoed through the tiled corridors outside the lab. Marybeth pulled back the rheostat handle. "He's clear."

Blaine whipped off the bypass skullcap. "Come on!"

Alex shook his head and refocused his eyes, then leaped up out of the chair. Both men pulled out their pistols and dashed for the door. The mysteries of the mental universe would have to wait for calmer contemplation.

Chapter 16

The two men that Captain Lawson held at gun point glared like cornered lions. One was dressed in a brown nondescript suit and beige cordovans. The other wore black from chin to foot: the high-buttoned jacket covered a turtleneck shirt, the soft-soled shoes were as quiet as cat's paws on the linoleum flooring. Each man held his hands at half mast, palms outward.

"That's him, Alex," Blaine alleged. "That's the one who came at us from around Langdon Hall."

"You're right." From the moment he stepped through the door, Alex's revolver was aimed straight at the one in black.

If the man had any qualms about having three guns aimed at his chest he did not show it. With a body the size of a compact car he did not appear to be the kind to wilt under any but the most dire straits. His ebony skin glistened in the light of the overhead fluorescents.

"Foley, cover the other one." Lawson pointed with his chin at the man in brown, leaning with his buttocks against the far end of the conference table, his feet crossed.

"You're wasting time. I'm telling you we're CIA." He spoke too casually for a man backed into a corner by a couple of six-shooters. He was so evenly tanned that he might have just stepped out of a plane from the tropics. He was large, but not imposingly so. "We're all on the same side, and we're all here for the same reason—to help Dr. Mitchell."

"Are you two together?" Blaine's finger did not ease off the trigger.

"We're from different departments and on different assignments. Our paths just happened to cross. I'm Hudson. And my big burly friend here is MacDonald." He flashed a toothy grin. "I've got identifi—"

"Don't do it!" Lawson yelled. "Don't move anything but your mouth, buddy, or you'll end up smiling out of the other side of your face."

Hudson froze. MacDonald just glowered.

The door burst open and Marybeth dashed into the room. "Thanks for wait—" She took in her friends with the guns, followed the line of sight, and inhaled sharply when she recognized MacDonald. "It's him."

"Angus, you really know how to make friends, don't you?" Hudson tried to be flippant but came off rather weak. "Look, if you'll just let me—"

"You make another move and I'll clip your ear, too." Lawson was clearly in charge of the situation.

"All right. All right. Don't get your dander up." Beseeching to Blaine, "Dr. Mitchell, I've been sent here by the CIA to look after your interests in light of recent developments concerning the neurometric feedback terminal. I can vouch for MacDonald if you'll just—"

"And who's going to vouch for you?" Blaine was having none of it. His life had been threatened so many times in the past day that he would be suspicious of his own mother. "Angus the fullback?"

Hudson scowled. "Look, you're just making this difficult—"

"No. You're making it difficult by not cooperating with the local authorities. I trust these two men. You, I don't even know. And this guy—" He waved the gun toward MacDonald. "—came at me with a gun last night, chased us into the woods, and beat up a reporter."

"Bullshit!" MacDonald exploded. "The lying little twirp ran into me. And if I get my hands on the bastard—"

"That's enough of that!" Lawson glanced at Alex. "Foley, take away their guns and their badges. I'll cover for you. But for God's sake make sure you're own piece is out of reach. These jokers are a bit too street wise for my tastes. Whoever they are, they're pros."

When Alex handed his gun to Blaine, Blaine realized the special agent had acted impulsively when he had frisked Carcione. Lawson covered MacDonald while Blaine kept one gun on each of them. Alex accepted

Lawson's cautionary notes with equanimity. He walked around the conference table and came up slowly behind MacDonald. Only then did Blaine realize how huge the black man actually was; Alex was a midget by comparison.

"Easy," Lawson drawled.

MacDonald's dark eyes glowed like twin pits of Hell. He stood as steady as a rock. Alex pulled MacDonald's coat over his shoulders and down to the crook of his elbows, a maneuver intended to immobilize him. Blaine did not believe for a moment that MacDonald could be rendered helpless by so simple a means.

"Don't do anything rash, Angus. Just let them check us out and we'll all be—"

"Shut up, you!" Lawson shouted. "No distractions. The man who's holding a gun on you is real testy today. And he can shoot out the legs from under a fly at a hundred paces. You want proof?"

Hudson made no reply.

Alex removed a Colt .45 from MacDonald's shoulder holster, five spare clips from a pouch on his belt, a knife from his right calf, and a single shot derringer from his left. He laid all the weapons on the table and slid them to the other end. "Not only is this guy a walking arsenal, he's wearing a bullet-proof vest." Alex ran his fingers over MacDonald's jacket. "With two holes in the material, I'd say he's been hit recently. And he's got more than a silver lining in his jacket. Lower your arms, please."

MacDonald did as he was told but with great displeasure. "Hurry it up, will you?"

Alex pulled the jacket all the way off, and hefted it with a frown. "It's full of interior pockets and Velcro flaps. He must think he's Doc Savage." He removed the wallet and identification folder. "It says CIA. MacDonald, Angus R. And there's no mistaking the picture; it hardly fits on the card."

"Check the other one," Lawson ordered.

Hudson submitted to the routine without demurring. He wore only a Smith & Wesson automatic and carried two spare clips in his pocket.

"CIA. Hudson, Stanislaw. He didn't make that one up." Alex let him keep his jacket on bent arms. "What do we do now?"

Before Lawson could answer, Hudson said, "You call Dickerson at HQ and get confirmation. He'll vouch for me."

"Dickerson's *my* boss."

"I know that. He's the one who passed the info on to us that you were on the job and needed backup. It only works if you call someone you can trust, someone who's voice you'll recognize. I could give you the number of the home office, but it won't do us any good. Look, Foley, we're here to help, and the sooner you get on the phone, the sooner we can start working together. You'll have to forgive Gargantua here. He's just pissed because a common police officer got the drop on him. No offense, Lawson."

Lawson scowled. "How did you get past my man at the front desk?"

"I flashed my badge; it gets me in more places than American Express. Angus sneaked in the back way and has been skulking around for hours. He caught me in the corridor, dragged me in here for a conference, and got caught with his pants down—"

"Shut up, Hudson." The expression on MacDonald's face could have killed a grizzly.

Hudson did not appear to mind being chastised. To Alex, "Would you call Dickerson, please, before we get any older?"

Marybeth plucked the receiver off the wall and punched in a four-digit internal code. The telephone was generally used as an intercom. "Just tap out your number, Alex."

He did. "Dickerson, this is Foley. I've got—" He listened for nearly two minutes. The soft rush of air from the floor ducts was the only sound in the room. "I understand—" Another full minute. "They're here now. . . . MacDonald and Hudson. . . . I will sir. . . . Yes, sir, thank you. . . . Yes, I'll keep in touch." Thank you. . . .

I will, sir. Thanks." Marybeth took the telephone from him and hung it on its cradle. "Okay, you can relax. He confirmed everything."

MacDonald did not look pleased. He scooped up his armament, donned his jacket, then without another look at his antagonists, began walking around the room looking under the furniture, behind pictures, and into the heating ducts.

"Now that *that's* over we can become acquainted." Hudson smiled at Marybeth. "How are you, sister?"

"Fortunately, not related to you."

He held out his hand. "Stan Hudson."

Marybeth offered hers uncertainly. "Marybeth Maples."

"I know—computer specialist." Hudson shifted his attention but did not let go of her hand. "That was nice shooting, Lawson. Couldn't have done better myself. Hey, Angus. Your ear okay?"

MacDonald continued his inspection of the conference room as if nothing else mattered. "Yeah." His left lobe was nicked, but he ignored it as if it were nothing more than a scab. Other than the whites of his eyes, the raw speck of red was his only exhibition of color. He never smiled.

"Tough as nails, that one." He still held onto Marybeth's hand. "And Foley, you gotta lot to learn if you're gonna stay in this business. Haven't you ever heard of fake ID? Next time ask for a description."

The special agent did not reply.

"Sharpen up, boy, or you'll get yourself killed. Worse than that, you'll muff your assignment. Thirty-five years in the business and I've never seen such a greenhorn. What was on Dickerson's mind, son, when he sent you out here?"

Marybeth yanked her hand free and came to Alex's defense. "Watch your mouth, mister. This man has done a heck of a job keeping us alive, no thanks to that mountain of flesh over there." She held her arm out stiff and pointed at MacDonald, now surveying the acoustical ceiling tiles. "Who's side are you guys on, anyway?"

"Whoa, whoa, whoa." Hudson held up his hands against her verbal assault. "First of all, little lady, keep your temper in check. I know this has been—"

"You don't know anything, mister." Marybeth intertwined her arm with Alex's. "Now you apologize to him, then start coming up with some explanations for your own conduct. And *his*."

Blaine could not help but smile. He had fallen prey to Marybeth's diatribes often enough to know how uncomfortable it was on the receiving end. He let her carry the ball.

Hudson started backpeddling. "I only got into the act this morning when the Bureau contacted the Agency about last night's incident—"

"Incident!" Marybeth screamed.

"—at the college. They gave me the run-down, told me to check in with Foley, and contact Angus, who was already on the job."

"What job?"

There was a momentary silence as Hudson waited for MacDonald to answer for himself. MacDonald took an electronic device from one of his inner jacket pockets and scanned the floor, walls, and ceiling; a red light in the casing blinked constantly. While he was performing his environmental ablutions, the door opened and in stepped Young. His normally impassive face registered anxiety and bewilderment at the goings-on.

"You're Dr. Young." Hudson held out his hand. "Stan Hudson. Nice to meet you."

Young was flustered. "Who—who are you? How do you know me?"

"It's all in the CIA dossier."

"CIA?" Young gulped loud enough to be heard. "You're from the CIA?"

Hudson glanced at the ceiling. "Is there something wrong with the acoustics in this room?"

His examination complete, MacDonald approached the knot of people but kept his eyes on Hudson. "Nothing. It's clean. Leastways, as far as I can tell." He said nothing else, volunteered no information.

Young was impatient. "Why is the CIA involved in this dispute with Dr. Mitchell? I thought the FBI was handling the matter."

"The CIA is involved because Mitchell works for the CIA." Hudson smiled smugly. The shock value of his statement gave him an out from Marybeth's accusations. He paused dramatically. "You all do."

Blaine felt a queer tingle at the base of his spine; it ran all the way up his backbone and raised the hair on the nape of his neck. There was little comfort in knowing that the reaction was not neurological. "What?"

"You're out of your mind," Marybeth said. "Where did you get that badge? From K-Mart?"

Lawson and Alex exchanged looks, but waited for developments. Young was simply in shock.

"Let me explain." Hudson seemed to be enjoying the situation, now that he was in control of it. "You're not on the direct payroll; your checks and retirement benefits don't come straight from the Agency. But this Institute is funded by dummy organizations backed by government tax dollars. It's a way of making it appear like a public enterprise instead of a military research and development center. But the bucks all come from the same place: Uncle Sam in the big white dome."

Now Hudson was talking in terms Young understood. "You are daft. This Institute operates on grants from the Franklin Foundation and the Ford Endowment Society, and receives contributions from hospitals, universities, local communities, and human services programs."

"And guess what? The Franklin Foundation gets its money from the Advanced Research Projects Agency—part of the Department of Defense. The Ford Endowment Society was established by the Central Intelligence Agency for one purpose only: to channel funds into Mitchell's neurometric feedback research. We thank all those other organizations for their donations; every penny helps. They may even choose to believe the Institute is doing pure research in the perceptual functions of the brain. But when you come right down to it this whole project is an instrumentality of war. The Cold War."

"Now I know you're crazy."

Blaine let Marybeth do the talking, but in the back of his mind lurked a creeping suspicion that Hudson was on the up and up. It certainly answered a lot of questions about why his particular line of research had received such a large slice of the pecuniary pie, why he had been given the go-ahead to expand his laboratory complex while the work space of other doctors at the Institute had been reduced, why he had been given a large crew of technicians and assistants at the same time the staffs of other departments had suffered cutbacks, and why Young had been powerless to divert incoming funds to his own pet projects—definite strings had been attached to the grants from the Franklin Foundation and the Ford Endowment Society.

Alex saw through Hudson's admission of facts. "If what you say is true, and all this is really a clandestine military project, how can you talk about it so freely without breaching security?"

"Because the project's security has already been compromised. There's been a leak, and the Soviets know all about it."

Young turned as white as a bleached shirt. "Russians?" The word came out like the quack of a duck.

"Russian is a geographical adjective, Soviet is political. But both are used interchangeably among the proletariat."

"Oh, shit, that's all we need," grumbled Lawson. "Now we got Ruskies in the picture, too."

At the moment, however, Blaine was more concerned about the projects of other people to end his life than the political ramifications of brain research. "We'll get back to that later. I want to know why MacDonald was trying to kill me last night."

"I wasn't." MacDonald's voice was as deep as an oil well. "I never even heard of you till a few hours ago. I was tracking a KGB agent."

"KGB?" Young was nearly apoplectic.

"Is there an echo around here?" chided Hudson.

Lawson threw his hands in the air. "We got everybody else in the picture, why not a Russian spy?"

"He's not a spy. He's an assassin." MacDonald hesitated. "Hudson, are you sure they've got security clearance for this?"

"Those are the orders. Remember, it's their party." To the others, "But nothing goes beyond this coterie. Is that clear?"

"Unless the KGB's got their snooper turned on," MacDonald scowled.

"Wait just a damn minute here." Blaine waved like a referee at a football game. "Did I sleep through something, or what? All of a sudden we're talking about broken security, Soviet assassins, the KGB, snooping devices. What the hell is going on? I'm just a doctor working on a method for pain relief; I'm not building secret weapons. How did I get involved in this international intrigue?"

Lawson raised bushy eyebrows at Blaine's denigration of his work, but remained silent.

"Which question would you like me to answer first?" Hudson smiled as if it were a game.

"All of them. But first, I want to know what was going on last night at Westmoreland." Blaine stared hard at MacDonald.

"You mean, before you shot me?"

"Goddamn it, I want answers—"

Marybeth disentangled herself from Alex and tried to soothe Blaine by running her hands over his shoulders. "Blaine, give them a chance."

He stabbed a finger at MacDonald. "Talk, Angus. And it better be good."

MacDonald flared like a solar prominence. He waited a full fifteen seconds before speaking. "Nabakov. Yevgeny Nabakov. Mean anything to you?" After ten seconds of silence, he continued. "He's a Soviet assassin. Not only the best in the business, the best there ever was. And ever will be. We got a tip he was coming into the country on a top priority mission. He danced around through a few European countries before making the crossing, but we knew his ETA so we were waiting for him at the airport. Only trouble is, nobody knows what he looks like. Leastways, nobody on *our* side.

"We photographed everyone who got off the plane, inspected every bit of luggage before putting it on the conveyor belt, ran all the passports through a computer check, and narrowed the suspects down to half a dozen possibilities: businessmen, vacationers, older men visiting stateside relatives. I put tails on all of them, but I was sure I had him pegged: a tall, thin aristocratic gentlemen carrying a big square box; it was red, and tied with green ribbon. One of my men slipped a bug in his pocket, but he was too crafty for that. He dumped all his clothes at a hotel and walked out the front door in a suit and overcoat from his valise, and wearing a disguise.

"He almost got away with it. I stationed myself in the lobby, looking for anyone fitting his approximate height and weight. Maybe his first appearance was a disguise; maybe both. I don't know. But this guy came down with a box; it was white and had no ribbon, and was a little smaller. I followed him on a hunch. He took a cab out to the 'burbs and disappeared in a park. I called the Boston police while I was cruising the neighborhood, but before they could surround the area I spotted him stealing a car. I got the make and model, but missed the tags in the dark. He had smashed the bulb.

"I chased him onto the interstate then lost him in traffic. He was headed west. So I got on the scramble horn and told the home office I needed help or I was going to lose him. They called every municipality along the projected route, and put them on priority alert. Finally picked him up in Greensborough. He pulled off—"

"Hey, hold the phone." Captain Lawson's jaw had just bounced off his chest. "Was that a bright green Fairlane? That would have been—Wednesday night?"

MacDonald nodded. "Taylor picked it up. Found it parked in the mall. I remember the APB, and cursing the goddamn feds—" He glanced at Alex and Blaine, then shrugged.

MacDonald went on without acknowledgment; he seemed to enjoy telling the story. "I checked all the motels in town, but he was too crafty for that. Must have been camping in the woods like a Siberian husky. KGB agents are trained to live off the land. My men arrived and spent all day pounding the pavement."

"Then you're the one who called in the bulletin?" Lawson's curiosity was piqued. "Made me stake out the car, and put extra men on the street looking for an escaped convict. Was that your cover story?"

"The home office made the call. We can't tell the local yokels we're chasing a Soviet super sleuth. First thing you know it'd be all over the papers and he'd read about it himself. 'Specially in this berg." MacDonald's dark eyes winced as if in pain. "I had tails on every pedestrian who was tall, thin, and fiftyish. With a convention in town that was no easy task. Practically every male doctor at last night's lecture fit the description. Most of my men ended up there. They had strict orders to stay undercover till Nabakov was singled out. I was outside when the shit hit the fan. I saw this character around the back of the lecture hall, lost him in the dark, then picked him up in the parking lot at the end of the fireworks. We were at opposite corners of the building. That's when I figured out who his target was."

Blaine inhaled deeply, awaiting the inevitable pronouncement.

"He was sent here to assassinate Dr. Mitchell."

Chapter 17

"Why me? How am I mixed up in all this fuge and subterfuge?"

Hudson supplied the answer. "The neurometric feedback terminal. That's the research the CIA has been supporting, it's what the Soviets are trying to prevent you from perfecting. They figure that with the genius behind the project dead, the project will die out as well."

"That's ridiculous. Why is an anesthetic device so important that everybody and his brother either wants to buy it, steal it, or destroy it? Give us a couple more months and we'll be giving it away."

"Not all of it." Hudson leaned against the conference table and crossed his legs. "We've been keeping tabs on you, Mitchell, and I don't mean just reading your progress reports. We've monitored your work for a long time, from way back when you were conducting occipital-parietal EEG-alpha-wave audio monotone binary feedback experiments at the VA hospital in Bedford. You might even say that we've groomed you—by offering you the facilities in which to conduct your research." Hudson spread his arms. "This place wasn't built by accident, you know."

Blaine's work in the psychiatric hospital had been done on a voluntary basis: his way of helping Vietnam veterans who had not survived their ordeal of combat as well as he had. "But—"

"I don't mean the Institute was constructed just for you. There were a lot of doctors whose work we were watching. Even Young here had some interesting proposals, such as the correlation between epilepsy and frequency modulation." It had long been known that lights flashing at certain intervals and sound propagated at certain frequencies could cause nausea, induce hypnosis, and trigger epileptic fits. "All lines of research on the perceptual functions of the brain are valid. Some are more valid than others because they have a greater potential for military use."

Blaine thought he was catching on. "You mean, because a portable neurotransmitter can stop pain and promote healing in the wounded?" Then he remembered Alex's prediction. "Or because biofeedback training can help soldiers perform superhuman feats in the field of battle?"

"Nothing so simple."

If Hudson judged such applications elementary, Blaine wondered what the CIA considered valuable. The human brain was regarded by most scientists as the most complicated construct in existence; the number of possible links between neurons—that is, the process and pathways of thought—exceeded the number of subatomic particles in the known universe. Brain research was undoubtedly the final frontier in understanding the grand enigma of life, death, and the cosmos. Yet they at the Institute were only just beginning to scratch the surface of such research; the possibilities and future potential were endless. So what kind of far-reaching concept was guiding government sponsorship? "What did you have in mind?"

"We're not as interested in what's in the mind as what we can get out of it. Take the Soviets, for example. They're way ahead of us—" Hudson squinted at Young. "Did I say something wrong?"

Young could not blanch any more than he already had. "I—I—you keep bringing up the Russians. And this Russian, er, Soviet assassin. Isn't there something we should be doing? I mean—"

"We're already doing everything we can. We've got a task force organized to storm this place that'll put the Normandy invasion to shame." Hudson glanced at his watch. "By now the Commissioner should be getting release orders from the home office. Most of Angus's men got locked up in last night's round-up because they were not authorized to break their cover." He swept the room with his hands. "As long as we're here in the basement, and Angus has got his gadgets set up, we're about as safe as we can get. Unless, of course, Nabakov is already here."

"I wouldn't put it past him." MacDonald checked the instruments he had placed in the corners of the room. "He could have gone anywhere after I lost him on campus last night. The forest was mighty black."

"Then you *were* chasing us through the woods?" Blaine shouted, in a burst of anger.

"I was behind you all the way, but it was Nabakov I was after. I didn't even know who you were at the time—or how important you were."

"It doesn't take a rocket scientist to figure out that the Soviets didn't send their number one cutthroat on a mercy mission. Whoever he was trying to execute should have been given priority protection. You could have told us what we were up against, instead of skulking after us and playing hide and seek. We could have been—"

"Bait!" Marybeth screamed. "That's all we were to you, isn't it?" She did not wait for a reply but waded into MacDonald with both fists, punching him on the chest with the heels of her fists like one would stab with a knife; it probably saved her from a handful of broken knuckles. She beat on him like a drummer pounding snares, but might just as well have been striking feathers against a stone wall.

MacDonald simply scowled as she vented her anger.

Alex pulled her away as gently as possible; it was like trying to extract an angry cat from a half-filled swimming pool. "Easy, Marybeth. Take it easy."

She slumped against the special agent. Her eyes were glassy, but she refused to let the tears flow. Her venomous "I hate you" was directed at MacDonald. Alex eased her into a chair and continued to comfort her.

"Look, I know we're all a bit on edge here, but let's get a grip on the situation. Events have been moving rather quickly for all of us." Hudson faced Blaine, "The CIA and the FBI have established a cooperative effort to protect you and the Institute from Soviet assassins and South American dissidents. We've got too much invested in you to let—"

"Is that all I am to you—an investment? Are you waiting for me to mature like some long-term savings bond?"

"Don't take it personally, Mitch—"

"I do take it personally because it's my hide these people are after. If I die, all you lose is another round in the Cold War game."

Hudson remained calm and somewhat contemptuous. "Oh, no, Mitchell. It's much more serious than that. The Soviets are way ahead of us in research of the mind because they haven't had to fight religious fanaticism like we have. Christ, whenever we set up a program to study extra sensory perception we have every kook from the Pope on down screaming hosannas as if we were killing their precious gods. Plus we have to contend with all the professional mediums and fake mystics who make their living by ripping off people through the perpetration of hoaxes such as communicating with the dead. Now we've gotten smart: ESP is called bioinformation. Duke University is doing most of that research; again, under government contract but through intermediate funding operations.

"The Soviets are working in areas we haven't even begun to explore. They've spent a lot of time, money, and effort on finding a rationalistic explanation for telepathy. They've developed an amplification device that enables people to 'hear' radio waves. As you know, the area of the brain most sensitive to field effects is the hypothalamus. Damage to the hypothalamus can increase the sensitivity many times. By intentionally restructuring the hypothalamus of human subjects they've got people passing Morse code messages to each other. And there's no telling how far the technique can be extrapolated. No telling *us*, anyway, because we're so backward we're asking chimpanzees to read minds when they can't even read. Then there's the phosphene effect, telekinesis, astral projection, and Kirlian photography."

Blaine had fooled around with the phosphene effect

earlier in his career. In perfect darkness a bar magnet of certain flux density held to the temple could induce a sensation of light. But the same response could be evoked by chemical and electrical means, by fasting, by meditation, and as a result of fatigue; it seemed to have no relevance. In Blaine's mind telekinesis was a bit far-fetched; moving physical objects by the power of positive thinking was more than even Norman Vincent Peale envisioned. Astral projection was an hallucinatory interlude: an out-of-body experience for believers only. Kirlian photography had long been debunked; there was no photographic proof that an 'aura' of life energy left the body at the moment of death, or that the body lost several ounces of weight that could not be accounted for by expelled air. All this was true, at least, among Eastern bloc nations.

It was obvious to Blaine that Hudson's knowledge of brain research was more than cursory. He had a mind and mental attitude that could only be the result of years of comparative study.

"So now we come to the Institute for Higher Research in Perceptual Functions of the Brain, and the work of the good Dr. Mitchell. How does all this tie in with Soviet assassination plots? The answer is simple: you've got some mind bending ideas that closely parallel their own."

"The spaghetti brain, no doubt," Lawson interjected.

Blaine ignored him. "Even if that's true, I fail to see any military advantage to the neurometric transmitter."

"I'm sure you don't, Mitchell, because you're a scientist. That means you have the mind of a scientist. Once you fine-tune your mind to a goal you have proven to be fantastically successful in achieving that goal. You work with admirable zeal and dedication. Nothing gets in your way. You overcome all obstacles. You created the concept of studying subjects on the point of death in order to learn more about the brain's natural protection from dangerously excessive external stimuli, you recorded the consequent evaluations of barely perceptible cerebral activity, you constructed a neurometric terminal that can record and transmit brain wave data through an array of electrodes, and you've developed the procedures for instructing patients in its use so they can control their own level of pain. Yet for all that you're not overendowed with a sense of imagination. You've been studying one tree for so long that you don't know that a forest has grown up around you.

"I've read your paper. I've read *all* your papers, even the ones you didn't submit. I've listened to phone conversations you've had with colleagues around the world—"

"You've got our phones tapped!"

"Of course." Hudson made it sound as if it were the most natural thing in the world. "We also have an agent on site who reports on a weekly basis. Apparently, so do the Soviets, because they've got hold of some pretty sensitive information about what's going on here."

This was more than Dr. Young could stand. As director of the Institute he was supposed to be its ultimate authority, to have total control of its projects, to have the last say on procedure, and to have all knowledge of its workings. Hudson's revelations made Young appear more a puppet than a puppeteer. Sweat poured down Young's forehead, and his body trembled. "This is insidious. You have no right to keep surveillance on a scientific institute as if it were a military installation."

"You don't think we can let a multimillion dollar operation run unchecked, do you? We own this Institute, Dr. Young. And we own you, whether you like it or not. Yet we've never interfered with your management policies as long as they were consistent with the original charter: to conduct research within guidelines prescribed by the agencies providing the funding. There's nothing unusual in that."

"Except that the CIA is pulling the strings." Blaine could not let Young argue alone. "You're manipulating the trend of scientific research to suit military objectives."

"We call it support, not manipulation. It's no different from Uncle Sam tricking the public into conserving energy by using the IRS to offer incentives for home insulation through tax advantages. By the same token, when scientists submit research proposals we channel grant money into those projects we think have the most potential to help achieve greater national security. We've never tried to prevent research in other areas. This very Institute is conducting experiments dictated by private subscription that have nothing to do with the CIA."

"Is that just a cover-up for the Institute's real function?"

"Now you're getting paranoid. There's nothing subversive about—"

"Paranoia is a mental disorder characterized by delusions. Bombs and bullets are real."

Hudson pushed himself away from the table and slowly sauntered to the far end of the room and back again. "Let's get one thing straight, Doctors. We are not the enemy; we are here to help you. The real enemy—"

"Sure, you want to save us so we can add to your armory, or help overthrow some foreign government." Blaine had a flash of insight. "That's it, isn't it? You leaked erroneous information about the uses of the bypass skullcap to the South American drug barons. They think it's a mind expansion device that will replace cocaine. They don't want people getting cheap highs because it'll cut into their trade, and widespread proliferation will put them out of business. So Montezuma's revenge is a herd of cowboys riding the range in pickup trucks, using Uzis and rocket launchers instead of lariats and branding irons."

Hudson was wonderfully calm. "You've been reading too many newspaper accounts of Agency activities. In fact, it was a newspaper story that brought the druggies into this mess. A local reporter did an exposé on your work here at the Institute. It purported to be based on your paper, but he glossed over your actual findings and concentrated instead on fantastic extrapolations that you mentioned only briefly as future lines of research—"

"If I ever get my hands on that Greenstein, I'll wring his neck like a chicken."

"Blame *him*, Mitchell, not the CIA. His story went out over the wire and was even picked up by the London *Times*. There's no telling how many languages it was translated into—"

"All right, already. I'm sorry. I apologize for jumping to conclusions. But what does my work have to do with strategic defense? Or how do you warmongers think the bypass skullcap could be converted to an offensive weapon?"

"We don't think it's a weapon at all. But if you'd remove your horse blinders I think you'd see that if the neurometric feedback terminal alters the level of consciousness the way you say it does, it can be put to uses that go far beyond your original research design."

Blaine was becoming more frustrated by the minute. "You're the one looking at life through a kaleidoscope. Why does everyone see in my work what they want to see? Carcione sees dream dens where people can come and have pre-selected fantasies. So he supplies information to help fight off monopolizing drug pushers who see people getting high without expensive chemical additives. What do you see? A telepathic transmitter that can send messages through the ether from one brain to another?"

"Eventually, perhaps. But for now what we want is a device to activate electronic equipment without physical contact."

"That's nothing new. Every solid-state television has one. It's called a remote control channel changer."

"I mean a device that can be activated mentally."

"In that case, take two aspirins and call me on Monday."

Hudson was deadly serious. "You think it's impossible?"

"I think you've let J.B. Rhine go to your head. What do you think I'm working on here? Pyramid power?"

"Mitchell, I prefer your predictions to your prescriptions. Look, we've got super sensitive relay switches that operate in the microvolt range, and we're developing nanovolt switches. If the neurometric feedback terminal—or its portable version, the bypass skullcap—can project only the minutest amount of energy generated by the neurons in the brain, it will permit the user to trip such relays. A person with a skullcap could then 'think' a properly equipped machine to work at a distance."

"I'll take back the aspirins. You need beta blockers. Shrinking blood vessels in the brain usually cause migraines, but I think your whole head has shrunk. The addendum to my paper was not a report on research in progress. It was levity. You see how I am, always kidding around. When you spend all your time with death and dying you've got to have a sense of humor or go mad in the meantime. Sure, I think the brain has untapped potential, but I didn't mean broadcast electrical potential."

"But you will admit that the brain is an electrical organ, that the mind, the consciousness, is maintained by the continuous generation of bioelectrical energy."

"*Your* brain's a pipe organ—one that's generating pipe dreams. We've come a long way in biofeedback training. Instead of controlling just heartbeat and blood pressure we're now initiating the release of endorphins and enkephalins. But whoever told you that we can discharge mental impulses like telegrams has us confused with Western Union."

"What would you say if I told you it's already been done?"

"I'd say you've been hoodwinked by a cleverly faked séance."

Hudson purposely made eye contact with each and every person, including MacDonald. "What I'm about to say is not to leave this room. Is that understood? You've all received special security clearance because of the gravity of the situation, but if anyone breathes a word of this I personally guarantee you'll be stuck in a dungeon so deep the devil will be sharing your bunk."

No one demurred.

"Angus?"

MacDonald double-checked his instrumentation. "Still clean as far as I can tell, but—"

Hudson held up his hand. "I know." He had everyone's attention. "Gentlemen, and lady, the Soviets have developed a spy device so advanced, so sophisticated, that it can see and hear through walls, and transmit signals to its mental operator up to five hundred feet away. We don't know what it looks like, we don't know how it works, but we know that if one of them was within range of this room we would be unable to detect it, and powerless to block it if we *did* detect it." He paused dramatically. "Furthermore, they think Mitchell has invented it, too."

Chapter 18

"This is preposterous." Bolstered by Blaine's retaliatory tactics against Hudson, Young had gotten over his diffidence and disquietude. "This Institute is conducting bona fide medical research, and Dr. Mitchell is one of the finest neurological researchers in this country— if not the world. But he is not working on any project involving occult shenanigans such as you suggest. Your insinuations are unfounded. Furthermore, Mr. Hudson, as director of this Institute, I deplore having our privacy invaded by phone taps and undercover men. I will not have it."

"Only those with skeletons to hide fear the disinterment of truth." It sounded like a statement Hudson had practiced throughout a long career of dealing with deceit and corruption. "Do you have a guilty conscience, Doctor?"

Young maintained a facade of forced indifference. The offhanded accusation, the challenge to his authority, and his inability to deal with life threatening situations, were all taking their toll on his equanimity. His stoicism had been stove in.

Blaine liked having Young on his side for a change, but thought that he was wandering far afield by objecting to matters of little consequence when weighed against the overall severity of the situation. "Hudson, you've let the Russians beat you at your own game. They're dispatching propaganda and you're eating it up. You should know better than that."

"Mitchell, this isn't Soviet misinformation. It's undeniable truth. We've captured top secret documents that were verbatim transcripts of conversations held behind so many closed doors that Houdini couldn't get through them all without getting caught. These conversations were not recorded, and no written records were kept. Only the participants themselves knew what they had said. Yet the Soviets reproduced the dialogue as if they'd had someone there writing it all down. And before you object, the participants are beyond reproach: two members of the Joint Chiefs of Staff. It was they who verified their own words, independent of each other. It is virtually impossible that the briefing room was bugged by the KGB."

"Doesn't the CIA have ultrasonic microphone guns that can pick up vibrations from window panes a block away? I read about it years ago."

Hudson refrained from comment, and went on as if Blaine had not even spoken. "We've also recovered documents that were reconstructions of Pentagon interoffice memoranda—paperwork that existed only long enough to be passed from one general to another, then shredded."

Blaine started to object, to make some droll comment about the invention of an unshredding machine, or a re-collator, then realized that he was not helping matters. Whatever the CIA believed about the Soviet spy network, whatever the Soviets believed about Blaine's neurometric feedback terminal, did not change the fact that an assassin had been ordered to terminate both him and his research. They might all be wrong, but he would still end up dead. So, although he did not want to believe what Hudson had to say, it was imperative that Blaine offer his cooperation.

"Okay, Hudson. I give up. What does it all mean?"

"According to our best intelligence, the Soviets have a thought controlled instrument that can penetrate any building, any office, even an hermetically sealed room. It doesn't come up pipes, it doesn't travel along electric wires, it doesn't use phone lines, it doesn't work on molecular vibration or infrared imaging or radio wave propagation or any scientific principle we know of. But it works. And if the controller can get within five hundred feet of his objective, he could be witnessing in audio and video, hi-fi and color, quadraphonic and three dimensional, everything that's happening in this room. He could watch you walk down the hall and follow you into the men's room, then tell you whether you washed your hands afterwards and what tune you were humming. It's the absolute, ultimate spy device. It's unstoppable, undetectable, and infallible. And I'm sure you'll agree that it's damned near unbelievable."

Only because of the abrupt and all-encompassing silence was the scuffing audible from the other side of the conference room door. MacDonald brushed Blaine aside as if he were a gnat. Gun in hand, he yanked open the door to reveal a startled, hunched over gnome.

"Greenstein!" Blaine yelled.

A fist the size of a country ham grabbed the reporter by the throat and dragged him inside. MacDonald kicked the door shut. "Just the nerd I wanted to see." He flung Greenstein across the room and bounced him off the wall, where he slid to the floor like a cartoon character.

"I want him first!" Blaine took the reporter's paisley tie, slipped the tail through the knot, and tightened it around his neck like a noose. "You little worm. You're the cause of all this grief. You—"

Greenstein's face turned cherry red, his eyes bulged out of their sockets. He tried ineffectually to push Blaine away but was no match against his strength or anger. He might have suffocated right there if Lawson had not stepped in and forced Blaine to release his strangle hold. The reporter started breathing in gasps.

"Take it easy, Dr. Mitchell," Lawson said smoothly. "We don't need another homicide on our hands."

Blaine clenched his fists. He backed away without taking his eyes off Greenstein. He did not talk because he was afraid the knot in his throat would garble his speech.

"You!" Greenstein stared past Blaine at MacDonald, who leered down from his inordinate height while slapping his gun in the palm of his hand. The second time it came out as a whimper. "You?"

"That's right, buddy." MacDonald leaned down threateningly. "Only this time if you don't tell the truth I'm *really* gonna pistol whip you." "Who—who—who—"

"Close your beak, Greenstein. Your feet don't wrap

around a branch."

Greenstein's owlish eyes registered horror and disbelief. He glanced at each person in the room, then focused through thick lenses on MacDonald. "Who—who—who are you?"

"Your guardian angel. And you better start praying because—"

"Forget that, Angus." Hudson took charge of the situation. He stepped between Greenstein and MacDonald, and crouched so his eyes were level with the reporter's. "How the hell did you get in here?"

Greenstein squeaked, "Well, I—"

"Speak up, man. Your presence here represents a major security breach."

The reporter cleared his throat. "It was Taylor, sir." He pointed a shaky finger at Captain Lawson. "His detective. He smuggled me in inside his trunk, then let me slip by the recept—"

"Okay, now you can kill him."

"Wait—"

Whatever Greenstein was going to say in his own defense was cut off by the fire alarm. The clanging sound galvanized everyone to attention, but Blaine was the first out the door. He raced to the stairwell with the rest of the group chasing him like Keystone Cops in a Mack Sennett comedy. He took the stairs two at a time. Seconds later he shouldered through the door on the first floor landing and into the main corridor.

The receptionist stood in the broad entryway just inside the glass double doors. "Back off, Lenny." Because she was so petite, the .44 Magnum she held in one manicured hand looked like a fifty caliber machine gun. She spun around as Blaine skidded to a halt on the waxed linoleum. "Don't come any farther, Dr. Mitchell."

Blaine was so shocked that he never even thought to draw his gun from its holster. His jaw dropped as if his jowls were full of lead sinkers. "Tilda?"

Detective Taylor stood in the alcove opposite the reception booth. He held his hands in the air. "I was only kidding about the bra. It was a joke. I always unsnap—"

Tilda ignored him. She faced Blaine but looked over his shoulder. "Sir, I just got the call. They spotted the pickup trucks: three from the north, two from the south."

"Good work, girl. Can you kill the noise?"

"Yes, sir."

Hudson followed her to her desk. She handed him the telephone, then leaned over the desk and flipped the fire alarm switch. Blaine's ears rang for several seconds after the raucous noise stopped.

"Dr. Mitchell, would you mind moving away from the glass?" Tilda kicked off her high heels and grabbed a pair of jogging shoes. She crossed the corridor, took him gently by the arm, and urged him into the alcove. "You, too, Ms. Maples. There's likely to be some shooting in a moment." She sat in one of the comfortable lounge chairs with the Magnum in her lap, and calmly slipped into her shoes.

Blaine did as he was told, but peered around the corner of the alcove. Alex, Lawson, and MacDonald stood guard in the middle of the entry with their weapons drawn. Only minutes before, Lawson had held MacDonald at gunpoint; now the two men prepared to fight shoulder to shoulder against a common enemy.

"Get over here, Taylor!" Lawson said harshly. When the detective hesitated, Lawson shouted, "*Now!*" Taylor got. "And stand in front of me. If you live through this, I'll kill you myself."

Peering around the corner of the alcove, Blaine saw half a dozen men slinking through the Institute's parking lot. They wore short dark jackets as protection from the cold; some were armed with Springfield carbines, some with Thompson submachine guns. Blaine pulled out his handgun. "What are we waiting for? Let's go after them."

"Those are our men, Dr. Mitchell," Tilda cooed. "They're preparing an outer defense."

"What do you mean 'our' men? And what are you—"

He pointed at the .44 Magnum.

"CIA, Dr. Mitchell. Has Mr. Hudson completed his briefing?"

Blaine was more confused than ever. "We were interrupted by—" He turned around, but saw no sign of either Greenstein or Young.

"You were right about the trucks, Lawson." Hudson dropped the phone in the cradle and turned to face the lawmen lined up across the entry corridor. "The South American gang must have hijacked that missing load. Two of them were taken out on the edge of town, but the rest of them—"

"Are here," Blaine blurted. The glass doors gave him a perfect view of the long driveway and closed entrance gate. Fred dashed out of the guard shack, checked the lock and chain across the wire gate, and ran straight for the double doors. Blaine suddenly felt sick about the retiree caught in the middle of something that he should have no part of.

Two of the Ford pickup trucks stopped at the head of the driveway; the low sun glinted off unmistakably new paint, and cast long shadows to the side. The other truck proceeded along the blacktop with ever quickening speed.

When Fred came in through the front door he had a Remington autopump 12-gauge shotgun over his shoulder. "Everything is set, Mr. Hudson."

"Snipers on the roof?"

He nodded. "And the rest of the staff was sent home early. Tilda took care of that."

"Good." Hudson appeared smug and complacent. "If the guys want war, we'll give it to them."

The green pickup made no attempt to reduce speed as it approached the locked gate. Three men sat across the truck's front seat, and an armed squad of cowboys, crouched for impact, lined both sides of the rear bed. When the Ford hit the gate it was going at least fifty miles per hour. Blaine expected to see the chain snap, the center posts spring apart, and the two gates flung wide; but that happened only in the movies, where the gates were rigged to separate. In reality, the truck tore only partway through the thick wire mesh, bent the anchor posts inward, and came to a grinding halt with the wire gates wrapped tight over its roof like a Christmas package for the Green Giant.

The man sitting in the middle crashed through the windshield wearing the rearview mirror on his forehead like a hood ornament. His body hung in the shattered glass, trapped by the reinforced wire mesh. The driver and passenger were saved by their seatbelts. The commando cowboys in the back were slammed against the cab by the momentum; they picked themselves up one by one. It was obvious from the way they ran their hands over their bodies that they had suffered injuries in the collision.

"They'll need more than a high-speed battering ram to get through that. The columns are reinforced concrete with twelve-inch I-beams buried ten feet in the ground." Hudson watched the assault as if it were a Sunday afternoon ball game. He would not have looked out of place sipping a can of beer. "The gate is high-tensile steel."

Blaine was astonished to learn that the barricade he thought was intended to keep out burglers and mischievous teenagers was in fact as impregnable as a castle rampart. He no longer wondered about the purpose of the strip wire stretched along the top of the fence.

"Fred, get ready to trip the claymores."

Without a word, Fred pulled open a white metal panel that blended in perfectly with the all-white decor of the lobby. The top half of the breaker box contained an array of disconnect switches that were labeled according to the circuits they controlled. The lower half was a locked compartment for which Fred produced a key. Inside were two rows of toggle switches. The left row was tagged "Perimeter Defenses," the right row "Entrance Defenses." The individual toggles had numbers only.

Since the Ford's cab doors were pinned shut by the fence wire, the driver and passenger smashed out the rear window glass and climbed through the jagged opening into the bed. The commando team only sluggishly pulled itself together. Someone kicked open the tail gate. The squad crawled out as if they were leaving the protection of an armored personnel carrier, and assembled along both sides of the pickup. One man, too injured by the crash to move other than feebly, provided cover from the bed.

Hudson nodded. "Just trip the odds, Fred. We'll save the evens for the next batch."

As soon as Fred flipped the switch, the electrical contact detonated a dozen canisters of C-4 explosive. The hedgerow disintegrated. Claymore antipersonnel mines cleverly concealed in the lower branches blasted thousands of steel pellets in a crisscross pattern that caught the cowboy team in a deadly crossfire. The only survivor was the injured man who remained in the back of the truck.

Blaine was speechless. He had seen similar ambushes in Vietnam; but that was a jungle, a war zone, not a pleasant New England farming community. Then he realized that war was where you found it. To the Montagnards, the central highlands was as pastoral as Plymouth Rock to the Pilgrims. Ideology created battlegrounds, not geography.

Marybeth wrapped her arms around Blaine's waist. "I don't believe this. I don't *want* to believe it."

The second truck started down the driveway, with the third one right behind it.

"What the hell do they think they're going to—"

Lawson was cut off as the embedded pickup truck exploded in a titanic ball of flame that vaporized the steel gate, obliterated the guard shack, and destroyed the reinforced columns. Sheets of fire lashed outward and upward into a fireball the size of a big bungalow. Molten steel and chunks of concrete followed the expanding gases by a fraction of a second. The glass doors of the Institute were pelted with flying debris.

Instinctively, Blaine fell back into the alcove, dragging Marybeth with him, and landed hard upon the floor. They were not alone, as everyone else had react-ed the same way. The whole group lay in a tangle of arms and legs and dropped weapons. When Blaine regained control of his senses, he discovered that he was uninjured.

A moment later Alex scrambled over Blaine. "Are you okay?" Blaine barely nodded. Then Alex scooped up Marybeth and cradled her head in his lap. "Marybeth?"

She coughed, and nodded weakly.

Hudson stood up brushing off his clothes. "Good thing the front doors are made of bullet-proof glass."

Taylor wasted no time in rushing to Tilda's aid, even though she was quite capable of taking care of herself. There was no time to do anything other than assume defensive postures, for the next truck, a red one, was bearing down on the still-burning opening.

"Shall I blow the driveway?" Fred asked.

"No, save it in case they bring in reserves. We can handle two lousy pickup trucks. But give them the other line of claymores."

Fred tripped the toggle. Another barrage of pellets blasted across the blacktop, turning the next truck into Swiss cheese. The driver lost momentary control when his window was blasted in. The truck swerved onto the grass, then swerved back onto the macadam, and man-aged to steer straight through the blazing remains of the demolition truck.

"Oh, no," breathed Lawson.

The second truck emerged from the smoke like a juggernaut, bound for destruction. It veered to the side, skidded when the driver applied the brakes, and slid into Captain Lawson's car. The CIA snipers on the Institute's roof pummeled the cab and bed with accu-rate gunfire that instantly decimated the gauchos. The survivors of the first enfilade hardly had time to raise their weapons before they were shot to pieces.

The last man fell dead about the time the third pick-up truck entered the fracas. It charged through the parking lot, bounced over the curb, and screamed along the sidewalk toward the front door as the rooftop sharpshooters realigned their sights. Blaine saw holes appear in the pickup's windshield, but that did not slow down the truck. At that point, even if the driver died of his wounds there was no way the white pickup was going to be deterred from its point of aim.

"*Get out!*" Hudson was the first to heed his own warning.

The Institute's defenders dived into the lobby alcoves just as the truck hit the front entrance. The terrible crinkling of glass was accompanied by the crash of fenders and door frames. When the front wheels bounced over the sill, the top of the cab gouged into the drop-ceiling tiles, snagged the metal framework, and dragged down the supporting grid, acoustical tiles, telephone wires, electrical cables, and plumbing conduits. The truck left a trail of sparks and spun glass insulation as it carved a path through the all-white furniture and gouged through the linoleum into the floor.

The truck smashed into the far wall where the next set of doors led into the corridor. Because the stairwell doubled as the fire escape, it was constructed of cement and cinder block. The pickup's hood crumpled like a child's toy; the driver was crushed when the engine sheered off its mounts and was driven backward through the dashboard. The center passenger became part of the building structure, and the cowboy riding shotgun was squashed under the collapsing block work.

Out of the cloud of smoke, dust, and flames came one of the gauchos with his Uzi aimed low. Before he had a chance to clear his eyes, Tilda very calmly blew his head off with her .44 Magnum.

"They may be wearing vests," she said calmly.

From the other side of the lobby Hudson leaped over the desk, blasting away. Lawson, Taylor, and Fred were slower, but just as effective. Alex and Blaine rose up together and added their guns to the firepower that was directed at the cowboys in the back of the pickup truck. Returning shots were erratic and misdirected; the cowboys were blinded by insulation raining from the ceiling and streams of water spouting from severed sprinkler pipes. The fusillade ended as suddenly as it began.

The dust was still settling as Marybeth grabbed a fire extinguisher and waded into the flame-filled lobby. She sprayed the small blazes that sprang up in the wake of the gunfight, put out a couple of electrical fires, covered the pickup's gas tank with white foam in case it had been shot through, and doused pieces of smoldering furniture.

Blaine stumbled across what was left of the lobby, holding his smoking Glock like a victorious gunslinger. He waved his hand in front of his face; it was difficult to get enough air to breathe. He stopped face to face with Lawson. The police chief was still standing poised for action, with his empty pistol held at arm's length, as if he refused to believe that the firefight was over. Water fell like rain from sprinkler heads and broken pipes.

"Lawson, you forgot to read them their rights."

Chapter 19

"I'm not a spy. I know it looks bad but you've got to believe me."

Joseph Young's office was brightly lit and crowded. Blaine paced nervously from one end to the other, like a tiger in a cage. Marybeth stood in a corner with her arms folded. Alex watched expressionlessly as events unfolded.

"Dr. Mitchell, would you move away from the window, please?" Hudson's deep voice was smooth but commanding.

With the overhead fluorescent's reflecting off the glass, the world beyond was a nether region of formless, impenetrable black. Only when he was close could Blaine look through it and see the horde of CIA agents in the parking lot, clearing debris and packing bodies by the light of the post lamps.

"Is it booby trapped, too?" Blaine found it intolerable that the Institute had been constructed with built-in defenses, that the hedges and pavements were underlain with mines, that the outer perimeter was rigged with explosives, and that there were probably other military expedients buried on the grounds or concealed behind false walls. Nevertheless, he did what Hudson suggested.

"No, but a good sniper on the road could easily put a bullet through a backlit body."

Blaine knew he was right; at one time he could probably have done it himself. He stepped to the side where he was protected by shadow and the brick facade. "What happened? Did they run out of bullet-proof glass?" The question was rhetorical but his next one was not. "Hudson, is the Institute bugged? Do you have hidden cameras and secret microphones watching us all the time, like Big Brother?"

"No, we rely on live operatives for intelligence." At least Hudson was frank. Tilda and Fred certainly had

Blaine fooled; he could never have envisioned either of them as gun-toting undercover agents. Hudson referred briefly to his notebook and continued his interrogation. "Dr. Young, according to our confidential files you've had quite a few telephone conversations with members of the Soviet scientific community. In particular, one Konstantin Kravtsov. What was the nature of the calls?"

Young was sweating like a steak on the grill. "You already knew about that?"

"We know quite a lot about what goes on here at the Institute. It's our business to know. What *you* don't know is how much *we* know. I suggest that you be truthful with us."

Now it was Blaine's turn to stick up for his boss. "Hudson, why would he have invited us up here to talk about this if he had anything to hide? We regularly correspond with scientists all over the world in order to share scientific knowledge. It's common practice in our field. It's you paranoid government types that—"

"Excuse me, Dr. Mitchell. You're obviously sensitive about the matter. But we do have to consider a Soviet assassin who at this very minute is probably skulking through the woods less than a quarter mile away, just waiting for a chance to slip a Ricin dart into your skin. Now, I'm not hurling any accusations yet. But I do need to ascertain how much of our organization has been compromised. And for that I need some straightforward answers."

Blaine scowled, but kept quiet.

"I swear you will have my full cooperation, Mr. Hudson. I just—you may find me guilty of naive indiscretion, but I am innocent of any charges of conspiring with the enemy. I do feel, however, that I may have been responsible in some small way for precipitating the, uh, Soviet, uh, contract put out on my colleague, Dr. Mitchell."

"Okay. Why don't you tell me how that came about?"

"Yes, of course." Young took a handkerchief out of

his suit pocket and wiped a gallon of perspiration off his forehead. "I think Dr. Mitchell will agree that Dr. Kravtsov is one of the Soviet Union's leading authorities on brain disorders. He has recently become director of the Institute for Psychical Research. We have met on several occasions, at international conferences, when we were both doing neurological research. As Dr. Mitchell suggested, it is not uncommon for scientists of all disciplines to meet and share the results of their work. It is, in fact, part of the scientific process of cooperative—"

"Please, Dr. Young. Quit rambling and get to the point."

"Yes, of course. I apologize. Well, in short, then, I've kept Dr. Kravtsov apprised of our progress through regular scientific channels, as he has kept me apprised of his. It is all very open and above board. We communicate through a computer network so that all our correspondence is saved for future reference—"

"Do you have hard copies available?"

"I seldom generate paper ephemera; all it does is take up filing cabinet space. I read incoming messages on my screen—" He indicated one of the monitors on the shelf behind him. "—then save them under a numerical entry code for later retrieval—"

"And now that your data banks have been completely erased, those records are nothing more than random magnetic bits. How convenient."

Young appeared stymied. He transfixed Marybeth with an incredulous stare. "Is this true, Ms. Maples? I thought you were working out the bugs."

"So much has happened today that I never got around to telling you. The computer has been sabotaged by a deadly virus that turned all our data into garbage. Even the subroutines were wiped out. I'm sorry."

"But, that's impossible. Why would anyone do such a thing?"

"For the same reason 'someone' has either stolen or destroyed all of Dr. Mitchell's paper files and has made repeated attempts on his life. With no records and with the project leader out of the way, our Soviet competitors stand to gain immeasurably. In my mind, the question is not why, but how. Access to your computer codes is limited to Institute staff members; this has to be an inside job."

"No, Hudson. You're way off base on that." Marybeth unfolded her arms and walked across the deep pile carpet to confront the CIA man. "It's true our data files have passwords as protection against illegal entry, but they can be broken by any really good programmer. I could do it myself. And because our computer is networked and tied in with so many electronic bulletin and mail systems it can be accessed in a variety of ways."

"You people really stick together, don't you?"

"I thought you weren't making accusations." Marybeth eyed Hudson defiantly, with her jaw clenched and her thin lips pursed tightly together.

Hudson glared, and was about to comment when Young suddenly stood up and walked around the desk. "I have backups, you know."

"Backups for what?" Hudson asked.

"For the data files." He said it matter-of-factly. He threw back his shoulders with a slight return of self-assurance. "In there."

"You do?" Marybeth cocked her head like a startled egret.

"Of course. You would not know this, but one of my responsibilities as director is to personally backup our computer files. Protocol, you know," he added, apologetically. He marched past Hudson to a closet-sized door behind which sat a tall office safe. He confidently spun the combination dial and unlocked the heavy steel door, then pulled it open to reveal stacked trays on which were piled notebooks, loose papers, printed reports, and cans of magnetic tape. "I do it on a weekly basis, usually on Saturday when I am here alone." He pulled out a flat can and checked the date. "Every six months I clean out the safe and place the tapes in our deep storage vault in the basement. I did not backup this week's work because the computer was down, but here is last week's cumulative backup."

Blaine could hardly contain his exuberance. He jumped on Young like a long lost army buddy, and hugged him hard. "In my book you'll always be the mightiest Joe Young. I love you." He planted a resounding kiss on Young's cheek, making the older man wince.

"I wish you'd treat me that way," Marybeth said wistfully.

Young was shocked into silent submission. He did not know how to respond to such an overture of exhilaration. For a man who did not like to be touched, Young appeared sorely affected.

Alex, however, was not emotionally involved. "Hudson, how is it that you didn't know about the backup system?"

Hudson smirked. "I did. I was just testing." He took the can, inspected it, and handed it to Marybeth. "Can you back this up and boot it into the computer?"

"Yes, but first I have to make sure the virus has eaten itself out."

Blaine breathed a huge sigh of relief, then gave Marybeth the kiss she asked for. He did not even care about Hudson's game playing. "That means that we're back in business, and that the only data we've lost are those statistical analyses you generated during the week."

She tapped her temple. "I've got that locked away in short-term memory. Give me a few hours and I can regenerate it."

"I love you, too, Marybeth."

"I know—like a sister." She winked to let Blaine know she was only teasing, then tapped a long fingernail on the can. "This also means we've got the previous week's brain wave function refinements and—" She stopped, and looked at Hudson. "We'll talk about it later."

The CIA man pursed his lips. "Thank you, Ms. Maples." To the director, "All right, Dr. Young. That may let you off the hook on that count. But what were you saying about being responsible for sicking a Soviet assassin on Dr. Mitchell? And be brief."

Young breathed deeply, and dabbed off a few more beads of perspiration. "Dr. Kravtsov warned me that trouble was brewing. As I said, we knew each other before each of us attained our respective directorships. We have always communicated freely despite the frigidity between our governments. Science exists on a level that spurns political overtones and . . . Anyway, as soon as Dr. Mitchell's paper was published in the *Journal*, copies of which are also distributed in the Soviet Union, Dr. Kravtsov called me. I would have expected him to be excited over our success, uh, over Dr. Mitchell's success, but instead he was in near panic. He had been temporarily suspended from his duties, and was under investigation for divulging state secrets. Apparently, Dr. Mitchell's discoveries closely approximated their own. The last thing he told me was that lives were at stake. I—I have not been able to contact him since Monday, and I fear for the worst. I was angry on one hand because the reputation of the Institute would undoubtedly suffer if it could be proven that Dr. Mitchell had used proprietary information without giving due credit, and upset on the other hand because I did not know *whose* lives were at stake.

"Believe me, I did not sleep at all that night. I tossed in my bed in a cold sweat. My wife tried to . . .Anyway, I was practically distraught. I knew I had to do something about the situation but had no idea what that would be. I am a doctor, a scientist, an administrator—not an expert on diplomatic relations. My position here is precarious; any incident that affects the Institute reflects on me. I did not want to get directly involved in any skullduggery. I . . . Anyway, on Tuesday I tried calling Dr. Kravtsov. His secretary told me that he had suddenly taken ill and was no longer available. The way she said it sounded ominous. Dr. Mitchell was incommunicado and, in my mind, possibly in danger. So, that evening on my way home I stopped at a phone booth and called the FBI."

"*You* called them?" Blaine exploded.

"Blaine, I did not know what else to do. I was scared. I realize now that I was thinking more of myself than of you and the Institute, but I was trying to preserve my anonymity in case the situation was nothing more than the paranoid delusion of an insecure old man." He turned to Hudson and pleaded with hands outstretched. "But I'm not a spy. You've got to believe that. I admit that I have exchanged numerous communications with a foreign national—"

Hudson cut him off with a wave of the hand. "All right, Young, all right. If your conscience is clear you have nothing to worry about. We'll see if your correspondence corroborates your story. Just don't leave the country. And we'll see what we can find out about Dr. Kravtsov. In the meantime we've still got Nabakov to worry about. He's out there, lurking in the dark, waiting for the right time. I know it; I can feel it."

"I can feel it, too."

All eyes turned to Marybeth.

She seemed in somewhat of a daze. She glanced around the ceiling as if she were following the flight pattern of a circling bee. "I've got the strangest feeling that we're being watched—that there's someone else in the room with as. Someone—invisible. It's—it's eerie." She shuddered, as if a cold draft of air had suddenly chilled her. She hugged her chest. "It's ghostly."

The Christmas presence, Blaine thought. But the moment was too serious for jokes. Whenever Marybeth had feelings that were not for him, he paid attention. He scanned the ceiling for giant insects or miniature hovercraft: anything that could be manipulated by minute telepathic energy beams. "Hudson, as a scientist I hate to admit this, but Marybeth sees things that normal people don't. Like a cat, you know?"

Hudson closed the notebook that he held in his hands, as if his inked scrawl might be read by a supernatural force.

"I had the same feeling last night in the dormitory."

"When Nabakov was chasing us?" Alex wondered.

"Yes. I know you think I'm a weirdo, but . . . "

"I believe you." Alex came up on her from behind and placed his hands softly on her shoulders. "I believe that some people have a sixth sense, an ability to perceive intangibles that other people, more materialistic people, can't. Maybe it's just a hunch, but—"

"I don't see anything, but I sure as hell won't deny your feelings." Hudson craned his neck as he looked around the room. "I *can't* deny your feelings—not in light of what I know about Soviet advances in parapsychology. They're way ahead of us in the more esoteric branches of mind research."

Marybeth spun her head abruptly, as if she were following a low-flying jet buzzing a landing field. "It's gone. It went right through that wall." She nodded with her chin toward the outside.

Young swallowed hard. "This is quite beyond—"

A gunshot sounded in the distance, from the direction in which Marybeth's sightless eyes stared. The noise broke her trance. She fell back into Alex's arms.

"It's Nabakov," breathed Hudson.

Blaine cringed instinctively as a horde of spiders crawled up his spine. His throat was a ball of cotton; he swallowed three bales before he was able to speak. "We must be using the same Ouija board."

"Okay, everybody, let's get back downstairs and find out what's going on. You too, Young. Nobody stays alone." Hudson opened the door and led the way down to the lobby where he had established headquarters.

Tilda was very efficiently handling the phone lines and radios: better than she ever had as the Institute's receptionist. "Sir, perimeter patrol reports a contact in the northeast quadrant. There were no casualties, but the intruder got away."

"Was he armed?"

"They said he was carrying a stick."

Blaine felt the tension run out of his muscles like melted ice cream. "Probably some kid out on a snark hunt. They always—"

"Nabakov."

Blaine turned and saw MacDonald approaching. He carried Greenstein by the scruff of the neck, and by the way the reporter swung his feet he must have been an inch or so off the floor.

"It's no stick. It's a blowgun."

Greenstein struggled silently, gasping for air.

"It's what he was trying to shoot you with last night in the parking lot."

"Oh, come on," Blaine started. "That's child's stuff—"

Captain Lawson appeared from around the wreckage of the pickup, which was still sitting in the middle of the lobby. Canvas shrouds had been hung across the doorway to keep out the bitter, nighttime cold. Clouds had rolled in after sunset and the sky appeared ominous. The weather was changing. "It's true, though. I sent Taylor to check it out. He just phoned in a report. Said he found a plastic dart embedded in the fender of the Cadillac at Westmoreland, not a bullet hole. Must have been from when the Ruskie fired at you and you ducked to see if the wop was dead. He took it out very carefully. We'll save it for analysis, but I'm sure it'll show traces of Ricin." To Alex, "It's a good thing we kept the area roped off, or somebody might have meddled with the evidence and killed himself in the process. And another thing. Ronson phoned in from Boston, said to tell you that Blaine Appleton Mitchell's house was full of thumbtacks, just like Dr. Mitchell's. This Nabakov is a real busy fellow." To MacDonald, "This other doctor lived right off the park where you lost the Ruskie on Wednesday night. I figure the Russians didn't know too much about Dr. Mitchell, about where he lived, or if he had more than one place. They looked him up in the physicians' directory, got confused with the names, and decided to cover all bets. Coincidentally, it turns out that *that* Dr. Mitchell had been dealing with the same South American gang that came after *this* Dr. Mitchell. Small world." He ended his report with a smug turn of the lips, then added, "Oh, and Hudson, thanks for the loan of the car. My department's getting real short of vehicles."

Hudson nodded. "Angus, where did you find the inkslinger?"

"Hiding in a stall in the downstairs lady's room." When MacDonald let go of the newshawk he crumpled to the floor like an unpotted plant. He rubbed his throat and tried to suck in some air. "Don't know what kind of story he was after this time, but I bet it'll be a humdinger."

"All right, Greenstein. I don't want you here, but you're here. And I've got every available operative beating the bushes for Nabakov. This building is under siege as long as we've got what he wants. I want you to stay out of the way and out of trouble; and if you give me any grief, Tilda and Fred have orders to zip you up in a body bag—permanently. Do I make myself clear?"

Greenstein croaked with an exaggerated nod.

"And no reporting. This entire operation is under government censorship. You violate that and you'll spend the rest of your life doing exposés in Leavenworth. Got that?"

He nodded again.

Hudson promptly ignored him. "Lawson, you're doing a good job here. This is the first opportunity I've had to say so. And not just because you got the drop on me and this big hunk of flesh, but because you're thinking ahead. I like that. I also like the fact that you're not bucking my authority with jurisdictional disputes. So many times the local cops won't cooperate with us because they view us as trespassers on their turf."

"To tell you the truth, Hudson, until yesterday I hated feds. They always come in highhanded, like they were more important than anybody else. I especially felt that way when I had to divert patrol cars to look for some runaway convict the other night. Now that I've seen what it's all about, I realize that sometimes your work is a little bigger than pulling speeders off the road and handing out tickets. And if it hadn't been for Foley here, half my men would be dead by now because of that crazy Russian and his poison darts. He's the one you ought to thank."

"Foley, I'll see to it that you get a very honorable mention in my report. Dickerson will get a signed copy. I realize you're pretty green in the field, but for an agent on his first assignment you've done quite well. Thanks to you, Dr. Mitchell is still alive. If you ever want to transfer to the CIA, I'll vouch for you."

"Well, uh, thanks to both of you." Alex cleared his throat in obvious discomfort. "But I think we should wait until this whole mess is over before we start writing accolades. Besides, I've been nothing more than a bodyguard. You're fighting the real battle: you with your men patrolling the grounds, Lawson with his troopers scouting the streets." He glanced nervously from one to the other. "Now, uh, if you'll excuse me, I've got to accompany Blaine and Marybeth to the laboratory. They've got some work to do, and I can't let them out of my sight."

Hudson smiled. "You do that, Foley. Mitchell is your responsibility; mine is protecting this compound."

Alex nodded wordlessly, then signaled Blaine and Marybeth with a tilt of the head. They followed him out of the lobby and down the stairwell. Because he walked so fast they did not have a chance to talk until they were halfway along the lower main corridor.

"Alex, let me stop off and pick up my jogging shoes," Marybeth said. "I thought we were just going to the lab."

"Yes, what's the rush? I had a few things I wanted to say to Greenstein—none of them printable. I'd also like to lock him up in a cage with the rest of the apes."

"Sorry, there's no time for jokes. I want to have another session with that skullcap apparatus."

"Uh, oh," Blaine whined. "Our first addict."

"Blaine, please. This is serious. I—I—" Alex stopped in the middle of the corridor and faced both his companions. "I was in that conference room with Lawson and Hudson and MacDonald."

"So, we all were." Blaine exchanged a questioning

look with Marybeth. "So what?"

"No, I mean I was in there before we ran in on them. Before our bodies got there—" He must have realized how irrational he sounded.

"Alex, are you feeling well?" Marybeth used her best bedside tone. "None of us has had much sleep, you least of all—"

"I'm wide awake—perfectly awake—more awake than I've ever been in my life. I've experienced something extraordinary, something that shakes the very foundations of my life—of my soul. I was in that room. Mentally. Projected there by the bypass skullcap, or by whatever chemicals are triggered in the brain from the frequencies that are generated by the skullcap."

"No, Alex. You were in there by the power of suggestion, or by memory." Blaine was gentle, as he always was with patients bordering on hysterics. "Don't you remember that I took you on a quick tour of the building this morning, before we took our showers? I mean, don't you remember consciously?"

"Of course I remember. But that has nothing to do with it. I'm telling you I was in there when Lawson clipped MacDonald's ear. I saw it happen."

Blaine slowly shook his head. "No. You heard the shot while you were having an electronically induced hallucinatory experience, Marybeth brought you down, we ran into the room, you saw Lawson holding a gun on MacDonald and Hudson, and in your mind the scenes all ran together so that afterward you confused the exact order of events and rearranged them in a highly imaginative fashion. It happens all the time. Did you know that people under anesthesia sometimes recall snippets of conversation between doctors and nurses? It's true. That's the reason that patients pronounced clinically dead, and who have out-of-body experiences, are sometimes able to describe what was going on around them before they were resuscitated. Just because the heart stops beating and the lungs stop taking in air doesn't mean that the senses cease to function. The ears still pick up sounds that the patient interprets subconsciously; he'll hear a clanging sound, and later report 'seeing' from overhead a surgeon dropping a scalpel."

"This was *real*, I tell you."

"Of course it seems real to you. Don't you think I remember Zarzinski working on my body as I lay there on the jungle floor? But I didn't actually see him. I heard him, and my brain converted those sounds into a visual image. The same way I 'saw' my buddies waiting for us in the Huey. It's easy to play tricks on the mind—"

"This was no trick. Just think back for a moment, to when we jumped into the room after Lawson fired the shot. Don't you remember that I had my gun pointing right at MacDonald's chest? That's because I already knew where he was standing."

"Alex, I think you're reaching for—"

"You don't believe me? Then watch this." Alex spun on his heel, and left Blaine and Marybeth momentarily in the dust. He shoved open the conference room door; they walked in behind him. He pranced straight to the other end of the room, rounded the end of the long table, and placed his finger down low on the wall where a tiny hole pierced the paneling. "I knew exactly where it was because I saw wood chips flying after Lawson pulled the trigger. MacDonald and Hudson were hiding behind the table."

Blaine breathed deeply. "Very good, Alex. But you could have spotted that hole when you took away their guns, and just put it in the back of your mind."

"Besides," added Marybeth, "It doesn't take much of a detective to figure out that if MacDonald was here and Lawson was over there, the path of his bullet would end up here."

"I don't understand you two. You've spent years developing brain wave functions and hormone triggering frequencies, you readily admit that the brain is an organ of incredible complexity, and that the mind is the most powerful, most complicated, and least understood biological mechanism in evolutionary history. You more than anyone know that the brain-mind has vast, untapped resources. Why, then, are you so quick to disbelieve that you may have tapped into one of its unknown abilities?"

Blaine did his best not to be conciliatory. "Alex, mind over matter is another matter—"

"I'm not talking about the mental movement of material objects. I'm talking about the mind instructing the brain to project the mind away from the brain. What is it in theory that makes that impossible?"

"Think about our Edison bulb, Alex. Can light exist away from the filament?"

Chapter 20

"I can't believe I'm doing this. I must be out of my mind."

Nevertheless, Blaine continued making the hardwire connections between the Institute's mainframe and the bypass skullcaps. There were two transportable units in functioning condition. The original, called BS-1, was the first production model made after the prototype chair unit cleared the design stage. BS-2 had only recently been completed; its electronics were more miniaturized, and the battery pack was enlarged to give it more sensitivity and longer range and duration. The batteries were rechargeable nickel-cadmium that could be rejuvenated only from the heavy-duty transformer lag-bolted to the floor in the basement assembly area. Self-contained direct current was more suitable than plug-in alternating current because of the delicate nature of the bypass units. Batteries ensured control over current flow, and obviated the need for an inverter and for protection against voltage drops and surges and against power interruption.

"Not yet, but you will be shortly. Blaine, mind my words: somewhere deep in your subconscious you know that mental broadcast is theoretically feasible, that the energy fields that define our perceptual existence can be projected like the beam of a searchlight. Don't ask me how it works. You're the scientist; you figure it out. But for now just accept the fact that it can be done."

"I'll keep an open mind, but if you really believe in mental transmission you've been reading too much Greenstein. Marybeth, how close are you to making the data transfer?"

"Just about done." Marybeth sat straight-backed at her terminal, a position from which she had hardly moved in the previous two hours. Her coffee cup sat on the desk next to her, empty but for an ugly, blackened smudge on the bottom that discolored the white glossy china. Her eyes were glued to the screen with an intensity that would have put most people to sleep after just a few minutes, or would have mesmerized them. "I've input all the updated statistical analyses. Now I'm just assigning entry fields and rearranging data files." Her fingers flew across the keyboard with the precision of a concert pianist, not slowed at all by the sidelong conversation. "Once the new data are integrated with the program I can transmit the renovated operating system in a few seconds."

Blaine aligned the pin connectors with the female socket, pushed them in, and tightened the knurled nut until it was snug against the bulkhead. "Alex, if you're even partway right, we could be on to a new interpretation of hitherto unexplained and largely ignored psychic phenomena."

"Make up your mind, will you, Blaine?" Marybeth shoved her chair back on its rollers and skated across the linoleum to a different workstation. She keyed in a set of sequential instructions. "One minute you're saying it's impossible, the next you can't wait to try it out."

"I can't help it. Part of me is thrilled to death by— uh, sorry, I didn't mean it quite that way. Part of me is thrilled to near-death by the possibility of ethereal mind transference, while part of me maintains the strictly reductionistic view that the very idea is insane."

"You're a man of two minds."

"Physician, know thyselves."

Blaine sighed more from trepidation of what he was contemplating than from exasperation over the banter. A taste of his own medicine made him realize how he must sound when he used the same tactic as bravado to counteract his inner feelings. "You two aren't helping my peace of mind." He cringed, and shook his head. "No, I didn't mean that."

"Blaine, darling, I've never seen you so on edge before. I think Alex is right in more ways than one. You're really nervous over what may turn out to be the biggest scientific breakthrough since Newton bit the apple, or Einstein put the universe in its place. And you're afraid that if it's true your whole concept of reality will be knocked off its pedestal."

"Makes sense to me."

"So does a mind-powered scanner like Hudson says the Russians have invented. Suppose this Nabakov fellow is using a device similar to our own? Suppose the Russians have a stronger mind set than we have? It could explain a lot about what's been happening—like the feeling I had last night in the woods, that we were being watched. You believed me then, what made you change your mind?"

"Who says I believed you?"

"Blaine, you know that we've always had a rapport. Oh, I don't mean a romantic affinity. I know you think I'm not your type, although I'd give anything to know what the hell your type is. But we've established a good working relationship and a bond of mutual trust because we respect each other's opinions. I'm your balance, Blaine, against your ingrained empirical view of life and reality. Last night, when Nabakov was waiting for us everywhere we went, I told you I could sense that we were being followed. I didn't know how; it was just a vague, uncomfortable feeling—because I was so distracted by the cold; but it was there. And you believed me. I know you did because you acted upon it. You've either forgotten, or you've buried it deep down inside of you because you can't explain it. But think about it.

"When we were in the dormitory and the fire alarm wires had been pulled out, you made a point of saying out loud exactly where we were going to go and what we were going to do. Then, as soon as we got outside, without a spoken word, you signaled for us to run as fast as we could in a different direction. It was as if you had some inkling that whoever we were up against had some way of listening in on our conversations. Logically that made no sense. But you did it."

Blaine felt a chill that was not inspired by low temperature; the basement rooms were adequately heated. "Marybeth, I don't know what was going through my mind at the time. I was as cold as you were; I wasn't thinking straight. But if I had to take a guess at my motivation, and rationalization, I'd have to say that I acted mostly on impulse, a hunch, a subconscious ratiocination that I picked up years ago during long jungle patrols. Whenever what you're doing doesn't work, anything different, no matter how radical, has more chance of success than that which has already proven itself unsuccessful. It's a logical approach to an illogical situation." He paused for a moment to collect his thoughts. "I've also learned to trust your instincts. I've never understood the mechanism of feminine intuition—no chauvinism intended—but I've come to accept it. Yours in particular. You have the kind of mind that sees things intuitively that I have to prove to myself. I can't explain it, and neither can you. It's just another one of the great marvels of the human mind that I'd like to understand." He took a deep breath. "And, now that you force me to think about it, I think Alex has your kind of sensitivity. You two are very much alike. You blend a certain amount of emotion into your thought processes—something that I just can't do. When I get a gut feeling it's just an upset stomach. Alex, you've had some pretty good hunches so far. I'm at least willing to give this one a try, and see where it goes. That kind of open-mindedness is the basis of scientific investigation."

"That's the spirit."

Marybeth picked up one of the skullcaps and checked the leads. "Maybe this is the spirit. Or the evocation of human spirit." She handed the BS-1 unit to Alex and motioned for him to sit down in the swivel chair that had been dragged in from the conference room for the occasion. "We'll soon know."

Blaine backed the other chair up to the power pack of the BS-2 unit, and sat down. He was adept enough to position the skullcap on his own head. "Out of body, out of mind, I always say. But I sure as hell hope I'm wrong."

"You know something? I almost hope you're right."

Alex let Marybeth affix the skullcap and adjust it properly. "Because if this experiment proves that the soul is an externalization of the mind, which is caused by chemical reduction within the brain, I could be facing excommunication."

"I'll vouch for your absolution. But right now, I'm more concerned with getting through *this* life than preparing for the next one."

"Let's not discuss theology until we have to." Marybeth held the control box where Alex could see it. "Hold this in one hand and place the fingers of your other hand on the touchpad. Like this."

Since the intended purpose of the bypass skullcap was not just for the termination of pain but for biofeedback training, the units were designed to be handled by a patient in bed. The skullcap was attached to the battery pack/central processing unit by means of a long extension cord; a second cable, about the diameter of a telephone wire, fed a touchpad with two tilt buttons to regulate voltage and to modulate frequency.

"The electrodes are self-seeking. That is, I've programmed the computer to automatically zero in on the specific points within the brain that trigger the hormone release functions." Marybeth guided Alex's fingers over the buttons, as she had done with so many patients since the unit first went on trial. "You govern the fluxion intensity and power output according to your tolerance level. Push up, or away from you, to increase intensity and output, push down, or toward you, to decrease. The lever on the side is a kill switch. Sorry, I didn't mean it that way. It turns off the unit, not the user. Once you get the feel of it, it's just like playing Space Invaders."

Blaine powered up and was ready to go. With the buttons at his fingertips he was master of his own fate. He felt instant relief from the nagging pain on his left palm, where the patch of skin had been torn off the night before. Also, he no longer felt the headache that had been building unnoticed, or the creeping numbness in his back where the exit wound of the NVA bullet had damaged the nerves. Normally, a few minutes of meditation would have enabled him to control these minor aches and pains, but he had been too busy to take advantage of his own biofeedback training. "How do you feel?"

"I don't feel a thing."

"The unit must be working," Marybeth announced.

"Now remember, I'll be the tour guide." Blaine boosted the fluxion intensity until he felt the onset of separation, then increased the power output. He snapped out of his body like a broken rubber band. After a moment of disorientation he had the vague feeling that his mind was floating just below the ceiling and that he was looking down on the occupants of the room. His hair was a mess. "I'll talk you through the procedure so you don't go schizoid on us. Let the power of my suggestion determine our course through dreamland."

He heard Alex gasp, and saw his body convulse as if electroshockers had jolted him back to life.

"I'm through. I'm up here under the lights."

"Don't get burnt. Marybeth, hold onto him if he gets rammy. Try to remember, Alex, that this is all an illusion. When we first experimented with the bypass units we found that people—research assistants, not patients—often swung their arms or attempted to walk because the hallucination seemed real until they accepted it for what it was. Like people wearing Walkman's singing along to music, forgetting that others were unaware of what they were hearing."

"You know, it's no brighter here next to the fluorescent tubes than it is on the floor."

"Of course not. That's because you're not really up here."

"Don't begin the trip with a closed mind," Alex said.

"You don't have to shout. I'm sitting right next to you."

"Sorry, but I flew down to the other end of the room."

"Don't let your mind wander." Blaine collected his

thoughts until he got used to the delusion. He did a slow pan of the laboratory. Once again he noted that the experience was not real; he did not feel as if he was soaring through the air as much as he felt as if he was watching late night television, or a poorly made home movie. There was no sense of being there; it was more like pushing a camera around on a boom. If he could show this to Carcione, the Italian businessman would understand why the device had little or no entertainment value.

The potential uses of the bypass skullcap were still under study. Blaine and his staff had concentrated nearly all their efforts on gaining insight into the mechanisms of pain relief, and so far had had no time leftover for peripheral research studies such as the induced hallucinatory experience. The very mention of such possibilities in his paper and lectures had already raised a furor among the scientific community—and had inspired the Soviets to terminate him as well as his program. There was little comfort in the fact that his colleagues on the other side of the Iron Curtain had more faith in his discoveries than his colleagues in the so-called free world. There was a message hidden there, if only he could decipher it.

"Wow, this is fantastic. I'm in the hallway outside the lab but I didn't use the door; I went right through the wall."

"Don't let your imagination run away with you," Blaine warned. He played with the buttons and auto-suggested a flight pattern into the brightly lit corridor. Naturally, he did not 'see' Alex because both of them were there only in their minds. "Let's check out the menagerie."

"Which way? I missed that part on the morning tour."

"Left. It's in the basement of the next building, but they're all connected underground." Blaine was feeling disoriented as well as dissociated. He knew where he was going, but he had the unsettling sensation that this experience was more realistic than any he had previously had. "Marybeth, has anyone tested the BS units since you made the brain wave function refinements?"

"No, it took me just about all week to input the corrections. Besides, we wouldn't undertake a major trial analysis without your supervision. If you hadn't been gallivanting with a mountain nymph . . . "

Blaine ignored her playful innuendo. "Something strange is happening. The sensitivity has been enhanced by the increased field effect. I don't know how to explain it. It's almost—"

"Ineffable?" Having dealt with many patients who had suffered the trauma of near-death, the one detail that stood out poignantly in her mind was that most people were so completely overwhelmed by the out-of-body experience that they felt inadequate to portray it: as if any description of a place beyond the world was necessarily beyond words.

"No, it's—"

"Unbelievable!" Alex called out. "Much better than the other session. Look out chimps, here I come."

"Marybeth, check his monitors." As a doctor, Blaine was concerned about Alex's exuberance. Patients often became ecstatic when severe pain that had tormented them for years vanished in a flash of insight, but Alex was acting out of accord. He popped back into the lab and 'saw' Marybeth walk around to the back of the bypass units so she could read the liquid crystal display.

"Intense brain wave activity, as expected; increased pulse and respiration, but not abnormal under the circumstances. Should I connect the doppler?"

"Yes. And watch it. If his blood pressure fluctuates I want to know about it."

"Blaine. Marybeth. This is no delusion of grandeur. I'm in here with the chimpanzees. I mean *in* here. I can even smell them."

In his wildest imagination Blaine never expected the results he was quite literally seeing. The refinements he and the team had been working on prior to his departure for California were expected to yield an incremental increase in the efficiency of the units, but this was a quantum leap. He zoomed out of the laboratory, down the corridor, and into the animal complex, feeling like a Steadycam in a low budget horror flick. Now the power of suggestion was working in reverse: Blaine had the distinct feeling that he too could detect the wild, musky odor of snoozing chimpanzees.

"How can they sleep with all the lights on?"

The room was indeed bright, but it was due to the mind's interpretation of the out-of-body experience: the anything-can-happen-in-a-dream effect. "If you'll look at the tubes you'll see that the lights are off."

"Oh, yes. You're right."

The cages and dozing chimpanzees were suffused with an all-around glow that could not have been achieved by any source of light, natural or otherwise. One chimpanzee awoke momentarily from her slumber to scratch a flea. She glanced through the wire mesh and appeared to be looking right through Blaine. He 'moved' aside with a creepy feeling that grew creepier as her aroused gaze appeared to follow him. He stopped at a wooden bench on which were strewn bowls and boxes of dry food that the volunteer students had not bothered to put away.

"Weakies, breakfast of chimps," said Alex.

"*What?*"

"It's right here, on the sign."

"Don't point," said Marybeth. "Remember, you're sitting in a chair with a control box in your hand, and you just banged the doppler against the arm."

"Sorry. But it's so real."

Blaine gulped. One of the college wits had left the penciled joke on the wall a couple of weeks ago, and it had never been removed. But Alex should not have known about it.

"Blaine, you're breathing pretty hard and—" Marybeth paused for a moment. "—your heart rate is up a bit. Are you okay?"

Blaine rationalized that someone must have mentioned it during the day, and Alex overheard it. "Fine.

I'm fine." He was glad that he was not connected to a polygraph, or she might have seen right through him. His throat was suddenly as dry as a box full of sand.

"This is too real," Alex said enthusiastically.

Yes, it was. Frighteningly so. The chimpanzee's eyes darted back and forth between Blaine's imagined position and another spot on the bench, below the sign. For Marybeth's benefit, he said, "The new refinement is a distinct improvement. The focus is sharper and the imagery clearer, almost as if we had been looking through a fogged lens before and now it's been cleaned."

"The recorder is on, Blaine, so if you want to take notes just speak out." Marybeth whispered in his right ear, low enough so Alex could not hear. With his mind on other things, he needed to be reminded that this was, after all, a scientific experiment; and that he was sitting in a chair, not floating freely throughout the Institute's basements.

He nodded, knowing that Marybeth could see him. "Alex, let's get out of here." That curious chimpanzee was giving him the willies. "Let's go upstairs and check on our jailers."

"Okay." Alex was taking the trip like a kid in a video arcade, with no holds barred. "Now what?"

"What do you mean, now what? Where are you?"

"I'm upstairs."

Blaine was only halfway to the stairwell. "How did you get there so fast?"

"I went up through the ceiling," he said matter-of-factly. It was obvious that Alex had a mind that was not bound by convention. People seldom realized that in multi-story buildings, entire parties could be raging only eight feet away from quiet contemplation, either up or down: a concept that required three dimensional thinking.

Blaine had a mental block against pushing himself through concrete because he still pictured his roving mind as a physical body. He took a deep breath and slowly poked his 'head' through the basement ceiling.

After a moment of blindness, when his mind was interspersed throughout the stone and cement, he found himself on the floor within the rungs of a stool. With an extra mental effort he rose through the seat, then spun around three hundred sixty degrees—rather like a periscope—so he could 'see' which room he was in. It was the women's lounge. He had never been in here, but he pictured the sinks and mirrors as he thought they should be, and noticed the magazines on the table (*Cosmopolitan*, *Mademoiselle*, *Playboy*, and a tabloid that could be found only at supermarket check-out counters). He spotted the note clipped to the stall door even as Alex read it out loud.

"Now available in very hardback, a novel detective who penetrates the mysteries of love: *The Big Dick*, by Hugh G. Rection."

This was absolutely the most bizarre out-of-body dream experience he had ever imagined. Freud would be proud of him. Then it struck him what Alex had just recited.

"*Alex!*" Marybeth screamed. "How did you know about that?"

"I'm looking at it. You don't think I made it up?"

"Blaine, are you getting all this?"

"Hell, yes. But I wish I weren't." He knew that his mind must be playing tricks on him, that in his heightened state of awareness he was as open to the power of suggestion as a kid in a candy store. "Marybeth, I'm getting some strange vibes about this new hook-up." In the back of his mind the thought was formulating that perhaps this was not all an electronically induced dream, that perhaps he had entered a realm where illusion was something that could be shared. He was suddenly terrified by the implications of what was happening—or what he imagined was happening. Was the interactive force of Alex's mind amplified to the point that his thoughts arced through the air into his own head? Was Blaine picking up Alex's mental wanderings through a form of telepathy? After all, they were sitting side by side. Or were Alex's wild flights of imagination flowing through the electrical circuits and merging with Blaine's recorded brain wave pattern in the Institute's mainframe, to which they were both still connected? "Marybeth, are our bodies okay?" He knew it sounded strange as soon as he said it.

"Alex is calm, but your heart is racing like a banshee. Blaine, what is going on?"

"God only knows. I'm experiencing some new kind of mental aberration, as if my mind is connected somehow with Alex's delusions."

"That'd make a great psychiatric tool."

"If the doctor doesn't go crazy in the process. Alex, are you still with us?"

"Sure. What's all the fuss about? I told you it was real."

When a patient began ignoring reality and went to live in an invented dream world, total mental collapse was not far behind. If Alex got lost in the intricacies of his mind, he might become hopelessly psychotic. He could, in effect, lose his mind. Irretrievably. But suppose Alex was right? Suppose his depictions were accurate, and Blaine was the skeptic who ignored Alex's observations because of their implausible nature? It was the textbook case of psychologist's fallacy.

"All right, Alex. Listen to me. We're going to try something different." What Blaine was really doing was talking him down in a way that was devious enough to trick him into thinking that this was another part of the experiment. "Let's go to the lobby where we can mingle with the crowd. You know, make direct contact with people."

"I don't think we can rub elbows, but I'll try. How do we get there?"

"Through this door—" Literally. "—and turn left. The wooden doors connect to the main building through the west corridor—"

"Right. I'm with you. Past the examination rooms, then left at the intersection. Hey, the door to Room 113 is open."

It was. Blaine's body shivered. Had it been open this

morning, when he took Alex on a quick tour of the complex? He could not remember, but Alex, being a trained investigator, would have noticed something like that. In his mind he pictured the route along the dimly lighted corridors. "Stay out of the lady's room."

"This is really weird," Marybeth said, in a hushed tone. "I'm in a room with two talking zombies. I think I'm the one who's deranged."

Her voice helped to steady Blaine's sanity. He remembered an early phase of development when they were working on the prototype bypass unit, with Marybeth as the volunteer user. He had reached under her dress and had unsnapped the stockings from her garter belt. With the neurometric feedback terminal blocking all physical sensation, she had not been able to feel his fingers doing their dirty work. She had not been amused, but it had sure tickled Blaine's funny bone; her bones, of course, had been numb.

"Don't go away, we'll be right back." Blaine forced himself to relax, to try to rationalize the experience in terms of scientific criteria. Every effect had a cause, and every cause led to an effect. Just because a scientist did not immediately understand an observed phenomenon did not mean that he had to start believing in the supernatural. How many millennia had man watched ships sail over the horizon before figuring out that the world was round? Now the concept was accepted by every school child.

He floated into the lobby like a Christmas wraith. The pickup truck was still parked in the wall, but the bodies had been removed. Small groups of people stood or sat in private conversation.

"Are you there?" said Alex.

"I'm imagining the lobby if that's what you mean, but why are you whispering?"

"I was afraid they'd hear me. It's all so real. It *is* real. Let's shuffle over to Hudson and MacDonald."

In his mind's eye the two CIA agents stood off to one side, engaged in an animated discussion. He drifted across the lobby to the alcove opposite the receptionist's desk. Hudson put a two-way radio up to his ear, listened for a moment, then spoke into the microphone, "Watch it. This guy's unpredictable. Stay in your quadrants. If you see any movement in the woods start shooting and don't ask any questions." To MacDonald: "They're not half as spooked as I am."

"I'm telling you he'll bring him right to us. He's got no choice. He's got to carry out this assignment at all costs. He's expendable, and he knows it."

"Taking out Nabakov is *your* problem, Angus. Saving this project is mine."

MacDonald noted the date and time in his black leather account book, and wrote, "Screw Greenstein, Jerry-296-49-1858. IRS." He snapped the book shut and stuck it in a jacket pocket. "You worried about your career?"

"Hell, no. I've been in the business too long for that. I'm worried about Mitchell. The guy's been thrust into a dirty deal that's totally out of his depth. He needs all the protection we can give him."

"Don't worry about him. He's safe down there in his lab, playing with his mad-doctor apparatus. Besides, now that my people are out of the holding tank we've got half an army patrolling the perimeter."

Hudson shook his head. "I don't like it. This device Nabakov has, whatever it is, enables him to hear what we say and read what we write. He can second-guess us the moment we make a move. He might even be listening to us now."

Hudson glanced up at the ceiling, his gaze sweeping across Blaine's imagined position. Although he could not actually feel it, Blaine was certain that his body in the laboratory had twitched.

"You really believe that bull?"

"You're damned right. The Soviets are doing things with mind control that we haven't even thought of."

"Stan, you've been studying screwy psychics for so long you've become possessed by their weird ideas. Hell, I'd rather believe that Nabakov can make himself invisible, or that he hypnotizes people into not seeing him, than this mind-at-a-distance crap. I think you're barking up the wrong tree."

"You're wrong, Angus. Why do you think the Soviets got so fired up when news of Mitchell's neurometric transmitter came out? Until now Mitchell's been quiet about it because he's the cautious type; not one to jump the gun until the evidence is all in. Maybe so cautious he'll plod on forever, afraid to make the last intellectual leap. But the Soviets know better. God knows how their device operates. I'd make a deal with the devil to find out. It may be completely different from Mitchell's. But the point is that the effect is the same. And the Soviets don't want us eavesdropping on them the way they can on us."

MacDonald snorted. "What about the Young-Kravtsov angle? You think they're in cahoots?"

"Naw. Young's a good man. A stiff-upper-lip type, but with complete integrity. I just threw out the Kravtsov connection to get him to open up. Kravtsov's not part of the inner circle; they've got him doing peripheral research: gopher stuff. That's why I think he's kept his association with Young to himself—in case he could pick up something useful that would make him look better in the eyes of his superiors. I also think the KGB found out about him and Young after Mitchell's article appeared. That's why they've got him on the wire. They won't retire him, though; he's too valuable to them. They'll just rough him up enough to throw a good scare into him. That's the Soviet way. But if they ever found out he tipped us off to save his democratic friend . . . "

MacDonald showed his teeth in a manner that was definitely not a smile. "I'd sacrifice the lot of them to get Nabakov."

"This is a job, Angus, not a personal vendetta. I'm not going to let you use Mitchell as a cat's-paw. First thing in the morning, I'm flying him out of here in an armored chopper. Put him someplace safe until this thing blows over. We can't afford to lose him even if the girl does get the computer up and running. He's too valuable."

MacDonald growled like an angry lion. "I want Nabakov."

"Then get him on your own. This set-up isn't going to work. You know Nabakov better than anyone. You know he'll get in here, somehow, someway. The whole Marine Corps couldn't keep him out forever."

MacDonald was insistent. "I want him, and I want him bad. So bad I can taste it."

"And I hope you get him. But it's going to have to be without Mitchell as your decoy. If he lives until morning, he's out of here."

"Nabakov will follow him—forever if he has to. That's his M.O. He won't give up until Mitchell is dead. He'll go after him, and he'll find him. And when he does, I'll be waiting for him."

"Just make sure he doesn't get you like he got your partner."

MacDonald's eyes were black coals, smoldering.

In the basement laboratory, Alex whispered, "Blaine, are you getting all this?"

"Yes, I'm—What do you mean? Getting what?"

"Hudson and MacDonald. I know you're here. I can feel you."

Blaine suddenly realized that he could 'feel' Alex as well. As he looked around the alcove he could sense the other's presence—knew, in fact, exactly where he was hovering: a globular shimmering in the air that was like a heat wave rising off a hot macadam road in the middle of summer. "I don't believe this."

"You mean, you don't *want* to believe it. But you have to believe this: 'I want him, and I want him bad. So bad I can taste it.' "

"What are you two talking about?" Marybeth interjected.

Blaine was too overwhelmed to respond. Instead, he floated across the lobby to where Lenny Taylor was conversing in low tones with Tilda.

"You know, Tilda, I've been wondering. After this case is over, you know, when everything dies down, maybe we could, you know, get together sometime. That is, if you're going to stay on this assignment."

Tilda was no longer the coy, scatter-brained receptionist. She had removed the fake fingernails because they got in the way of the trigger guard. "Sure, Lenny, I'd like that. But how come you never asked me out before? I used to see you at Greasy's Grill. And Pop's Top Tavern. I even said hello a couple of times."

"Well, I—I—I don't know. I guess I never really noticed you before. I mean, I saw you, but I thought you were just another dumb floozy. No offense, but, well, you always struck me as an airhead."

"Thank you, Lenny," she said demurely. Instead of sitting at her desk polishing her nails, an act that was part of her cover, she checked her bullets for cleanliness before inserting them in the clip. "I'll take the comparison as a compliment. I'd love to go out with you."

"Great. Uh, Tilda, just so we don't get off on the wrong foot, I'm sorry about that bra strap routine. I'm not usually like that, but—" Taylor shrugged. "I was just trying to distract you so Jerry could slip by. He's my kid sister's husband. I'm just trying to help him get ahead."

"Uh, oh," said Alex. "Greenstein's getting a double barrel."

Blaine shook his mind free, glanced around, and saw the special agent's shimmering coalescence in the corner above Dr. Young, Captain Lawson, and the quaking reporter. He moved closer.

"What's going on?" Marybeth wanted to know.

"Shhh," Alex said.

"—thermore, if you *ever* print anything again that's in the least bit derogatory about my department I'll see to it that you get tarred and feathered and run out of town on the cowcatcher of the evening train. Do I make myself clear, young man?"

"Y-y-y-y-y-yes, Captain Lawson. Thank you. I'll remember that. I-I-I didn't really mean to put anyone down, it's just that I was trying to make the story interesting so the readers—"

"It was your infernal meddling that *caused* most of this adversity." Dr. Young was in his best Mighty Joe mood. "Perhaps the Russian agent was not your doing, but the Mafia and the drug dealers came here as a direct consequence of your misinformed dispatches. Not only that, but the entire scientific community has been incensed by your dastardly misrepresentations of scientific research. By comparing the Institute to Frankenstein's castle you have made us out to be ghoulish quacks who rob graves and steal brains and body parts."

"I—I—I know I got a little carried away with my prose, but that was just to—"

"Your calumniating rhetoric is despicable. Be advised that first thing Monday morning I intend to file charges of libel against you and your newspaper, and I will ask Captain Lawson to revoke your license."

"That's private investigators who need licenses, Dr. Young, not investigative reporters." Lawson looked grimly at Greenstein. "But I can put that pencil of his someplace where he can't write with it." To Greenstein, "If you use a typewriter it's *really* gonna hurt."

Despite the cold air blowing in from under the folds of hanging canvas, Greenstein was sweating like a marathoner in the last mile and breathing twice as hard.

Fred slipped in between two sheets of canvas, carrying his shotgun in the crook of his arm. He was dressed in a heavy overcoat that went down to his knees. His head and shoulders were covered with white fluff. "All quiet outside. Pretty, too," he announced.

Blaine shot past Fred like a beam of light, and found himself in the parking lot. There was already an inch of snow on the ground with a steady fall that promised a large accumulation. He had no sensation of cold. *Of course not*, he thought. *I'm not really here. Only my mind—*

No, he corrected himself. *Only my imagination.*

He suddenly felt confused and very lonely. Was he a phantom in a snowstorm, or a schizophrenic lost in the crevices of his brain? Did he really see those armed men who were patrolling the parking lot, or was he imagining them? Had he heard that dialogue in the lobby, or had he created in his mind the words he thought appropriate for each character? Was this fantastic reality, or phantasmagoria?

He could not decide. He wanted to believe, but all his life had been spent dispelling beliefs; his skepticism was too ingrained to cast it aside on a single, unexplainable episode. Yet, there was Alex's corroboration of sight and sound; and there was scientific principle that could account for the strange circumstances. The exploration of the human mind was the final frontier in man's search for knowledge. By its very definition exploration meant the search for the unknown; if there were no unknowns there could be no exploration. Was that truth, or cleverly constructed tautology?

He pushed himself to the limit. He ordered his detached fingers to increase the fluxion intensity and power output. His mind, the incorporeal entity that was the embodiment of his conscious being, soared high above the Institute's interconnected buildings. He looked down from the snow-filled sky with new insight.

The grounds appeared as bright as day, but without the shadows that were cast by a beam of photons. His mind 'saw' the world in all its nakedness: from hunched-over sentries who were squatting on the roof, to those patrolling both sides of the Institute's fence, to the rabbit scurrying around a bush, to the man skulking—

Blaine plummeted toward the fence at the rear of the Institute. He stopped directly over a CIA operative who was oblivious to his presence, oblivious to the man crouched at the tree line across ten yards of untrammeled snow, oblivious to the blowgun aimed at his midriff. Blaine cried out as he dived at the unsuspecting man's head—*and went right through him.* It terrified Blaine, but the operative did not appear to notice. Blaine was only a ghost, a spirit, unable to warn the man of impending danger because his body was several hundred feet away in the basement laboratory.

Blaine noted how the bottom of the fence had been torn away from the cement foundation. The damage was not obvious from ground level because of the bushes around it, but it was clearly visible from overhead. His mind lunged at the dart-wielding sniper but fell short of his goal; he had reached the limit of his projective power. He hovered atop the roll of strip-wire, straining against nonmaterial bonds that refused to let him go any farther. *And the sniper looked right at him.* Not through him, not past him, not above or below him. The deep-set eyes, lighted by eerie, ethereal radiance, were focused exactly on the spot which his mental energy occupied.

Blaine nearly jumped out of his skin.

From the fencepost a foot away he heard Marybeth's hysterical voice. "Blaine, what's happening? You screamed, and your read-outs are practically off the scale."

The sniper spun around and high-tailed it through the woods like a frightened deer—only instead of antlers on his head he wore a white plastic crash helmet overlain with a wire grid.

Blaine altered the focus of his concentration so he could see Marybeth standing next to him in the lab. She wore a look of panic. Through his mind's eye he could still see the snow-covered forest, but the sniper was no longer in 'sight.'

"Alex, get back here! *Quick*! I've just spotted Nabakov."

Chapter 21

Cold air crawled into the crowded lobby, but the discussion was so heated that no one seemed to notice.

"You're a doctor, Mitchell, so I don't have to tell you that one of the most common causes of hallucination is lack of sleep. How long have you and Foley been on your feet? A day and a half? Two days? Add a bad case of jet lag and your suggestion level hits the top of the charts."

"Hudson, this was no ordinary out-of-body experience. This was *real*."

"Since when did out-of-body experiences become ordinary?"

"Since we integrated our first near-death brain wave pattern into the bypass program. With the additional data that Marybeth input—"

Hudson held up his hand and put the radio to his ear. After a short squelch the transmission came out loud and clear. "—fence has definitely been pulled out, and the snow is flattened all around it. Someone's been through here recently; the snow hasn't filled in the tracks, yet."

"But I saw him running away. He couldn't have had time to—" Hudson waved for silence. "Where do the prints lead?"

The radio squelched again. "—mixed in with our own. Can't tell." After a moment of strained silence a different voice got on the radio. "We're beginning a sweep from the front." Another team moved in from the rear of the complex. The first operative came back, "No windows broken along the side of the building."

"Keep a sharp lookout on the roof. He may have scaled the wall." Hudson turned to Blaine, "I take it all back, Mitchell." To MacDonald, "Angus, it looks like you may get your chance. If we can trap him inside the fence—"

"Are you buying this load of crap? Do you really

believe Mitchell saw Nabakov in his head like a god-damn spiritualist?"

"Mediums communicate only with the dead," Mary-beth explained. "Not the living."

MacDonald glowered.

"What I believe doesn't matter," Hudson said. "But there's no denying that the outer perimeter has been breached. How do you think Mitchell found out about it?"

"It's got to be a trick. This is nonsense—sending his mind out on a tour of the grounds. He's dotty, and so are you for falling for it."

"Then the Soviets are dotty, too. They have enough faith in Mitchell's device to send their best assassin to terminate him."

"And to raid my files and destroy the computer program," Blaine added.

Hudson swept that thought aside with a wave of the hand. "His description would explain how the Soviets have been able to steal classified information without being seen. Don't you see how perfect it is?" Hudson raised his arms and his voice like a Sunday morning televangelist. "Christ, all you have to do is get close to the installation you want to penetrate, put on the mind set, and roam mentally through the rooms and hall-ways listening to conversations and reading printed matter left in view. If the place has a parking lot or is close to the street, you can sit in the comfort of a heat-ed vehicle while your mind wanders at will."

"Not only that," added Alex. "If he has to lam it on foot he can control the release of endorphins to the point that he can quite literally run until he drops. If he gets wounded in action, he's got the ultimate pain con-troller right at his fingertips. He can write his own pre-scription and not have to worry about the handwriting."

Lawson tugged his coat a little tighter around his waist. The water on the floor of the lobby was beginning to freeze. "If you had told me this last night I'd have locked you all up in the loony bin. Now I may have to lock myself up. I'm beginning to believe you."

Dr. Young was not yet convinced of his colleague's diagnosis. "How would such a device operate without a large energy cell and an unwieldy central processing unit?"

"It doesn't need the memory capacity and data storage of our bypass units because it wasn't designed as a research tool. A spy device only has to induce the out-of-body response. Last night we saw him first wearing a bypass hard-hat, then a Walkman. My guess is he keeps the mind set in the bowling ball bag when it's not in use, and carries the batteries around his waist in a belt or cummerbund."

"Like bullets in belt loops." Greenstein scribbled notes as fast as he could.

"Give me that." Lawson snatched the pen and pad out of the reporter's gloved hands.

MacDonald's huge left fist landed on Greenstein's shoulder like a sack of cement. He shoved the little man aside. "Okay, wise guy, take a gander at the pictures we shot at the airport." He slipped a package of photographic prints out of one of his jacket pockets and fanned them out like a deck of cards. "We'll find out if you really saw him. Which one is Nabakov?"

Blaine selected one of the portraits without hesitation. "Him." MacDonald stared at the picture long and hard. His face was a blank.

"Is he the one you followed from the hotel?" asked Marybeth.

He said grudgingly, "Lucky guess."

"Oh, you stubborn fool." Marybeth punched him. It was not likely that he felt it. "Can't you accept anything beyond the limited bounds of your experience?"

Blaine could care less what MacDonald believed. "Hudson, listen to me. You won't find Nabakov inside the complex because I saw him running away. He's long gone by now. But he's out there watching—with his mind. Waiting for the right moment. Your men won't be able to find him because he'll see them coming a block away. Our only chance is to know exactly where his body is so we can surround him."

Hudson shivered as if he had gotten a sudden chill. "Goddamn it, Mitchell, this operation is giving me the creeps." His face creased with indecision, he shouted into the radio, "Naidoff, check out that break in the fence again. Look real close and tell me what you think."

"Don't play up to them, Stan." MacDonald stuck the photographs back into his pocket, and nodded his chin toward Blaine and Alex. "One lies and the other swears to it."

Young took a more analytical approach. "Could it be that the increased fluxion intensity induced a shared delusion by making your minds more suggestible?"

"Could it be that we're just ghoulish quacks who rob graves and steal brains and body parts?" Without waiting for a response, Blaine turned to Lawson, "Or that you're going to have Greenstein tarred and feathered and run out of town on the cowcatcher of the evening train?" To MacDonald, "So Nabakov killed your partner, did he? And you want him so bad you can taste it. Then you'd better start accepting the fact that I'm your ticket to revenge. We can use the new portable unit to—"

The radio squawked. "Hudson, it now appears that the perimeter has not been breached. Repeat, not been breached. The fence has been pulled out, but the tracks around the bush are probably small animal tracks, and the snow outside the fence appears smooth and unbroken."

"Get some men and go check out the tree line." Hudson clicked off the radio. "Mitchell, so far you're batting a thousand. Can you get back on the neurometric feedback terminal and locate Nabakov for us?"

"Not from here. We don't have the range. But if we form a posse we can go after him."

Hudson squinted. "How do you mean?"

"I'll take the portable unit into the woods and conduct a mental search. We'll start from where I saw him last. But we need a tracker, someone who can tell the difference between rabbit spoor and a human footprint."

"I can't let you go after a seasoned assassin. He'd take you down so fast you'd never know what hit you."

"He won't get that close. By projecting my mind I can spot him in the distance, and your men can close in on him."

"It's too chancy. I can't permit it."

Alex took a step forward. "With all due respect, Hudson, it's not within your authority to deny permission."

Hudson might have been jolted by an electric shock. "Not within my—just what the hell are you talking about, Foley? I'm in charge here."

"No, you're not. This is a cooperative effort, remember? Your responsibility is to protect the Institute and its ongoing research projects. Now that Marybeth has cured the virus and reinstalled the computer program, your duty is to preserve the security of the building. Dr. Mitchell is my responsibility, and I believe the best way to ensure his safety is to remove Nabakov as a threat."

"Foley, you've got a lot to learn as a field operative. You never put your mission in jeopardy. Never."

"I think Dr. Mitchell is in jeopardy as long as Nabakov is on the loose. You know that if you fly him out of here in an armored chopper, Nabakov will follow him—forever if he has to. That's his M.O. He won't give up until Mitchell is dead. He'll go after him, and he'll find him. Isn't that right, MacDonald?"

Having his own words thrown back at him was more than he could stand. MacDonald's eyes darted rapidly from Hudson to Blaine to Alex. "How did you know about that?"

"The same way I know about the notation on page 27: 'Screw Greenstein, Jerry — 296—49—1858. IRS.' Is that how you get even with people? By having their tax records audited?"

MacDonald's eyes glared in amazement; he was too stunned to speak.

Blaine made a pitch in his own defense. "Hudson, I've been thrown into a dirty deal, but it's not out of my depth. We can get this bastard. I know it. What's more, when we get Nabakov we also get his mind set. And that's something you want. Not only will we know exactly how advanced the Soviets are in neurometric feedback research, we might learn something ourselves. That's a much better deal than you'll get from the devil."

Hudson gnashed his teeth but said nothing. He looked like a man in turmoil.

"Thanks, Stan." Alex slapped him on the shoulder in a gesture of friendliness. "Thanks for not getting in the way. Angus, get your people ready. We'll need guns, flashlights, radios, and plenty of warm clothing. We're going on a witch hunt. Blaine, how much time do you need to rig the mind set for transport?"

"Fifteen minutes."

"Okay, let's do it. Nabakov's getting farther away every second."

Three minutes later found Blaine and Alex in the basement laboratory, jury-rigging hospital bed straps to the BS-2 unit. They soon had it rigged like a backpack, with two straps crisscrossed over the shoulders and another around the waist.

Marybeth entered with her arms piled high with white hospital garments. "It's snowing pretty hard so we'll need all the protection we can get."

Blaine noticed the use of the collective pronoun, started to protest, then thought better of it. There was no time to argue with a woman who was headstrong under the best of circumstances and capable under the worst. She had proved herself valiantly during the previous night's adventure. Wishing he had time for vespers, Blaine struggled into the sleeves that she held out for him. "This thing weighs a ton."

"It's a smock from radiology. Alex, here's one for you. I brought the OR mats, too. Wrap the towel around your neck like a scarf." The rubber gauntlets she handed out would have been at home on King Arthur's knights. "From the chem lab. They're insulated. And the galoshes are courtesy of the janitorial department."

Fully dressed, Blaine backed up to the BS-2 unit and slipped his arms into the shoulder harness. He leaned forward so the unit came off the dolly. The weight was about the same as he had carried in Yosemite (Was it only two days before?) but the rigid battery box made it much less comfortable. He tightened the waist strap.

"How do you feel?"

"Like a Galapagos tortoise."

Marybeth smoothed back his hair, fitted the skullcap, and checked the digital readouts. "Everything looks good. Let's make you mobile." She unplugged the mind set from the charging unit. "Okay, you've got full function and power. Go ahead and give it a try."

The control box swung on its cord like a pendulum. Alex handed it to Blaine. He held the box in his left hand and placed two fingers on the buttons. The pressure of the straps biting into his shoulders faded rapidly as he calibrated the fluxion intensity; he kept the power output on minimum wattage. "It feels good so far."

At the lowest power setting, the mind forced the release of just enough endorphins to eliminate the discomfort of minor aches and pains; preliminary experimentation had shown that this was sufficient for people with arthritis, muscular disorders, and upper or lower back pain. As the electronic stimulus was increased, the amino acid breakdown became more pronounced; neurotransmitters flooded the brain and locked onto the pain receptors, offering relief equivalent to that given by the injection of potent drugs except that there was no accompanying feeling of euphoria.

"It's working fine. I'm going to pop out now."

Blaine separated mind from body. Once past the initial jolt of disorientation he again felt that the out-of-body experience was mere hallucination. He looked down from a point just below the ceiling, noting the placement of equipment and the movements of his companions. "I'm through, but it doesn't seem any more real now than it did before. Alex, it was only your confirmation of observable events that lent validity to the phenomenon. Now I'm not so sure it wasn't self-delusion."

He watched Marybeth lean close to the left ear of his body. "Try to be objective, Blaine, and take an intellectual approach based upon the evidence of your previous excursion."

Blaine caused his head to nod. On the floor, the body that stood between Alex and Marybeth moved its head up and down. Blaine then performed several maneuvers designed to test his coordination. If he closed his mind's eye he could easily swing his arms in circular sweeping motions. Direct observation, or optical feedback, offered the same sense of reality as when he closed his eyes and relied on imagination. But when he watched his gestures from above or from the side, as he allowed his mind to coast around his body, he quickly got out of synchronization. The various points of view caused him to lose his sense of oneness with his body: like using two mirrors to clip curls from the back of one's head. Remote self-observation was not as easy as it sounded.

"I wish I had time to study this transphysical effect before engaging in a battle of the minds, but it'll have to wait. Let's get going." He missed the doorknob on the first try because his mind was still out of his brain. He concentrated on watching where his hand was reaching, realigned the motions, twisted, and pulled. He walked into the corridor with the faltering gait of a baby learning how to walk. Confusion was enhanced by double vision: one physical and one mental. It was like looking with one eye through the lens of a periscope while looking straight ahead with the other. He found it difficult to actuate his body properly unless his mind was in his head.

Even the descriptive syntax was disturbing: he thought of himself, his persona, as the locus of his mind; his body then became a disparate entity, like an automobile, that he could leave at will and trade in for another. After walking into the water cooler he turned off the power completely and re-merged with his body. "This is going to take some getting used to."

"Remember that Nabakov is an expert at this," Alex said. "He's had special training and a good many field exercises."

Blaine negotiated the corridor and stairs more confidently without the power of the bypass skullcap. He regulated the rheostat experimentally. "I can't seem to walk and project my mind at the same time. After a lifetime of watching my footsteps from eye level, looking down from overhead makes me feel as if I'm floating above someone else's body, or like an inexperienced puppeteer. If I try to look way in front then I feel like a blindfolded child playing pin-the-tail-on-the-donkey."

When they arrived in the lobby he found Lawson and MacDonald dressed in winter garb, complete with rubber boots. MacDonald seemed to like the all-black look.

"An advance squad is already on the trail," Hudson said. "They reported that the only tracks leaving the area where you said you saw Nabakov were deer tracks. Looks like a doe might have been resting there." There was no accusation in his voice, just information.

"This Russian is a crafty fellow. I wonder how he managed that."

Hudson appeared to take it in stride. "Beats me. I'd also like to know how he managed to cut the bottom of the fence out of the concrete footing without leaving footprints of his approach."

"He could have done it earlier, before it started snowing," said Lawson. "Then for some reason decided to come back later."

"Let's stop gabbing and go get the son of a bitch." MacDonald slammed a full clip into his Colt .45, cocked it, and slipped it through the unbuttoned front of his coat into its holster. "*If* he's really here. And *if* you can really find him with that tinker toy of yours."

"You don't sound convinced," said Blaine.

"I'm convinced that one of us is crazy, and it ain't me." MacDonald spat out the words in a base guttural overtone. "Is *she* tagging along?"

"Try and stop me, buster." Marybeth shook her fist at him.

"All right, let's save the belligerence for the enemy." Hudson gave a radio to Alex. "I'll have my ear glued to the other end of this. Keep in touch. You too, Angus. I want an open line of communication."

A minute later found them trooping single file through the wind and snow. MacDonald took the lead. Captain Lawson followed close behind, then came Blaine, Marybeth, and Alex. Two operatives, picked up at the remains of the front gate, acted as a rear guard.

Snow covered the ground like a soft white llama skin; more was piling up rapidly. The armed squad plowed through the broad sward between the tall, cross-linked fence that surrounded the Institute and the wooden barrier that was one side of the corral. Fat bushes sprinkled through the separation zone looked like white-capped mushrooms with their undersides bare.

Blaine punched the power button to get an overview of the situation. He popped out of his body and soared into the sky. The land was suffused with a mellow brightness that was no trick of optic's, but a perception by the mind that was extrasensory: on a wavelength other than that of visible light. He flew on ahead, into the forest that bounded the side of the Institute, and promptly stumbled and hit the ground. He pulled his mind back into his brain.

"Blaine, are you okay?" Marybeth helped him to his feet.

"Yes, I just lost my balance." He did not tell her why, but knew that he could not think ahead and maintain his motor coordination at the same time. He brushed himself off. "Is it cold?"

"Worse than last night, and biting because of the wind-chill."

He hurried to catch up with MacDonald and Lawson. "I can't feel it." With all his pain receptors blocked by endorphins it was impossible for him to distinguish between hot and cold. A person could easily get frostbite or die of hypothermia without noticing the symptoms.

They reached the corner of the fence and made a sharp turn to the right. A gust of wind blew snow and particles of ice nearly horizontal to the ground. Blaine covered his eyes with his hands, wishing he had his ski goggles no matter how badly they fogged. The severity of the storm was increasing and, while he could not feel its effects, he knew that the drifting snow might soon cover any chance they had of following Nabakov's trail.

"Sit rep, Naidoff." MacDonald's gruff voice was practically lost in the howling wind.

They huddled in a close circle in order to hear the operative's situation report.

"Hard to tell." Naidoff held his carbine tight against his parka. He had to scream to be heard. "There's a spot here in the snow where something laid down, and there's a trail leading off to the east. The team's out checking it now."

Captain Lawson pulled up his collar as he bent down on one knee and inspected the area. "Deer sleep under trees in places like this." The overhanging pine boughs offered some protection from falling snow, and served to break up the wind. "Mountain lions and bobcats, too."

Rifle shots sounded in the distance, followed by automatic weapons fire. There must have been twenty to thirty shots in all.

"What the hell—" MacDonald had his radio out in a flash. "Who fired? Who's that shooting?"

The transmission came back barely audible. "Got 'im, sir. We got 'im. Wounded, at least."

More rifles cracked in the air.

"You civvies stay here. The rest of you come with me." MacDonald took off like a fullback at the snap of the ball, and was quickly swallowed up in the swirling snow.

The muffled report from Alex's radio was, "He's down."

Chapter 22

Lawson continued to study the tracks in the snow.

"Anything wrong, Captain?" Alex's question was nearly blown away by the blizzard.

The policeman stood up slowly. "Hard to tell because they're partly filled in."

Alex squinted as he turned into the wind. "What can you see through the mind set?"

Blaine heard the voices, but his mind was hundreds of feet away. "MacDonald just went out of range to the east. I can't reach the action."

"What about this other trail?"

Feeling like a ghost slipping effortlessly through the trees, he brought his mind back to his body, then took off in the direction of the trail. Again he was assailed by doubts, as if this were just another figment of his imagination. It no longer seemed real. After a cursory check he rushed back into his brain, where he could realign himself with his physical senses. "They head south as far as I can see. Why?"

"Something strange about them," Lawson shouted. "I'd like to say they're deer tracks. Done a lot of hunting in my day so I should be able to tell. But if you did 'see' Nabakov lying here—and I'm not saying you did—there wouldn't be any deer close by."

"Captain, you wouldn't be having an intuitive feeling by any chance, would you?" asked Marybeth. "Sensing something instinctively that isn't readily apparent to the normal senses?"

"Just call it a hunch. I—"

The rat-tat-tat of automatic weapons fire sounded dim and distant, deadened by the howling storm. Then came a detonation that Blaine recognized as that of a grenade. None of the CIA operatives carried launchers or hand grenades. His experienced ear also picked out the distinctive burping of Uzis.

The high-pitched squeal of the radio cut through

the noise of wind and whipping snow. Alex pulled the radio out of his pocket. MacDonald's frantic voice was easily recognizable.

"—wasn't Nabakov. We got two goddamn cowboys and a twelve-point buck. And there's more of them out here, flanking the grounds from the northeast. They're all around us in the snow. Can't see the bastards."

"Take care of it, Angus. I got a tractor-trailer coming down the driveway at ramming speed."

Confusion reigned. The radio crackled with commands and counter commands, shouts, reports, and partial messages that were cut off by everyone pressing transmission keys at once. The South American gauchos were making a frontal, last-ditch assault on the Institute.

Visibility was reduced to twenty to thirty feet. Blaine peered through the blinding snow but could see only searing whiteness. It was not until he was knocked backward that he realized Marybeth was pounding his chest with her fist.

"What can you see, Blaine? What can you see?"

In the sudden fear of impending battle he had forgotten about the mind set. Even then he hesitated, afraid to leave his body helpless in order to let his mind wander through the surrealistic world of mental perception. He forced himself to submit to the separation of mind and body. In a flash his perspective changed, and he found himself looking down on four people standing in the snow-swept forest.

His feet were firmly anchored to the ground by his inability to actuate coordinated body movements from a distant mind, but he was free to roam mentally wherever he wanted; no obstacle could get in his way. An ethereal brightness suffused the world with shadowless emanation; darkness did not exist in the mind's eye. Free as the wind he soared over the fence, cut diagonally across the Institute's grounds, flew over the parking lot and along the driveway. He saw Hudson and his men taking defensive positions in front of the lobby as the truck barreled along the snow-covered blacktop.

"It's a long distance carrier. The kind that delivers cars from the factory."

"Must be the one hijacked by the South American gang," said Lawson. "That's where they got all the pick-up trucks."

"And there are men on foot—"

Half the length of the driveway suddenly exploded in a titanic ball of flame and melted tar. The eruption of Vesuvius could not have been as awesome. Blaine's mind was hovering directly above the truck at the time of detonation. He caught a whiff of C-4 mixed with burning rubber and gasoline. A split second later the expanding fireball drove right through his mind, engulfing him in an incinerating cloud of heat and vapor.

Blaine screamed louder than he had ever screamed in his life. He jerked back in a flash, and hit the ground screaming in pure terror. He must have blacked out, for in his next moment of awareness he saw Marybeth and Alex and Lawson staring down at him in a near-death montage of life review. He screamed again, and tried to shut death from his mind.

Sometime later he felt Marybeth's cool hand on his forehead; she had a mother's touch. He was bathed in sweat despite the bitter cold. She daubed away his fears with care and soothing kindness. "Take it easy, Blaine. Take it easy. You're all right. Just take it easy."

"Let's get the hell out of here," Lawson called out. Rifle and automatic weapons fire were getting louder and more intense. "There's a full-fledged battle coming our way."

Blaine opened his eyes—his real eyes—to find his head cradled in Marybeth's lap. He sucked in some air. The sharp iciness helped to revive him. "I—I—I was right on top of the truck when they blew the driveway. The flames went—" He choked for a moment. "The flames went right through me. God, it was so real, as if I were actually standing there when that sheet of flame overtook me like a napalm attack."

The sounds of gunfire and exploding grenades filled the air.

"Just think of it as a 3-D movie," Alex said.

"But this was *real.*"

"I'm sure it was. But you were only there in thought. You were merely observing. Whatever happens to your mind during remote sensing can't hurt your body. Remember that. There's no actual contact between pure mental force and the physical world."

A rifle cracked nearby, and someone screamed.

Blaine took a deep breath. He knew Alex was right, but it was difficult to shrug off an encounter that was so vivid. He nodded in acquiescence. "Help me up." He felt drained, as if all his energy had been sucked out of his body by a mental vampire.

Alex and Marybeth lifted him to a sitting position. He leaned back against the battery pack of the BS-2 unit. If anything, the snowstorm was increasing in severity.

"Goddamn it, Mitchell. Get on your feet." Lawson spun around and pointed his gun into the woods. "We're gonna get caught in this mess."

"Someone's coming, Blaine," said Alex. "Use your mind to see who it is."

"No!" Blaine could not think of letting his mind go, of leaving his body again so soon after—

"I hope that's MacDonald out there, or we're in trouble," yelled Lawson.

"Blaine, you've got to," Marybeth pleaded.

Through his eyes Blaine saw indistinguishable shapes that could have been planted shrubs or crouching men. Was that a tree limb waving in the gusts, or a rifle seeking a target? He steeled himself for the dissociative feeling that he was beginning to hate. A second later he popped out of his body, and cruised toward the figures skulking in the forest.

"*It's a cowboy!*"

Lawson fired three times. One of the saplings keeled over like a felled Christmas tree, and lay still.

Blaine cowered in his body. Circumstances of extreme stress took so much psychical energy to maintain the out-of-body experience that he was quickly becoming drained. His brain had a limited supply of endorphins just as the body had a limited amount of adrenaline. One could not run on natural chemicals forever. Furthermore, the rapidly changing viewpoint as he jumped back and forth between mind and matter threw Blaine into a state of confusion. Like an untreated schizophrenic on the verge of breakdown, he was losing his sense of reality.

Slowly he climbed to his feet. He put his hands on his head as if that would help keep his mind intact. "There are more of them out there, between us and the entrance. But I don't think they know we're here. I think they're attacking the Institute. They probably think I'm inside."

"There's someone else coming," Lawson announced.

"Let's get the hell out of here." Alex's eyes darted like the tongue of a snake. "Come on. This way." He tugged Blaine away from the sounds of battle.

"Wait a minute." Blaine protested, but let himself be led through the woods. "Tell MacDonald to come and get us."

"I can't. When you went into that convulsion you knocked the radio out of my hand. It's broken."

Marybeth took Blaine's other hand. Together she and Alex led him through the forest as if they were walking a sick patient. Marybeth said, "Blaine, take a look back and see who's after us."

Blaine was still in shock over the mind-blowing experience of the exploding truck. It required every effort to dissociate himself from his body, from his only touch with physical reality, and to make a mental reconnaissance in search of their pursuers. He actuated the mind set for only a few seconds. This time he did not stumble when he left his brain. His legs moved automatically. Alex and Marybeth kept him from running into trees when his eyes went blind. Working with the bypass skullcap in the field was different from operating it in the safety and comfort of the lab. "There are a couple of gauchos on our tail about a hundred yards back." With great relief he slipped back into his brain.

"All right, let's make some tracks." Alex pulled harder on Blaine's hand. "Can you manage by yourself?"

"Yes. I'm okay." But he knew in his heart that he was not. The continuous process of bouncing out of and into his brain induced debilitating disorientation. The effect was as dizzying to his equilibrium as it was to his equanimity. He was experiencing double vision similar to what a person might have after stepping off an amusement park ride. He felt nauseated.

Lawson came running up from behind. "You were right. It was one of them cowboys." He brandished a captured Uzi. "And they mean business."

"Thanks," Blaine said distractedly. "Thanks for believing me."

"At this point I'll believe anything you tell me. There's more to this mind-roving stuff than meets the—" Lawson stopped, and shone his flashlight into a pile of drifting snow. "Hold on, there."

"What is it?" Marybeth wanted to know.

"This doesn't look right." Lawson got down on one knee with his back to the wind. His long coat flapped around him like twin banners. "This is the trail we've been following." He ran his gloved fingers over the tracks. "See the two deep depressions? They're the hooves of a white tail deer. But this—this doesn't make sense." He indicated how the snow had been leveled around the print.

"The next one's like that, too." Alex ran his flashlight along the trail to the succeeding prints. Each one showed a deer print surrounded by a flattened area the size of a paperback book. "What could cause it?"

"Nothing in a deer's hoof, that's for sure." Lawson scanned the area before them. "Looks like its headed for the old quarry. As good a place as any to hide from that South American gang. Let's go."

Blaine had never hiked in the woods behind the Institute. Whenever he took the time to go backpacking, he went to the States west of the Rockies, where the mountains were high and the canyons were deep and the air was clean and dry.

"I've got the strangest feeling that we're being followed," Marybeth said in a loud voice, so her words would not be lost in the wind. They were far enough away from the Institute now that the sounds of battle were no longer audible. "It's like last night, in the dorm."

"Lady, I'm so cold that I can't feel a thing, but if you think we're being followed I'll take your word for it." Lawson doused his light. He held his gun firmly in hand.

Alex said, "Blaine, how about taking another trip and sweeping the area?"

Blaine was reluctant to leave his body. "I don't know—"

"Come on, Blaine, this is no time to get cold feet."

That sounded funny, since Blaine could no longer feel his feet due to the bypass skullcap. But he was in no mood to laugh. "I'm not feeling well." The initial euphoria of mind travel had worn off in light of the dire consequences that it could bring about.

"Jesus, Blaine, come on! We've lost our backup, so it's up to you to establish a safe perimeter. Nabakov is still out here somewhere, and he's dangerous."

"Come out of it, Blaine," Marybeth urged. "This isn't like you. Where's your fighting spirit?"

What was wrong with him? Was he really that traumatized by the truck explosion? Yes, he was. They could not possibly understand how it felt to be overcome by violent death, to be blown to atoms, to cease to exist, then to regain consciousness moments later in another place, in another body. Although he had survived physical dissolution, perhaps a piece of his mind had been obliterated by the blast: a momentary discontinuance of the energy pattern that was responsible for the existence of consciousness. The neurons of his brain were intact, but was the flow of thought?

"I'm—I'm okay. I'll give it a try."

Marybeth placed the control box in his hand. He did not even realize he had dropped it. He breathed deeply.

Then he placed his fingers on the two buttons. Instead of pushing the rheostat to its fullest extent, he tapped the buttons in reverse until he felt the stinging cold of the winter storm. He had to do that first; it was important to feel pain in order to understand what it was like to be alive. Mankind was descended from animals that had no concept of self, whose lives were governed by instinct and physical contact with the world around them. The mind was a latecomer to the evolution of life. Blaine felt a need to return to that basic element of life before once again forsaking it for transcendentalism. If the mind was a construct of universal transience, there was a chance that his persona, his soul, might get trapped outside of his body and never be able to return. He was afraid of that much more than the darts of a Soviet assassin, darts that could do little more than relieve him of the burden of struggling to maintain sanity in a world that no longer made sense.

"Okay, I'm out. I'm—" Blaine hovered a few feet over his head, afraid at first to get too far away. He gradually increased the power. "I'm in a glade about thirty feet in front. There's a big hole just ahead. A hole with steep sides of exposed rock that the snow can't cling to. It— it must be that quarry you were talking about, Captain."

"Let's get over there, then. There's some overhangs where we can get out of the weather while Blaine 'thinks' out the area."

Blaine watched his body being pushed along by Alex and Marybeth. The snow was not very deep in the open because the strong gusts swept it away, but six or eight inches had accumulated in the bottom of the quarry, and there were deeper drifts due to the vagaries of the wind. As his body neared the edge of the cliff, Blaine coasted mentally down the thirty-foot-high walls. He saw the overhangs that Lawson had mentioned. They looked like good hiding places: good enough for them, good enough for Nabakov.

"We'll have to walk around the other side so we can climb down."

"I wouldn't be surprised if—" And then he felt it: a stabbing presence that struck him to his very core, as if his inner being were suddenly contaminated with evil. "He's here!"

He zipped back into his body in a flash. But as soon as he did he realized that he was mentally blind, that Nabakov's body was hidden from view, that the only way he could locate the Soviet assassin was by going after him with his mind. He halted at the edge of the cliff face.

"Where! Where is he?" Alex panned the forest with his pistol.

"I've lost him."

"Get out there and look for him," came Marybeth's frantic voice. "He knows we're here. He knows exactly where we are."

Blaine had not 'seen' Nabakov's body, he had only felt his mind. The Russian had touched him with his lonely, loathsome soul, and had called him out for a duel. Blaine, so recently full of fight and looking forward to personal combat, found that he was terrified of the choice of weapon. He could ponder a showdown with guns, knives, or fists. But mental jousting was a method of warfare with which Blaine was not only unfamiliar, but found repugnant. He had as little chance of besting his opponent as a badminton player had against a black belt in karate. Nabakov had experience as well as the psychological advantage.

"Come on, Mitchell. I have faith in you." Lawson shouted in Blaine's face. "We came out here to get this Ruskie, so let's get him."

Blaine steeled himself mentally. "Okay, I'll do it." As soon as he tapped the power control he found himself out of body. The separation was painless and instantaneous. He hovered about twenty feet in the air. His mind's eye took in the scene below: his body with his back to the quarry, Marybeth by his side, Alex and Lawson protecting him in front by panning their guns along the line of trees shrouded by falling snow.

In his mind he saw through the forest with crystal

clarity. The blizzard did not affect his mental travels; his mind was quite literally as free as the wind. He hovered in the tree tops like a hunter sitting on his platform, watching for game below. The fluxion intensity increased his second sight, his mental awareness, to the point where he could sense Nabakov's mind. He was close. He was real close.

Blaine swept the area in an expanding circular pattern; he felt like a soaring eagle looking for prey. He saw snow and rock and pristine forest, and the jagged scar of a quarry so old that trees growing in the bottom rose to a height of forty feet. When he swooped down to the ground he saw deer tracks in the snow: tracks that went in all directions and seemed to come from everywhere. Such large herds of deer inhabited the county that farmers often complained that they decimated their fields and trampled their gardens.

Then he felt it: that flutter in his heart that signified the presence of another roving mind. There was nothing below him but whiteness. Nabakov was there, hiding his body in the snow, but his essence was up and about. Suddenly the Russian appeared before him as a swirling globe that could have been a rotating oil slick on the surface of a pond, or an evanescent soap bubble. The evil mind glided past him, slowed, and hovered like a hummingbird over a spring blossom; the long beak emerged, seeking nectar.

"He's here!"

But where? Where was Nabakov's body? As if in answer to his question, the Russian's mental essence retreated in a straight line to a snow covered lump on the ground, and quickly thrust aside the long white overcoat that concealed his body. Blaine whirled around to get his bearings, to shout directions. He found himself among the trees.

"He's in the quarry!"

Nabakov placed the end of the blowgun to his lips. He looked straight up at Blaine, hovering twenty feet in the air, and puffed.

Blaine saw the poison-tipped dart speeding toward

him. He screamed, and jerked back instinctively. His mind plummeted to the ground at an accelerating pace, coming to a halt with a bone-jarring crash. He lay stunned, broken, paralyzed, unable to think straight. He gasped for air, feeling a sharp, searing pain in his chest. His mind spun dizzily out of control.

His new mental perspective stood only inches above the snow. He tried to fly away, to escape before Nabakov put another dart through his mind. Then he realized that he could not move, that he was trapped in his body as securely as a mouse caught between the steel jaws of a spring-loaded snare. It took all his strength just to raise his head.

Nabakov's white-clad body emerged from the misty, swirling snow like a ghostly image from the past. He stood smugly with weapon in hand, knowing—*knowing*—that his victim was powerless to move. Nabakov was a professional assassin, and as a professional he did not take time to gloat. There was nothing personal between him and Blaine. Killing was merely a job.

Blaine fumbled for the Glock that he had shoved in his outer pocket. He pulled out the gun and pointed. The barrel wavered from side to side as if he were trying to hold a ten-foot length of lead pipe. He could not concentrate his thoughts, his will, his energy, his strength; he could not align the sights.

The sallow faced Russian inserted another dart in his blowgun, inhaled deeply, raised the mouthpiece to his lips, took careful aim, and puffed.

Blaine pulled the trigger.

The dart hit Blaine in the chest and plunged through the fabric of his coat like a high-speed bullet cutting through flesh. He squeezed his eyes tightly shut. His head lolled. His body was a huge, amorphous mass of pain. Where was the control box? No sooner did the pain reach the limits of tolerance than it slowly left him. A delicious painlessness crept along his central nervous system like a shot of sodium pentothal. He entered a world of bliss and blackness.

Once again he found himself rising out of his body.

He saw himself lying crumpled on the floor of the quarry at the base of the sheer rock wall. Nabakov approached his body as lithe as a cat. Alex and Lawson and Marybeth raced along the edge of the cliff, looking for a way down. It's too late, now, he thought. Too late for anything but revenge. Nabakov had accomplished his goal, and I am dead. I am leaving this world for a better one where there is no pain, no strife, no longing, no suffering.

With cold-blooded determination, Nabakov knelt in the snow, wrapped his fingers around Blaine's throat, inserted his thumbs into the larynx, and quickly exerted pressure.

Blaine slid along the smooth walls of a long, black tunnel toward a circle of light that was the essence of peace and purity. The light grew brighter and brighter until its sheer whiteness was glaring; but it did not hurt his eyes. Then he was surrounded by a brilliant, all-encompassing sphere of light. He felt no pain or emotion. Out of the intense whiteness appeared his wife. Blaine felt comforted.

"Carol, what are you doing here?"

"I have always been here."

"Wh—why? Where is here?"

"I am the light at the end of the tunnel—at the end of *your* tunnel."

"Where—where are we? What is this place?"

"It is not a place. It is a part of your mind. I have been waiting for you."

"When you could have passed beyond the light? Why?"

"I knew that someday you would come for me. That a part of you needed me. And I had to be here when that time arrived. You need help if you are to go on."

"What kind of help?"

"Guidance for your soul, surcease for your sorrow. You still grieve for me."

"I let you die."

"That is not true, Blaine. My death was beyond your control—beyond anyone's control."

"I could have saved you if I had had the skill."

"You are a doctor, Blaine, not God. No surgeon expects every brain tumor operation to be successful. You did the best you could with the medical technology available. Do not torture yourself."

"It was my fault. I am to blame."

"That is not you talking, Blaine. It is your guilt. You think that because you loved me you had more of an obligation to save me than a doctor who was a stranger to his patient. Life does not work that way. It was not your love that failed me, or your faithfulness; it was my body. You cannot reproach yourself for that."

"But, Carol—you trusted me. And I let you down."

"You did not let me down. You did your very best both as a devoted husband and as a conscientious doctor. You did everything possible to ease the pain of the final months. And then you dedicated your life to easing the pain of others. No more penitence is required, Blaine. Let go the hurt that wells within your heart, and let your soul find peace."

"I love you, Carol. I always have."

"I know that, Blaine. I have never doubted it. Your heart is full of love. But it is time for you to build on that love, to share your love with others. You did not become a doctor just to practice medicine, but to give what you have to offer to the great gestalt that we call humanity. You cannot forsake that, Blaine. You cannot forsake your destiny."

"But the light—"

"Will always be there for you. You need not fear for that."

Blaine knew that she spoke the truth. As the light grew brighter around him, he felt a calmness, a tranquility, the like of which he had never imagined possible. He bathed in the light, luxuriated in the light, became as one with the light. He was dying to see what was on the other side of the light.

And so he passed beyond.

Chapter 23

Awareness came to Blaine like the gradual brightening of an incandescent light controlled by a slowly rotated dimmer switch. He felt dreamy and languorous—not the cozy Sunday morning sensation of knowing that he did not have to get out of bed until he was good and ready, until the sun was high in the sky, until the church bells began clanging in the distance—but the soporific, mind-numbing response brought about by sedatives.

The scene before him was pure white. No, not quite pure, he noticed, as his awakening mind brought the world into better focus, but blemished. He saw patterns that resolved themselves into recognizable shapes, and shapes that became three-dimensional objects, and objects that evolved into living, breathing creatures.

One of the creatures moved in close, and spoke in a deep vibrant voice, "He's coming to."

Blaine closed his eyes. The last person he wanted to see in his new life was Angus MacDonald. But when his lids fluttered open again, the CIA man was still there: standing above him and peering down with white, gleaming teeth. It was the first time Blaine had seen him smile.

"It's about time," said Stan Hudson. "I thought he was going to nap all day."

There was a scuffle of chairs as other people swam into view. "Don't tell me I'm alive."

"That's the bad news. The good news is that everyone else managed to survive the ordeal. That is, all except a gang of gauchos that we rounded up in the last rodeo."

Blaine's voice was viscous. "Is the Institute still in one piece?"

Marybeth leaned close, took his hand in hers, and placed her other hand on his forehead. "Reasonably so. The driveway needs to be repaved and part of the fence has to be replaced. It was blown up in the attack."

"By us or them?"

"Both," said Hudson.

Alex's face came into view. He was clean-shaven and dressed in a clean set of clothes. "And you won't have to worry about them causing more trouble any time soon. Carcione gave us enough information to nab the lot of them. Ronson coordinated the raid against the Boston faction this afternoon, and another team is intercepting the Miami shipment."

Blaine managed a weak smile. He found it difficult to move because of the weight of the blankets; but he recognized post-operative chills, and did not want to have a single layer of wool removed. "Why don't you thank him by taking him off the FBI hit parade?"

"I'll see what I can do. Dickerson has already promised me a promotion. If I decide to turn down Hudson's offer, I may take it."

The drowsy feeling was beginning to wear off. As Blaine reached a higher level of consciousness his mind overflowed with questions. He recognized the intensive care unit so he did not ask the obvious. "So what happened out there? In the quarry? Did I get him?"

After a strained silence and a complicated exchange of looks among Blaine's visitors, Captain Lawson supplied the answer. "No."

The wave of disappointment that swept over Blaine was like a Diamond Head curl tumbling an inexperienced surfer.

"Your shot went wild."

Blaine took a deep breath, then winced in pain; his chest was taped. "Damn."

"But he didn't get away."

For the second time in as many minutes, MacDonald grinned. "I got the bastard. Shot him through the head."

"And the Soviet skullcap," Hudson added with a sneer.

Blaine was relieved that the menace to his life had ended, but he also felt cheated because MacDonald had

had the satisfaction of pulling the trigger. The desire to want to be directly responsible for the death of a fellow human being was not within the creed of the Hippocratic oath; but under the skin of the doctor was the soul of an ordinary man, with commonplace emotions and deep-seated longings. Vengeance was not base, it was simply an innate human trait. Two decades of impotent flashbacks about not getting his man in the jungle would continue unabated.

"But, Nabakov got me with his blowgun. I saw it. Unless—did I dream it?"

Alex put his arm around Marybeth's slender shoulders. "You can thank your bright assistant for that." He gave her a peck on the cheek. "The smock from the radiology lab was lead-lined. It stopped the dart from going through."

Marybeth smiled and shrugged her shoulders. "I thought we might need the protection."

"I got there just as Nabakov put his hands on your throat to make sure that you had given up the ghost," said MacDonald. "A moment more and he would have strangled you. I shot him from the top of the cliff. He never knew what hit him."

Blaine nodded. "Then I guess you owe me one."

With a one-eyed squint, MacDonald said, "Don't you mean that the other way around?"

When he tried to hold up his left hand so he could stick out two fingers, he found that his arm was in a plaster cast. Marybeth still clutched his right hand. "First, it was you who pulled the plug on the dormitory fire alarm. Nabakov was still in the woods when we broke into the dorm, and couldn't possibly have run around the building before Alex reached the break station. You didn't want him scared off by the noise."

MacDonald's smile faded.

"Then you tried to lure him into the Institute by ripping open the fence and offering him a way to sneak in. I remember Hudson saying you had come in the back way, but it didn't mean anything to me at the time. I just thought you did it as an exercise to keep your stealth skills in trim."

"You bastard!" screamed Marybeth. The sudden pain that Blaine felt in his hand came from Marybeth making fists when her fingers were still wrapped around his. She let go of him and reached across the bed for MacDonald, but Alex held her back.

"Take it easy, honey. Take it easy." Alex held her tight and pulled her back from the bed. "It's all over now." She let herself be mollified.

MacDonald's face was as expressionless as ever. To Blaine, "Okay, but remember what Foley said: as long as Nabakov was alive your life was on the line. It was the truth. I had to get him before he got you. After I lost him at Westmoreland, I reported the situation to the home office. I was alone because Lawson locked up all my men and wouldn't let them go until he had positive ID from the FBI. My men followed instructions and stuck to their cover story. When Foley's report was relayed to the home office, Hudson was brought in on the job because the Institute is his baby. I staked out the place and waited for him. I was keeping an eye on you in case Nabakov came in for the kill. Then Hudson showed up and Tilda told him where you were. I damn near blew him away when I caught him sneaking along the basement corridor. I pulled him into the conference room, but Lawson spotted the door closing and got the drop on us." His hand went up to his ear, where Captain Lawson's well-placed bullet had nicked the lobe. "Since I saved your life twice I guess that makes us even."

"Twice! When was the second time?"

Again came a strained silence. Marybeth was flushed with anger. Alex had his hands full trying to control her. Hudson raised his eyebrows. MacDonald simply stared. No one seemed willing to divulge the secret.

"Is someone going to tell me?"

Captain Lawson consented. "When we got to you— at the bottom of the quarry—you had stopped breathing. You were pretty broken up by the fall, and there was Nabakov with his hands still on your neck. We thought you were gone, especially knowing how fast Ricin affects the central nervous system. I guess I was too stupid to know any better so I stretched you out and started CPR and mouth-to-mouth. I did the breathing, Alex and Marybeth took turns on the compressions. I'm not as young as I used to be. I get out of breath pretty fast. So when MacDonald got to the bottom of the quarry he took over for me. He finally brought you around."

Blaine was goggle-eyed. "I think I'm going to be sick."

MacDonald smiled once more, nearly making it a habit. "Twenty years I've known CPR, but this was the first time I ever got to do it. When I practiced on the dummy they never told us about how the victim vomits when he's coming around."

Blaine tried to sigh, but the deep inhalation hurt too much. "Okay, Angus, we're even. So let's shake and make up." He reached out and grasped MacDonald's giant-sized mitt.

"Fair enough."

"I hate to break up this lover's spat but we've got work to do." Hudson patted Blaine gently on the shoulder. "We've been hanging around waiting for you to regain consciousness, and say thanks. But we'll be seeing a lot more of you, Mitchell, after you get back on your feet. For now you just concentrate on getting well."

"Thanks." Blaine had an uneasy feeling about his future involvement with the CIA, but he kept his thoughts to himself.

After Hudson and MacDonald left, Captain Lawson held out two color photographs where Blaine could see them. "Look familiar?"

The pictures sent a chill up Blaine's spine. He gulped. "Don't tell me he's come to life again?"

"Not this time. They're the Brazinski brothers: Karl and Conrad. Information salesmen. Corporate thieves who stole company secrets and sold them to the competition, or to foreign countries—whoever bid the highest. According to the FBI dossier, they've broken more computer codes than have ever been invented. That's their stock in trade. They siphoned off restricted data files without the owner ever knowing he'd been robbed. Only, when they tried to break into the Institute's computer, there was a surprise waiting for them. As Marybeth tells me, a self-destruct program that consumes all data if it is tampered with. That's why Dr. Young had orders to back up the files once a week.

"The Brazinski brothers knew from last week's published accounts that you were on to something big— something someone somewhere would pay a lot of money for. But this time their modus operandi went astray. They destroyed the files they were trying to steal. So, before the sabotage was noticed, one of them went to your house to steal your printed files while the other hung around the lecture hall to make sure you didn't come home early. Karl sat on a poisoned tack intended for you, Conrad tripped a booby trap placed in your car by the South American gang. Mystery solved and case closed."

In light of everything else that had occurred during the past two days, the Brazinski brothers were small fry. Blaine humphed. When he tried to shake his head in disgust he discovered that his neck was in a brace.

"Oh, and get a load of these." Alex showed him a pair of rough-hewn wooden clogs. "Nabakov made them himself when it started to snow. He took two logs and carved the bottoms in the form of a deer's hoof, then shaped them to fit his shoes and lashed them on with thread from his pants that he plaited into laces. He was quite a resourceful fellow."

Now that his life was no longer in danger, Blaine was bored by it all. Or were his troubles just beginning?

"But he never reckoned on American ingenuity."

Blaine humphed again. "I feel like such a fool. I went out there to be the big hero and bring down my nemesis, and I was nothing more than a babe in the woods. I guess I'm not the soldier that I used to be. I never had a chance against Nabakov. Operating the bypass skullcap as a mobile out-of-body tool is like flying a 747: it takes training and practice. If you push the unit too far it'll kill you."

"You'll get used to it."

"Not me! As far as I'm concerned, I've had the last out-of-body experience I'm going to have in this life." There was slight emphasis on "this."

"You're not going to have it in any other," Alex said excitedly. "Don't you know what you've done? What you've proven? In a single night you've overturned the writings of thousands of years of misguided missals. You've completely disproved all religious claims to afterlife. It's a milestone in science."

"At the expense of religious faith. Look, Alex, I'm not so sure—"

"Religion will survive, Blaine. It always has. But it won't survive on unfounded faith. It can do just as well promoting humanitarianism without the Biblical connotations and ecclesiasticism and fear of God. I wasn't implying that you've put an end to religion, or the need for religion. What I'm saying is that you've liberated it. Ancient canon has no place in today's world of science, technology, and education; that's why it's been foundering. If people have lost faith in religion it's not because they don't believe in what it stands for, but because they're no longer credulous enough to accept orthodoxy with blinded eyes. Religion is teaching Santa Claus fables to children smart enough to question how the fat man got down the chimney.

"The kingdom of heaven has never been anything more than a bonus, a treat, a reward for living a good life on Earth. People of deep faith have always looked forward to the day when their strife could be traded in for heavenly concessions. But nowadays, educated people just can't accept angels and afterlife. They're more concerned with the here than the hereafter, and how to make this world a better place instead of ignoring its troubles and waiting for the next world to come along. Once you burst the bubble of life-after-death you force religion to restructure itself toward realistic goals more in keeping with the parishioners' mentality and sophistication."

Blaine was not in any mood for Alex's revelations of truth. Besides having his mind dulled by drugs, he was in turmoil from his own intrusion into the beyond. "Alex, now isn't the time for articles of devotion. I'm too tired—"

Captain Lawson interrupted, and for once Blaine did not mind. "I know we're supposed to let you rest. You've been through a lot. We all have. But before I go, there's something I have to say." The police captain turned the photographs around and around, and, contrary to his usual manner, had a difficult time maintaining eye contact. "And—and this is for you, too, Marybeth."

He made several false starts before getting himself in gear. "When my mother was dying—when I knew she was beyond help—I felt—despair. I know that adults, especially older men, aren't supposed to have deep feelings like that. We're supposed to grow out of it, accept death. I see death all the time in the course of my job, and I guess I've gotten used to it. Calloused, you might say. But the deaths I see are strangers, not someone close, not someone I—not someone I care for."

The captain swallowed continuously; his eyes glistened. "When they took my mother to the Center—for the Terminally Ill—and I knew there was no hope for recovery, I couldn't take it. I only went to see her once. She was so shrunken and sickly that—it made me cry—and I couldn't stand to see her that way. I just couldn't. I know it seems like I abandoned her, but—I just couldn't. And I want you two to know that I appreciate all you did for her—in her final moments. I'm glad that two people like you care enough to . . . "

Captain Lawson hurried out of the room before he broke down completely. In the doorway he bumped shoulders with Dr. Young and Jerry Greenstein, who were on their way in. The reporter allowed no time for a change in mood.

"Hi, there, Dr. Mitchell. I'm glad to see you're all

right after your operation. Kind of different, wasn't it, being on the blade end of the knife instead of the handle?" No one smiled at his feeble attempt at levity. He seemed not to notice. He dropped a newspaper and a stuffed manila envelope on Blaine's night table, "Hey, I got some great pix from the photo lab." He dumped the eight-by-ten glossies out of the envelope and fanned them in front of Blaine's face. "Here's you on the ground. And here you are on the stretcher. And this one's you getting in the ambulance. Well, four-wheel-drive vehicle really, because they couldn't get the ambulance down the old quarry road with all that snow. These are spare copies—for you." He put them down and held up the *Morning Chronicle*. "Plus, there was time to write the whole thing up for the Sunday edition—"

"Greenstein, I'm not really interested in your mindless, self-serving journalism. In fact, I'm surprised someone hasn't wrung your neck for you—"

"No, it's okay, Dr. Mitchell. Everything's been approved. Ask Dr. Young. There's no mention of the CIA or the neurometric feedback terminal or levels of consciousness or—or anything like that. Hudson and MacDonald created a cover story. We stayed with the terrorist angle that has the attack on the Institute as a reprisal for the FBI breaking up the drug ring that the other Dr. Mitchell was involved in. We used the confusion over the names as the reason you became the target. Plus, I've written a retraction that—" His smile changed to a frown with the speed of an electron changing direction in an alternating current. "—makes my other articles a cover story for this one, until the terrorists were caught. Pretty clever, huhn?"

Blaine rolled his eyes. "Clever enough to entitle you to live, against my better judgment. Are you going along with this, Joe?"

"In light of circumstances, and after detailed discussions with Mr. Hudson, I have decided not to sue the paper for libel. That decision is also part of the cover story."

"It sounds as if while I've been asleep, you people have tied up all the loose ends like a neat Christmas package."

"Not only that, but I think you'll like the present that's inside." Marybeth flashed the conspiratorial teenage smile that she used so often.

"What's that supposed to—"

"Blaine, I have—my wife is waiting for me outside." Young did not fidget, but he leaned toward the door obviously eager to leave. "Now that she has read about our, uh, difficulties at the Institute—at least, the part of our work and the recent events that are not classified—she is beginning to understand some of the pressures I am under, and, well —I hope there are no hard feelings between us." He straightened his arm and extended his fingers stiffly.

Blaine gently shook his hand. "No hard feelings, Joe."

"Thanks, Blaine. And I'll see to it that we work together more closely in the future." He nodded to the others on his way to the door.

Greenstein followed Dr. Young like a faithful puppy dog. "I'll keep in touch, Dr. Mitchell."

"You do that." Inside, Blaine was groaning. He hoped that the reporter would forget to write. He turned to Alex and Marybeth. "Is there anything else I should know about?"

"Your doctor will fill you in on the rest."

"Speaking of rest, I could sure use some." Alex's eyes were bloodshot from lack of sleep. "I've spent the whole day either on the phone or filling out reports."

"The whole day? What time is it?"

"Bedtime." Marybeth slipped her arm through Alex's, and winked. "For everyone. We've got to let you have some time with your doctor. Come on, Alex. I'm taking you home to bed."

"Say hello to your mother for me."

Marybeth stuck out her tongue at him.

Chapter 24

Dr. Frances Crowley was dressed in a white hospital uniform, white smock, and white shoes. Her silky blonde hair was done up on top of her head and tied in a knot. She wore the stereotypic stethoscope around her neck like a badge of office. When she eased the door shut behind her the latch made only the barest click.

"How are we feeling tonight, Dr. Mitchell?"

Blaine was still wondering why everyone had suddenly hurried off and left him. "Fran!"

Smiling broadly, she sat down on the edge of the bed. "Darling. I thought your friends would never leave us alone."

"Wha—what are you doing here?"

Fran placed her fingers on the veins of his wrist. "Taking care of you. I've been given visiting doctor status."

"But—how did you get here so fast?"

She flapped her arms. "I flew."

Blaine's jaw dropped. "You are amazing."

Fran glanced at her wristwatch. "Your pulse is fine, but now I'm suspecting brain damage. Your cognitive responses are clearly subnormal. Let me listen to your heart." She pulled down the blankets, placed the stethoscope to her ears, and slipped the diaphragm between the buttons of his pajamas.

"Fran, I—you know what I mean. I'm just surprised—shocked, actually—that you're here. After I talked with you yesterday—was that yesterday?"

"Yes."

"After telling you I was okay and to stay put I didn't expect you to jump on a plane and head east."

She removed the stethoscope and placed it on the nightstand. "So how do you feel?"

"Like Ray Milland in *The Lost Weekend*. I've been through two days I'd rather forget. Uh, how much do you know?"

"Enough. Alex and Marybeth gave me a personal narrative, and Hudson briefed me on the classified material. You've been through a lot."

"You don't know half of it. I'm surprised Hudson let you in on any of what's been going on."

Fran's blue eyes sparkled. "As it turns out, you and I both work for the same outfit."

"What?"

"My grant money comes from the Ford Endowment Society. It's no coincidence that our research projects encompass similar aspects of brain stimulation. Sooner or later you and I were bound to meet. That it happened last week was more or less inevitable, given the status and progress of our work."

"Yes, I'm beginning to believe what Alex said about nothing being a coincidence. Everything that's happened in the past week has been interrelated." Blaine tried to nod, but winced in pain instead. "By the way, how badly am I hurt? I haven't seen a medical report, yet."

Fran took the chart from the foot of the bed and read it in her best physician's manner. "You've got hairline fractures of the left fibula and ulna, fractures of the left transverse processes T10 to T12, two broken ribs (T2 and T3), minor dislocation of the cervical vertebrae but not bilateral, although there is partial detachment of the nuchal ligament of C1, and compression fractures of C2 and C3, possibly C4, either of which may exert pressure on the transverse foramen." She looked up. "We'll have to watch that carefully." From the chart, "Some superficial damage to the left superior articular process of C5, and concussion. Now that you're conscious I can do a complete neurological workup, but on the whole I'd say you're a very lucky man."

Blaine ran his right hand over his head. "The ground broke my fall. How about subdural hematoma? Shouldn't you drain—"

"Let's get one thing straight, darling. I'm the doctor, you're the patient. I'll do the prescribing and you'll take your medicine. I'm not as concerned about your head as I am about injuries to your extremities." She ran her hand along his lower abdominal region. "As far as I can tell there's been no internal damage, but certain organic functions will have to wait until your bones have healed before I can perform the necessary tests."

"Plural. I like that." Despite Blaine's grogginess, he smiled at the prospect of Fran's aid to recovery. "It'll certainly give me something to look forward to." Fran leaned down and kissed him on the lips. "This isn't my usual treatment, you understand. But you're a special case."

Blaine felt a comfort greater than the drug-induced euphoria that was slowly wearing off. "So are you. Very special."

"Uh, oh." Fran backed away pouting. "Now I've done it." She checked her watch for several seconds, then said, "Your pulse has increased twenty beats per minute. That's not good for a patient on complete bed rest."

"But not unexpected under the circumstances." The increased circulation brought with it a return of physical sensitivity. His leg and arm throbbed dully, his chest and neck ached, and, oddly, he felt a sharp burning sensation on the palm of his left hand where the patch of skin tore off when it stuck to the door handle in the Westmoreland University parking lot. The full cycle of events was recapitulated in pain. "Fran, why am I on opiates instead of the bypass skullcap?"

"For one thing, the unit you were wearing was smashed in the fall. For another, your body is so depleted of endorphin-producing amino acids that no amount of electrical stimulus could produce the desired effect. You're worn out." She patted his inner thigh. "You've got to build up your hormone level."

Blaine lay still since he was practically incapable of moving. His face clouded. "You know we've had a mind-expanding weekend?"

Fran's seriousness matched his own. "So I'm told. You've undergone some fairly bizarre phenomena, although, taking a strictly rationalistic approach, I see

most of it as hallucinatory. Alex described his experience in detail. He still appears to be suffering the effects
of schizophrenic dissociation; his grip on reality is tenuous at best. What's your explanation? What's really
happening in the recesses of your mind?"

"I wish I knew." Blaine stared at the ceiling in order
to collect his thoughts. "One moment I think it's real,
the next I think it's illusory. And then I think it's real
again. That final episode was definitely . . . "

"Yes?"

Blaine remained thoughtfully silent.

Fran took a different tack, "How much do the others know? Or think they know?"

"Hudson's a pretty smart cookie, with a good grasp
of neurometric feedback theory and its potential uses."

"He's a neurophysiologist by education. That's why
the CIA put him in charge of the brain research program."

Blaine humphed. "It doesn't surprise me. He also
knows a hell of a lot about Soviet psychic research,
which I think is just a cover for their own neurometric
feedback program, although he probably wouldn't own
up to it. Alex and Captain Lawson know only what I told
them. I gave them an overview of brain stimulus without going into the scientific details such as brain wave
characteristics   or   beta-lipoprotein/methionine
enkephalin interactions: stuff I didn't think they'd
understand. I wanted to clear up Lawson's misconcep-
tions because he's the police chief of this burg and I
have to live with him after this is all over. He thought
we were still playing with autonomic brain reflexes. I
gather he's heard from the college students about Lilly's
mapping of the dolphin brain, and their self-stimula-
tion of the pleasure center; and early rodent experiments." Mice with implanted electrodes that stimulated
the brain's pleasure center would activate an electrical
pushbar that evoked the pleasure response until they
starved to death. "I needed to set him straight. Alex I
truly wanted to educate. He's bright and inquisitive,
and I thought the more he knew the more he could help

me understand why so many people were willing to kill over the bypass skullcap. As it turned out, he taught me at least as much as I taught him." Parenthetically, "Greenstein doesn't know a damned thing, but he sure stirred up a hornet's nest by making believe he knew and making up what he didn't."

"Getting back to our discussion of last week: is the mind a nonphysical entity, and can it exist away from the body? What is your medical opinion of that?"

"You get right to the point, don't you?"

"Life is too short to beat around the bush."

"After spending a week with you I should know that." Blaine humphed. "But I can't give you a straightforward answer because I'm still of two minds—sorry, I didn't mean that literally. It's just that my medical opinion differs from my subjective impression. Call it mental diplopia." Double vision was not an uncommon disorder. "As a scientist I can't accept anything but a pharmacological explanation of the near-death experience, but as a person who's been through an artificially stimulated near-death experience, I can't explain it scientifically. There's so much we don't know about the mind—so much that we can't explain given the present state of technology—that it would be presumptuous to make rash judgments. I can describe my latest experiment, I can't rationalize the results."

Fran intertwined her fingers with Blaine's. "Did you externalize your mind as Alex described?"

"Oh, I went much farther than that. I went through the light at the end of the tunnel. I saw what was on the other side."

"And what did you see?"

"I can't—I can't remember. There was nothing physical—that's not what lies beyond the light. It wasn't even a place. It was a concept. Of eternal tranquility and infinite peace, of goodness, of painlessness, of sensuality, of belonging. Of belonging! And my wife was there waiting for me. She told me not to blame myself for her death. That it was all right for me to love someone else—someone alive. That . . . " Fran's expression brought him back down to earth, to the world of material existence. "I know how crazy it sounds when I put it in words, but it's all true. I spoke with her. It's just—it's difficult to describe. But it happened."

Fran nodded. "I believe you. I believe you saw something in your mind that you interpreted as—"

"No! This was no hallucination. Carol was there, as real and as substantial and as touchable as you. Look, Fran, I know you'd like to rationalize this from the standpoint of a psychiatrist treating delusions. I would do it myself if I were in your pantyhose. But you have to accept my observations just as you take the word of a patient when he tells you where he hurts. Sure, you can't always find an organic reason for his pain, but he feels it just the same."

"Amputees feel phantom pain because the missing limb's neuroreceptors continue to transmit impulses."

"Don't patronize me by quoting elementary neurology."

"I'm suggesting that you be more objective. You've been through an incredibly powerful experience that has affected your mental outlook, and as a doctor you should understand that. In time, I'm sure the feeling will fade like any other flush of excitement—like coming down after a drug rush. As a scientist you have to recognize that possibility."

Blaine sighed as deeply as he could with two fractured ribs. "I hear what you're saying. I really do. But I can't get out of my mind the sense of the reality of the experience." He was practically pleading. "Fran, I didn't have to come back from the other side. I could have stayed in the realm beyond the light. I could have continued my existence there—supported by noncorporeal mental energy."

"Blaine, you're justifying an aberration of the mind by—"

"No, think about our concept of physical reality. This bed seems solid until you look at it under an electron microscope and see that most of it is empty space: nuclear forces that maintain the distance between an atomic nucleus and its electrons. The amount of actual matter is infinitesimal."

"What does that have to do with—"

"It's a point of view. Our concept of reality—that is, the concept of reality that our brains are capable of perceiving—is not the same as the actual reality in a non-relativistic sense. All I'm saying is that we can't deny the existence of nonperceptible dimensions of the universe simply because we don't have the type of brain to perceive them or the technology to detect them." His voice rose in crescendo until he was practically yelling. "The mind is an energy pattern that can exist in an externally-generated universal force field. It grows within the brain like a fetus within the womb, but when it reaches a certain level of consciousness it becomes self-sustaining: independent of the brain and body that was once necessary to support it."

Fran was not so easily persuaded. "That sounds like the classical definition of transmigration of the soul, with biblical connotations of life after death." She glanced at her watch. "It took you only a minute and a half for your convictions to shift one hundred eighty degrees—from the questioning scientist to heroin addict, each arguing against the other. Complete self-dialecticism. Can't you hear yourself?"

"You just don't understand, Fran. You haven't experienced it."

"And you sound like a psychedelic drug user trying to convince the world that he just got back from the Moon. This isn't like you, Blaine. You're a sane, rational man not given to flights of fancy."

"Then why don't you believe that my experience was real?"

"Because it's dangerous for a doctor to share her patient's delusions. Besides, if this realm beyond the light was so attractive, so peaceful and painless, why didn't you stay there? Find out more about it?"

Blaine had to think for a moment. "I guess because I knew that further exploration would trap me there—"

"You mean, you would die?"

"No, I can't die. None of us can die. At least, not in the conventional way we've come to think of dying. I remember being—confused. Unsure of myself. It's like—remember when we were climbing the back side of Half Dome, and we came to that tricky place where we had to let go of one handhold in order to reach out for the next one? And you were afraid to let go in case you didn't make it? It was like that. The life before me was an unknown—a great unknown. But to reach it I had to let go of this life. And I didn't have the conviction to do that."

Smiling, Fran patted his hand. "I'm glad you didn't, or you wouldn't be here with me now." Then she dropped her smile. "And now that I've found you, I don't want to lose you."

Blaine squeezed her hand as if he were clinging to the edge of a mile-high cliff and her grip was all that prevented him from falling into oblivion. "There were other considerations, too, Fran. For one thing, I knew that whatever I learned about the dimension beyond the light was useless knowledge: I could never share it with anyone in the physical world; it would do no one any good. In that moment of passage I had a choice to make—*my* choice; you might call it my 'last rights.' And in that final introspective moment I beheld in my deepest inner being considerations that forced my return."

Fran stared deep into his eyes. "You came back with revelations?"

"Let's say I came back liberated. Until I stood poised on the brink between life and afterlife, I didn't realize that I had too much definitely established in this continuum to give it up for the uncertainty of the next. The path beyond is always open to me, as it is to all of us. For now I belong here. But there were two things on my mind that brought me back."

Fran waited expectantly.

"The potential for misuse of the neurometric feedback terminal is frightening. With the wrong frequency programmed into the computer a person could accidentally induce his own brain death, as I nearly did out there in the quarry. He could—"

She shook her head slowly. "Your near-death experience did not occur as a result of the bypass skullcap. It was broken in the fall."

Blaine had hardly absorbed the impact of her statement before she went on.

"Furthermore, at that point you had used up your stored supply of endorphins. Something else must have triggered your out-of-body experience—some mechanism of the brain that we haven't discovered yet."

Blaine's mind was vacillating again. What to believe?

"But," she was quick to add, "Something with a pharmacological explanation."

Now was not the time to argue the point. With his pain receptors open again, his brain was being stimulated by raw nerve endings. He squirmed uncomfortably. "Honey, how soon can I have another dose of Demerol?"

Her long lashes fluttered. "That is one of my responsibilities as your doctor." She filled a syringe from a small glass vial, and slipped the needle into a vein in his arm. "This will make you feel better. Make you forget your confusion."

But Blaine desperately did not want to forget. The drug started taking effect right away. He felt that he had to talk fast, before he got so drowsy that he could no longer formulate his thoughts. "There's another abuse of the bypass skullcap that's more important than a program fault. The reason for its development was strictly therapeutic: to control pain and promote healing; a use that is for the good of humanity. But suppose our financial backers are more interested in population control than pain control."

Fran squinted. "What contraceptive value does—"

"I didn't mean it that way. We're—" Already, his tongue was becoming thick. "We're at the beginning of a new science: the study of the electrical stimulation of the brain and its untapped potential. And, as in any new study or exploratory venture, we don't know what we'll discover. The only thing I can guarantee is that the rate of discovery will be exponential. Look how far we've come since the first researchers inserted electrodes through the skull in order to apply an electrical stimulus to the brain. Next we did it by taping pads on the surface of the scalp at predetermined locations. Now we have a skullcap with hundreds of electrodes that are hardwired to fire a preprogrammed stimulus through the skull to the brain only a fraction of an inch away. That is only a short step from triggering the electrodes remotely: from an inch away, two inches, half a foot, across the room, from the next building, from the White House." His voice again raised in crescendo. "Or the Kremlin."

Fran rubbed his temples with her warm hands. "Slow down, Blaine. Slow down. Don't let your imagination run away with you."

"Hudson said the Soviets were working on mind control, but I didn't take him literally. Now I'm scared. Now I'm afraid I may have been responsible for opening the way to electronic domination of the world. It's the ultimate propaganda device, because people can be forced to do whatever those in power want them to do. It can turn people into mindless slaves—"

"Shush, baby. Shush." Fran leaned forward and placed her cheek against his. She whispered in his ear, "It will all seem different in the morning. We're a long way from the kind of mind control you're predicting. Anyway, for every weapon there is a defense. If a method is ever developed to transmit controlling signals directly into people's brains, a method will be found to deflect the signals."

"But there's no guarantee—"

"Yes, there is, darling. There's always American know-how and ingenuity. Personally, I think Hudson is paranoid about Soviet intentions. There's a big difference between a spy device and mind control. But, as long as he's paying the bills, I'll do what I can to develop his neurometric interference propagator."

Blaine was really getting groggy. "You mean—"

"I've been working on it for years. It's very hush-hush. But now that you and I have become part of the family, I guess it's all right if you know a little something about it."

His eyes were drooping. That dreamy lightheadedness caused by artificial opiates was slowly clouding his mind. "Before I pass out on you, I have to tell you the second reason I came back." He had to moisten his mouth with his tongue before he could say it. Even then, the words were difficult to pronounce. "I came back because—I love you."

Fran leaned back, smiled, and winked. "Same here."